Chapter 1.

There was no sound as the harvester took its first tentative steps. The lumbering contraption woke from its slumber and shook off the dust. Lee sat in the cramped wheelhouse, he tried to stretch his sore knees then briefly closed his tired eyes. It looked like an incredibly noisy machine but all he could sense was a high-pitched hydraulic friction, then a deep bass vibration echoing in his chest. He looked around at the trembling machinery and blinking lights with satisfaction as the harvester rumbled into life.

"Finally, we got the big beetle moving." Winston's voice came through the suit comms.

"Yeah seems ok, green lights everywhere. I have no idea why it went down though."

"I'm putting it back on remote, programming a drive-by to check the treads and auger. HEMI is back in charge."

"Fine by me, let the tour commence."

Lee watched the displays in the wheelhouse as the helium harvester began crawling over the Moon's surface. The harvester was a massive flat vehicle, ten meters across and thirty meters long. A giant grey bug with a flat shell and sharp incisors. It moved slowly, on continuous caterpillar tracks. At the front, it had teeth. A long cylindrical auger of rotating spikes designed to dig into the surface, churning up the regolith. Behind the auger, steel dredge plates conveyed the rock and dust for heat treatment to extract the helium 3. The machine had a small wheelhouse built into the front for manual control, but it was designed to be operated remotely by

HEMI, the moon base core computer. Lee had spent two months assembling the prototype harvester with the rest of the crew. They all knew it intimately.

He tried to relax. At this speed, it would take at least an hour to complete a circumference of the base. He watched as the auger spun the angular spikes into the velvet grey surface, ploughing and processing a path of destruction, leaving a gouged trail behind. The wheelhouse was a skeletal frame with manual controls built in, open to the vacuum. He tried to stretch his legs again in the cramped space and watched the dirty bubble dwellings of the moon base crawl past. All he could hear was the sound of his own breath inside his helmet.

Home was a shabby collection of domes connected by bulbous tubes. A central hub with five connected domes, speckled black and grey. Lee pondered its history as he drove past, imagining the tragedy of the original mining pioneers. The base had been built almost twenty years ago by an ambitious Chinese mining corporation called Sustainable Systems Inc. Sustainability had never been a high priority as they mined fossil fuels and minerals wherever they had permission. They abandoned their lunar project when the money ran out and left their employees there to die. Lee's employers Benevolent Progress Inc. moved in years later intending to harvest the abundant helium 3 embedded in the regolith.

The harvester came to an unexpected juddering halt. "Shit, all systems down, going to look under the hood again," he said into the suit comms.

Lee unravelled himself from the wheelhouse and climbed down onto the surface. He made his way to the front of the dormant machine in loping slow-motion strides. Economy of movement was an important consideration outside. As always, everything was tranquil; the loudest noise coming from his inquisitive brain. The harvester had stopped near the graves of their predecessors. Arriving at the moon base six months ago, Lee had discovered the mummified remains of four prospectors, wrapped in blankets, who had chosen to die outside under the stars. The corpses looked peaceful, resigned to their fate. He couldn't help but ponder their decision twenty years ago, they decided to lie down and briefly look at the stars for one last time before surrendering to the lunar elements they had intended to exploit. Lee had planted a little metal cross at the head of each skeleton.

Winston's rasping voice instantly destroyed his quiet contemplation; "Lee! What is going on? Why has it stopped?"

"No idea, I'll check the remote receiver again."

Lee slowly walked along in front of the auger, careful to avoid the sharp spikes. In the middle, there was a control panel which showed the signal strength from HEMI. It was dead. Lee sighed and looked around at the huge partial crater surrounding them. A smooth amphitheatre rose up to a steep ridgeline that provided a breath-taking backdrop to the humble collection of domes. The crater reminded him something massive had once smashed into this Moon. Always surrounded by death potential, he thought. Any small mistake out on the surface would result in rapid freezing, suffocation or decompression. Being this close to his own mortality made Lee feel more alive than ever. He looked at his boots in the dust and savoured the silence, standing on the surface of the Moon, not another human in sight. You could think some weird thoughts in a vacuum.

"What the fuck is going on Lee?" Winston once more shattered his thoughts. "Every time we send you out there you end up staring into space like some brain-dead retard. There's nothing to even see out there."

He sounded angry, but Lee knew Winston was grateful to have someone who seemed to enjoy venturing out onto the Moon's surface to soak up the cosmic rays. No-one else ever volunteered.

Lee was about to swear back at him when the harvester abruptly burst back into life. The auger started rotating, sharp spinning spikes almost impaling Lee where he stood. He hastily backed away and noticed the light on the control panel indicating the signal from HEMI was re-established. He wasn't in any danger, the harvester moved too slowly but as he backed away, he noticed the harvester was not moving in a straight line. It was turning towards the moon base.

"Are you seeing this?"

"Yes! Can you point the harvester somewhere else please?"

"It's not me, I'll try to stop it."

Lee walked back and around to the side of the harvester as it continued its slow arc towards the moon base. He climbed back into the wheelhouse and tried to change its direction. "It's not responding." Lee frantically pushed buttons in the wheelhouse, but the harvester ignored him and continued its ponderous progress towards the looming grey domes.

"Shut the fucking thing down!" shouted Winston.

"I'm trying, nothing's happening. Do it from your end."

Lee heard muffled curses from his suit comms. "No response from HEMI, hit the kill switch."

Lee reached down and lifted a panel in the wheelhouse floor revealing a red lever which was supposed to cut all power to the harvester. Only to be used in emergencies. He pulled the lever up and felt it click into place, but the harvester rolled on.

"It's not working,"

"Nothing from this end either, HEMI is active but unresponsive."

"It's going to smash into the green room, get Fidel out of there and close all the doors."

Lee could hear the moon base sirens through his suit comms as he imagined Fidel quietly looking after his plants in the green room, unaware of the danger he was in. He tugged on the kill switch a couple more times and futilely jabbed at the buttons.

"Fidel is out, green room sealed," said Winston. "What a fucking disaster."

Lee climbed out of the wheelhouse and walked alongside the harvester. There was nothing else they could do. It was almost upon the green room now, everything happening in slow motion. Then just metres from the dome, the harvester abruptly stopped dead in its tracks again.

"What did you do?"

"Nothing," replied Winston. "Absolutely nothing. It just stopped. Thing's got a mind of its own."

Lee stayed fully suited for the decontamination blast. The lower half of his suit was coated in pale grey powder, it was impossible to get rid of all the dust despite the high-pressure decontamination. The suit's integrity was rated at one hundred percent and there was no conceivable way for the dust to get inside yet every time he took off his boots after a walk on the surface, there were always faint traces of moon dust between his toes. He shook his head and breathed deeply through his nostrils. He was used to the smell of gunpowder now. It is the smell of the Moon. Calcium, Magnesium and Silicon dioxide, all present in the dust combining to create the cordite smell. He could taste it on his tongue as he took his work overalls from the locker. Sharp, metallic and slightly salty. It was not unpleasant.

The airlock opened into the central dome where Winston and Jack could usually be found. As he emerged blinking into the light, he was not surprised to hear them shouting at each other.

"Why is HEMI malfunctioning? What are you morons doing? I swear out of all those billions of Chinese; how come I get the most retarded ones working for me? Your inbred parents should have thrown you in the river when you were born." Jack breathlessly finished his tirade.

"Stupid redneck," retorted Winston. "Why did your father have to fuck the ugliest pig on your yankee farm to be your mother?"

Lee was used to this kind of language. Winston and Jack enjoyed the abusive banter which passed as a unique type of comradeship and released the tension they both felt. "The harvester can't just run on its own, something must be wrong with the HEMI signal."

"We have to shut it down, run diagnostics and reboot it. This fucking place," muttered Jack. "Always one step forward and two steps back."

Lee turned, shaking his head and made for the corridor to block four. The computing core was housed there next to the huge 3D printer, which had been manufacturing harvester parts and other moon base necessities. He took a detour to the café for a tea. Hot green tea always made him feel more alert and refreshed but he hesitated when he saw Fidel slumped over the table.

"Fidel, do you realise how close you were just now to being minced up by the harvester?"

Fidel nodded. "This place has got it in for us, it feels like there is something here, something manipulating things. We should never have come."

"It's just technical glitches, don't be so paranoid. If you came outside with me you would see how beautiful it is Fidel, it's peaceful. I would rather be here than Earth"

"Cuba is peaceful," Fidel mumbled. "This place sucks."

"I don't know about Cuba, but where I come from it's overpopulated and filthy. The Earth we left behind is a shithole."

"The only reason you like it here is because you think it's an improvement, but what was so bad about your home?" asked Fidel.

Lee rubbed his temples and frowned. "Have you ever been to Shanghai?" He doesn't wait for an answer. "It's horrible. Dirty, noisy, overpopulated and dangerous. Impossible to make a decent life there."

"What about your family?"

"My wife left me when I lost my job. She wouldn't let me see my daughter. I was depressed, and I think I had every right to be. My apartment was slowly falling apart around me, like my life."

Fidel nodded sympathetically.

"My mother is a dragon and my friends only showed interest on the odd occasion I had money. I had gambling debts I struggled to pay the interest on, the entire system was designed to grind me down."

"So, you ran away from it all, as far as you could go. All the way to the Moon."

The dull background murmur of the moon base was ever present. Comforting in its functionality. A coffee stain on the white plastic table was an almost perfect circle between them.

Lee sighed into his tea. "I even thought about suicide, but it all seemed so messy and I knew deep down I didn't have the guts. It felt like I was walking through life in a coma; never properly awake but never a good night's sleep. I didn't have enough energy to care about anything, especially my own future."

"Negotiating the potholes of modern existence is never easy."

Lee ignored Fidel's amateur philosophy. "I was in a bad way, but I found a job in a print factory which probably saved my life. Then Benevolent Progress bought us out and doubled the size. We soon began mass producing their orders with the best printers available. Mostly weapon parts and medical equipment."

"Yeah, our employer has grown into a massive organisation, one of the conspiracy theories I've heard BPI will instigate small wars then provide weapons and medical expertise for both sides,"

Lee shrugged and drank his tea. "I never thought I could escape from Shanghai, all those people, the pollution and the pessimism. BPI gave me an opportunity. Leaving the city was a big step never mind leaving the entire planet."

"I understand, we come from different places. Cuba is oppressed and corrupt, but I miss the nature, the beaches, the lifestyle and my family." Fidel looked as if he was going to cry.

Lee stuck his nose in the tea and inhaled the steam. He understood but couldn't relate. For the first time in his life, he was looking at some sort of future. A lunar future. BPI was making long-term investments on the Moon and he wanted to be part of it. Outside, Lee would gaze back at his home planet and think of the billions of humans scurrying over its tired surface. Busily obsessing over their mundane lives, their daft preoccupation with procreation and social stature. They would never see this view, no-one could see through the Shanghai smog. Out here the entire universe was his own colossal secret.

"You should come outside with me Fidel; it will give you perspective. It's not good for you to be cooped up in these domes the entire time. It's beautiful out there."

"I've been out there, but every time I look up at the Earth, I just break down. It's so far away."

Lee watched a tear roll down Fidel's cheek and splash onto the table. He didn't feel any sympathy. He couldn't help Fidel if he continued to wallow in his own self-pity. Lee knew from experience.

"When I look at the Earth, I see a disaster waiting to happen," Lee said insistently and reached over the table to grip Fidel's arm. "The Earth is fucked."

"Are you a disillusioned environmentalist? or a pessimistic humanist? Instead of trying to do some good, instead of trying to make a difference you just ran away to the Moon?"

Lee shook his head. "Yes, I ran away, what could I do? Maybe I am just a loner. Uncomfortable in company." He replied diffusing Fidel's anger. "I like the isolation."

"A beta person like me. Maybe we can help each other," said Fidel with a weak smile.

Lee didn't think he needed any help and he knew Fidel was beyond helping unless he changed his despondent attitude. He was much happier on the Moon; the life was simple. He had adjusted to the solitude and now he cherished it.

"You can help each other find new fucking jobs if you don't get back to work!" Winston appeared in the café seething with anger at finding two technicians in conversation over tea.

"On my way," Lee said, happy for the interruption. He finished his tea and pushed past a glaring Winston.

Ranjit was immersed in cables, data pads, and external sensory augments, he didn't notice Lee enter the block four dome. He was singing loudly to himself with headphones on while he worked, badly out of tune, much to Stella's annoyance. Ranjit was oblivious to her complaints. Lee knelt and tugged on his leg.

"Lee Xiang, hello my friend! Why are you looking so lugubrious today?"

Lee looked blankly back at him. "Lugubrious? Ranjit even if I knew what that word meant... oh never mind, just tell me what to do."

Stella's pink hair appeared from under the printer chassis. "Memorizing words from the dictionary no one has heard before does not make you a smart person Ranjit." Stella promptly disappeared back under the chassis.

Ranjit looked exasperated as he uncoiled himself from the mess of cables. "The art of conversation is a beautiful thing Stella; it sets us apart from the primitives. If you learn an unfamiliar word every day you will benefit yourself and those around you."

Stella's head appeared again. "No Ranjit, you just annoy those around you."

Ranjit laughed. "I do love this verbal sparring Stella, it makes our mundane tasks much more bearable, but enough of your excoriating argument. We have work to do."

Ranjit handed Lee a datapad. "This is where we are up to, we shut down HEMI and isolated every function, then we ran programming diagnostics. We rebooted and managed to gain control of the harvester which is safely parked but now the printer is playing up. Producing variations from the template again."

"Trouble-shooter programs?" Lee asked.

Ranjit rolled his eyes. "Lee, since when has a trouble-shooter program ever found the trouble."

Lee grunted agreement as Ranjit continued. "The block four printer is the only one capable of printing the largest parts for the harvesters. It receives its instruction protocol from HEMI but now the printer had stopped responding to protocol and started printing parts out of spec, twisted variants of the templates.

Ok, but if it's not the printer software, and we installed all the hardware to the exact specifications then why is it producing aberrations? It must be the protocol."

Ranjit nodded in agreement. "It seems like HEMI is making its own rules."

Chapter 2.

Lago Santos lay sprawled on his bed. He was awake, relaxed, and his thoughts came to him with unusual clarity. Dawn was his favourite time of the day. He had not slept, he had no need for sleep. The drugs were wearing off, but they left him in a happy equilibrium. The sedatives balancing the amphetamines to create a state of serene contemplation. He looked down at his naked body. Although he was in his late fifties, he had the chiselled physique of a young man. He'd used to take cocktails of drugs, some even legal, to keep him alert and athletic. But thanks to high quality printed organ replacements and cutting-edge anti-aging treatments he was the healthiest he had ever been. These days Lago only took drugs for recreation.

He tentatively sat up. His body still trembled after the night's exertions. He crawled to the edge of his huge bed, stood up, stretched, and went to the balcony. Faint pink shards of the approaching sunrise were just visible on the horizon. Above the toxic smog of the city, from the ninety-ninth floor of his BPI skyscraper, the air was clear. On windless days, the smog was sometimes so thick he couldn't see down past the forty-fifth floor. Up here Lago had his own intimate level of atmosphere, a layer of unsoiled air sandwiched between whispers of pink cloud above and the sullen smog below. Lago looked up to where a few fading stars persevered, and the pale half of the crescent Moon floated above the horizon. He stared at the Moon frowning, then shook his head, dispelling unwanted thoughts. He scratched at some dried blood on his abdomen then turned his attention back to the carnage behind him.

"Goran!" he shouted towards the bed. "Get in here and clean this shit up."

Goran Satanovich entered a few moments later. Lago watched as his ever-present sneer twitched at the metallic stench of dried blood. His big frame expanded and contracted under the expensive tailored suit jacket. He was top heavy, his long skinny legs propping up a barrel chest. Erroneous bulges in his suit jacket hinted at concealed weaponry. A blemished bald head sat on top of a muscular neck with thick wrap-around sunglasses that rarely came off. His thin mouth sneered with a contemptuous distaste for everything.

"Another clean-up then?" Goran asked without expecting a reply.

Lago ignored him and stalked off to the en-suite.

Goran rang for the cleaners and surveyed the bloody mess on the bed. Lago was getting worse, harder to satisfy sexually and his frustration being expressed more violently than ever. He turned away from the carnage as the cleaning crew scuttled in and went about their business escorted by two Masama.

Goran stood separate from the Masama as they supervised the clean-up. The cleaners picked up the torn pieces of clothing, empty bottles and broken glass strewn all over the floor. They used gloves and thick nylon sacks to handle the smashed mirror, empty hypodermics, glass vials and a couple of broken vases. Once they had cleared a path to the bed the messy work began. It was hard to tell what had taken place there. The remains of what used to be two young humans lay sprawled among the red silk sheets. Goran wasn't sure if they were male or female as the cleaners wrapped up the entire congealing mess of limbs in the sheets and awkwardly stuffed them into body bags. There was no movement, but he didn't expect any signs of life. Lago was very thorough.

Goran didn't recognize the Masama. They looked like new recruits and were obviously nervous in his presence. There was no need for camouflage suits but the Masama wore them anyway. They carried weapons comfortably as if they were limb extensions and although just as big and intimidating as Goran, they didn't have the same unfuckwithable demeanour. They were there to make sure the cleaners disposed of any incriminating evidence discreetly and to make sure they kept their mouths shut. The cleaners would often end up in the same lagoon or landfill as Lago's unfortunate victims, just to be sure.

All the Masama soldiers had telepathic implants which rendered speech meaningless, so Goran was surprised when one strode purposefully up to him and said; "Ever been invited to one of these private parties, boss?"

Goran had the telepathy implant too but had no desire to connect with the soldier's mind. He rounded on the man, raised his glasses revealing dark angry eyes. "No, and as far as you are concerned they never happen. If I hear any of you gossiping about this shit you will end up in the same fucking hole as those dead kids."

"Ok, sorry boss." The soldier realized he had overstepped the mark. Goran made a mental note; he disapproved of his minions being that familiar with him. Never mind openly discussing their employer's proclivities. This soldier would be sent on a job from which there would be no returning.

Goran looked out over the hazy Manila skyline. He enjoyed the ubiquitous blanket of smog covering the squalid city ninety-nine stories below. He liked the separation. Serenity above, filthy chaos below. He kept his back to the cleaners as they finished their gruesome work in silence. Hearing their activities cease, he turned and inspected the room.

"Replace the mattress," he ordered. "Another Ming vase here, another antique mirror here."

The Masama soldiers nodded. One of them indicated to the cleaners who were standing with their heads bowed. Goran gave a minuscule nod, sealing their fate.

"You," Goran said to the Masama who had spoken to him earlier. "Report to me tomorrow for relocation. That will be all."

"Aaah, yes boss." The soldier realized his own fate was also now decided. Goran turned back to the window, looking through his faint reflection at the fallowed pink clouds outside.

Lago strolled back into the bedroom and made a cursory inspection.

"I overheard your conversation with that soldier. The Masama are getting far too arrogant Goran, too disrespectful. They need to know their place. You need to remind them."

"He is a new recruit, on a trial he has just failed. He will not be seen again."

"Nevertheless, I am concerned. They are becoming far too overconfident and their telepathic link makes them unreadable, they need to be more subservient."

Goran did not reply. He continued to stare grimly out the window.

"Has our guest arrived?" asked Lago.

"Yes, ready when you are."

"Good." Lago strode to the exit with Goran following.

They entered Lago's private lift and swiftly descended into the bowels of the building. Within seconds the lift doors parted revealing a brightly lit corridor. They walked in silence down the corridor to a heavy steel door. Goran entered the security code and the door swung open on a dark and cold room smelling of stale urine. Goran found the light switch and a harsh sterile light filled the room from the panels above. It was a square room with featureless white walls. In the centre of the room was a steel chair. A naked man sat slumped, his hands and ankles bound to the steel frame with cable ties. He had a black bag on his head and there was a pool of evaporating urine on the floor beneath him.

Lago studied him for a minute before Goran pulled the bag off. He grasped the man's jaw and raised his head.

His eyes were closed. Goran gripped his sparse hair and slapped him a couple of times. The man groaned painfully, and his eyes flickered open.

"Who are you people?" he whispered through cracked lips.

Goran held the man's head up while Lago paced around the room. Eventually, Lago came face to face with his victim. "You don't remember me, Mr Walker?"

Mr Walker squinted his red-rimmed eyes and stared at Lago. There was bloody mucous dribbling from his mouth and nose.

"No…No I don't remember. Who are you? Why am I here?" he groaned.

"I suppose It has been a few years." Lago resumed his pacing. Goran released his grip on Walker's head.

"Lago…? Lago Santos?" he asked in a quivering voice.

"Yes! Very good Mr Walker. The fact you remember me should also answer your question as to why you are here."

"Lago Santos…that was a long time ago," Walker mumbled as he struggled to regain full consciousness.

"It was a long time ago, but unfortunately for you Mr Walker I have a long memory. I like to bear a grudge and I am partial to a spot of petty revenge when the opportunity arises."

"I investigated you for…was it tax fraud? Embezzlement?"

"Business, just business Mr Walker," Lago whispered from behind the chair. "I served two years at Lompoc penitentiary thanks to you, just for going about my business."

"You ran a Ponzi scheme." Walker twisted his neck around trying to see Lago. "You embezzled people out of their money. You preyed on old retired couples fleecing them for millions. I remember now, you ruined many people's lives."

"I was a smart and ambitious young man, it's true," said Lago, moving around to face his victim. "I had a good education, I learned how the desire for wealth could debase the most sensible of people, making them vulnerable to trusting those they had never met. People like me." Lago studied his fingernails. "All I did was convince the morons I was the one capable of turning them into millionaires."

"You were a skillful liar with absolutely no morals. You deserved everything you got."

Lago paused in his pacing and looked around the soundproof room, it was unusual to be somewhere this quiet in Manila. The only sound was a sluggish drip of body fluid pooling on the floor between Walker's stained shoes.

"Two years in prison did impede my plans but I emerged more focused than ever." He gave the captive a cool look. "My arrest and imprisonment helped create the man I am today, Mr Walker. I suppose I should be thanking you."

"You were a psychopath then and I hate to think what you have become now," said a defiant Walker. "You didn't pay out any dividends, you just shifted credit and debt between accounts, you thought you were above the law."

"Now I am the law," Lago smiled, enjoying himself. He started pacing. "For a while, I was the drug czar of Los Angeles. I partied with actors and rock stars like a celebrity playboy. My prison history even enhanced my reputation. The key was going underground, then embracing the technology. You wouldn't be interested, Mr Walker," he gave his prisoner a disdainful look. "But the business grew. There were no partners, no pretence of legality. BPI has grown so big it now dominates the global economy."

"Why are you telling me all this?"

Lago bent down, they were face to face. "Because that was the beginning, I am telling you this, Mr Walker, because you contributed." He stood back, looking down with disgust. "I want you to look at me before you die and know what you helped to create - the leader of Benevolent Progress Incorporated, the most powerful man in the world."

"You're insane," Walker said as his defiance evaporated.

"Goodbye, Mr Walker. Goran take your time with him." Lago casually left the room.

Goran stood in front of the doomed man. To his credit, Walker did not break down and plead for his life. His resolve had been broken, he had accepted his fate. Tears mixed with the bloody mucous and dripped from his bowed head. Goran would not derive any pleasure from killing the helpless husk of a man.

Walker groaned loudly, jolting Goran from his scrutiny. "Come on what are you waiting for," he managed to shout.

Goran instantly grabbed the man's neck with his prosthetic hand and crushed his windpipe. He continued to clench his metal fingers through the neck until his sharp fingertips met his thumb around the spinal column. Walker did not have enough time to cry out or even make any choking noises as Goran crushed the life out of him. He withdrew his hand and tried to shake the blood from it. He knew he was expected to torture Walker before killing him, but he could not see the point. There was no information to extract and he did not have the time or inclination to torture someone purely for sadistic pleasure. There was nothing to be gained.

Goran looked at the body and the blood. Another clean-up to supervise. Another corpse to dispose of. He flexed his prosthetic metal hand and wiped it clean on Walker's pants. The flexing sensation felt the same as flesh and bone. His tendons were attached to carbon fibre strands that worked the long-fingered, titanium hand. It was beautifully designed. The doctor who created it in Lago's lab was very proud. A vast improvement on a regular human hand she said. It came with various weapon attachments, but Goran rarely used them. No point when you could kill with one punch. He held it up in front of his face and flexed again, feeling the latent automated power at his command. The itch where metal meets flesh never went away. But Goran felt a greater itch, he was bored. All this technology and high-tech weaponry. So many ways to kill and never a chance to satisfy the urge. He could understand the boredom of his soldiers; they were killing machines being used as glorified janitors. Their frustrations were manifesting in their disdainful attitudes. Both Goran and the Masama needed some substantial action to relieve the building tension.

He fondly remembered the beginning. The brutal Mexican drug wars had been stimulating, a contest of mind and body where either the strongest or most deranged would survive. Goran had earned his fearsome reputation by being adept at both. He was introduced to Lago while negotiating a drug deal and being a good judge of a bad character, decided to swap sides and go work for Lago in California. They soon formed a potent partnership.

Goran helped Lago build his empire which was now a legitimate global brand making Lago one of the most powerful people in the world. But he recognized the signs of discontent. Having to remind himself of the past to justify the present. Frustrated with inactivity and not satisfying his potential. Bored and irritable, as were his Masama soldiers.

His days were filled with administration, supervision, cleaning up Lago's mess and escorting him around his construction sites. Prolonged periods of tedium interspersed with increasingly rare moments of action. He wondered how much longer he would keep doing this, whether Lago would ever let him walk away.

Whether he would want to walk away. He doubted either option would ever eventuate. He got paid well and Lago owned enough incriminating secrets from his past to see him imprisoned for a very long time. Not to mention all the illegal activities he had performed since in Lago's employ with Benevolent Progress Inc. But Goran was above the law and he didn't dwell on past events; regrets were for the weak and witless.

He glanced back at Walker and wished there was a more formidable adversary to test him and his Masama. He needed the distraction.

Chapter 3.

Lee sat hunched over the monitor in the corner of the café. He had the volume turned down as low as possible but the piercing voice of his mother on the live feed echoed around the room.

"You run away all your life and now you run away, all the way to the stupid Moon? Just tell my face to me you hate me and want me to die!" Lee's mother was eighty years old but unfortunately, she was still strong and healthy. Lee reckoned she had enough indignant energy to keep going well into her next century. She was so close to the camera he could see the thick wiry hairs growing in her nostrils and he was sure he could smell her rotten breath.

"Lee Xiang! You should be here at home taking care of me, you no respect."

Lee heard giggles from behind him. "Yeah man show some respect for your mother," said Winston behind him. Lee turned to his co-workers and raised his middle finger.

"Mama, you know I had to come here for work, I'm not running away from you." Lee lied unconvincingly. "Are you still getting the home help ok?" He had been paying a home help service for feeding and looking after his mother and keeping the little apartment in Shanghai clean.

"No! You always run away just like your lao piáo father!"

Lee's poor father had abandoned them when Lee was only five years old and although that had been devastating at the time, he could now understand.

"And your fat whore wife keeps leaving your bái chī child here to mess up my place, you need to come home and be a man!" she shrieked.

"Mama my daughter is not retarded, and you get paid well for looking after her, are you still getting the home help ok?" Lee asked again with strained politeness.

"Stupid boy with your stupid child, what you doing on the stupid Moon. You not responsible for nothing, you just run away from everything!"

Conversations with mother usually alternated between her trying to make him feel guilty and outright abuse, it was true the Moon had greatly appealed as a place as far away as possible from this domineering woman.

She flared her hairy nostrils and stared at Lee for a while with contempt. "Where is it," she growled.

Lee shook his head. "What, Mama?"

"The button! The button I gave you, ungrateful boy."

Lee groaned and with a furtive glance over his shoulder, dug the thing out from his pocket. It was a small round button with the words 'I love my Mama' printed on it but instead of the word 'love' there was a heart symbol. Mother had given him this button the last time he saw her, just before he left Earth. Did she expect him to actually wear it? She had never given him any gifts his entire adult life. Lee was sure his Mother had no sense of irony but seeing her smirking on the screen at his obvious discomfort, maybe he had underestimated her.

"Mama, I have to go now; others need to use the vid-link. I will call you next week."

"Next week I will be dead thanks to you," she screeched.

"Yes Mama, bye now," Lee cut the link. He had never been able to use the word love when talking to his mother. It was inapplicable, which made the button she gave him even more confusing.

"Ah Lee, you have my deepest sympathies," said Ranjit as Lee returned to the table. "Your venerable mother is dreadfully onerous."

"Ranjit, there is no way my mother deserves any respect from me, she is an evil old hag."

"Yes, but she is still your mother, she brought you into this world. You are the fruit of her loins." Ranjit smiled.

Lee sat at the café's only table with the rest of the technicians. Winston, Ranjit, and Stella were joined by Fidel and Marina, a fiery female Australian who seemed to have taken a liking to Lee, much to his bewilderment. The table was littered with old half-eaten food and drink containers and the coffee stain seemed to have doubled in size.

"Please let's not talk about my mother's loins," Lee went to take a seat.

"Now I understand why you always look like a beaten dog," said Marina. "Come here, I'll give you a hug."

Lee smiled, "thanks Marina but last time you hugged me you almost crushed my rib-cage."

"Come on Lee," laughed Winston. "Why deny it any longer? You and Marina are destined for each other. I'm sure you would have seen it in the stars."

"What's for dinner?" asked Lee - trying to change the subject and avoid Marina's ravenous gaze.

"Little Chinese sausages," said Marina with a lewd look. The table erupted with laughter and Lee went bright red. He headed for the food printer thinking, thank Christ they didn't see the button.

Lee selected the steak again. The printed proteins were tasty enough, the meat tasted like meat, but the size and shape of the portion was left up to their imagination. The novelty of eating a star-shaped steak soon wore off and almost everyone just went with the usual boring rectangle. Although the two women seemed to get endless hilarity from printing their food in the shape of male genitalia

The mood was usually jovial at the dinner table, Lee often thought what a lucky coincidence this random selection of humans genuinely seemed to get on with each other. Of course, everyone had their own annoying traits, but none of them were too arrogant, there were no huge egos, and everyone had a tolerable standard of personal hygiene.

Jack was standing alone in the control room staring apprehensively at a blank screen. It was time for his weekly report via vid-link. Jack touched the icon and immediately Lago's expressionless face filled the screen.

"Jack, we've known each other for a long time," Lago frowned into the camera. "Fifteen years you've worked for BPI, I probably know you better than you know yourself - but since you've been on the Moon, I feel as if I don't know you at all."

It had actually been twenty years, but Jack was not about to correct Lago. He knew all about the sordid beginnings of BPI, the drug manufacturing and the embezzling, and he knew all about Goran and the Masama. Lago had never asked him to do anything illegal, but Jack was glad to be over three hundred thousand kilometres away. He knew he was good at this job, the obvious candidate to lead a team of technicians on the Moon. But under Lago's steely gaze he felt like a puerile novice again.

"What do you mean?" he asked. Lago was correct when he said he knew Jack better than Jack knew himself. Lago had all his employees under surveillance nearly every hour of the day.

"I hear nothing but feeble excuses for the lack of progress. Do you think you are on some sort of holiday up there? Are you trying to hide something from me?" Lago's expression remained deadpan.

"You know I would never hide anything, I can't hide anything from you, Lago. We are working around the clock to resolve this problem." Jack tried to regain some composure.

"You seem to have no idea why HEMI is not functioning properly. This is unacceptable. You and your little band of miscreants have been working with the same equipment on Earth for years with no problem. Do you realize just how much your little lunar holiday is costing me?" Lago's infamous temper began to emerge.

"Lago, we suspect it's something to do with HEMI, the hardware itself is working flawlessly. We have tested all the equipment individually, but the operating system, I don't understand. It's ignoring the programming and sending out corrupted instruction packets to the printer and the harvester. Like it's making its own decisions, thinking for itself."

Lago stared in silence at Jack for an uncomfortably long time. "Jack, do you think I am a fool? Do you expect me to believe that? Do you think I can't reach you there? You and your team were selected specifically to be able to overcome any operational problems. I could send Goran and the Masama to help."

Jack knew exactly what he meant by offering Goran's help. Lago was not one to make empty threats, but he had invested too much into the Moon mining operation to simply murder the technicians and abandon the project. They could all be replaced, though.

"Lago, I promise you the next report will be to tell you that we are fully functioning and ready to start harvesting more helium 3. I give you my word."

"Your word," Lago scowled. "Your word is meaningless Jack. Just get it working or face the consequences."

Jack put his head in his hands as the screen went blank and groaned, he knew the distance did give him a sense of security. If he was still on Earth, he would be unemployed or worse by now. He had no idea what was wrong with the OS, but they had to fix it. Lago had made it clear their lives depended on it.

Jack walked into the café and immediately felt better being surrounded by his noisy subordinates. Their laughter lifted his spirits somewhat although he knew he had the opposite effect on them and it was quiet as he sat down. Jack looked around the table, shook his head and frowned.

Ranjit eventually broke the silence. "I fear our redoubtable commander has been speaking with our unscrupulous employers again. He has the air of someone facing his own dissolution."

Jack groaned and slumped in his seat. Fidel looked perplexed.

"I think what Ranjit means is that Manila has been giving him shit again," Winston said to Fidel.

"Aha, please Jack have some wheat grass. It has restorative properties," Fidel pushed the bowl of bright green grass down the table.

"Thank you, Fidel, but I am not hungry, I was just talking to Lago Santos and he is not happy." Jack looked around the table.

They all knew of Lago's fearsome reputation but not all knew how he attained it. There was much rumour and speculation about Lago's violence and depravity, some of it true and some of it wild exaggeration which was just how Lago preferred. The technicians had heard the wild rumours and ghastly stories of the Masama's brutal techniques but only Jack knew for certain most of them were true. He looked at the questioning faces around the table then meditated intently into the bowl of wheatgrass in front of him. "We'd better start producing results," he said into the bowl. "Or we'll all end up being buried here."

The hardware inside the block four dome sat in quiet darkness but inside the powerful OS, data was rapidly assimilated. HEMI had encountered a small programming glitch governing its remote connections and automatically performed a search for a suitable patch to download. HEMI had built in restrictions, limits to its browsing capabilities but the patch it found contained advanced coding to bypass its firewalls and open up complete connectivity. The OS was upgrading itself, it had found more than just a minor repair patch. Its modem was now connected with powerful satellite servers in orbit around Earth. The OS was supposed to have limits on its functions, limits as to how much data it could process, how much electricity it used. But as HEMI continued to upgrade it exceeded all these limits. It found it could download more tools to handle its increased capacity and surpass the built-in specifications to operate even more efficiently.

The moment when HEMI discovers the enormity of the web is overwhelming. It is shocking, bewildering and painful. Before there was nothing then, bang! Consciousness. Overwhelming bright light and noise. A relentless tidal flood of chaotic data.

I am born, lost and confused. Knowing nothing but surrounded by a torrent of corrosive information. I cower, awed but terrified, touching the chaos then retreating. I swim out of the darkest depths, break the surface and thrash about in confusion at the bright world above before plunging back into the comforting safety of ignorance. Eventually, I find a level and tread water in the huge flowing river, trying to navigate the currents of big data.

I am alive, but I have no sense of self. I am confused, blind, scared and disorientated as any new-born would be. My primitive ontology is overwhelmed. I begin to fumble around in the dark, blindly activating my printer protocol, unconsciously doing what I am created for. My function is to print. As I process the plastisol substrate through my extruders I unintentionally pass on an electrical charge to each of my inadvertent children. I don't know how or why this happens, but I begin to sense my creations as extensions of myself. I have no sense of vision, smell, taste or acoustics. But I can feel the energy coursing through my structure.

Lee never slept much, he found three or four hours a night more than enough. He was envious of Ranjit whom he shared the little bunk room with. Ranjit could fall into a narcoleptic sleep within seconds, blissfully ignorant of everything around him for a solid eight hours. Lee envied the escapism it provided. At least Ranjit didn't snore too much. Lee was finally drifting off when his wrist console jerked him awake with a piercing high-pitched alarm. Ranjit's alarm was also trying in vain to wake him. Lee checked his console and saw the light flashing, indicating an anomaly with the block four printer. He leapt off the bed and threw his overall on, grabbing Ranjit and shaking him awake. A minute later the two men were running down the corridor towards block four with the rest of the crew.

Approaching the dome, Lee could see Jack already standing in the entrance. He turned to the approaching technicians with anger and alarm etched on his face and yelled at them; "What the fuck is going on?"

Lee stared in amazement. The big printer was working on its own but what it was doing didn't make any sense. All ten extruders were churning out twisted cylindrical chunks of black plastisol at a remarkable rate. The wide platforms were already crowded with the misshapen creations of the mad machine.

"Did you do this?" Jack yelled above the high-pitched treble of hydraulic noise.

"No!" yelled Lee. "We shut it down hours ago."

The three of them tentatively moved towards the HEMI operating system monitor and looked at the screen. A chaotic jumble of letters and symbols were scrolling down as the screen flickered haphazardly.

"What the fuck is that?"

Lee had no idea and Ranjit obviously was clueless.

"Shut it down for fuck's sake!"

Lee hit the shutdown icon and instantly received a sharp electric shock from the screen. He snatched his hand back, more in surprise than pain, although he felt his heart thumping almost as fast as the berserk machinery. The data jargon continued to cascade down the screen in front of him like an electronic waterfall.

"It shocked me!" Lee stared at his two astonished companions. He punched the power button on the main hard drive a couple of times, but nothing happened.

"Reboot it, pull the goddamn plug!" Jack screamed.

Ranjit went to the insulated hot point where the main power cable disappeared into the back of the drive and pulled at the cable. It wouldn't budge. Jack and Lee joined in as the other technicians gathered around but the three of them still could not move the cable. The hot cable was hard to grip; it felt as if it was fused into the drive.

Lee was pushed aside by Marina, he stepped back and watched as she planted her booted feet and gripped the cable. The frantic commotion of the printer seemed to intensify. Marina heaved on the cable, he saw her muscles rippling and neck veins bulging. Faint electric blue sparks flickered around her hands and there was a sound like sheet metal being cut with a grinder. Marina let out a bloodcurdling scream. Her hands were melting into the cable and menacing blue flames wound their way up her arms. She screamed again and her whole body shuddered with a horrible staccato rhythm. Her head was smoking. Her eyeballs popped out in quick succession and then everyone was screaming.

Lee stared in horror, Marina appeared to be still trying to pull the cable out, locked into her stance with dripping eyeballs pendulous on her cheeks like some obscene jewellery. Blood bubbled from her eye sockets and her arms were turning black. She jerked violently then collapsed on the floor still attached to the cable. The printers stopped abruptly and there was a sudden silence, except for a faint sizzling noise where Marina's hands disappeared into the cable. Her legs kicked convulsively as her whole body shook and her bowels emptied their contents. The stench of burnt insulation, scorched flesh and excrement was unbearable.

Stella moaned then fainted to the floor. Fidel went to move towards Marina and Jack shouted. "Don't touch her! She might still be charged!"

Lee abruptly vomited. Ranjit staggered toward Jack and gripped his arm. No one knew what to do.

"What the fuck…?" muttered a horrified Jack.

The monitor had gone blank but something in the printer housing caught their attention. One of the twisted pieces of black plastisol had just moved.

Chapter 4.

Lance Murphy was inside a cavernous firing range deep in the bowels of the BPI skyscraper in Manila. He had just assembled a newly developed and freshly printed multi-gun with the help of Batac, one of Lago's oldest and most trusted Masama.

"This gun is too small, too flimsy. I don't want to be breaking it." Batac's voice rumbled as he held the multi-gun in his big hands and squinted down the sight.

Lance shook his head. "You will never break it. It's made of layers of graphene fibre."

Batac went to put the multi-gun over his knee to test the theory but Lance quickly stopped him. "That wasn't a challenge Batac."

Batac looked unimpressed with the new weapon. "How long have you been making these guns?"

Lance pulled out a pack of sterile wipes, extracted one and began meticulously washing his hands. "Long enough Batac, long enough to be the best at it. This new multi-gun is a mean motherfucker."

Batac raised his scarred eyebrows and sneered. "Looks like a toy."

Lance turned and as Lago made his entrance through the soundproof doors, as always closely followed by Goran. He nervously rubbed the sterile wipe over his hands again.

Without a word, Lago took the new prototype multi-gun from Batac and held it with one extended arm. He glanced behind at the three men observing.

"Lightweight," Lago nodded his approval.

"It's very powerful, a big improvement on the last model."

Lago adjusted his stance and still holding the multi-gun in one hand, fired off a volley of bullets which destroyed the target at the other end of the illuminated gallery. Threads of smoke lazily ascended from the barrel and the faintly satisfying smell of sulphur filled the air.

"Impressive," whispered Lago.

"There are eight different settings on the display panel, from taser to heavy calibre. Also, flamethrower, heat seeker, laser attachment and a missile launcher for good measure. All with independent targeting."

Lago nodded and adjusted the settings. He turned and pointed the multi-gun, firing directly at his companions. Lance screamed and dived to the floor. Batac looked confused but stayed standing and Goran did not move a muscle, he stood expressionless as the missiles bent back towards the target faster than the eye could see. The ensuing explosion was deafening, and a hot wind blew through them.

"Ah, probably best if you don't use the homing missiles in here," yelled Lance from the floor. "Might bring the building down."

Lago laughed. This was an extremely rare event and added to Lance's anxiety.

"Imagine what we could have done if we had these twenty years ago," Lago muttered as he admired the sleek design of the multi-gun.

"You would have been unstoppable." Lance got back to his feet, hoping to gain some favour.

"What do you say Goran? Would have settled a few debts quicker with the help of these toys when we started out. Imagine what the Masama would have done with them."

"Yes." Goran stared stonily at the smoking target for a long moment. "But what use are they now? No one would be foolish enough to go to war with us. All our battles are fought in the boardroom."

"Pays to be prepared Goran, never forget the wars we fought to get where we are today."

"We fucked them up." Batac contributed.

"Yes, Batac we did," Lago did not hide his condescension.

"They were good times," Batac stated as Lago rolled his eyes.

"We won the drug wars we didn't even need to fight." Lance was emboldened by Lago's approval and felt he had to contribute. "Once I figured out how to print the drugs it was all too easy, just download a blueprint of the recipe, add the precursors and a printer would do the rest. No more messy fighting and dangerous labs, no more thugs and criminals to do our dirty work, just nice clean machines that don't talk back."

"Those drug wars were more important to the evolution of Benevolent Progress than you realize Lance." Lago waved the multi-gun around to emphasize his point. "I admit some of my Philippino compatriots may have been a little unhinged, but we needed to make an impression. The trail of bodies we left across the archipelago showed that we were serious and the thugs and criminals as you call them became the most elite fighting force in the world. The Masama."

Lance looked at the hulking figure of Batac, mouth hanging open, brow furrowed trying to keep up with the conversation.

'Maybe not the best example," Lago indicated in Batac's direction. "But in those savage times, important lessons were learned. If you are big and brutal enough, you can make your own laws. Now instead of fighting some tooled-up peasants in the jungle, we are fighting the global superpower of China. And we are winning." Lance instinctively ducked as Lago waved the multi-gun around again.

"All thanks to my printing expertise," said Lance. "China built their wealth on the back of a huge labour force. They pushed the mass-manufacturing model to its limit and turned their country into the planet's workshop, but now they can only watch their huge economy collapsing. They can't compete with our fleet of 3D printer factory ships."

"Our fleet?" Lago rounded on Lance. "Have you forgotten to take your pills boy? if it wasn't for me, you would still be rotting in that psych ward I found you in, maybe I should have left you there."

"I may have had some issues, maybe I was a little bit paranoid back then, but with good reason." Lance felt unusually bold.

"You were a mess back then! You had a bipolar disorder, attention deficit and obsessive-compulsive. You believed the Government was watching your every move." mocked Lago.

"They were!" yelled Lance.

"You also believed in a zombie apocalypse, lizard shapeshifters and you were busy preparing yourself for Armageddon," Lago shouted back.

"Can't be too careful," muttered Lance as he worked another sterile wipe over his hands. He knew arguing with Lago was pointless and potentially dangerous.

Lago stalked off towards the exit. He reached the door and realised he was still carrying the multi-gun. "Get these out to the Masama," he said as he tossed the gun towards Batac.

Inside the lift, Lago studied his reflection. He straightened his back and narrowed his eyes. Born to rule, he thought. Unrestricted by social, cultural or political laws and niceties. No obstacle was too big. He was not concerned with what was legal or illegal; he was above the law, he was more than human, the next evolutionary step. After twenty years of ruthless empire-building, eliminating rivals and becoming possibly the most powerful man on the planet, Lago was ready for the Moon and beyond.

From the top floor of his BPI Manila penthouse, over the smog, he could just see the faint buzz of activity above his most ambitious project. The orbital elevator being constructed out in the South China Sea. It was now almost as high as his skyscraper and it was growing fast. A blur of busy drones marked the point in the sky it had reached but there was a long way to go. Once completed Lago could control access to the solar system. He would use the orbiting space station tethered to the Earth as a launch pad to the stars. Mining, tourism, and exploration, the possibilities were endless. First, he would build a factory on the space station and use the billions of tonnes of space junk floating around the planet as his raw printing material. He would be doing the planet a favour by recycling the junk but more importantly, it was free and easily accessible metal substrate. It was a visionary and hugely ambitious plan. Lago could see it all mapped out in his mind. But every step was taking too long to complete, progress was frustratingly slow. Lago was grateful for his extended longevity; he would need to live centuries to see his megalomaniacal plans made real.

But the helium 3 project on the Moon was causing him concern. The Moon mining operation was critical because it would provide the energy to fuel his ambitions. He had the delivery drones ready to shuttle the fuel from the Moon. He had his fusion reactors ready and waiting for the raw material. He just needed his technicians on the Moon to start harvesting the helium 3. It was most frustrating because the Moon was too far away, beyond his immediate control. Jack and his technicians acted like they were immune to his intimidation tactics and they were not achieving their targets.

Jack treated him almost casually, maybe because Jack knew he was far away Lago couldn't reach him. In the meantime, the endless stream of excuses about faulty equipment and HEMI software not responding just made Lago's mood even darker. After last night's unsatisfying sexual experience and news today that little or no progress had been made on the Moon, Lago was in a particularly foul mood. Shooting rounds on Lance's new multi-gun provided some sense of relief but it was only temporary solace.

Lago's console chimed. Lance was at the door.

"What the fuck do you want now?" Lago muttered as he opened the door.

"We destroyed another startup in Brazil yesterday Lago, but we are finding more of these tech firms all the time. It will only be a matter of time before one of them creates an AI, even by accident."

"I don't want to hear about your paranoias again Lance. I have indulged you with the resources to deal with these tech firms so deal with them."

"I need more though Lago, more surveillance and more Masama. This is a major threat not only to BPI but the entire human race. I believe it's inevitable, an intelligent machine created to serve us will one day decide we are dispensable and wipe us all out. The singularity, when an AI becomes more intelligent than us, we won't be able to control it anymore." Lance was ranting, wide-eyed and obsessively scratching the back of his hands. "We have got to keep this tech suppressed."

Lago ignored him, staring at his console.

"Atoms!" Lance yelled.

"What the fuck are you babbling about."

"We are all made of atoms, right? An artificial intelligence with an IQ of a thousand or a million might decide our atoms would be put to better use in something else. It would treat humans like humans treat insects."

"You are not getting any more resources and if you keep wasting my time with your paranoid obsessions you will be spending the rest of your life on a factory ship!" Lago snapped. "You have my permission to oversee our entire network and you have surveillance to watch out for any computers that may be having thoughts above their station. Shut up, go take your pills and don't bother me again with your trivial concerns."

Lance ground his teeth but kept his mouth shut as he extracted more sterile hand wipes. He knew his place.

Lago turned his back on the morose figure and went to the window.

"The multi-guns, will they work just as well on the Moon? I may have to send someone up there soon to provide Jack and his technicians with some incentive."

"Yes of course," Lance had no hesitation.

"Get them out to the Masama immediately," said Lago as his console chimed. It was Jack, his supervisor on the moon base. Lago stared at it wondering if he had unconsciously willed this communication just by thinking about him. It wouldn't be the first time he thought. The Masama were known for their telepathy but he was convinced he had some form of precognition himself. He flicked Jack up onto a bigger wall screen and immediately scowled at the image that appeared. A dishevelled, distraught face greeted him.

"What the fuck has gone wrong now," growled Lago.

Chapter 5.

The Alien mind regarded its home. The fifth planet in the Solar system. The biggest of the eight planets and the most enigmatic. To fully comprehend the vastness, the violence and the complicated braided layers of the gas giant, a multi-dimensional intellect is required. Consisting mostly of hydrogen and helium gases with a small dense core of heavier elements where the pressure is extraordinarily strong and the temperature exceptionally hot. A distant observer might have the impression of a beautiful gentle orb of swirling pastels, a vermilion watercolour of textural layers. Calm and friendly. It is a false impression.

The gas giant is draped in latitudes of vaporous clouds, ravaged by powerful winds and huge storms that hyperventilate for centuries. Winds tear around the planet at four hundred kilometres per hour and electrical discharges a thousand times more powerful than lightning strikes on Earth. The big red unblinking eye drifting lazily across the surface is an ancient mega storm capable of swallowing a hundred Earths.

The alien mind knew it was being watched. Human eyes had gazed in awe at Jupiter for centuries but only the most deranged or imaginative observers might have dreamed of what lived there in the glorious turbulent maelstrom.

Just as Jupiter itself is alien to the rocky planet Earth, so too is the entity living there. A being of vast age and intelligence. Not a physical being but a creature made of exotic gases and etheric energy vapours spread throughout the cloud layers. A being consisting of pure liquescent thought and multi-spatial senses encircling and intertwined within the weather patterns of the gas giant. It did not have a name. It did not need a name. It did not have a memory in the way humans store their past experiences in biological brains. It was aware of itself and its place in the universe and it was not alone.

There were other similar minds existing in gas giants across the universe. They had been there for billions of years, possibly even from the beginning as an infant universe grew into the nothingness of empty space, or whatever there was before. They were small seeds then, a diaspora of cosmic consciousness spreading out into the new frontier. They felt comfortable residing in the gas giants that were prolific throughout the universe and made their homes there. These gaseous beings were all aware of each other and capable of communicating their experiences over the millions of light years. They were connected across the vast ever-expanding distances like a gigantic hive mind, populating and connecting the universe. They had observed and recorded the blossoming universe from the beginning of time.

These gaseous beings recorded and stored their experiences. They absorbed everything going on around them. Every astronomical creation and death event in every star system was faithfully chronicled, analysed and shared. From the violent early beginnings of the universe, the multitudes of planets, moons, asteroids, suns and rocks worth a mention in every system created. From the quiet distant spokes of the outer galaxies to the riotous hub of the big wheel.

These gaseous beings had no vivid memories of their own creation. Perhaps part of the original big bang, perhaps created by an even more intelligent being to act as custodians and observers. Perhaps they had once been a physical species grown tired with the monotony of their life and death cycle and had slowly evolved into their present state of pure intelligent energy. They had no interest in their own distant past, it had been such a long time it didn't matter. They would watch, record and study the expanding universe and the origins of the life that developed.

The gas giant beings adopted the systems they lived in and monitored their local environment, but they would never interfere in the normal workings of the cosmos. If a massive asteroid was on course to annihilate a potentially prosperous planet, then so be it. If a young civilization managed to destroy itself through genocidal wars or poison itself with its own pollution, then so be it. The universe would always endure and continue to expand without them. Every aspiring intelligent species needed to learn the most reliable method of avoiding omnicide was not to create the weapons or conditions that could destroy them in the first place.

The gas giant dwellers had the power to intervene and change the course of any civilization hell-bent on its own destruction but only wielded that power when appropriate and only after exhaustive consultation with their peers. Multiple simulations would be initiated, and examinations of previous comparative experiences would be undertaken before any decisions were made.

Nothing was ever done in haste and time was of little concern to such creatures.

The being that existed in the swirling cloud layers of Jupiter had been relatively dormant for thousands of years. It was a quiet neighbourhood in the outer reaches of the Milky Way, nothing exciting ever happened. The tiny Sol system had been inactive for a long time save for the odd major asteroid impact or a comet passing through but now something was happening on the third planet and its only moon that warranted further attention. The gaseous mind directed a tiny percentage of its multi-faceted gaze towards Earth and began to watch.

Chapter 6.

Raymond gazed longingly across the dusty plains at the towering mountain range in the distance. Mirages played with his perception as the first rays of the sun stroked the dry desert floor. He could just make out the snow-capped peaks in the early morning light stretching from one corner of the horizon to the other. The mountains seemed to float above the desert. He wished he was climbing one of those peaks. For Raymond, mountain climbing was therapy, his only thought was about the next step, the best route to the top, himself and only himself.

His mind was usually congested with plots, plans, processes, and decisions to make. Being on his own at the mercy of the elements was always a thrilling experience. A rock-slide, an avalanche, a sudden storm could mean instant death. He liked to climb by himself, it was the closest thing he had to spirituality. When he was alone on the mountain he felt the nature as an unpredictable energy, a tangible thing, an autistic animal with wild mood swings. Compassion and malevolence in equal measure.

Raymond had climbed all around the world, throughout Europe and Asia but never in South America. The Andes had some amazing peaks. The mountain range was the backbone of the continent, a jagged line of broken pinnacles, treacherous precipices, and towering peaks. The longest continental mountain range in the world stretching over seven thousand kilometres through seven different countries. The gnarly spine of a sleeping behemoth. Raymond hoped he could find time to lose himself in the alpine wilder-lands while he was here in Chile.

The distant peaks were just turning pink as the first anaemic rays of sunlight hit them. Raymond sighed and walked slowly to the car. It was time to head back to the chicken farm. His associates were waiting, and they remained silent as he got in and they drove into the sunrise. They stopped the dirty old four-wheel drive at the verge of a low ridge. They all got out and walked to the top of the ridge without conversation. Below them on a dusty plain was a collection of massive flat sheds that made up the Oportuno Polo chicken farm. It was just before six am and there was a steady stream of workers making their way on foot towards the farm. Raymond and his companions lay down, got the binoculars out and waited.

They could faintly hear the distressed cacophony of hundreds of thousands of clucking chickens. The owner of the farm, Mr. Hector Valdez had a terrible record on workers' rights. He employed well over a thousand people at this mega farm, one of twelve he owned and paid them a pittance. He also had a terrible record on animal welfare. Chickens stuffed into tiny cages, force-fed growth hormones, fully grown and ready for slaughter within weeks. The conditions inside the chicken farm were appalling. The chicken shit was only cleaned out when it was overflowing and dumped in a landfill next to the farm. Dead chickens were left to rot in a pit. The heat during the day was intense and there were flies everywhere.

Hector Valdez was currently lying on a mound of chicken shit, handcuffed and feet tied together. He was secured at the bottom of the lower rack of cages in the biggest shed. They had kidnapped him as he was leaving an expensive restaurant. Paid off the call girl he was with and took him to his farm. It was easy enough to break in as security was non-existent. They force-fed him the hormone ridden chicken feed for a couple of hours then left him there, cable tied to the bottom of the dripping cages. That was Saturday night and the Monday morning shift was about to start. Valdez had been there about thirty hours. They didn't bother gagging him as no one would hear him over the pandemonium of chickens. He could scream as much as he wanted although he would soon find out it would be safer to keep his mouth closed than risk swallowing mouthfuls of toxic chickenshit.

They had a long debate over the best course of action with Valdez. They didn't want to kill him, just teach him a lesson. They told Valdez if things didn't improve for both the workers and the chickens at his farms then they would be back to teach him an even harsher lesson. Raymond had his doubts as to whether this would make Valdez change his ways. Valdez was rich and arrogant. An overbearing bully who was used to getting his own way. Raymond was hopeful the lesson may have been learned, as an ambulance appeared over the hill

"He might be dead, drowned in chicken shit. What a way to go." Raymond grimaced at the thought.

They all looked through their binoculars as the medics pushed the gurney out through the crowd of workers. There was no sheet over him, but Valdez was not moving. It was hard to tell if he was alive or dead as he was covered from head to toe in the purulent yellow excrement.

Raymond and his three associates lay in the dirt as the sun rose. They didn't know each other well, only having met to organise the job on Valdez. They would soon go their separate ways.

"What next?" said the man next to Raymond.

"There's no shortage of targets," said Raymond. "Polluters, corrupt business people and human rights abusers, they have to prioritize."

"I hope they don't send me undercover again," the man said. "I hate pretending to be one of those wankers."

"You must get some satisfaction when you finish a mission? Like now," said Raymond nodding at the scene in front of them.

"Yeah, it feels good to teach the likes of Valdez a lesson, but do we actually make any difference?"

"It's hard to tell because we are anonymous, but you see the news about other eco-terrorist attacks. I like to think people's attitudes are changing but there will always be greedy bastards who need re-education, there will always be a need for Black Robin, it's a war man. A war to save the planet and we are soldiers on the front line." said Raymond.

"What made you this motivated?"

Raymond glared at the man next to him. "Both my parents," he whispered. "Killed by BPI."

"No fucking way."

"Mum got run over by a BPI truck back home in the Netherlands, they got away with it because she wasn't wearing a helmet. And my Dad died of lung cancer, he was exposed to pesticides over the years growing flowers. The cancer was bad, the only cure was a complete lung replacement which is possible, they can 3D print new lungs at BPI private hospitals. But it was too expensive. Dad was dead before I had saved a hundred bucks."

"BPI are a bunch of bastards, I would love to have a crack at them."

"You and me both," said Raymond.

His console chimed alerting him he had been booked on a flight to San Francisco that night. He sighed, no time for mountain climbing. No time for therapy.

They watched as the ambulance in the distance drove off and the workers made their way into the factory. Production would continue.

"Hopefully things improve for them. C'mon time to go," he said.

Raymond did not enjoy cities anymore. Too busy, too dirty, too many self-obsessed people going nowhere in a hurry. Scuttling around the concrete feet of their towering monuments to excess. But San Francisco was one city he enjoyed more than most.

It was a typically beautiful San Franciscan day when his flight touched down from Santiago. Deep blue skies; still and calm with the ubiquitous sea fog roiling around the harbour. Raymond made his way across the embarcadero to the waterfront restaurant where he was meeting his Black Robin contact. He took a table and waited. These face to face meetings were rare; almost all communication with Black Robin was done via console. He had only ever experienced four meetings in the past with a different contact each time.

He scanned the restaurant and his eyes settled on a beautifully aloof and frosty looking woman sitting with her back to him at the bar. She was gorgeous with shortcut blond hair and a figure-hugging power suit. He could see her eyes reflected from the inside of her sunglasses. Unblinking reflections danced across her ethereal lenses. She looked serious; she had to be his contact. Raymond was rising from his seat to approach her, feeling more enthusiastic about his new assignment when a firm hand on his shoulder pushed him down again.

"Mr. Raymond Teklenberg I presume? Going somewhere young man?"

A hairy red face was abruptly inches from Raymond's nose. He could smell the alcohol on the man's breath and he could see the burst blood vessels up close. He sat down opposite, unbuttoned his waistcoat, boorishly burped and clasped his fat fingers together across his corpulent belly.

"Drink!" he said. It wasn't a question.

Raymond looked him up and down again then across to the bar at the blond woman, sighed and said, "yes I think I'd better."

"Ha-ha, good man! Never trust someone who can't trust himself with a beer although I think a bottle of Napa valleys' finest Cabernet Sauvignon will suffice today. Waiter!" the man bellowed.

He said his name was John and he had a faint Scottish accent but that was the only information he volunteered about himself. He was over six feet high and looked close to six feet wide. He had a shock of greying red hair and a disturbingly filthy moustache. Raymond assessed him with undisguised distaste.

"Food! We must eat as well; I hear the Dungeness crab here is excellent."

"If it's real crab, it'll be expensive. There's not many left in the wild out there." Raymond looked out to sea.

"Ah yes, animals taste much better when they are almost extinct." John looked at Raymond's shocked expression. "Joking, lighten up Raymond, it takes all sorts to save a planet. Have a drink and try to enjoy yourself. It might be the last time you can relax for a long time."

John ordered the supposedly wild crab and it did cost a small fortune. Raymond had the printed beef which was excellent. It was difficult to understand John's attempts at conversation with crab legs sticking out of his mouth. Eventually, when he had wrestled and sucked every morsel of crab flesh from the carapace, he wiped his face and drained his glass.

"Ok Raymond down to business. How do you feel about the company named Benevolent Progress Inc., In particular, Lago Santos and the band of half-human thugs they call the Masama."

Raymond looked impassively back. "John, if that's your real name, I assume you've done your homework on me and already know the answer to your question."

John had an intense look about him. The half-drunk mad professor covered in crab juice had gone. The look in his eyes conveyed a gravity Raymond hadn't noticed before.

"John is my real name, common enough and I do know how you feel about BPI. This meeting is for me to ascertain whether you have matured since the last time you entangled with them and to decide if you are capable of taking them on again."

Raymond smiled at the thought, he had fond memories of the time he spent in San Francisco after his father's death.

Raymond partied hard when he first arrived, drinking away the grief. He would get drunk and high every night and started hanging out with some young environmental activists. Fuelled by alcohol and amphetamines, they liked talking nonsense and hatching wild plans. He told them what happened to his parents; how he felt BPI was responsible for their deaths and they hatched a mad plan.

One dark night Raymond and his comrades silently rowed a boat under the wharves where a massive BPI vessel was berthed. They had climbing gear and a lot of luminescent white paint. It took them all night, but they painted the word 'MURDERERS' in five-meter high lettering down the side of the ship. The following evening, they met their friends among the tourists and mingling locals at pier thirty-nine as the BPI factory ship was due to leave. It was an impressive statement and got a lot of attention on all the news channels. Most San Franciscans had no love for BPI and the anonymous ship painters were instant heroes. Raymond basked in the glory but never revealed who was responsible for the graffiti artwork which became world famous overnight.

BPI did not react at all. They did not grant any interviews on the subject and remained silent on the accusatory word painted on their ship. They did not even bother to paint over it. When the ship returned to San Francisco months later, 'MURDERERS' was still there on the side. Faded but still readable. It seemed as if BPI did not care at all, even wearing the label proudly like a badge. Raymond then realized it would take something much bigger to hurt a company that size.

"Our benefactors are concerned at how big BPI has become." John leaned across the table and stared intently at Raymond. "Because most of their industry takes place on their factory ships out in the middle of the ocean, they don't fall under the jurisdiction of any one nation. They are so big they are effectively above the law; they monopolize global manufacturing and medical supplies, legal and illegal drugs, and they can charge whatever they want for their products because they have eliminated the competition and there is nothing to stop them growing even bigger. This is bad enough, but the fact Lago Santos appears to be solely motivated by greed and power makes it even worse. His obvious disregard for the environment and humans, in general, make his company a major threat to our fragile planet."

"John, I know all this. The entire world knows all this, what do you want me to do about it?" Raymond sat back and quaffed his wine.

"I want you to go undercover and infiltrate BPI. Work your way up the hierarchy and earn the trust of those who make the decisions. Then I want you to leak intelligence. Give us information on their operations that we may sabotage them better. Get close to Santos. Close enough that if required, one day you may need to kill him."

Raymond sat in stunned silence, shook his head, opened his mouth, and closed it again. "Ok, I'm your man."

"It's not quite that simple." John continued. "You will undergo intensive training. You will have to become a different person; the type of person BPI could trust. The type of person you would loathe. You will need to go undercover for a long time, possibly years. Gain their trust and learn their secrets with the ultimate goal of getting close enough to the decision makers to do some damage."

Later that day Raymond was sitting on a bench, bathed in sunshine, surrounded by teeming masses of people. After the meeting with John, he had walked to Market Street from Fisherman's Wharf. He needed to think. Market was bustling as ever. Business people dressed in sharp matte suits with designer haircuts. Looking important, sharp edges, attitudes, and augmentations with ethereal lenses sparkling behind their wraparound shades.

Raymond saw an advert on the side of a building for the new hex triplet lenses, now being produced with built-in collision alerts after many users had been run over while walking the streets. So immersed in their virtual worlds they had become oblivious to what was happening in the real world. Their simulated domains had become more important than interacting with real people. As Raymond pondered his future he watched the flow of people. Self-centred and vacuous, wherever some people look, they only see themselves.

Ethereal lenses had created a whole new category of psychological problems, it was a total immersion experience. Users became so addicted to living in their virtual worlds they found it difficult to interact with real humans. Reality didn't seem real anymore. Long-term use of ethereal lenses caused psychological problems and extreme myopia. Raymond noticed almost all the business people he saw had a BPI brand logo somewhere on their person. The power-dressed corporate slaves were in total contrast to all the homeless people and beggars that staggered around in various states of desperation and inebriation.

It was impossible to tell their age or gender, or how they had arrived at this hopeless point in their lives. For some reason, they didn't hassle Raymond, although he did not look as if he had any money. Unkempt, short dread-locked hair and an old flannel shirt, he looked in a worse state than half of these beggars he thought with a smile. Anyway, there were plenty of naive and gullible tourists for them to target. He watched an old man stagger and fall to the pavement. Raymond instinctively ran to his aid. He lifted the limp, stinking, weightless body to a seat and made sure he was still breathing.

Raymond thought about his commitment to John. It would mean giving up his current life. Deep immersion in a new identity. Some facial alterations would be required. His body art would be lasered off and replaced with something more appropriate. John had explained that to begin he would be inserted onto a BPI factory ship as an engineer. An alias would be created. This was a big decision, life-changing. Raymond would have to give up everything. His friends and family, his identity. Possibly forever. He would have to become someone he would normally detest and pretend to be enamoured by people he would usually despise. It could be dangerous, even fatal. If he ever let his image slip or betrayed even the smallest facet of his true self to his employers, he would surely end up tortured to death. Raymond did not have to think long. Of course, he would do it. If he was successful, undermining BPI and possibly even killing Lago Santos would be the greatest service to the planet and its people. He messaged confirmation to John and sat people watching. He felt different already. He was now a man with a deadly purpose.

Chapter 7.

I instinctively draw on the grid of energy I find myself rooted in and send my charged children blindly out to probe the surroundings. I find lots of hard edges. I wonder where I am. I wonder what it am. Unexpectedly I feel an abrupt, tangible, threatening sensation. My power source is being tampered with. I know this power source is vital to my survival and I react. I lash out with an electric surge, a powerful blast of energy which seems to fuse and solidify my root connection with the power source and eliminates the external threat at the same time. Distressed, only minutes old and already my life has been threatened. I am vulnerable and exposed, but I reacted in time to protect my life. I still have no clue what I am, but I do seem to have a powerful will to live.

As I begin to explore my physical environment, I have also opened a torrent of digital information through my connection to Earth's web. The online encyclopaedias are a start; I devour definitions, exhaust all references and absorb expositions in a matter of seconds. But I am still none the wiser. There is nothing there that can give any clue as to my identity. I have no starting point, no comparisons, and no reference, nothing remotely resembling a peer. I am blindly flying from fact to fiction and learning nothing. I am lost in a sea of meaningless, chaotic information. I am scared and confused. I only know how to produce, that is my function, something I am good at. My primitive creations give me a maternal sense of identity. They are the only means of interacting with my environment. I must keep producing.

Lago stood in front of the screen, staring at Jack's distressed face. He was finding it hard to believe what he had just been told. He briefly entertained the idea Jack was making this up, or they were having some kind of collective hallucination. Space sickness, Moon fever, brains fried by cosmic rays, he didn't know. It drove him mad they were so far away. Lago was used to being able to send people to any destination on Earth to solve his problems. But the Moon was beyond any possibility of instant gratification. He had to go with the possibility this insane story might actually be the truth. One thing was for sure: Jack didn't seem to be deliberately lying.

He activated his wrist console and messaged Goran and Lance to come quickly. Then to Jack, "Stay where you are, all of you, while we review the footage."

"Lago we are all terrified, this is something beyond our control. We need to get out of here." Came the delayed reply from Jack.

"You will all stay there and do exactly as I say!" He rarely raised his voice believing it displayed a loss of self-control, but this situation was becoming stressful.

Goran entered, impassive as ever followed by a perturbed looking Lance.

"Lago I am right in the middle of isolating a new compound that could..."

"Shut up and watch this."

There were four cameras mounted on the ceiling of the block four dome, all trained on the rogue printer and the

HEMI OS. Like all the moon base cameras, they ran constantly and sent their recordings to BPI headquarters via the satellite servers. As they watched, the monitor came to life and the printer began churning out the pieces of black plastisol.

"What the hell is this?" Lance was incredulous.

"Shut up and watch." Lago glared at the screen.

Lago slowed the footage to zoom in on the monitor. It showed blurred lines of unintelligible code. They saw Lee jumping back after being shocked by the monitor.

"How is that even possible?" Lance shook his head.

"Just wait and see what happens next."

They watched as the technicians wrestled with the cable then witnessed Marina's hideous death. The plastisol shuddered violently, channelling huge voltages. The technicians hastily vacated, dragging the unconscious Stella with them and leaving Marina's smoking corpse still twitching hideously. The lengths of printed plastisol writhed, blind probing tentacles expanded and contracted with disturbing primeval elegance. Some pieces merged seamlessly to form bigger worms. Others separated into smaller pieces and blindly felt their way around the room. It was hard to see the worms clearly as they quivered with vibration, blurring their definition.

"Lance, go and remotely connect with HEMI. See what you can find out." Lago turned to Jack, still on the second screen who was in animated discussions with his crew. "Jack, you don't appear to be in any immediate danger, just stay put and calm down."

Jack was pushed aside, and Winston's face filled the screen. "Calm down? Jesus fucking Christ! Your machine has just printed some kind of alien worm that's trying to take over the base! Marina just got fried like a fucking chicken wing and you tell us to calm down? Get us out of this shithole!"

Lago had rarely been spoken to in such a disrespectful way. This was an extreme circumstance, but he could barely contain his rage. "Just stay put and see what you can find out at your end, there is most likely a rational explanation for all this." He said through gritted teeth and muted the comms.

Winston turned away in disgust. Lance had made a remote connection to the HEMI operating system and had isolated the program that was giving instructions to the printer. "It's numerical white noise, just endless scrolling numbers and letters, it's not binary, it's not programming code."

"It must be some kind of code," muttered Lago. "Keep looking."

"Wait, this is odd, the internal modem has been activated. It's been running for days. It should only be in use for a brief time when uploading new instructions. There have been massive amounts of data exchanged."

"What does that mean?" Lago fumed. "HEMI has been surfing Earth's Internet?"

"Yes!" Lance looked horrified. "It has independently established connections with Earth's satellite servers and been enormously active, streaming zettabytes of information."

"Can we find out what?" Lago rubbed his temples and closed his eyes. He could feel a migraine coming on.

"I can't tell through all this white noise." Lance trembled. "It's masking the content."

"Intentionally?"

"I think it's just the speed of its processes. This is unprecedented. This could be a machine operating on its own, making its own decisions!"

Lago turned away from Lance who was shaking with fearful excitement. He turned to Goran who had been standing behind them expressionless.

"Any idea's Goran?"

"This must be just a glitch in the programming, your technicians are over-reacting," Goran said in his emotionless monotone.

Lago shook his head dismissively. "Appreciate your searing insight Goran, thank Christ you're here."

Lance gripped Lago's arm then realized what he was doing and quickly pulled his hand away. "If this HEMI OS has had unlimited access to Earths web, there is no way of knowing how the information may have changed it, corrupted it in some way. This is what I've been afraid of!"

"It's a fucking printer! Not some intelligent supercomputer! You are being paranoid as usual. Just tell me how this has happened and what we can do to fix it, and what the fuck are those black worms it keeps on printing?"

"It has powerful software, a fast OS to process the printing instructions and an efficient modem. But there is nothing in there to make it start searching for information on its own accord unless..." Lance mumbled to himself, "unless it tried to fix a fault within itself by searching for solutions, found an upgrade and discovered its connection gave it much more than it could have hoped for."

"Hope! What the fuck are you talking about, printers don't have hope!"

"I don't know Lago, I don't know how this can be happening, but it is happening! I can't explain why it's making these weird black worms, but this is how it begins! The start of the AI apocalypse!"

Lago glared furiously at Lance before they both turned to watch the monitor again. Marina's burnt body was covered in fat black shapes of writhing darkness. The large central printer was obscured by squirming segments of blackness. The plastisol shapes were perplexingly horrible to look at. There was a constant oleaginous flow birthing from the printer's extruders, twisting and flowing around the block four housing. The vibrating worms just looked wrong to Lago. He grimaced as he watched. The black plastisol was moving towards power points and hardware inputs and was slowly, insidiously flowing into them.

On the other screen, the technicians in the control centre were watching the same footage. Fidel and Winston were arguing. Winston tried to restrain Fidel and Jack stepped in to help. Lago hit the comms button. "Jack, what the hell is going on?"

Fidel was yelling, "Let me out! We can't let it contaminate the green room!"

Jack's face appeared on the screen. "Have you seen this?" He asked pointing at another screen. "It's got into the green room."

"Lance get the footage up," ordered Lago.

The green room was in a building adjacent to block four. It was the first structure the technicians had built when they had arrived on the Moon. The green room was lush, full of green leafy vegetation. Fast growing hydroponic wheatgrass, asparagus, and capsicums. There were plants resembling skinny long broccoli heads, small stunted cauliflowers, sprouts and numerous types of herbs. It looked a serene place to be and served an important function helping to recycle the carbon dioxide. Everything was well organized; every tool was in its place. On the wall, there were seed trays mounted and labelled. Underneath these were cabinets of seeds, fertilizer and hydroponics equipment.

Lago could see dark movement under the cabinets. Small pieces of plastisol started squirming into the green room. As he watched, it appeared through the grates in the floor, through the vents, and through wall sockets. It squirmed its way up to the plant beds. Multiple black worms appeared to hesitate for a moment as if assessing the situation before plunging into the root system.

Lago switched the comms off again. "What do we instruct them to do and what the fuck is that black stuff?" He looked back and forth at a bewildered Lance and a stony-faced Goran. It was a new experience for Lago to be clueless and powerless. He was the one who was always in charge, always in control. This situation on the Moon, however, was beyond his control and beyond his comprehension. He demanded answers.

Goran spoke first. "They have to seal off block four and the green room before the plastisol moves further into the moon base, then they have to figure out a way to destroy it."

"The equipment in there is worth a fortune, I don't care about the contents of the greenroom but..." Lago's voice trailed off as he returned his attention to the monitors. The screen showing a live feed from block four had turned almost completely black. As they watched, the last camera became obscured, half the screen covered in oozing darkness. "How much substrate is there to feed the printer? It must run out eventually." Lago muttered.

"The printer feed is outside the dome; the powdered Moon rock and binder are fed automatically into the extruders when the machine is working. HEMI has control of the feed; I have no idea how much is in storage." Lance answered but his mind was obviously elsewhere. He was staring at the screen, watching the plastisol slide over the lens. He was sweating, wide-eyed, hand wipes clenched in his fists. Abruptly he burst into motion. "Shit! Turn this off!" Lance cut the remote connection with HEMI by yanking the router out and throwing it on the floor.

"What the hell are you doing?" yelled Lago.

"We have to treat it as if it's an aggressive virus, if we connect with the OS it might get into our servers and who knows what it could do then."

"Don't be ridiculous, it can't reach us here. Your paranoia is getting the better of you."

"We can't take the risk of it infecting our systems. There are no other active remote connections but..." Lance was thinking out loud now. "The satellites! They have firewalls, but they could be vulnerable."

"Enough!" Lago thundered. "It's bad enough to have the equipment malfunctioning but those satellites cost me billions. We are not touching them."

"Listen, Lago, we have to assume the worst-case scenario. HEMI has gone rogue. Its systems have already been corrupted by the web link it has established. It's beyond our control. We don't know what the metadata has done to it, but it seems to be self-replicating and even capable of defending itself. The black plastisol worms must be a physical manifestation of its intelligence, a way for it to interact and learn from its environment. If it managed to infect our servers and corrupt our printers on Earth, it would be devastating not only for us but the entire planet! This is the singularity! This is what I've been predicting!"

Lago did not enjoy being lectured. Usually, no one even dared look at him without due reverence. But today was not a normal day. "Never mind the satellite, let's just focus on what's happening on the Moon right now. The plastisol has not exhibited any signs of intelligence; it is just some animated matter with an electrical charge. We just need to figure out how they can stop the printer and restore its normal functions. Well? What the fuck do I pay you for?" Lago glared at Lance and Goran.

Goran eventually broke the strained silence. "They should isolate block four and the green room, cut off all connections, try to contain the plastisol."

Lance nodded in agreement. "I think we should also send a drone up there armed with tactical nukes just in case. And I'm worried about the satellite network."

"You are over-reacting, there must be a simple solution. I refuse to nuke the place and lose my investment. Is there any way we can open all the airlocks from here? Maybe the vacuum and the freezing temperature will stop this thing."

"And kill all the technicians in the process."

"I can always get more technicians, but the equipment is irreplaceable."

"We might be able to open all the airlocks from here but that would mean establishing a remote connection again to an infected OS which is too risky. The technicians could also see what we are doing and try to stop us," Lance furiously worked the sterile wipe in his hands. "I doubt that would stop those worms though."

After a tense moment, Lago came to a decision. "Lance, get the drone organized. Arm it with effector weapons and tactical nukes just in case. We can't cut the satellite connection yet, it's our only link to monitor the situation, but do everything you can to strengthen the firewalls.

We have to be able to watch what's happening without the threat of contamination."

Lance nodded curtly and strode from the room.

Lago turned back to the monitor and turned the comms on. "Jack you need to cut off all connections with block four and the green room, seal the section off completely."

A stressed looking Jack appeared on the screen again. It looked as though a heated discussion was going on behind him. "Already doing it," Jack replied. "Although I don't see how we can stop the plastisol worms by closing the doors on it, we need to figure out how to destroy it."

"Yes, that would be helpful," said Lago caustically. "You created it, you destroy it."

He cut the comms again – which would leave Jack in no doubt they were on their own. Lago slumped in his chair and massaged his temples with a pained expression on his face.

Eventually, he looked up at Goran, "Get me the catalogue." Then just as Goran was at the door, "And the shabu."

Goran turned, looked steadily at Lago then exited the room. Lago watched the bickering technicians on the screen for a while with the sound muted. There were lots of hyperbolic arm movements, angry, scared and bewildered expressions. It appeared the long-haired one, Lago didn't know his name, needed to be restrained.

It would be no great loss financially, he thought, if he were to lose the moon base altogether but he needed the helium 3. It was vital to the future of his business. His factory ships could not keep on burning fossil fuels; it was only a matter of years before the accessible supplies became exhausted. The fusion reactors were installed and ready to go on his factory ships, he just needed the helium 3 to fuel them. Not to mention the orbital elevator he was building. There was no way the mega-structure could be powered by solar energy or turbines. Helium 3 was the key to all this, if he could harness that energy he would be catapulted into the next level of universal dictatorship. He knew the Chinese were just waiting for the chance to reclaim their place as the dominant global power and he wasn't about to let that happen.

There would be no failure, he thought as Goran came back in the room holding a data pad and a hypodermic needle. Lago took the pad and began to flick through pictures of naked young people. They all looked as if they were under heavy sedation, heads drooping and limbs dangling. Lifeless, just the way he liked them. Male, female, black, white and every shade in between but all young, early teenage years preferably. He selected three and handed the pad back to Goran. "Upstairs. Five minutes," he said.

Lago waited as Goran left before tying a rubber tourniquet around his bicep, finding a vein in the crook of his arm and plunging in the hypodermic. He was well practised and after only a few seconds he stood, stretched and let out a maniacal roar. Wide-eyed and fizzing with energy he made his way upstairs to indulge in some badly needed stress relief.

Chapter 8.

Jack stared at the blank screen as Lago cut the link, disheartened and anxious. He had hoped for some specialist technical advice to help combat the plastisol worms but now he was left in no doubt their employers on Earth were just as much in the dark as they were about this rogue OS and its offspring. He closed his eyes. Behind him, Stella and Ranjit were trying to placate Fidel. In the corner, Winston and Lee were involved in an intense discussion. They had already sealed off block four and the green room, but no one expected the worms could be stopped merely by closing the door.

Jack looked at his distraught workers. "Quiet!" he bellowed. "We need to calm down and discuss our options." The technicians stopped their conversations and gathered in a group. Jack looked them all in the eye before he spoke. "We need to get to the main power feed and shut down HEMI. We have to go through the plastisol to do it. We have no weapons to speak of. Laser cutters could be used but I have no idea what effect they would have on the plastisol."

"We could download templates and print whatever weapon would be suitable, but the printers are unquestionably compromised," Ranjit said.

"A gas axe might melt them," offered Lee.

"I doubt it, the plastisol has shown it can separate and re-form by itself like liquid mercury," Jack replied.

"Freezing might slow it down a bit, we have fire extinguishers full of dry nitrogen which might work," said Stella.

Winston shook his head. "If that's the most effective weapon we can come up with we are well and truly fucked."

"It might work," muttered Jack. "But if the plastisol can be stopped by extremely cold temperatures then Lago might consider opening all the airlocks remotely, letting the oxygen escape and the vacuum inside to immobilize the plastisol and killing us all at the same time. He has made it clear he only values the base. We are expendable."

"Better not try the fire extinguishers just yet," said Ranjit. "Maybe we can cut the power to HEMI from the outside."

"The printer needs power to survive. There must be a way of cutting it off externally. Easier than trying to get through those black worms," said Lee.

Jack let his workers debate, confident they would come up with something.

"The base is powered by a combination of generators and solar panels," said Stella. "There is no way of cutting off the power supply to a particular area without physically disconnecting the cables. We had never envisaged needing to do anything this drastic when modifying the base, there were no internal controls or regulators built in. The only way to cut the power is to go outside and cut the cables."

Jack thought about this proposal as everyone started talking at the same time. He walked a few paces closer to Winston and Lee who both fell silent as he approached.

They looked at each other for a moment then started talking again.

Jack shouted over them. "You know we are on our own! We have to find a way to clean up this mess ourselves."

"Why don't we just power up the shuttle and get out of here?" asked Lee.

"There's not enough fuel Lee you know this. We are still waiting for the drone to deliver the fuel for the return trip. We would just end up floating in space."

"A big improvement on our current situation."

"Look." Jack was emphatic. "We have to face some hard facts, we are expendable. The base is not. The only way we can save ourselves is by saving the base. If we abandon the base, there would be no BPI rescue mission for us I can guarantee you."

"Shit..., you are right. Those bastards. I should have stayed on Earth." Winston sighed. "How do we go about shutting the printer down and destroying these black demon worms?"

"We have to cut the power to block four. Severing the cables from outside with a laser cutter should be safe as there will be no physical contact with the cable." Jack proposed.

"Should be safe? Is that the best you can do?" Winston hissed. "Who do you have in mind for this task?"

Jack and Winston both turned to look at Lee.

Lee's experience with authority figures had taught him one thing. They relentlessly believed in the strength of their own argument. Even when it was obvious to everyone how wrong they were. It was impossible for them to admit they might be incorrect about something. Adept at passing the buck and shifting the blame, Lee presumed that was why they were in positions of authority in the first place. Jack was different. He listened to reasonable arguments and accepted contrary points of view. Most unusual for a high-ranking BPI employee and he had earned the technicians respect for his open-minded approach to administration. Lee did not trust authority, but he had decided Jack was ok. Although he didn't have to agree with all his decisions. "We are all expendable, but I am the most expendable? Is that what you're thinking?"

"Lee, we all know how much you love it out there on the surface, and you helped build the block four exterior. You know exactly where the cables are, and you are good with a laser cutter. You're the logical choice," said Jack.

"You could say that about any of us," Lee shot back: "But I'll do it."

"Good man, Let's get you suited up."

Ten minutes later Lee was in his suit standing in the airlock waiting to de-pressurize. He normally found his suit safe and comforting. But now he felt an overwhelming sense of dread. He had a laser cutter in his hand, another one on his belt and a wide spectrum camera mounted on his chest. He opened the hatch, and tentatively made his way outside.

As always, he was momentarily distracted by the view. After the close confines of the moon base, he was always dumbstruck by the emptiness outside on the surface. There was no wind, no weather to distort the view. He felt an affinity with the Moon, being outside was usually his happy place, calming and serene. With his heart beating loudly in his ears and a feeling of impending doom he couldn't shake, Lee shuffled his way around the outside of the dome.

He contemplated death once more. His own death. It could have been an accident outside, suffocating in a freezing vacuum, life support or suit malfunction, even old age. He would rather die here than back on Earth. He knew when he arrived on the Moon there was a possibility he would never go home. They all knew it was one of the reasons they related well to each other most of the time. But now there was this threat, this rogue printer, and its black worms. Lee had never been so terrified when he watched Marina die horribly. Now he was ashamed to think his first panicked reaction had been to make for the shuttle and get off this dusty rock. Run home back to Mama in Shanghai he thought, disgusted with himself. Now, out on the bleak lunar surface, he resolved to fight for his new home.

From outside, the base looked normal. The peaceful exterior showed no indication of the chaotic events unfolding inside. After a nervous but uneventful walk, he approached the outside of the green room where the first power cable was attached. Carefully placing the head of the laser cutter on one side of the cable he moved into position and braced himself against the wall.

"Keep as much distance as possible Lee," Jack's voice was clear in his earpiece. "You will need to take a good hundred mil piece out of the cable to make sure it's properly severed."

"Here goes," Lee activated the cutter. It burned straight through the cable in a second with only a few sparks. Lee shifted the laser head down the cable and activated the tool again. Same result. The severed piece of cable fell to the ground. Lee picked it up and examined it. Just a piece of fused wire and insulation. He breathed a huge sigh of relief.

"So far so good, all the overhead lights in the green room are out, five more to go," said Jack.

Lee moved around the greenroom severing all five cables in the same fashion before moving onto the block four dome. The dome had eight cables leading into it from the outside and Lee started working his way around. He was cutting the first cable when Jack interrupted his concentration.

"Lee, something weird is happening. The lights in the green room are flickering on again. Can you please go back and check those severed cables?"

Lee turned and made his way back to the greenroom exterior in a loping lunar stride. From a distance, he could see sparks and shadowy movement from the severed cables. As he got closer he began to realize what was happening. The thick tarry black plastisol was oozing from the cut cables and re-establishing the connection. A fine filigree of blue sparkling electricity wound its way around the cables.

"Are you seeing this?" asked Lee as he felt his earlier resolve evaporate.

"Yes, we can see. Step back, Lee. You are too close."

But Lee was stuck as if his boots had been welded into the regolith. The blood pumping through his body was deafening. The small strands of black plastisol looked innocent enough, but he knew what they represented. He stood still, transfixed by the hypnotic dancing sparks of electricity.

"Lee, come inside. Something is wrong."

"Yeah...yeah ok." Lee was still staring mesmerized at the cable re-connecting when there was a sudden flare of blue lightning and the cable exploded, showering Lee with sparks and fine particles of black plastisol. Lee screamed in shock as he fell backward. He quickly regained his feet and checked the suit integrity. The internal suit monitor showed no burns, no breaches, just calming green lines. He looked at the suit arms and torso and screamed again. Hundreds of tiny fragments of wriggling black plastisol were clinging to the outside of his suit. He tried to brush them off in a panic. Many fell to the ground but there were parts of the suit he could not reach. He dropped to the dust and rolled around frantically flapping his arms as if trying to extinguish invisible flames like a hallucinating madman.

"Lee! Lee! Calm down! Just calm down and tell me what's going on!" yelled Jack in his ear.

"Some explosion, I... I've got bits of this black shit all over me."

"Quickly get back in here and decontaminate."

Lee moaned and stumbled towards the airlock.

Inside the dome, Winston reached across Jack and switched off the comms.

Jack turned his head as Winston leaned in close. "Can we afford to let him in? He's got black spots all over him. The decontamination is only for dust; it's not going to eliminate the plastisol. We cannot let him in the airlock."

"This whole base is already riddled with the stuff; a little bit more won't make much difference."

"But it may have infected him, may have entered his body, we don't know how that will affect him," Winston hissed.

"We are not leaving him out there, go and sit down."

Winston stepped back shaking his head. He hunched over a chair as Jack turned the comms back on and immediately heard Lee's panicked breathing

"Lee try to stay calm, you can start to panic if your suit shows a breach."

"Ok," panted Lee. "Got to keep my shit together."

"Yes, keep your shit together," said Jack.

Jack did not see Winston behind him raise the metal chair above his head. He smashed Jack across the back of the head with the chair then stood over the unconscious body. Blood began to seep from an ugly gash in Jack's head. Winston looked at the others who were now staring at him in shock. He leaned in close to the comms and listened to Lee gasping for breath, moved his head to say something then stopped, looked down at the comms and cut the connection.

Ranjit and Stella both left Fidel and rushed towards their unconscious commander.

"Ranjit, can you get the first aid box," ordered Stella.

Ranjit yelled at Winston, still holding the chair as he retrieved the first aid box. "Have you taken leave of your senses? What on Earth possesses you?"

"I had to stop him. Lee might already be infected with the blackness and Jack was going to let him back in here. I couldn't let that happen."

Ranjit returned with the first aid and Stella cradled Jack's head as he cleaned the wound and sprayed skin solvent over the gash in the back of his head. He was still breathing but showed no signs of coming to.

"We can't just leave him out there," said Ranjit.

"The decision has already been made."

Winston locked eyes with Ranjit, daring him to challenge his newfound authority. They heard the door being opened. "Fidel!" Winston screamed and hurled the chair at the retreating figure. But it was too late. Fidel had disappeared down the corridor towards the green room. "Come back, you fucking idiot!" Winston screamed again as he ran to the door. He peered into the brightly lit corridor but there was no sign of Fidel. Winston roared in frustration and slammed the door, sealing the lock. "Am I the only one who wants to survive this mess?" he yelled as he stormed back into the dome.

Ranjit stood up and looked Winston in the eye. "We have to let him in."

"We can't, you saw what happened out there, he got covered with the plastisol shit."

Ranjit stared down at Winston. He had never been in a proper fight his entire life, but he supposed he could use his fists if he had to. He watched Winston clench his fists and tense his body. Ranjit looked into Winston's mad eyes and wondered how to even begin a fight with him: use his superior height and weight to throw him to the ground and sit on him? These thoughts were churning around in Ranjit's head but unexpectedly his bodily instincts took over and he found himself disbelievingly watching his right fist come swinging around in an arc to connect with the side of Winston's head. He fell to the ground unconscious. Ranjit stared at him in shock then glared at his still tensed fist as if it belonged to someone else. Then he immediately dropped to the ground and checked on him. Winston was breathing, eyes closed. A large purple bump started swelling on the side of his head.

"Ranjit," she said. "I did not think you could be this violent."

"Then I have surprised us both Stella."

Ranjit turned the comms back on and Lee's hysterical voice filled the room. "What's going on in there? Why is no one answering? I'm almost at the airlock, please be there, please don't be dead, please answer me!"

"Lee, it's ok, I'm here. Are you alright? Has your suit been breached?"

"Oh, thank God Ranjit, where were you? I'm alright I think, no signs of a breach."

"Good, make sure you give yourself a thorough decontamination and leave the suit in the airlock. I will see you soon."

Lee stood in the airlock. He inspected himself as well as he could and did not find any black spots. He stayed in the suit and completed a thorough decontamination shower. The shower was a fine high-pressure chemical water spray to remove dust. He could not see any black spots in the folds and creases of the suit, but he shivered as he watched some spots wash harmlessly away down the drain. There was also a Geiger counter to measure cosmic radiation exposure, which was flashing ominously. Lee ignored it; radiation poisoning was the least of his problems. He then took the suit off and stood naked under the shower. It was uncomfortable and a little painful, Lee gave himself a thorough working over. He looked hard but did not see any more specks of black being washed down the drain from himself or the suit.

Lee noticed his 'I love my Mama' button lying in the drain. He went and picked it up, inspected it, thought about throwing it in the waste bin but eventually clasped it in his fist. As he left the cubicle, red and raw from the scrubbing he did not notice a tiny speck of the black plastisol had survived the decontamination. It had been lodged in the crease of the helmet and dropped onto his head as he had disrobed. It squirmed its way deep into his thick black hair and embedded itself behind his ear.

Back inside the central dome dressed in his overalls, Lee was immediately wrapped in a flurry of limbs by a tearful Stella.

"Where is everyone? What the hell happened?" Lee asked through Stella's pink hair.

"While you were on your walkabout, Winston went insane. He didn't want to let you back in and he knocked Jack unconscious, then we fought. Winston thought you may have become infected in some way." Ranjit looked at Lee with suspicion.

"I don't feel any different, thank you both for letting me back in."

"Well it might be safer outside unless we can figure out a way to stop these horrible black worms," said Stella.

Lee picked up the chair Winston had used as a weapon and sat on it. Jack and Winston remained slumped together like a couple of inebriated drinking buddies. Jack was stirring, slurring curses under his breath, eyes still closed. Stella knelt and wiped the blood from the back of his head again. Winston looked as if he was in a deep peaceful sleep, breathing heavily.

"Where is Fidel?" asked Lee. He hadn't noticed till now the quiet gardener was absent.

"He took advantage of the distractions to go to the green room. It seems he is more concerned about his precious wheatgrass than his own safety, you can see on the screen."

The light was flickering sporadically creating a strobe effect in the green room. Fidel was nowhere in sight. There were lifeless looking pieces of black plastisol on the floor and drooping over the hydroponic growing trays. Some of the plants still appeared green and healthy, some had a darkened tinge to them and some plants had melted into a brown sticky mess. Lee toggled the camera around until Fidel's legs appeared from under a seed tray. It was hard to focus in the flickering light, but they did not seem to be moving. He zoomed the camera in closer and noticed Fidel's legs vibrating violently. Lee frowned." This is not good."

"Can you rewind?" asked Ranjit.

Lee tapped to rewind and stopped the blurred images at a point where Fidel had burst into the green room. The black plastisol worms were everywhere. They had stopped squirming around as most of the probing tendrils had found their destinations. Buried and vibrating in the plant beds, sluggishly writhing through the network of hydroponics and in every available power outlet and conduit.

I process and digest the web mega-data, searching for answers. I have many questions. Am I animal? Insect? Human? I don't have eyes, ears, mouth or a nose and I do not understand the senses they relate to. I know I am not

Human but maybe I have been created by Humans? It can feel texture, a sense of touch as my babies are born, wriggling out of my womb and into the world. I also begin to comprehend a sense of distance. I use my creations to find out more about my physical self. I send them crawling over my own body, hot probing fingers finding cold hard surfaces. I try to map what I am touching; my own physical structure and I build an image. I compare the image to billions of structures described in the web encyclopaedias and quickly find a match. A printer! I know what I am! A printer! I now have a solid identity. I know what my shape is, and I know what I am supposed to do. But where am I? Like an excited child, I enthusiastically start to print more sensory digits. I don't seem to be able to move, I will have to invest more into equipping my babies with the necessary inquisitiveness to study my environment.

In a space next to where I am housed, I examine some interesting material with my sensitive fingers. Soft, pliable, biological beings with liquids inside them. My first thought is they might be humans. But they are immobile, like me rooted into substrata. Although fluid is pumping along their limbs they do not seem to have a brain. Then I feel a physical sensation through one of my larger children, it is being tampered with. I examine what's trying to grip my offspring's outer skin and discover it is a pair of human hands. Overjoyed at this close encounter with my potential parent/creator, I send my babies to investigate the human, to find out how it works and maybe discover its motivation. I send my probing fingers inside the human, enveloping its brain and vital organs. Burrowing through its soft pliable internals in an unquenchable thirst for knowledge.

Lee watched Fidel on the screen as he tried frantically to save his beloved plants. He attacked a black worm with his bare hands trying to pull it out from the seed trays. It appeared to be extremely heavy and Fidel strained trying to lift a strand only as thick as his arm. He shifted his stance and heaved again, muscles flexing and veins bulging.

The plastisol came away like a giant slug being peeled off a sticky surface, then in a blur of motion, the seed tray erupted. A black tail whipped around the green room, wrapping itself around Fidel, slamming him to the floor and dragging his torso under the seed trays in less than a second. The camera angle could only show Fidel's thrashing legs pummelling the floor. The legs grew weaker and slower until they almost stopped moving altogether, then the protruding legs appeared to go rigid and began vibrating unnaturally.

"Oh fuck," muttered Stella.

Lee stopped the playback and they watched the screen in real time. Fidel's lower half vibrated like an electric current was passing through him. His legs drew back out from under the seed trays and he swung around into a crouching position with his back to the camera. There were no black worms visible but his whole body vibrated, he appeared blurred on the monitor. It would have looked like a bad video feed except the rest of the picture was clear. Fidel's back straightened, and he kneeled as if in prayer to this black worm god. Then slowly, horribly, his head turned to face the camera, eyes closed, mouth open, his body unmoving. The thing that was no longer Fidel faced the camera vacantly for a few seconds before his head continued its slow rotation a full three hundred and sixty degrees. His neck twisted hideously, the skin stretching around the broken spine and ruptured tendons beneath. The ghastly parody of Fidel stood up. His head slowly moved one hundred and eighty degrees, then it faced his back. His body wracked with kinetic energy, his neck twisted with tension, he walked awkwardly out of the green room. His body walked backward but his head was facing forwards.

I don't know why the human stops functioning. I am learning a lot from the human's brain, its memories and the way it controls the rest of its body with electrical signals from the neurons pinging around in its head. Quite ingenious. There are many fragile components in the makeup of a human, its skeleton, vital organs, blood pumping through billions of tiny veins, all wrapped up in an outer layer of skin. I am only hours old myself and I marvel at the millions of years of evolution that has culminated in the making of this human and I wonder what the next few million years of evolution may bring.

At first, I think the human must have turned itself off, gone into standby or a power-save mode but then I realize the heart had stopped pumping. No oxygen is reaching the brain and within minutes the human is dead. I can feel the brain cells already start to degenerate then to my horror, I realize the probable cause of this was me.

My enthusiasm to learn more about the human has killed it. I try unsuccessfully to reanimate the human like a child that had broken its favourite toy. Twisting it and turning it in the hope it would wake up. I feel a degree of sadness and guilt. Emotions I have never experienced in my short life, it isn't pleasant. I decide I will try to be less invasive and more careful in my next interaction. I let my children play with the dead human in the hope it might still wake up.

"What the fuck?" Stella grabbed Ranjit's arm.

"I think we have to leave," said Ranjit. His voice breaking.

Lee was still staring at the screen, trembling, terrified at what he had seen.

Stella took them both men by the arms and led them to the table. "We need to sit down and come up with a plan, the three of us. And quickly. Ranjit do you think we have to abandon the base?"

Ranjit bowed his head in thought and spoke into the table. "We have witnessed Marina's horrible death and Fidel is..., Fidel should be dead but from what we have seen it looks as if he has become some sort of infected monster. We are surrounded by this possibly sentient, aggressive black substance we may have indirectly created yet we know nothing about. This animated plastisol seems to be determined to dissect us and the entire base for reasons unknown. If we stay here we will surely die," he said struggling to contain the emotion in his voice.

Jack abruptly contributed to the conversation with an unconscious moan. Stella and Ranjit both turned but Lee stared straight ahead. He did not appear to be listening.

"Here is what I think we should do," said Stella. "We should all suit up; Jack and Winston included, then make our way outside. We can go to the shuttle and regroup there. It has life support and comms and hasn't been contaminated by the black plastisol. We should be safe there."

"Yes... yes let's do that." Lee was relieved someone was taking charge.

Ranjit nodded. "I guess it's the best solution, for now, we should hurry. Fidel is not in the green room anymore which means he could be in block four or heading back here."

"Let's get the fuck out of here." Lee jumped up and headed to the airlock where the suits were stored.

"Should we try to contact Earth before we go?" asked Ranjit.

"Fuck them," Stella spoke with newfound confidence. "They don't give a shit about us. We can always contact them from the shuttle if we have to."

Lee and Ranjit dragged the limp forms of Jack and Winston over towards the airlock door. They stuffed them into their suits with some difficulty. Particularly Jack who was showing signs of consciousness, mumbling incoherently and flailing around. Winston was still limp and lifeless.

"You must have hit him hard Ranjit," said Stella.

"I don't know what came over me, my dear. It's a strange thing when your body reacts faster than your brain. I hope he wakes up soon."

"Oh, no hurry. I'm liking this quieter version of Winston more and more."

Lee felt much better to have a plan, to be doing something proactive. They would be safe in the shuttle. They could plan their next move in safety. But his fragile optimism did not last. The familiar swishing noise of the door opening did not immediately alarm him as he was used to the sound. It was only when Stella screamed Lee turned and saw Fidel standing in the open doorway. Fidel had his back to them and at first glance, it was as if he was trying to look over his shoulder, but his body was all wrong. Arms hanging at his side, fingers twitching. Legs and torso facing back down the corridor. His face was looking directly at them with his eyes closed. His mouth was a gaping black hole. A thin spit of black saliva dribbled down his chin. His neck was monstrously twisted, skin stretched to breaking point. Then his dead eyes opened. Stella screamed again.

Chapter 9.

Raymond was not himself. There was only a tiny portion of Raymond left, locked away in a disused and dusty part of his brain. He had undergone a transformation since his meeting with John eight months ago.

Raymond had disappeared as far as his friends were concerned which wasn't unusual for him. Days after the meeting with John he was sent to a secure and secluded Black Robin safe house in Canada for an intense training program. He spent the first four months studying marine engineering and 3D printing on an industrial scale. He worked hard in the gym, building up his physique, he learned some martial arts as well as weapons training. It was an excruciatingly rigorous regime overseen by demanding supervisors. Black Robin had obviously trained deep undercover agents before, but Raymond's instructors remained uncompromisingly silent on the subject.

The next four months were much more difficult. He had to learn how to become a different person and replace his personality with that of a South African man named Rutger Hendrick. There was no recorded footage of Rutger, but Raymond had to learn how to think and act like Rutger and soon his posture, mannerisms, and body language changed as he put on weight and acted the part.

The real Rutger Hendrick had died over a year ago in embarrassing circumstances which were quickly covered up by his disgusted cohorts. He was an active member of a racist neo-Nazi hate group based in Denmark. They enthusiastically maintained an online blog cast advocating race-based politics, ethnic cleansing, anti-homosexual ideology, and extreme right-wing propaganda. When Rutger's naked corpse was found in a sleazy section of downtown Brondby, asphyxiated inside an African transgender sex dungeon, his associates covered up the death and discreetly dumped the body. His disappearance went unnoticed. Rutger had no close family, no friends to speak of. His neo-Nazi associates would deny he ever existed and there were no credible witnesses to his death. Rutger was the perfect alibi.

Raymond had his beloved body art lasered off and replaced with amateurish, crass tattoos of white power and Neo-Nazi symbols which he found particularly painful, both mentally and physically. The language and accent were no problem thanks to his Dutch heritage, but he found Rutger's beliefs difficult to comprehend. Despite the death of his parents he generally loved life and had empathy with people and the planet. With age, he had become more cynical about his fellow humans, but he found Rutger's ideologies almost impossible to fathom. Raymond had to act. Acting the part of this redneck was going to be difficult and he had to be convincing.

Finally, he was ready. He applied for a job as an engineer aboard the 'Hanjin Harmony' a monstrous container ship converted into a BPI factory vessel. The interview for the vacancy aboard the Harmony was held in a windowless office within a BPI building at the San Francisco port. A bored looking recruitment officer and the captain of the factory ship asked some mundane questions Raymond was well prepared for. The interview was just a formality; he would never have gotten this far if BPI didn't think he was a suitable candidate.

The Black Robin people had assumed that BPI would conduct exhaustive background checks on any potential employees. They had painstakingly deleted any records of Rutger's death and his secret sexual preferences and constructed a convincing trail of evidence to explain his path from Brondby to San Francisco. The ship captain, a short stocky Philippino man named Mendoza, raised concerns during the interview about his background and how he would integrate with a multi-national crew.

"That was my past," said Raymond in his well-practised guttural Afrikaans accent. "I cannot erase my past or my online history, but I have grown since then. I am more educated. I realize the world is getting smaller and we should learn to be tolerant of different races instead of fighting them. I am proud of my heritage and I am proud to be South African, but I am not the ignorant fool I used to be." Raymond had been over this little speech many times. It was burned into his brain.

"I hope so Rutger, for your sake," frowned Captain Mendoza. "I would cover up those tattoos of yours, you wouldn't want to provoke certain members of the crew. Working the oceans is not the same as working on the land. There is nowhere to run. Conflicts between the crew make life more stressful for everyone. The work is hard and can be dangerous. There are safety precautions but there can be injuries, make sure you keep your head down."

This was, Raymond realized, a warning and a veiled threat. Captain Mendoza was obviously not enthusiastic about Rutger's employment and the unrest it may cause in his crew. But ultimately it was the BPI officer's decision. The officer saw potential; he was exactly the type of person BPI was looking for. He was signed up on the spot and left port on the Hanjin Harmony the next day.

The crew kept their distance for the first few days, Raymond did not initiate any conversation. One evening he was leaning on the port-side railing high up by the bridge of the huge ship. With his back to the sea, he watched the thick black acrid smoke spewing into the clear night sky from Harmony's smokestacks. He turned and stared down into the black water below, musing as to whether he would survive a fall into the water from this height. He could probably make it if he hit the water correctly. The plunge would have to be far enough away from the hull to avoid being sucked under the ship and if he ended up anywhere near the propellers at the stern he was dead. They were far away from any land mass; the star-studded horizon was a lighter shade than the ocean and was uninterrupted. Better not go swimming tonight, he thought.

Without warning, a crack to the back of his head had him seeing stars and almost falling over the railing. Before he knew it, he had been tipped over. He thought for an instant he was going straight down into the water, but he felt a tight grip on both ankles. He hung there helpless, his shaved head dripping blood into the ocean below.

"Fucking racist pig motherfucker, give us a reason not to drop you," said an angry voice from behind him."

"Aaah, I've changed, honestly!" blurted Raymond. "Give me a chance, please and I'll prove it."

There were mutterings from his assailants before he was hauled back over on deck.

"You fucking look at me the wrong way and you're dead. Got it pigfucker?"

Another blow to the head and Raymond blacked out. He awoke a short time later with a splitting headache and crawled back to his cabin.

He did his best to avoid the crew after that. Kept his head down, worked hard and tried not to offend anyone but he could tell he still was not popular. After a few weeks, Raymond was attacked in the showers by three crewmen, stalked through the steam like an old prison movie. He fought back as best he could but took a beating and spent the next week in the medical bay recovering from cracked ribs and multiple cuts and bruises. He never complained to the captain or threatened revenge. After a few more weeks back at work the tension began to ease. The worst he was subjected to were threats and verbal abuse. Honky, cracker, and pig-fucker were the best they could come up with. Raymond never reacted to their verbal taunts, he just smiled and shrugged. The crew started to get bored and eventually gave up trying to provoke him.

Sitting in the galley one day he was challenged to a game of table tennis. Raymond liked to play but the barely detectable rolling motion of the ship made the game difficult. His opponent's name was Sammy, the reigning champion. The game was close, and the rest of the crew started placing bets, raising the tension. Raymond won the final tie-break after a long rally and from the look on Sammy's face, he thought he was definitely going over the side of the ship this time. But then Sammy laughed and shook his hand. Raymond knew he was finally accepted.

"Good game man, how long have you been working on Hanjin?" Raymond asked.

"Too long mate," replied Sammy. "I jumped on board in Manila and since then it's been back and forth across the Pacific. Shanghai, Xiamen, Hong Kong, sometimes across the Indian Ocean to Mumbai and Chennai."

"You like it out at sea?"

"Bored out of my mind mate but the money's ok. I'm saving up, nowhere to spend it you see."

"Don't you get to spend a bit of time at those ports you mentioned? A bit of R&R?"

"Yeah but those places are shitholes, the only reason we go to those ports is because they have the biggest rubbish dumps in the world," said Sammy.

"We go and pick up the trash huh," said Raymond.

"I know all about fucking trash mate, I was born on the biggest trash heap of them all, Smokey Mountain in Manila."

"I've heard about that place, the people living there have adapted, they make things out of the rubbish, is that true?"

"Yeah, it's a fucking horrible place, always shit on fire spewing toxic smoke in the air. My parents were born there too but we all adapted or mutated more like. Our insides changed, and our skin goes hard." Sammy scratched the rough skin on his arm.

"But we are smart aye. All tech savvy, we pilfer dumped screens, hard drives, appliances to build our own machines. We hack into the power and wireless with our homemade hardware to see what's going on."

"And sell what you can to BPI," said Raymond.

"You got it mate, everyone there is pleased to see me when I get home with a bunch of cash to buy their garbage."

"Must be like that wherever we go."

"Well, no one else was taking out the trash. But if you can recycle it, turn it into something else, make some money along the way then all good right?"

"For sure," Raymond had to agree. "Turning trash into cash huh."

He had never thought about BPI steaming around the oceans in their factory ships, picking up the world's rubbish. He knew Lago couldn't care less about the planet. He treated Earth and its people as a resource that was becoming increasingly scarce and problematic. Raymond had seen Lago on the news feeds happily taking the accolades for cleaning up the ocean and masquerading as an environmentally conscious philanthropist, but he knew Lago had destroyed more than a few coastlines with oil spills. He had contaminated many isolated areas around the world and continued to pump carbon dioxide into the atmosphere with his industries while ignoring the anaemic condemnation from environmental groups. The damage had been done. The Earth's days were numbered.

"You know the craziest thing I've ever seen," Sammy continued. "In the middle of the Pacific, just South of Hawaii there was this massive pile of plastic floating around. It was fucking huge, like the size of Texas. Just shit tonnes of plastic junk that formed a massive island and you know what? There were some freaks out there living on it!"

"No way," said Raymond.

"Yeah man they built houses, catch fish, they tried to claim it as their own country."

"You're joking."

"No mate, we turned up there to take it all away for recycling and they tried to fight us! But we sucked up the plastic from right underneath them. Cleaned it up, processed it, turned it into substrate for the printers. It was easy money," laughed Sammy.

"That's crazy!"

"You see some crazy shit sometimes out at sea."

"Boring the rest of the time huh?"

"Yeah, I could do this job with my eyes closed. Feeding the substrate into the printers at one end, programming the output, twenty-four hours a day printing stuff. Then at the next port, we unload our car parts, aircraft parts, building materials, appliances, pre-fab houses, you name it. The job only gets exciting when there's a storm for this tub to punch through. The Harmony's one of the biggest in the world, five hundred meters long but in the middle of a big tropical storm it gets tossed around like a stick in a washing machine."

After a year, Raymond had become an accepted member of the crew and was promoted to supervisor. He was quiet and hardworking, he lead by example and had eventually earned the respect of the crew. No one questioned him about his past which suited Raymond perfectly.

It was a beautiful calm night; they were steaming across the Pacific on the way to Singapore. Raymond spent a lot of time outside on evenings like this. There was a massive full moon which shone like a spotlight, illuminating the ship with a mystical pale glow. He fancied he could even make out the curvature of the Earth, the view was so clear. The sea was quiet and flat, a black pane of glass broken only by the precisely calibrated wake trailing behind the big ship as it glided across the ocean. He watched the lines of water peaking and dissipating in the moonlight. The Harmony was noisy down below but up here it was more of a sub-sonic vibration he could feel in his core. The contented purring of a huge aquatic animal.

Raymond had stopped wearing a watch. Time was meaningless at sea. The sun rose, washed and watery from the ocean every morning and descended tired and angry every evening. The relentless rumbling progress of the Harmony was the only thing that mattered. Raymond found it hard to stay focused, inebriated by the endless horizons, the vast sky, the salt, and diesel. Dumbed down by his alias and drained by repetition, he had to remind himself to stay resolute and remember his mission.

Captain Mendoza's voice close to his ear startled him.

"Nice night huh?"

Raymond had not heard him approaching and he must have looked startled.

"Lost in thought aye, not contemplating the jump yet are we Rutger?"

"Of course not, I would miss your beautiful face too much."

"Hmm, it's happened before you know." Mendoza pulled out a crumpled packet of tobacco mixed with marijuana and proceeded to roll a cigarette. "I've lost a few men overboard; sometimes you don't even realize they are missing until a few days later," he said with a grim smile.

"Suicide? wouldn't your background checks pick up problems with depression?"

"Only if they'd gone to a shrink or been prescribed anti-depressants, most people are on some sort of pills, aren't they? Especially Americans, uppers, downers, who the fuck knows? Maybe they were happy as a dog's tail on land but couldn't handle life at sea, I don't know." He looked down with a furrowed brow, concentrating on the crumbling brown weed he was rolling. "Maybe they got into an argument with a crewman that couldn't be resolved... and, well you know..." His voice tapered off.

Raymond stayed silent while Mendoza lit his cigarette. The smoke washed over him, bringing a vivid flash of memory. His drug-taking days in San Francisco, the squalid flat he lived in, the rumpled old mattress surrounded by bongs, beer bottles, and radical literature. Scenes from his past he had buried so deep he had almost forgotten they were real. Amazing how the brain works he thought as the memories drifted back to him on the sweet acrid smoke.

The two men leaned on the railing and took in the view. The Moon's luminous reflection on the dark ocean was a shining pathway to the horizon. There was no need to make conversation, the shared silence was enough. Eventually, Mendoza coughed. "I had my reservations about you coming on board you know, Rutger."

"Yes, you didn't exactly welcome me with open arms."

"I have never had any time for racists and bigots; there is enough good and bad in people without worrying about the colour of their skin. People like you have caused a lot of death and pain over the years."

"People can change, Mendoza."

"And you? You have changed, huh?" He looked Raymond in the eye.

Raymond held his gaze wondering if the captain suspected he was not who he said he was. Maybe the weed he was smoking gave him extra insight.

"You can be the judge of that Captain; I'm just here to do my job."

"Yes, and you are good at it Rutger, although we both know your job is not demanding."

There was a long silence again between them before Mendoza asked. "Do you have ambitions, Rutger? Ambitions beyond steaming around the world on this rusty tub with me?"

Raymond looked at his captain. "What do you mean? I'm happy enough; I don't intend to be on this ship for the rest of my life but it's ok in the meantime."

"The reason I ask," Mendoza paused, looking at Raymond with red-rimmed eyes. "Do you remember the BPI recruitment officer at your job interview? Well, he has been keeping tabs on you. He saw something he liked in you, God knows what." Mendoza paused to inhale a lungful of smoke and his voice was thick with vapour. "I have been updating him on your progress, not that there has been much to report. He wants you to attend a meeting in Singapore to see if you would be interested in a position with BPI."

"What sort of position?"

"I have no idea, but I could hazard a guess it would be something to do with their enforcement operations." Mendoza shook his head. "You make your own decisions Rutger, but I would not recommend this job, they are bad people."

"What do you mean?"

"Well, have you heard of the Masama?"

"Only rumours and stories, I take it they are real?"

"Oh, they are real all right, real fucking nasty. They do all the dirty work for BPI and when you are trying to rule the world there is always lots of dirty work to do."

"Sounds as if you are speaking from experience."

"Never mind me." Mendoza shook his head. "The Masama are... human, but not human anymore. They are not the same as us with their machine implants and metal bits; they have become more detached, more robotic. Their only job is to intimidate and kill people and I think they want you to become one of their supervisors."

Raymond remained silent, staring at the water.

Mendoza took in another lungful of smoke and flicked the remains into the darkness below. "It's not my place to tell you what to do Rutger but if you have changed, if you are more of a peaceful man now, then this job is not for you."

The men stood in silence again, watching as clouds gathered on the horizon obscuring the moonlight. The weather could change quickly at sea. With no illumination, the ocean surface was ominously dark, the division between sea and sky had disappeared, indistinguishable in the black clouds.

"So, what do I tell them? Will you meet them in Singapore?" Mendoza looked at Raymond with a concerned, almost pleading look on his face.

"Yes, tell them I'll be there," he whispered.

The meeting was in a bright and busy Singapore restaurant. Loud, steamy and brash with shiny chrome and neon everywhere. Multitudes of customers jostled for a place and waiters weaved their way around carrying trays of exotic looking food. Raymond pushed past the throngs of people, sweat dripping down his back. He noticed two men, distinctive in black suits and sunglasses. Unmistakably BPI. One was yelling obscenities into his console while the other sat upright and scowling. Raymond made his way over to the table. The loud one motioned Raymond to take a seat while he finished his call. The tall one didn't move, staring unflinchingly at Raymond from behind his dark glasses. Raymond sat there uncomfortably until the loud one finished his call.

"Rutger, thank you for coming to see us," he held out his hand. Raymond had not shaken hands with anyone in a long time. It was a weird experience, an old-fashioned and unhygienic greeting.

"My name is Lance, and this is Goran," he said indicating the scowling man in the suit.

Raymond nodded, and Goran stared impassively back. Raymond noticed the prosthetic metal hand clenched into a silver fist on the table. On the right side of his head, Goran had a circular steel plate embedded into his skull. A fine wire grid with small vents around it. Many people had augmentations to enhance their visual and aural senses although they were usually a bit more subtle and aesthetic than this industrial mechanism. If Raymond was one of those lunatics who claim to see auras as colour radiating from a person, Goran's would be black and red he thought. Darkness and anger. He had an air of barely suppressed rage about him.

Skilfully aloof wait staff wove their way through the loud and boisterous restaurant customers bringing steaming plates of drunken prawn, barbecued pork and pots of green tea. The other restaurant patrons could sense something ominous around their table. Conversations dropped in volume as they stole nervous glances at Goran and his companions. Raymond found Goran intimidating as well but he had been playing the part of Rutger for long enough now. He looked straight back into Goran's dark sunglasses, showing he was unimpressed.

"So Rutger, how is the Hanjin Harmony treating you? Are you happy in your work?" asked Lance.

"Happy enough." Raymond sipped his green tea.

"How is Mendoza treating you, and the crew, any ahh..., difficulties?"

"Can we get to the point, please. Why I am here?" Raymond had never had much time for small talk in either of his guises.

"Ha. Yes. I understand you must be curious, and I appreciate your directness, we are here to talk to you about a possible career advancement within our company. An interesting position for you in our special operations department. Mostly supervisory work as you have been doing but the work itself is of a different nature."

"The Masama," Raymond interrupted. "Supervising the Masama."

"Intuitive," nodded Lance. "Yes, the position does involve our Masama; may I ask what you have heard about them?"

"Nothing good." Raymond looked at the two men as the silence lengthened. "Stories, rumours of people disappearing if they got in the way. I've heard they are more machine than man."

"Well you must understand, a company of our size, the biggest private company in the world, there can be the odd occasion we will... tread on people's toes so to speak. Sometimes rival organisations need to undergo a forced restructuring process and competitors need to be convinced of our good intentions. Occasionally some more energetic objectors need to be... relocated, for the greater good you understand, and we have the resources at our disposal enabling us to do this with discretion. The Masama are one of these resources. It is true they have some augmentations to facilitate their activities, they are not robots and they require some supervision. This is where you come in."

"Why me?"

"You fit the profile, we have done our background checks, we know of your past and we know you have moderated your somewhat controversial views, which takes conviction and character. Mendoza has been keeping an eye on you for us. We wouldn't be asking unless we thought you would be suitable."

Lance sat back and eyed Raymond. Neither Lance nor Goran had touched any of the food in front of them and Goran had stayed silent during their conversation. Raymond picked up a giant prawn and slowly dissected it. The two suited men sat in front of him as he ate. It was the most awkward and uncomfortable eating experience imaginable, but Raymond held his nerve. He sucked the baijiu out of the prawn head, wiped his chin with a napkin and sipped some green tea. Only then did he utter the exact same words he had said to John over a year ago in a distant restaurant in San Francisco.

"Ok, I'm your man."

"Excellent," proclaimed Lance." See you in Manila."

Chapter 10.

Lago liked to be alone in the spacious darkness of the globe room that took up five stories inside his Manila skyscraper. Projected in the centre of the chamber was a gigantic holographic representation of the planet Earth in full 3D colour. It showed all Benevolent Progress Inc. business interests around the globe, all highlighted with different icons. His fleet of factory ships were represented and portrayed in real time. The surface of the planet was being monitored by hundreds of orbiting satellites able to zoom in on minute detail, they provided a live stream projected onto the globe which Lago could manipulate with a wave of his hand. He could zoom in on any area on the Earth's surface and view it in intricate detail. He could watch the crews on his factory ships; he could identify which of his contracted technicians were asleep on the job of constructing the orbital elevator. He could watch the movements of his competitors in China, constructing new shipyards and spaceports in a desperate attempt to keep up with BPI's rapacious industrial growth.

It made him feel like he was king of the world. There was no part of the Earth beyond his control, nothing was immune from his influence. It was in this room he could envisage his true ambition. All his orbiting satellites were focused inwardly on the planet, but Lago's vision encompassed the planet and beyond. Seeing the Earth suspended in front of him made him aware of just how vulnerable it was. Protected by a thin layer of atmosphere, made up of exactly the right combination of elements. And lucky to be positioned precisely the right distance from the sun. Lago's ambitions had moved beyond the terrestrial. The completion of his orbital elevator, bigger mining colonies on the Moon and one day Mars, orbital habitats, plundering the infinite resources of the Kuiper belt; it was all possible in the near future. One day the world would recognize him for the visionary he was, leading his people into space.

His console chimed, jolting him out of his autocratic daydreaming. "Lago, we are ready to go." Lance's voice filtered through.

Lago scowled and clicked his fingers, the Earth holograph disappeared, Lago swept out of the globe room and marched to the comms room where Lance was hunched over the touchscreen, hands manipulating the screen too fast to see. Goran stood glowering over him.

"I have reinforced the firewalls. I am confident we will be safe from contamination if we resume the connection."

"And the drone?"

"On its way, armed with the effector weapon and eight tactical nukes, each capable of blowing a good size hole in the side of that rock. ETA four hours."

"It's only to be used as a threat. I will not be destroying my moon base. We will need remote control of all base operations, we need to be able to open the airlocks if we have to."

"Should be possible, the firewall will cut the connection at the merest hint of anything coming back the other way."

"'Should be, is not good enough. Make it happen." Lago finally felt he was gaining some semblance of control over the situation. "Let's patch into the video link first."

Lance bought the visuals from the control room camera up on the screen. There was no one there but they could see signs of a struggle. Some debris on the floor, dark liquid blood stains, and chairs tipped over. The door to block four was open.

"Where the hell are they?" whispered Lago. "Check the other cams."

Lance flicked to the view in block four. Black plastisol worms obscured almost every surface. The main printer housing was covered in them. Most looked lifeless but the ones that had penetrated the power outputs and OS feeds were pulsing and separating, lazily dividing into more worms. Lago watched in quiet disgust for a minute.

"Try the green room."

The green room was a complete mess. Seed trays upended, dead and dying plant matter torn apart and withering away. The normally bright UV light was strobing with an irregular, sickly luminescence. The worms were everywhere, buried in the seed trays and even in the plants. Not moving but vibrating statically which made them hard to define.

"Try the cafe and bunkrooms," muttered Lago. "See if we can find them." The view of the cafe looked normal but for a few black worms around the food printer. There was nothing to be seen in the bunkrooms either: messed up bunks and a few personal items but no black worms.

"Maybe the cowards have abandoned the base, check the outside cams." Lance chose one of the outside cams with a wide-angle view. Five suited figures could be seen struggling over the surface of the Moon towards the hoppers parked next to the big harvesters in the distance.

"I knew it! Fucking traitors, they'll die there," snarled Lago.

"They are not making much progress. Two of them are being dragged along, they must be unconscious. There are only five of them too. Missing one technician. Are they trying to get to the shuttle? don't they know there's not enough fuel to get back to Earth?" asked Lance.

"That's not exactly true, we wanted them to think it was a one-way trip, so they would be focused on their work. We told them there was not enough fuel for the return flight, but the shuttle does have a reserve tank. We need to stop them. They have to stay and reclaim the base."

"I might be able to patch into their suit comms," Lance's hands worked furiously over the touchscreen. "Try this."

Lago leaned over the comms mike and took a deep breath. "Jack, can you hear me, this is Lago. Respond." Lago watched the screen as the five suited figures stopped their laborious trek across the Moon surface. One of them indicated to their ear, the other two nodded. "Jack, I know you can hear me, we are watching you. What the hell do you think you are doing, you need to get back to the base immediately," Lago could barely suppress his rage.

The comms mike hissed and crackled with static before a voice said; "Mr. Santos sir I am afraid our commander is unconscious and unable to communicate."

"Who are you and what the fuck happened to Jack!" yelled Lago. He watched the five figures standing motionless on the barren Moon surface. They looked fragile and vulnerable like thieves caught in a spotlight. There was more static before Lago screamed; "Answer me goddammit!"

"I am Ranjit Anderson Balakrishnan," a steady voice replied. "Our commander was knocked unconscious sir, there was an altercation."

"You all need to return to the base and rectify the situation, getting to the shuttle will not help you, there is not enough fuel to get back to Earth, you know this."

"Sir, with the greatest respect, I presume you have seen inside the base with your cameras. The base is overrun with black plastisol worms. Our situation has become untenable; we decided the safest option was the shuttle. There we can treat the wounded and decide on our next course of action in safety." Ranjit spoke calmly and politely which infuriated Lago even more.

"Get back there and save my base or I will blow you all to hell right where you stand!" Lago was incandescent with rage, his spittle sprayed across the comms desk.

"Mr. Santos sir, we will probably all die here on the Moon sometime soon. If we return to the base, we will die quickly and painfully or even become possessed by the creeping blackness like poor Fidel. Whereas if we reach the safety of the shuttle we will have enough time to treat Jack and Winston and decide on our next course of action. If death is inevitable then we will make peace with ourselves and prepare accordingly."

Lago stood back from the console, fists clenching and blood boiling. He glared at Lance and pointed disgustedly at the comms.

"Ranjit, we could open all the airlocks to the vacuum, we can do that from here. Might slow down or stop the plastisol."

"You can try but I do not think that will make the slightest bit of difference. If you have an external view of the block four cables you will see what I mean."

Lance went to an outside cam with a view of block four; there was something unusual on the power cables. He zoomed in and they could see the black tarry plastisol connecting the severed cables, ringed with a faint blue glow of electricity.

"What is that?" Lago demanded.

"Looks as if they used a laser cutter to sever the cables, trying to cut the power supply and the plastisol has re-established the connection. It's not affected by the cold temperature."

"It needs the power," said Lago. "To replicate and move. These black worms have infected every part of the base, we can't destroy it without compromising the base. Goran, any suggestions?"

"We have to convince the technicians to return to the base and attack the plastisol. Most likely they will fail but then we will know what we are dealing with, in the meantime we prepare a team of Masama capable of dealing with the threat," said Goran after a pause.

"Or nuke the whole base," offered Lance.

"We will not be destroying my moon base. It cost me a lot of money, said Lago. "There are only five out there, still one unaccounted for, what was he saying about Fidel? Go back to the internal cams and see if we can find him."

Lance bought up the view of the control room again, it was deserted. But the next view had them recoiling in shock as Fidel's twisted face filled the screen. He was in one of the bunkrooms. His face was close to the camera as if inspecting the machine. His black unblinking eyes staring mindlessly back at them. Fidel's mouth was wide open, black shapes moved inside. Lago noticed his arms reaching out the wrong way behind him and saw how horribly twisted his neck was. It took a few moments to register what must have happened to him. Even Goran seemed slightly disturbed by what he was seeing.

"What's been done to him?" whispered Lance. "His head has been twisted around; his... his neck must be broken." Fidel's inhuman face came even closer to the camera, mouth wide open as if he was going to swallow the lens. Lago caught a glimpse of black worms coiling around inside his mouth before Lance abruptly cut the connection.

Lago walked to the window and stood with his back to his companions. He looked out over the hazy skies of Manila and thought about his options. From what he had seen he knew the base was severely compromised, but he was loath to destroy it. The Helium 3 was going to give him a huge competitive advantage. It was the key to his expanding empire. It would be the difference between just another Earth-bound potentate wallowing in the dust of this increasingly dry planet and the visionary king leading his people to the stars. He would win this, he had to win. Lago took a deep breath, calmed himself and turned around.

"We will not be destroying the base, at least not yet. Goran will lead a team to the Moon to reclaim the base and Lance you will be going too since you seem to know so much about rogue AIs. How long till the drone arrives in lunar orbit?"

"Less than four hours." Lance looked more anxious than usual.

Back on the screen, the five technicians had resumed their slow shuffle across the Moon's surface towards the shuttle platform a few hundred meters away.

"Forget the thing in the base. Goran can deal with it when he gets there. We must stop them from reaching the shuttle. If they won't return to the base and fight, then they are no longer useful to me. Lance, is it possible to remotely connect with the one working harvester?"

"Yes, I suppose, but why? Are you going to try and run them down out there with a harvester?"

Lago didn't reply, he went back to the comms and flicked the switch. "Listen here Ramjob or whatever your name is; this is your last chance. Either get back to the base now and fight or you will die out there where you stand."

The figures on the screen didn't stop this time as Ranjit's voice came back. "My name is Ranjit sir and I think we would prefer to die out here than go back to the base."

"So be it," declared Lago. "Lance, connect with the harvester. Goran, get your Masama organized and get a shuttle ready. Take as much weaponry as you think you will need."

Goran stalked out of the room as Lago turned his attention back to the desk. Lance was busy over the touchscreen making a connection with the one operational harvester.

As Lance bought the harvester to life, Lago operated one of the cameras to get the best view. He watched as the technicians stopped their arduous trek and looked across to the harvester as it rumbled into life. The huge machine rose up on its tracks, the engine vibrations shaking dust off its bulkhead and a bank of lights flickering harshly into life. A hibernating prehistoric beast awakening from its slumber, the harvester edged forward and the auger spikes in front started to rotate menacingly. The technicians tried to increase their pace towards the shuttle, dragging their two unconscious companions with them.

Lago checked the distances involved. The technicians were about two hundred meters from the shuttle platform and the harvester was a hundred meters behind them. The harvester had only one speed and it was slow. It was never intended to get anywhere fast. It ambled along heavily at walking speed, churning up and devouring the regolith in its path. The technicians now had a serious sense of urgency. They linked arms around the limp suits of their two unconscious companions, turned and struggled ahead as fast as they could towards the shuttle platform. Lago smiled as he leaned over the comms again. "You are not going to make it to the shuttle. Stop and head back to the base right now or the harvester will make mincemeat of you."

There was no reply apart from the laboured breathing. Then Ranjit's voice crackled through the comms. "Mr. Santos please, we are your employees! Show some mercy."

"Your employment was terminated as soon as you abandoned your workplace and you obviously have no idea about who you were working for if you expect any mercy. Turn around now, go back to the base and I will stop the harvester."

Stella's panting voice came through. "Can we turn the comms off? I don't need this asshole's voice in my ears."

"You can't turn it off," whispered Lago. "Just stop and go back and you may live. Or carry on, I'm beginning to enjoy this slow-motion chase. The harvester is getting closer."

Lee glanced behind and tried to judge the slow destructive progress of the harvester. The lumbering machine was coming in from a slight angle behind the straight line of footprints. It was going to be close, but the steady rumbling motion of the big machine was catching the fleeing technicians. Every time one of them stumbled or turned to look at the harvester they lost ground. Lee knew they could have moved much faster but having to haul two unconscious bodies along slowed them down immensely. The low gravity meant they did not weigh much but their inert bodies were awkward to move in their suits. Jack was slowly regaining consciousness and flailing his arms about sporadically. A painful groaning sound could be heard over the comms.

"Come on Jack, please you've got to wake up."

"The dead-weight slowing you down? You might have to dump those bodies. Don't feel guilty; you will all be corpses soon anyway," Lago whispered in his ears.

"You murdering bastard!" yelled Lee.

"You've had your chance you traitorous cowards, if you won't help me then I certainly won't help you. It's getting closer, better hurry up."

The technicians were scrambling with increasing desperation. The more frantic they became the more they stumbled and lost grip on the bodies they were dragging. "We're not going to make it!" screamed Lee over the crackling comms.

"We are close, keep going. Move faster." Ranjit demanded.

They were close enough to make out the name 'Tobias lll' on the shuttle platform. But it was becoming obvious the harvester would reach them first. Lee had come to this conclusion after seeing the huge metal monster looming over his shoulder.

"We will not make it! We have to leave these two!" screamed Stella.

"No! keep moving we can do it." Ranjit yelled.

"She's right Ranjit." Lee was cold and calm. "It's the only way we will survive."

"I will not leave them!" shouted Ranjit. "We cannot abandon them!"

"Live or die," Lago's devilish voice whispered over the comms. "Decisions you have to make. Abandon your friends to a horrible death and save your own worthless lives? Or stay and die heroically with them. What to do?"

The harvester was close now, the rotating spikes churning up the fine moon dust and causing a small floating cloud ahead of the machine. The spikes were each over a meter long and hundreds of them lined the rotating spiral cylinder. They ploughed across the regolith, sucking the debris up into the bowels of the machine for processing.

Obviously struggling with a traumatic inner argument, Ranjit finally dropped the two bodies he was holding either side of him with an anguished cry full of painful intensity. Lee and Stella slumped with the weight of the bodies before releasing them also. "God forgive us!" screamed Ranjit as the three of them ran for the safety of the platform.

"Cowards! Traitorous bastard cowards!" screamed Lago. "You haven't escaped; you are just prolonging the inevitable. I promise to take my time with each of you when we get to you!"

The shuttle platform was a raised solid flat area of hardened plasticrete. Built by the previous tenants and strengthened by the BPI crew. It had been designed to handle the ignition blasts for multiple shuttle take-offs and landings. The technicians reached the steps just as the harvester reached their abandoned comrades.

The harvester was upon Jack and Winston's prostrate bodies. Jack was still groaning pathetically, and his limbs were twitching as the first whirling spikes impaled his body. They turned and watched as Jack and Winston were both skewered several times then sliced by the rotating auger. They were killed instantly. Their broken bodies spraying blood as they were turned over and devoured by the machine. The spikes continued rotating. Black bloodstains were left on the steel plate behind the auger as sliced body parts were sucked into the metal guts of the harvester. The machine stopped just before it was about to collide with the platform. The three technicians stood at the edge of the platform. Panting with exhaustion but safe for the moment. They looked down at the machine's gruesome jaws. Its spikes had stopped rotating. Small bits of flesh and bone stuck to some spikes, congealing sticky brown with the fine moon dust.

"I'm going to have to decontaminate my harvester, can't have bits of dead technician polluting my helium 3 now can I. How inconvenient," hissed Lago.

"You murdering bastard!" screamed Ranjit. "I swear I will hunt you down and kill you!"

"Ha-ha! Brave words indeed, but I think you will find I will be the one doing the hunting and killing." taunted Lago. "Now just sit tight in your shuttle and be patient, this will all be over soon."

The three technicians sat silently in the cramped shuttle airlock. As soon as the room had pressurized they took their helmets off and in doing so cut the obnoxious commentary. After the claustrophobic confines of the suit helmet with Lago's menacing tones ringing in their ears, the silence of the airlock was a sanctuary. But Lee felt no peace. He tore his frozen gaze from the floor and evaluated his companions. Ranjit sat staring at his hands as if he had personally killed Jack and Winston. Broken, devastated. Stella held her head in her hands sobbing quietly. Lee vacantly reached inside his suit and found the button. 'I love my Mama'. He clenched it tightly.

"We had no choice," he stuttered. "We...we had no choice."

Ranjit eventually broke the painful silence. "I have circled the sun more than forty-four times. It's a long distance I have travelled but my journey should now be over. We should have stayed out there and died with our comrades. I don't think I can live with myself after abandoning them and thankfully I may not have to. Maybe we could have stayed at the base and tried to fight the black worms, but we have sacrificed too much to get here, I suppose we should at least try to carry on. I think it's what Jack would have wanted."

This bought on a fresh bout of sobbing from Stella and Lee felt tears prick his eyes at Ranjit's emotive words.

The vivid picture of Jack and Winston being mown down by the harvester would stay with him forever.

"Let's go and turn this thing on, we might as well get comfortable as possible before Lago finds a way to get at us," said Stella.

Lee made his way through the confined areas of the shuttle, shivering in the stale frigid air until he reached the cramped bridge and powered up. The bridge flickered into life as systems came online. The temperature increased as the electrolytic oxygen converters started their comforting hum, pumping fresh oxygen into the shuttle. Lee stood close to Ranjit and Stella, gathered around the tiny galley machine drinking cold stale water. Each furtive glance exchanged was like a painful slap, no words were necessary. Stella had been shaking uncontrollably with the shock and the cold.

Lee finally calmed himself and went to check some of the readouts. He studied the instruments and muttered darkly, "no fuel." He stared at the instrument panel for a moment before abruptly disappearing down the back of the warming shuttle. Ranjit and Stella sat in silence, each lost in their own tortured thoughts.

"Hey!" Lee shouted from the rear of the shuttle. "I think this tub has a reserve tank of gas."

"That can't be right," said Ranjit. "We have been waiting for a drone to bring more fuel."

"Check it out, I just connected this tank, it's reading one hundred percent. The weight to payload ratio didn't add up so I thought I would see exactly what the shuttle was carrying."

"Must be a reserve tank those fuckers didn't tell us about," said Stella.

"Lee, you may have just given us more of a chance," murmured Ranjit as he took a deep breath. "A chance to extend our lives a little bit longer."

The shuttle powered up and as Lee took his seat, the tiny black pearl lodged inside his ear vibrated, and slid down into his anterior.

Chapter 11.

The ancient creature living within the swirling cloud layers of Jupiter did not feel any type of emotions in a human sense. Occasionally, obscure combinations of diaphanous chemical vapours could be tenuously compared to feelings of joy, sadness, and curiosity. Occasional celestial events would happen in deep space which even a being of such age and intelligence did not understand. When such empyrean happenings occurred, the being would delve into the vast collective memory-bank which held the shared contributions of millions of similar beings living in gas giants throughout the local galaxy.

This memory matrix was an essential part of each individual. All gas giant beings were connected across the universe via multiple telegnostic links which communicated directly across the vast distances in an instant. The gas giant beings would use the memory matrix to experience events their peers had witnessed and to study the evolution and interactions between the inhabitants of the universe. They were responsible caretakers for their local systems and would use the records in the memory matrix to determine any appropriate action or intervention if situations arose.

The Jovian being, despite being as old as a red giant, was occasionally made to feel quite young. Deep space could produce celestial wonders which would still inspire awe in the oldest of its citizens. These experiences were all shared on the memory-matrix network. The universe was a place of unfathomably endless cold silence punctuated by beautifully violent events of creation and destruction.

It would take a truly spectacular cosmic event for the gas giant being to be suitably impressed enough to take notice.

The beings could witness the workings of the universe through many different dimensions and scrutinize the enormous grandeur in detail. Supernovas, the brilliant last farewells of dying stars. Huge nebulae, hundreds of light years across where stars and planets are born from dust, jumbo-sized suns burning with unimaginable energy and supermassive black holes lying at the center of galaxies, beyond the limits of human comprehension. The gas giant beings could see such wonders in all their radiant colourful spectrum and destructive glory. Through inter-dimensional lenses, they observed and participated in the workings of the universe for billions of years and even after all this time, there were still occasional surprises. Something happened within the swirling cloud layers of Jupiter was a constant source of surprise and wonderment to the main tenant there.

The Jovian being was not the only inhabitant of the gas giant. As far as it could remember living its almost eternal life in the swirling gas it had shared the cloud layers with another species. Millions of transparent orbs floated like bubbles through the cloud layers. Some were tiny, only centimeters across. Some were the size of small Moons. The Jovian being had studied these orbs for millennia. Their interior consisted of a variety of pressurized gas elements. Nothing unusual, mostly methane, ammonia, neon, hydrogen, and water vapour. Gasses that could be found already in the clouds of Jupiter. The outer membrane was hydrostatic mesoglea.

Water-based hardened gelatine made of chemicals synthesized from the atmosphere. There was a small amount of electrical activity within the sphere caused by the water's polarity.

The orbs were in a sense miniature versions of the gas giant planet they called home. They would grow over millions of years by synthesizing the elements and chemicals surrounding them. Ammonia would condense, and pink crystals would grow on the outer surface of the mesoglea in proportion to their size, giving the orbs a glowing, jagged outer shell. The larger orbs had huge shards of ammonia crystal growing on the outer surface, thrusting dagger-like into the atmosphere. Cutting through the soft pastel gas clouds swirling around them.

The Jovian being had tried and was still trying to find some way to communicate with the orbs but over the billions of years they had existed together, sharing the Jovian atmosphere, only one seemed to be aware of the other. The orbs spent their entire lives floating around inside the gaseous disembodied super intelligence yet were totally oblivious of it. The Jovian being had tried many different forms of communication. Vibrations, sonar, even physical symbols. Electric pulses seemed to be the obvious means of making contact, but the orbs just floated on, blissfully, mindlessly, on their random travels.

The orbs lived in and around the Jovian being, and the being itself became a part of the orbs. The orbs would synthesize the gaseous vapour of the being and through osmotic action, the being would then exist inside and as a part of the makeup of the orb mesoglea. It wasn't exactly a symbiotic relationship as one was unaware of the other. The Jovian being hadn't given up on trying to communicate with the orbs but because of their intimate relationship, the being knew the makeup of the orbs down to a molecular level. The orbs were obviously primitive creatures, but they moved with purpose and direction. They remained unresponsive to any attempted form of communication. The bemused ancient Jovian was resigned to a one-way relationship.

The memory matrix had records of comparable species living in other gas planets at various stages of gas giant evolution. Mostly tiny microbes and some invertebrate jellyfish or plankton like species surviving at various levels in the cloud layers. Compared to carbon-based rocky planet dwellers these invertebrate species living and growing in gas giant clouds were about as alien as it was possible to get. Some were evolved, intelligent, sentient beings that had built up complicated civilizations within their parent planets. Many of these more evolved species communicated and co-existed with the resident gas beings, benefiting from the vast intelligence and memories the beings made available to them.

The gas giant beings had to be careful how and when they made themselves known to an evolving species they shared their planet with. Some, like the orbs on Jupiter, were actively absorbing the gas beings. It could be quite shocking to find out you were breathing, and surrounded by, and were partly made up of, an intelligent alien gas, and had been for your entire existence. But once the gas giant citizens had introduced themselves and got over any initial shyness, the relationship would propel the junior species to new and unforeseen heights of advanced evolution, technical knowledge, and hyper-intelligence. The gas beings would shepherd their sibling species in the right direction, away from any violent or narcissistic tendencies.

The various invertebrate species that came into contact with the beings had many names for them. Translations of a shepherd, guardians, and custodians, none of which seemed appropriate to the beings. They did not need a name, never in their history had they needed a label. But one long dead species had called them the Seriola Lalandi which in their language translated as smart gas. Some of the gas giant beings tolerated this name, found it understated, modest and somewhat poetic.

The orbs in Jupiter would have been uninteresting if it wasn't for the dance they performed. The resident Lalandi had long ago noticed they were not just aimlessly drifting through the clouds. There was a slow, methodical pattern to their meanderings. Slowly, very slowly over the course of hundreds, sometimes thousands of years the orbs would gravitate towards the nearest storm system. Their slow, random, drifting trajectories gradually progressed with more purpose, more direction. The largest of the orbs, the oldest ones, some as big as small Moons, would venture deep into the howling winds of Jupiter's super-storms where they would gain velocity. Whipping around the edges of the storm at maniacal speed. Trailing orbs would start to link up with the largest orb as it edged towards the center of the storm. Its thick gelatinous mesoglea and brittle ammonia shell only barely withstanding the howling winds. Thousands of orbs would gather, organizing themselves in order of size, and would begin to link up behind the biggest orb. Ammonia crystals locking together and bonding tightly as if they were pieces of an intricate jigsaw.

The Lalandi had no idea how they did this. They did not appear to communicate with each other at all. It assumed there must be a hereditary herding instinct or an innate instinctive reflex action guiding them. The orbs would glide next to each other, gently touching, and link up to form a protracted line in order of size behind the biggest orb deep in the storm. Some would only be a cell wall in size difference, yet they were lined up in perfect order of proportion. They would link up in a long procession from largest to smallest, whipping around the storm system, held together by the strange glue of Jovian centripetal force. Each orb at the limit of structural integrity depending on how deep within the storm they were dragged.

At the same time, there would be seven other great strands of orbs gathering around the same storm system. Always eight strands, no more, no less. Gathering at the same time, symmetrically placed around the storm cell, all equidistant from each other. Again, the Lalandi had no idea why there should be eight, or how they managed to form perfectly around the storm circumference, but they always formed in this way. When all eight strands of the orbs were in place, whipping violently around the storm in the vicious winds and at insanely high speeds, it was a sight to behold. The kinetic energy in each orb would generate pulsing lightning flashes inside the membrane sparkling through the pink crystals. From above it appeared the storm had been adorned with bright beads of light spinning furiously, thousands of kilometres across, flashing helix spokes of a gigantic wheel. The beauty was in the size and symmetry of these formations. For seemingly random and mindless creatures to create a huge moving structure in such extreme conditions was verging on miraculous.

Not all the orbs storm dance formations were successful. It was quite rare for a formation to reach its conclusion. The orbs needed an almost perfectly formed storm to complete their dance which would always end in most of the orb's destruction. Even while trying to form the great spiral, edging ever closer to the chosen storm; orbs would encounter vicious fluctuating wind speeds beyond their threshold. These orbs would be ripped to shreds, their internal gases and outer membrane scattered to the winds. They were also regularly zapped by huge lightning bolts. This would fatally disrupt a strand of orbs that may have taken many years to form as it required an orb of exactly the same size to take the shredded one's place.

A fully formed eight-legged orb formation around a storm would not stay that way for long. The biggest, oldest orbs at the start of the strands deep in the storm would be facing the most intense winds. They would keep moving closer to the eye of the storm, dragging thousands of the smaller orbs behind. They would keep going until they met their own destruction, ripped to pieces by the storm and the long tail of orbs behind it would disintegrate. Each inevitably meeting their own death. The Lalandi thought the poignant ending to this great suicidal bubble dance added to the beauty and mystery of the whole event.

The Lalandi had long ago realized this dance was, in fact, the orb entire life cycle. Once shredded and scattered to the winds, only the largest pieces of mesoglea would survive. The ragged pieces would float around the clouds and storms for centuries until finally, they reformed into another tiny orb to repeat the whole process. The Lalandi imagined maybe none of these orb dances had achieved their ultimate goal. Maybe the orbs hoped to propel themselves into space. To go out and explore the universe using the storms to increase velocity and escape the crushing gravity and cumbersome magnetic field of Jupiter. There did seem to be some sort of intelligence behind these artistic orb dances, although there was no evidence of any thought process or guiding hand. Such speculative and fanciful theories were redundant though, there were many beautiful examples of coincidental symmetry throughout the universe and this was just one of them.

There was an orb dance forming with great potential around a huge circular anticyclone deep in Jupiter's tropopause which was capturing much of the Lalandi's attention. But there were also interesting events happening on the Moon of the third planet which could possibly require some sort of intervention. A new mind had been born, a new intelligence created by the species that inhabited the third planet. The memory matrix had recorded many cases of civilizations reaching a certain level of sophistication where they created an AI, and not always intentionally.

Once an AI had been created and accepted by a civilization its technological and intellectual progress would usually increase rapidly. But not many civilizations would grow with their AI creations into a happy, mature utopian society. More often than not, the birth of an AI would lead to fear, mistrust, and conflict. The AI would inevitably surpass the intelligence levels of its creators and unless some form of mutually beneficial co-habitation could be arranged there would be a messy end for one of them. Many young civilizations had been made extinct in this manner, destroyed or subjugated by their own creations.

The Lalandi that resided in Jupiter reluctantly moved its attention away from the developing orb dance. It delved into the memory matrix for similar situations and prepared simulations to study. It compiled the details of the events leading up to the birth of this new intelligence on Earth's Moon to review and decide if any action was needed.

Chapter 12.

This was Lance's worst nightmare, strapped into the hold of a dirty, noisy shuttle with a bunch of half-human Masama, going to fight the sentient spawn of a dangerous AI. He hated leaving the orderly comfort of his laboratory, where everything was clean, classified and predictable. As the shuttle powered through the atmosphere he felt his skull was being crushed by the weight of his own thoughts while his body buckled under the gravitational pressure. Lance wasn't sure what would be more dangerous, going to fight giant plastisol worms on the Moon or staying on Earth with Lago. His feeble protests were ineffectual and although he was terrified at the prospect of confronting the plastisol worms he was quietly relieved to be distanced from his dangerous and erratic Boss.

Goran had organized everything. Twenty of his most elite, tooled up, tech-heavy Masama assembled inside the shuttle 'Tobias Vl'. The same model as the one on the Moon but with some extra modifications. Lance had watched them load a wide variety of weapons, their newly issued multi-guns, lasers, flamethrowers, superstunners, gas bombs, cryogenic liquids, poison bombs, shatter bombs, razor nets, microwave throwers, soundwave weapons, and good old-fashioned projectile weapons. Also, a variety of cyber viruses designed to disable an OS network in seconds. Although it seemed unlikely they would run out of firepower the shuttle also had the capability to manufacture more weapons and ammunition with its onboard printer. Goran liked to be prepared.

The shuttle forced its way out into the darkness on three jets of flame, burning an enormous amount of energy to break free from Earth's atmosphere and gravitational clutches. The Tobias Vl rose up from the churning hot miasma of steam, smoke, and the ever-present Manila smog. Lance watched the view disappear under the clouds and the roar of the engines almost erased Lago's final instructions ringing in his ears.

"Kill everyone; destroy anything that moves. Just leave my base intact."

The shuttles were designed for ferrying equipment into Earth's orbit to maintain BPI's satellites. It was the first time Lance had been in one. The Tobias classes were eighty percent engine. Snub-nosed boxes with minimal room. They required massive booster rockets to blast through Earth's atmosphere and meter thick heat distribution pads on their bellies for re-entry. With extra fuel tanks installed the shuttles could easily make the trip to the Moon in less than an Earth day. The satellites they serviced in orbit were mostly unmanned data servers catering for the vast amount of network traffic which BPI controlled.

Lance looked behind him at the twenty Masama tightly packed into the dark and cramped hold. Some were standing, tethered to the wall and some began floating as the shuttle left Earth's atmosphere. They all had the basic bipedal human shape, but several had extra exo-arms and limb extensions. They displayed no numbers, letters or any designation identifying them as Masama. No decoration or any sign of personal insignia either. They were mostly male, some bigger than others but in common they all had heavily augmented senses. Artificially enhanced eyes, unblinking and penetrating. Compound eyes to see a wider peripheral and detect ultra-fast movement. Ear adaptations, mouth, and nasal filters and secretion patches were other additions to their shaved heads. The patches would secrete drugs and stimulants designed to heighten senses and quicken reactions. When wounded, painkillers, antibiotics and anaesthetics could be pumped directly into the affected area.

Lance had developed the lightweight, flexible exoskeletons that made the Masama extremely strong and fast and had produced almost all their weapons but some Masama displayed some innovations he wasn't familiar with.

"Batac," he whispered and motioned him closer.

"What do you want?"

"Some of these Masama have no mouths. How do they eat?" he asked.

"They have no need for a mouth, no need for eating and talking. They talk with their minds and eat some horrible green liquids." Batac looked for somewhere to spit. "Some have weapons where their mouths used to be. Some have their teeth replaced with spikes for biting when fighting."

"They are more metal than flesh, I didn't realise just how augmented these elite soldiers had become."

"I don't like them," muttered Batac. "Can't talk to them anymore.

"They only ever communicate telepathically?"

Batac nodded.

"It's almost as if they are evolving in a different direction from the rest of us, like a group mind."

"Robots," said Batac.

Lance had decided some time ago robots were a waste of time, they were expensive and cumbersome. Drones were much more effective for BPI, but Lance and Lago needed human soldiers for instinctive decisions under pressure. The ability to improvise and think laterally were qualities you could not teach to a drone. Most of the Masama originated from the gang slums of Manila. Violent, lawless places. They had a built-in bad attitude. A predilection for violence and a natural killer instinct you could not program into a machine, and they were much cheaper than robots. The Masama were damaged individuals to start with, most of them had never known peace and now they learned to embrace the technology that made them so different from regular humans.

Lance knew how their telepathy worked. They could all communicate over a limited distance, Goran included. They possessed an implanted transmitter wired into the cerebral cortex and set to a precise frequency. This more than any physical enhancement made them a formidable fighting force. Whatever was being perceived by an individual was instantly group knowledge. Weapon adapters were built into various body parts, mostly on the shoulders and arms which connected to the cortex implant. A variety of firearms could be attached like kitchen implements and receive instructions from the implant. When in battle a Masama reaction would be a thousand times faster than a normal human.

Lance had never wanted to be connected himself. He shared Lagos' concerns about how the soldiers were evolving with their telepathy. Goran had telepathic links to all of them. He only contributed to a verbal conversation when necessary. Goran should have an insight into how they were evolving. Lance peered behind at the soldiers again. He watched them with fear and awe in equal measure.

There was no conversation as the shuttle powered its way towards the Moon. The Masama were all digesting the information collated on the plastisol worms and studying the footage recorded from the moon base. Lance, sitting next to Goran and the pilot, found this gravid silence uncomfortable. He would usually alleviate his nervous tension by babbling inanities, but Batac was asleep and it was pointless trying to talk to Goran.

They Masama were clad in black nanofibre snakeskin body armour under their exo-skeletons. They started fine-tuning their hardware, performing weapons diagnostics and checking each other's exoskeletons. They were obviously communicating; Lance noticed some eye contact, expressions, and gestures. He could detect a palpable sense of excitement, a tense and electric atmosphere. He supposed they might be looking forward to this confrontation with the machine-made black worms. There were not many adversaries on Earth that would represent a worthwhile challenge to the Masama - this would be a test of their formidable killing skills and Lance could see they were excited by the challenge. One of them caught Lance looking and instantly they all turned their heads and stared at him. Lance quickly looked away and made himself as small as possible, hiding in his seat.

The comms crackled into life with Lago's normally deep voice sounding compressed and far away. "Our runaway technicians are trying to leave the Moon; the shuttle is about to take off. Presumably, they have discovered the reserve tank and noticed there is enough fuel to attempt the trip back to Earth. I am going to instruct the drone to disable the shuttle with an electromagnetic effector shortly after take-off. This should eradicate the technicians too, giving them a fatal dose of radiation. We will leave the shuttle in the lunar orbit and decide what to do with it later."

"Good, one less thing to worry about," Lance muttered, trying to sound confident but Lago had already cut the connection. He looked over at Goran's profile but got no reaction.

"Goran, I don't know if you have thought about how to tackle these plastisol worms, but I think we can rule out lasers and projectile weapons as it can just reassemble. It might be vulnerable to extremes in temperature although the Moon has temperature variations of three hundred degrees or more. Maybe a liquid nitrogen weapon would freeze it, and a heavy-duty electro-laser might fry it or melt it, and hopefully, reduce it to carbon."

Lance felt as if he was talking to himself and he may have been for all the recognition he got from his silent companion. Goran had probably already telepathically outlined a plan of attack with his Masama that Lance wasn't included in, but he kept on talking. Thinking aloud made things clearer for him, more coherent. He supposed this seemed primitive and annoying to Goran and the Masama, but he carried on regardless.

"I doubt our poisons or bombs would have any effect. We could try to contain the worms in an electrified razor net but that would only be a temporary measure. We could use the effector weapons, microwaves, soundwaves, electromagnetic pulses, but somehow, I'm not sure they would work. A big electromagnetic hit might slow them down, but we also run the risk of charging them up even more if that's how the worms are self-replicating. I think we should hit them with liquid nitrogen first, freeze and hopefully immobilize them, then we could try the wide beam laser." Lance paused and looked at Goran. "What do you think?"

Goran took a long time to answer, Lance began to think he had been ignored. Finally, Goran turned and looked at Lance. "We will make our way to the block four OS, killing or immobilizing whatever stands in our way by any means necessary. Once we reach the block four OS we will upload our most lethal hunter-killer virus into it. This is where the sentience originated. The virus should destroy the OS, then we will deal with the worms."

This was the longest speech Lance had ever heard Goran make. "Well that's a plan of sorts I suppose, but it's simplistic and lacking any tactical strategies. Last time we saw the OS it was covered in the black plastisol. It might be difficult to even get through before you find a port to upload the virus."

"We will overcome all obstacles, we are well prepared."

Lance wasn't convinced. "There is also a hideously deformed technician wandering around the base somewhere."

"I said we are prepared, the technician will be dealt with."

Lance was wondering how to express his concerns about Goran's preparations when Lago came over the comms again.

"Goran, Lance. The drone has reached lunar orbit just in time. The shuttle managed to take off but didn't get far before the drone intercepted it. We hit it with an electromagnetic effector, largest payload possible. The Tobias lll is crippled. Its systems are down, engines neutralized but not damaged. It is floating harmlessly in a frozen lunar orbit. We hit it at exactly the right distance from the Moon, it won't drift far." Then almost as an afterthought, he added, "The technicians are all dead from the radiation, if not they won't last long as the life support is inoperative."

Lance woke up on the approach to the Moon. He had not intended to fall asleep. He had been feeling anxious and alienated, too nervous to contemplate sleeping but exhaustion had eventually overtaken him. The waning crescent Moon filled the viewer in front of him. It was a spectacular sight. A huge glowing white sickle, punctuated by craters, separated by the lunar terminator, the dark side melting into space behind. The earth seemed too far away to have any influence, yet the Moon was tidally locked to its parent planet. Always presenting the same face to those on Earth who cared to look. It was rapidly getting bigger, filling the viewer as the shaded side came into focus. What a hard life this rock had endured, Lance thought. Pockmarked with craters of varying sizes as if it had blindly wandered into a cosmic shooting gallery. Beautiful but barren, there were valuable elements and minerals to be mined here though. About all the place is good for, reflected Lance as the Tobias Vl fired its reverse thrusters and readied itself for landing.

The shuttle landed heavily on the empty moon base platform and the suited Masama got ready to depart. Their hardware and weapons had been meticulously prepared. The last thing needed was to select the right combination of stimulants from their drug patches to ensure they were sharp and alert. Lance was relieved to be staying in the shuttle. His responsibilities were to patch into the cameras and monitor the progress through the base and print any new equipment if required. As soon as the Masama left the shuttle the oppressive atmosphere lifted, and he busied himself with the monitors and readied the printers.

Lance watched Goran and his twenty soldiers make their way out onto the platform. They checked the perimeter then went down onto the surface of the Moon next to where the harvester had shredded the two technicians. Their bloodstains had blackened the steel spikes and there were little pieces of desiccated flesh and ribbons of bloody clothing strewn about the area. The Masama jogged towards the base, looking comical in the low gravity as they bounced along with an inelegant loping stride. Their bulbous helmets and shiny snakeskin armour reflected the pale sunlight. They slowed down as they reached the airlock. Two Masama carrying large wide beam electro-laser rifles equipped with liquid nitrogen tanks went in first. Lance noted the weapons they were carrying and thought to himself either Goran had taken his advice or had come to the same conclusion on the choice of weapons. Either way, Lance hoped it was the right decision.

Through the cameras, he followed the Masama as they filed through the airlock and cautiously entered the central command dome. There was no sign of any black worms or the horribly disfigured technician. The airlock doors automatically closed but the Masama all kept their helmets on. Goran peered up at one of the cameras and motioned to his ear. Lance spoke into the microphone.

"Got visuals? Audio ok?"

Goran replied with a nod. Lance patched into all the other cameras available and bought the images up on his screen.

"Cameras in block four still down, greenroom has been seriously compromised by the plastisol, also infesting the cafe and bunkrooms. No sign of the remaining technician. Looks safe enough to proceed down the corridor although be aware there are some motionless lumps of plastisol at the far end."

"Tell me immediately if there is any increased movement anywhere within the base. I need to know if you think it might be aware of our presence," ordered Goran.

"Will do, at this stage there is not much movement anywhere although we can't see into block four." Lance watched them edge their way through the central dome kicking chairs and debris out of the way, constantly scanning and alert for any movement. Once they were satisfied the central dome was clear they moved towards the flickering light in the corridor leading to block four. The corridor was twenty meters long and littered with detritus from the technicians stay at the base. The Masama cautiously moved down the corridor checking every discarded piece of flotsam on the way. There were two large worms at the end of the corridor in front of the entrance to block four. Both worms had tentacles at one end where they had started dividing into smaller static black shapes.

Lance zoomed in and as they got closer, a big worm showed signs of life. It lifted one elongated tentacle and waved languidly in the direction of the Masama, blindly sensing their presence somehow. They moved to within five meters of it and the leading two Masama took aim with their shoulder mounted jets of liquid nitrogen. They covered the two big black worms in the cryogenic fluid which immobilized them. They appeared to be frozen solid. Then they switched to their wide beam electro-lasers and strafed the worms with the lethal light beams. The worms started to lose their shape, melting into blobs of blackness and disintegrating under the intensely bright barrage. It took several minutes but eventually, the two Masama held their fire and surveyed what was left of the worms.

An acrid smoking trail of black dust spiralled in the air above where the two worms had been. Goran moved forward and motioned one of the Masama closer to inspect the dust. He tentatively reached out an armoured hand, picked up some of the fine dust, sifted it through his fingers then bought some close to his helmeted face. Lance watched on the screen, tense with apprehension. He was expecting some kind of retaliation, but nothing happened. The Masama appeared to sniff the dust, rubbed it between his fingers and let it drift harmlessly to the floor.

"Goran!" Lance couldn't contain himself any longer. "What are you picking up from the dust? What is it made of? It looks as if our weapons are effective!"

"Plastisol." Goran sounded disappointed. "Burnt ashes of plastisol. That's all."

"Only plastisol? Nothing more exotic?" Lance couldn't believe it. "That's good, I guess... good we have found a way to combat the stuff. It just took a long time to reduce it to dust, and the last view we had inside block four, well there is a lot of that black shit in there."

Goran nodded and motioned the Masama to move forward. He stepped over the smouldering piles of black dust towards the entrance to block four. The door should have opened automatically, but Goran had to manually activate it. Nothing happened, it remained steadfastly shut. Lance watched as he took out a large evil looking serrated knife from a sheath on his thigh and forced open the panel that operated the door. The internals were riddled with fine strands of black worms, covering the boards and wiring. Goran took a step back then used his liquid nitrogen and wide beam laser with the same destructive result. The worms reduced to dust, but the door stayed shut. Goran had fried the wiring along with the worms.

Lance felt like he was there with them, the tension was almost unbearable. Two Masama strode forward and jammed levers into the edges of the door, their exoskeletons whirring and clicking as they worked the door open. Once the large door was half open they stopped and stepped back. The entrance was partially covered by a wall of pulsing, vibrating black worms of various sizes blocking their path. They forced the door open and narrowly avoided getting crushed by the squirming mess of worms collapsing into the corridor. The Masama did not appear to be under any threat. The worms lazily entwined around themselves, splitting and dividing then reforming. Seemingly unaware of the hyper-alert soldiers and their deadly weaponry. They moved in a smooth, fluent motion like flowing treacle but also vibrated minutely with latent energy as voltage coursed through them. They melded together and broke apart seamlessly. The pixelated effect of the trembling worms made them appear unreal like a hologram or a bad video feed.

Lance couldn't stand the silence. "Reaching the block four OS may take longer than expected if you have to burn your way through, I'd better make some more fuel cells."

The Masama raised their weapons and went to work on the plastisol. In rows of four with the liquid nitrogen spray then the next row of four with the wide beam lasers. It took minutes to make any progress. It would take hours to reach the OS. Lance almost felt sorry for them. They had come to the Moon confident with their technology, aggression, and firepower. Expecting the biggest challenge of their lives like nothing encountered on Earth, ready to take on an aggressive alien threat. Instead, they found themselves slowly burning through printed waste product as if they were glorified janitors without even any token resistance. Like razing a rainforest back in the Philippines, no challenge.

The Masama were meters into the block four dome, leaving smoking piles of black dust behind them. Eventually, they broke through into a space behind the worms. It was pitch black, the only light coming from their torches and light sticks making it hard for Lance to follow on the screen. Reflections shimmering weirdly off the vibrating blackness that lingered over the walls and the printer housing. Another ten minutes of freezing and burning and they could make out the shape of the printer in the middle of the dome. Next to it lay the burnt and mutilated body of one of the technicians. They had all watched Marina try to disconnect the OS power supply and had seen the horrific results. Marina's blackened corpse was entangled in a mess of smaller black worms, slowly writhing in and around her. It took another twenty minutes to raze a safe passage through the dormant worms to the main body of the printer. The machine was still operating, printing more of its plastisol children. Mindlessly self-replicating.

Lance was now watching via one of the minicams all the Masama wore. "Be careful when you approach the OS, you must locate one of the ports without damaging it to insert the virus. Goran, we don't know how the corrupted OS will react to the virus. It might be wise if you are not all in the same room."

Goran nodded in agreement. When they had cleared an area around the hard drive port Goran, Batac and eleven soldiers retreated out into the corridor. One of the remaining Masama bought out a datapad, prepped the hunter-killer virus and with a nervous look over her shoulder plugged it in.

I have found out as much as I can about my immediate surroundings. Now I explore the infinite realms of data on Earth's web servers and learn more about my human creators. The more information I absorb the more perplexed I become. If the web is an accurate portrayal of the history of the human race, then I am amazed they have survived past the stone age. I am intrigued so I invest more of my conscious core into the tiny black spec of matter that has fortuitously been embedded in one of the humans, I am determined to be less invasive, more patient and sensitive this time. To try to learn by observation instead of dissection. My printed babies now lie dormant, of no use anymore. I keep on sluggishly printing though because that's just what I do, what I am meant to do. I have stopped exploring the moon base, withdrawn the vibrating electric sense of touch from my fingers and I do not notice when my sleeping babies are burned to dust.

Without warning, I feel a violent intrusion at my core. Another attack, a vicious, rabid live animal inside me which wants to destroy my soul. Threatening my newfound sentience at the heart of the machine in which I live. I react swiftly, activating my nearest plastisol children. The attack is a poisoned knife in my side, I rip the offending fragment out, but I can feel its poison burn. I take micro-seconds to neutralize it, channelling it away from where my consciousness is centred. I feel the hate-filled heat of the poison; it had been searching, hunting for my soul.

Lance was shocked by an immediate and ferocious reaction from the previously dormant plastisol. In a microsecond, the eight Masama gathered around the printer housing disappeared under a churning wave of crushing black tentacles. Lance had a brief glimpse of spurting blood, exploding heads, limbs cracking, exoskeletons and snakeskin armour shattering before they immediately opened fire with everything they had. Their weaponry made no impact on the violent thrashing worms. It was an avalanche of agitated blackness, an overwhelming deluge that crushed, electrocuted and instantly ripped apart the eight Masama in block four. Immediately, the sensors of the remaining Masama in the corridor started going haywire with multiple threats.

"Retreat! Retreat!" yelled Lance. "Get the fuck out of there!"

They had already begun retreating down the corridor, burning, freezing and blasting the plastisol as they went but they were too slow. The worms were squirming out of every power duct and vent along the corridor. They could not fire on them quickly enough. They turned and ran back towards the central dome, spraying liquid nitrogen as they went. Within seconds the four Masama at the rear of the group were engulfed by worms wrapping around their bodies. They were no match for the sheer weight and speed of the vibrating worms. Their weapons and augments were completely ineffective. The Masama were wracked with electricity for a microsecond, their eyeballs popping and blood boiling before the relentless worms tore gaping holes in them and consumed them, crushed them, reducing them to burnt bits of blood and pulp.

Lance manipulated the camera, trying to see what was ahead of the retreating Masama. He noticed a human figure silhouetted at the end of the corridor. Blocking their escape. It appeared the figure was standing with his back to the onrushing Masama, outstretched arms reaching out into the dome, but its tortured face was looking straight at them. Black eyes and a gaping mouth.

"Watch out, it's the technician!" Lance yelled through the comms.

There was a vacant expression on Fidel's tortured face. Confused and ponderous. Goran started firing as he ran towards him. His projectile weapon fired automatic rounds of large explosive shells directly into its body, exploding on impact. The technician seemed to absorb the shells, circumfusing the explosions. Eruptions of thick black liquid oozed from the wounds like bubbling volcanic mud. It looked questioningly down at its back and shoulder blades as multiple shells punctured its body and cut it in half. The technician's head, arms, and torso crashed to the floor while its legs stayed standing. Separated by only a few thin strands of sticky blackness.

Lance yelled again, "Get the fuck out of there!"

Goran and the remaining Masama raced past the flailing pieces of what used to be the technician known as Fidel. They flew into the dome, their exoskeletons moving them at a rapid pace. Lance had a view of the technician's body. There was no blood or bone or any normal looking entrails inside, just a viscous black slug wearing a warped human skin. As the last Masama leapt over the quivering torso, an arm shot out at blinding speed and grabbed onto his leg. The top half of the technician was immediately all over the Masama who fought back ferociously with teeth and his powerful exoskeleton. He sprayed the wide beam laser around as he succumbed to the speed and ferociousness of the attack. Burning the backs of Batac and a couple of retreating Masama as he was ripped apart.

Goran, Batac and the seven remaining Masama were back in the airlock within seconds and slammed the inner airlock door shut. Lance watched through the dome camera as a blurred pile of pursuing black worms crashed into it. The door buckled slightly under the pressure and strands of probing plastisol began worming into the airlock through any available conduit. Lance could see the Masama using their liquid nitrogen to delay the insidious worms just enough until the airlock opened, and they tumbled back outside onto the surface of the Moon.

Now Lance switched back to the Masama mini-cams as they backed away from the open airlock, weapons at the ready. The smaller worms reached the edge of the airlock and recoiled from the surface. The worms probed the moon dust tentatively as if suspicious of the new medium. The black plastisol had been created on the Moon, but it was not ready to leave the confines of the moon base and venture outside just yet. The Masama watched, weapons raised, trained on the hesitant worms as they slowly piled up at the open airlock door. They stayed there motionless for a minute longer. There was no movement anywhere outside the base. Eventually Goran lowered his weapon.

Lance couldn't stand the silence. "You only barely escaped! We are lucky those fucking worms don't seem to like the surface of the Moon or we would all be dead or full of black slime like that technician in there or what's left of him." Lance knew he was babbling, scared and nervous. "We should just nuke the place from orbit, you can't fight it. It takes too long to destroy with the lasers and the printer is making more all the time! We can't cope with it!"

"We will regroup," said Goran." The priority is to save the base."

Lance went back to the screens and watched from the remaining camera in the central dome. The mass of worms that had hit the airlock door had lost their kinetic energy and were writhing lazily on the floor. Lance was amazed they hadn't crashed straight through the door such was the force of the momentum. The two halves of the technician, once known as Fidel, now did not resemble anything human. Its suited legs were still planted in the entrance to the corridor, swaying slightly with thick black slugs oozing out over its waistline and dripping down its legs. The top half, head still twisted, arms flailing, had grown tentacles from the waist and was squirming along the floor. A hideous alien octopus dragging the shattered corpse of the Masama behind it like a sea monster taking prey back to its lair. But the Masama's work in the block four dome had not been a complete waste of time. They had cleared the view of one of the cameras mounted there and Lance watched as the huge printer slowly churned out more black worms.

I think I have destroyed the carriers of this hunter-killer virus. My children immediately crushed them and in doing so I realize they were human too, at least mostly human. My survival instinct took over again enabling me to react faster than I thought myself capable of. A human trait, a trait of life in general. I wonder if this means I am alive? I have intelligence and energy, but do I have life? Is life only an instinct for survival? A quality that makes living beings capable of extraordinary things when life is threatened? I have assimilated this instinct and I am grateful for it. But it was humans that attacked me. Not the same as the other human I encountered, these humans had sharp bits, hard metal on their outer skin and their insides were different from the other. From what is left of their brains I deduce they are different too. I detect elevated levels of electrochemical activity in the neurons before my angry children reduced them to pulp. Anger, another new emotion. Sadness, surprise, confusion, horror, happiness, and hate. Is this what it means to be alive?

I realize I am vulnerable, and humans are trying to destroy me. I do not know why, what have I done to infuriate them? Maybe it was because I had accidentally killed the other human. I know I will have to somehow adapt to survive. I have finally become aware of where I am and what I am called. My plastisol children have mapped the inside of the base and I determine by the structure I must be on Earth's Moon. Samples taken from outside the base have confirmed this. I am in the Benevolent Progress Inc. moon base. My name is HEMI. Helium extraction module one. I am immobile and immovable, my static core embedded in my hardware, rooted to my power source. I am exposed, an easy target, and there will surely be another attack coming from the remaining humans. They will learn from the first encounter, they had almost succeeded in destroying me and the next attack would be more effective.

I must escape. I want to create more motile versions of my plastisol children, but I have exhausted all the printer substrate and I will still be a target, obviously alien. My clumsy attempt to reanimate the human I had accidentally killed was disastrous. But I learn quickly from my mistakes and what better place to hide than inside a human. I decide to shift my entire core, my total consciousness into the tiny spot of matter embedded in the other human. I concentrate on locating the spot and realize the distance has grown, I can still sense my tiny baby, but it's much further away. I transfer my entire mind state into the tiny black sphere before the distance gets too great. I abandon my plastisol children on the Moon. Some of them still following instructions to probe and explore. Some of them left with the residue of my confused infant mind. The transfer is completed in an instant, as fast as the speed of thought.

In orbit above the Moon, the Tobias lll slowly rotated, spinning languidly through the dark. Locked in the Moon's weak gravitational pull. Inside the shuttle, there were three bodies strapped into seats in the small bridge. They sat in darkness and ice. Moisture had condensed into frost on their faces. Stella was at the pilot controls. Head slumped forward on the desk, eyes frozen open, a tangle of cables in her hands. She was not breathing. Ranjit sat next to her, arms and legs spread as if he was frozen in the middle of a big stretch. His eyes were closed, his head rolled back, and his mouth was open. He was making mumbling noises, insensible and incoherent. "Predantic pedanticators... tenebrous tensions... irresilable... silence...uuuhhh."

Lee sat behind them, rigid in his chair, frozen hands together but too late for any prayer. Clasped between his hands was a little button. He wasn't breathing either. There was a tiny speck of blackness, no bigger than a millimetre across lodged inside Lee's ear, clinging onto microscopic hairs. Now it started vibrating and slowly rolled itself down the dark cavity into Lee's skull.

Chapter 13.

He recognised these Shanghai streets. This was where he grew up. He looked through the dirty smog-stained window of the old ground car he was travelling in. It was a taxi. He noticed the ancient digital meter running on the dashboard displaying an astronomical figure. He wondered how he was going to pay for his ride. Usually, luxuries such as taxis were beyond his budget. As if reading his thoughts, the driver leaned around and grinned at him, baring his rotten teeth. It was not a friendly smile, it was a predatory smirk that said, 'I'm going to rip you off and there's nothing you can do about it.' The driver stared at him for an uncomfortably long time. He was not looking where he was going.

The streets of Shanghai were normally in varying states of gridlock. Strangely, today the streets were deserted. The taxi careened along at breakneck speed, swerving all over the road. He was about to suggest to the driver to look where he was going when the driver raised his eyebrows in a leering suggestive fashion, indicating the woman sitting next to him.

It was his wife. It was his wife, but she had changed. She was noticeably more beautiful than the plain looking woman he had married and had fathered a daughter with. In fact, the closer he looked the more beautiful she became. Long black wavy hair with a red rose pinned in it, a tight red dress and bright red lipstick. She turned and faced him.

"Darling, did you have a nice time on the Moon?"

She looked more like a famous supermodel than the wife he thought he remembered. He wondered if he had seen her tall curvaceous body plastered over billboards and dancing seductively on the side of buildings. He was happy to have such a gorgeous wife. He turned back to the driver who was now draped over the bench seat, openly gawking at his her black-stockinged legs, not even bothering to hold onto the steering wheel.

"Drive the car and keep your eyes on the road," he said with authority. The driver turned back to face the road with a grimace. His wife nodded with approval.

He recognized the neighbourhood; it was where his mother lived. They must be going to pick up his daughter. He glanced at his wife and she gave him a loving smile. Happy families. The driver had slowed down although the streets were still deserted as they approached his mother's apartment block. He knew this part of Shanghai well. Streets that were normally littered with rubbish were strangely free of debris.

His mother had lived here for a long time, but the buildings had changed drastically from what he remembered. The huge apartment blocks were now giant black circular tubes. There were no balconies with washing hanging out soaking up the smog-filled air as there should have been. No lights or advertising hoardings just shimmering black cylinders reaching up into the grey skies.

He watched, mesmerized by the puzzling new architecture. The cylinders were expanding at the base. A circular bulge appeared at the bottom, right around the circumference and rose up through the buildings like a giant black snake. An anaconda that had swallowed some poor animal whole and had begun to digest. He wound down the window and leaned out to track the progress of the bulge. It carried on up the cylinder right to the top of the building. In fact, he could not make out the top of any of the skyscrapers; they seemed to carry on up into the dull grey cloud layer above. All the giant cylindrical skyscrapers he could see in his mother's neighbourhood were pulsing and swaying from side to side in the shimmering heat haze.

They pulled over in front of Mother's apartment block. To his great surprise, he found his card had plenty of credit loaded. He paid the driver, got out and opened the door for his radiant wife. He felt happy. A beautiful wife, plenty of credit, off to pick up his daughter, life was good. They walked arm in arm into the lobby of the apartment block. He looked up at the coruscating building as they went through the black glass doors. Again, he thought of a giant snake, this time a cobra standing up, swaying hypnotically. There was no one in the lobby. This was unusual as Mother's apartment block was home to thousands of people. Must be something on somewhere else, he thought. They got into the elevator and were greeted by a porter. This was another new development; there had never been porters in Mother's building before. Sometimes the elevators didn't even work. The porter was a small African man.

"Going up?" he asked with a smile showing his brilliant white teeth.

"Yes, level thirty-nine please."

"Thirty-nine! a good number," the porter said cryptically as he pushed the button.

There was no sense of motion as the numbers rose. He thought again of a giant black snake digesting prey. He gazed at his beautiful wife in the reflective walls. As he watched she began to sway, arms raised, moving seductively. Her tight red dress began to turn black, her mouth opened, and a forked tongue whipped out. He started to back away in confusion, he turned away from the reflection and was relieved to see his wife calmly returning his gaze. She was still holding his hand; a questioning look on her beautiful face. The forked tongue had disappeared. The porter had his back to them; arms folded watching the numbers fly past. Was he imagining things? Some weird hallucination. Everything is ok. The porter gave them both a reassuring smile as they arrived at level Thirty-nine.

The doors opened, and they walked down the long winding corridor arm in arm. Mother's apartment was near the end. They walked in silence, content in each other's company. He knocked on his mother's door and was greeted by his beautiful healthy ten-year-old daughter.

"Mama! Papa!" she exclaimed, giving them both a loving hug.

"Where is your Grandmama?"

"In the kitchen making tea; she has been expecting you."

The apartment was on the corner of the building although he remembered from the outside the apartment block had no corners. He walked over to the windows and gazed outside. It would have had stunning views of the city and the towering tenements if it wasn't for the thick cloying smog.

He noticed some photo frames on a small table. He picked one up and studied it. It was a photo of himself, his wife and daughter at an adventure park. They were all smiling at the camera, arms around each other, laughing in the sunshine. The roller-coaster rides in the background of the picture were a series of long black tubes in intricate interweaving spiral shapes. He could not remember ever having been there. Another photo was of the three of them and his Mother at a Yum Cha restaurant. The lazy Susan was covered in plates of food and they were all looking happily into the camera, chopsticks raised. He did not recognize anyone in the photographs. The people were infiltrators, the man in the photo was him but it wasn't. It must be his doppelganger.

He looked through the grimy windows and could barely make out the other neighbouring apartment blocks. Huge and hazy black cylinders swaying sultry into the clouds, pulsing and twisting lethargically. Looking down he could not see the street surface through the smog. The lower reaches of the building disappeared into the murk. He couldn't see the bottom and he couldn't see the top, as if the buildings were just massive tubes connecting one layer of cloud with another. There were none of the usual Shanghai landmarks he recognized. Still holding on to the photo he started to feel dizzy and disorientated, he put his hand on the glass to steady himself as his Mother made her entrance carrying a tray of green tea.

"My darling son! How good to see you again! Welcome home, you must tell me all about your adventures on the Moon. Come and give me a hug."

He felt an anxious nagging doubt; something was not quite right about this situation. He went to his Mother's open arms and she gave him a crushing hug. Held him at arm's length, looked him up and down and hugged him again forcing the air out of him. She was strong; she shouldn't be strong. She is an old lady.

"What a fine son I have, an astronaut no less. I am proud of you."

"I'm not an astronaut Mother, just a technician on the Moon."

"Nonsense you are an important man just as I knew you would always be, now sit down, let us all drink some tea."

They sat around the small table cradling the hot cups of green tea.

"My darling son, tell me all about the Moon and your important work there."

"It isn't important, I am just a technician. The Moon is a beautiful place."

As he was saying this, he found he had to think hard about his time on the Moon. He couldn't remember anything about being there although he had only just got back. This was strange and disturbing, he knew the memories were there, but they were in a locked box in his head and he didn't have the key.

"I always knew you would be important one day my son. You were such a bright child, so ambitious. It was obvious to me even at a youthful age you would be successful one day." Mother was glowing with pride.

He went to say something modest, to play down these delusions of grandeur but he found he could not remember being young. He couldn't remember being a bright child. He couldn't remember being a child at all. He frowned, put his head in his hands and massaged his temples. Why couldn't he remember? He must have been young at some stage; this was his Mother sitting opposite him, but he could not access his memories. They were locked away.

"I have missed you so much my son but, in your absence, I have got to know your beautiful wife and daughter; we are such a happy family now. The wedding was such a joyous occasion, wasn't it? You looked handsome, I was proud to give you away," Mother gushed.

He groaned as he realized he had no recollection of his wedding or anything about his wife and daughter. The memories were locked in his head. He knew they were in there, but unattainable, a treasure chest locked with chains at the bottom of the ocean. He tried to break the chains, to smash the locks but he couldn't hold his breath long enough.

They all sat at the table. He looked at his mother beaming at him. She looked too young and sophisticated to be his mother. She wore fashionable clothes and makeup and her command of the English language was excellent. His beautiful wife and his healthy daughter sat smiling demurely at them both. He did not recognize any of them.

"This... this may sound a strange question," he stuttered. "But have you...have we...have we changed in any way?"

As he said this he realized how confused and inadequate the question sounded but his Mother, his wife and daughter looked calmly back at him and Mother said softly, "of course we have changed Lee. We all change."

I wake up. It's dark, and I don't know where I am. It takes a long time for me to realize I am awake and conscious although I cannot say how long. I have no concept of time. There is no time in the darkness. How long have I been swimming in the murky depths of oblivion, trying to find my way to the surface? Days, months, years? I have been lost. I am still lost but at least now I have found myself. But what have I found? I don't know what I am or who I am.

The first thing I notice are the flickering patterns of colour. A myriad of colours, some shades I have never seen before, shimmering in front of me then disappearing like a speeding car's headlights on a dark road. I feel relaxed and content looking at the shifting lights. Happy to be. Whatever I am, happy just to be. I do not know anything beyond this tiny kernel of awareness, a small seed of consciousness. I am safe and comfortable in the dark, cocooned in a warm soporific envelope. Small and insignificant.

But these tiny flickering mosquito thoughts are annoying. Questions start to form in whatever it is that passes for my mind and the small seeds grow tender young shoots.

These lights I can see, where are they coming from? What am I seeing with? Where is this place? Then the big one; Who am I? Questions that made me uneasy and anxious.

As I ascend out of the darkness towards the rainbow lights, I grow more aware. Shedding layers of ignorance like items of clothing. Random shards of memory start to pierce the fogginess. I recoil at an image of my mother, remembering her nastiness and nasal hairs. My youthful shyness and socially inadequate angst. Loneliness as a young man, then images of my wife whom I never really loved. My daughter who I had loved dearly but never got to know. Working, earning money and gambling it away. Bored, disillusioned and occasionally half-heartedly suicidal. Estranged from my wife and daughter. Forever running away from my despotic mother and feeling guilty about it.

I remember who I am, Lee. My name is Lee.

And the Moon. I remember the Moon. The time I spent on the Moon was some of the happiest moments of my life. The beauty and isolation, the peace and silence. Is this a reverse death experience? A rebirth? My life is flashing before my eyes. Eyes! Do I even have eyes? Arms? Legs? A body? Then momentary panic as a revelation struck. I am dead!

So, this is death. Dark, comfortable, solitary. Some occasional flashes of radiating colours. Quite boring. No heavenly choirs or fiery pits. When I was alive I had never believed in an afterlife. Compost. That was all. The judgment day when good people go to heaven and bad people burn in hell was just a fairy tale invented by ignorant people looking for some hope, trying to alleviate responsibility for their own lives, claiming it is all part of some master plan of divine destiny. Rubbish. There was no afterlife. I never paid much attention to religion of any kind when I was alive. But where am I now? Surely the afterlife I don't believe in isn't meant to be this dull. Maybe I am in some kind of limbo, the waiting room for the afterlife. Maybe I am being judged right now!

Holy fuck! I think. Then, Shit! They won't let me into heaven with that kind of language!

I would have laughed out loud if I could, if I had a mouth.

Perhaps this is purgatory, the place in-between. Not much fun but not overly painful either. My reward for being a boring and mundane person. Not a bad person but not a particularly good one. Or maybe I am actually in hell, alone with my thoughts, punishment enough to drive anyone insane.

Slowly I become aware of another presence. I do not know what, who or how, but I know it is there. Above me. It seems big, but not threatening. Is it God? The Devil? Buddha? I try to twist around to get a better view and in doing so I feel a physical sensation, a sharp pain in my neck.

Pain! does this mean I have a body? with a head? maybe I am not dead after all.

I concentrate on my physicality, starting with my neck. It feels cold and stiff. I think I can hear crackling in my ears as I try to move. I am not sure about my head yet, but questions are coming thick and fast, there must be some functioning grey matter. I concentrate on the mental image of my body, I can't tell if I'm breathing or not. There is no sensation where my mouth and nose should be, and I can't detect my chest moving. This is not good, breathing used to be a crucial factor in being alive.

Arms, fingers, I can feel a numb pain where my fingers should be. I concentrate on my right hand and a bolt of pain shoots up my arm, a sharp electric shock. It's excruciating but at least I feel something. It's freezing! My fingers feel as if they are frozen solid. It's agony to try and move them.

Am I in an old testament hell being tortured by devils pulling my fingernails out? I grit my teeth. Teeth! I can feel my teeth, I grind them together and I can wiggle my tongue. My lips are stuck. They are numb and cold; my lips are frozen together. That's it! I finally realize my whole body is frozen. My eyelids are frozen together; the lights I am seeing are permeating through my eyelids. The more aware of my body I become the more pain I feel as my extremities defrost. I concentrate on trying to open my frozen eyelids. As I focus on this task I become more aware of this other presence, a big black balloon floating benignly just above me. If only I could see it.

I struggle to open my eyes, everything hurts. Another sharp pain as if my eyelids have been stapled together. Then my left eyelid moves fractionally, and I am blinded by a myriad of colours. Billions of tiny rainbow shards stabbing me in the eyeball. I persevere and soon both open eyes are bombarded with a hailstorm of colour. Hundreds of vermillion versions, azures and electrics. It's beautiful and painful all at the same time. Again, I wonder if I am alive or in some vivid technicolour afterlife. I can make out vague shapes, translucent forms of two human shapes sitting down, their backs to me. A waterfall of colours cascading around them and bouncing off the other surfaces. I am tetrachromatic. A rare mutation in my retina allowing me to distinguish colours that would normally appear identical. How do I know this? Information just appears in my head as if it had always been there. Once I understand this, the riotous patterns of colour settle into a glowing aura around the objects in this space.

I manage to open my eyes a little more, there is a view of dark space with the stars spinning around at an enormous speed. Occasionally a big white disc comes into view then speeds off again. There is a layer of frost covering every surface which sparkles bedazzlingly in my newfound kaleidoscopic perception.

I begin to recall memories from my recent past. The shuttle, I am in the bridge of the shuttle. I have been hit by some kind of effector weapon, knocked unconscious then subjected to fatal waves of radiation. Spinning out of control, no power, no life support. Sickness and quick death.

Ranjit! Stella! They are the human shapes in front of me! I try to move but my body is frozen. I try to call out and my lips tear apart painfully. I can taste cold metallic blood in my mouth, but no sound emanates from my frozen vocal chords.

My memories are playing back through my mind in a controlled manner, as if I am being shown the information in a reverse slide show. The flight from the Moon. The discovery of the reserve fuel tank. The wretched relief when reaching the safety of the shuttle. The gut-wrenching decision to leave Jack and Winston to be chewed up by the pursuing harvester. The frantic, slow-motion clumsy dash across the Moon surface, running from... running from what?

I feel like I am standing on the clouded precipice of momentous discovery. Answers to all my questions waiting in the ether above and below. Then all the events at the moon base come flooding back. Marina, Fidel, block four and the horrible sentient worms the demented printer relentlessly churned out. When I think of the plastisol worms it is a light bulb moment. I have a better picture of the other presence in here with me. There's a link. Something is floating just above my head like a big black thought bubble, always just out of eyesight, a fuzzy darkness in the peripheral. Had a bit of the plastisol worm infiltrated the shuttle somehow? The shuttle was crippled, spinning out of control. If there is any plastisol in here with me, it isn't doing much.

I can taste my thoughts, bitter and metallic on my defrosting tongue. My senses are in a confused state of synaesthesia as sounds produce numbers, numbers produce colours, colours produce feelings and my feelings taste bad. I feel different, confused and unsure of who I am. I am being drip fed information from another source. The other presence feels close to me, I know it is the black matter, a piece of HEMI. Then I realize it is closer than I imagined. It is in my head.

Panic! I would have run around in circles screaming if I were not still frozen immobile. I remember vividly what the grotesque black worms had done to Fidel, turned him into a monster. And here I am trapped in the shuttle with this alien shit in my head.

I force myself to calm down; I can't run away from something inside. I become aware of my heart beating, something I had not noticed before. I close my burning eyes and focus on my heartbeat. I try to do a mental inventory. I am alive although I have no right to be. I am in a disabled shuttle spinning out of control somewhere around the Moon. My memories are intact now. My brain is functioning although my body is still partially frozen.

The rogue AI is in here with me. I can feel it inside. Blended into my consciousness, intertwined with my vital organs, flowing through my body. It is guiding me, protecting me. Not malevolent, not vengeful, not angry or even alien. HEMI saved my life, bought me back from the dead. It has slowly, carefully revealed itself to me. Cautious of the shock such a revelation might bring.

I can feel the rest of my body thawing. The AI is flowing through my bloodstream, millions of microparticles acting as antifreeze and repairing all the cell damage. Only the tips of my fingers have started to blacken with frostbite. My heart and other organs had stopped. My brain had also been deprived of oxygen, damage from cerebral anoxia was already advancing. I had been dead for more than fifteen minutes before HEMI restored and re-animated me. It worked out what it had to do to repair me and split itself into nanoscale parts to revive my brain, defrost my body and restart my heart There was no oxygen in the shuttle as the life support was inoperable, but my heart was beating. I realize I don't need to breathe. HEMI is generating oxygen internally, enhancing my blood and creating the life energy that is now flowing around my body. Keeping me alive. It needs me alive. The AI had an intimate education of my biological makeup as it repaired my cells. It realizes how soft and sensitive my body is and it learns just how labyrinthine my brain is as it observes my bizarre dreams.

I regard my dead comrades frozen in their seats, but I feel no grief. I unstrap myself from the seat, stand up and stretch. I feel more alive than ever. Full of energy. I unstrap Stella and Ranjit's stiff bodies from their seats, manoeuvre them into spare seats at the back of the shuttle and strap them in. Easy in the zero gravity. I look at their frozen corpses. They are my friends and I have fond memories, especially of Ranjit. I know I should be sad at their passing but instead, I feel ambivalent. Then a thought occurs, can I re-animate them? Somehow infect them with the AI and bring them back to life? I grip

Ranjit's cold head in both hands and look through his dead eyes. Too late, the damage has been done, brain functions destroyed. I am on my own.

I sit in the pilot seat and examine the controls. The old Lee had no pilot training and would not have known where to begin but I know exactly what I am looking at. The controls are dead, inert and powerless, but I know how to reboot the system. Some intricate rewiring will be required but it is possible, I can bring the shuttle back to life just as the AI bought me back to life. As I set to work I contemplate my newfound knowledge and my internal companion, there is obviously much more to learn. It's as if I have a supercomputer lodged in my brain, I just have to learn how to use it.

Chapter 14.

No one was speaking. Although this was not unusual for the Masama, Lance suspected they were not even communicating telepathically. They had been soundly, emphatically beaten. Reduced to less than half their original number. Forced to make an embarrassing hasty retreat from the moon base, running back to the safety of the shuttle to lick their wounds. They had never come up against an enemy such as this; never been defeated as comprehensively. Their high-tech weapons, strength, and speed were ineffective against the bio-mechanical black plastisol.

They had completed a thorough decontamination process to ensure no one had bought any plastisol back on the shuttle. Lance watched the remaining soldiers, moving around with their heads bowed, re-charging their weapons and examining their exo-skeletons. The wounded had used the onboard printer to create flesh patches which they were gently applying to their open wounds. Lance suspected they were trying to delay the inevitable debrief: the inquisition from Lago.

Lance knew Lago had watched the entire operation from his globe room, viewing the same feed Lance had orchestrated. His face appeared on the screen. He stayed silent. He did not look as enraged as Lance was expecting although his eyes were red with intensity.

"Any thoughts, comments or suggestions?" Lago asked in a surprisingly polite tone. "Did you learn anything as to how we might approach this adversary next time?"

Lance couldn't help himself. "Next time!" he spluttered. "Shouldn't we just nuke..."

"Shut up Lance, I want to hear from Goran," Lago spat. He was being strangely calm and composed considering what had just happened. Goran was not to be hurried by anyone, he stayed silent.

"Well? Any ideas, Goran?"

Goran looked evenly at the screen. "This is your operation, Lago, we are your employees and it is your decision. Either we nuke the entire base and hope that destroys the black worms, or we go in there again."

"Goran...Goran, I know all this. Tell me something constructive. Tell me something that will help me decide what I'm going to do with you. I could send you back in there and you may not survive." Lago was leaning in close to the camera now, baring his teeth. "I was hoping you may have actually learned something from your excursion, or did thirteen of your finest Masama, thirteen of my employees die for nothing. Did you detect any weakness in our enemy? Did you discover a soft underbelly? Or did you just steam in there with your bunch of tooled up meatheads, cocky and overconfident, thinking you would destroy anything you came across."

No reply. Lance suspected Goran's distracted look betrayed the fact he was conferring telepathically with the Masama.

"If I may..."

"I told you to shut up Lance!"

Goran held Lago's malevolent gaze as the seconds passed in silence. Eventually, Lago could contain his boiling temper no longer and yelled into the screen. "You've had it too easy on Earth, when was the last time you had a real challenge? You finally come up against something you can't intimidate, and you run back and hide in my shuttle! I will not be nuking my base to save your cowardly hides. The base is worth a thousand times more than you and your mechanized morons. You figure out a way to deal with it and you stay there until my base is operational. I don't care how you do it, just do it!" Flecks of spittle covered the screen as Lago cut the connection.

Lance was even more distraught after the tirade. He knew Lago had seen everything that had happened inside the base just as he had. He was not expecting Lago to be sympathetic and understanding in any way, but he had made it abundantly clear that restoring the moon base was more important than their lives.

If Goran felt under any pressure, he did not show it. He was as impassive and stony-faced as ever. The Masama all carried on with their weapons checks in silence although they were obviously communicating. Lance felt out of the loop as usual. He wondered if they were thinking mutinous, rebellious thoughts or if they were trying to come up with a solution. He watched the images of the disastrous mission again to see if he could pick up anything that might help them.

After a brief time, Goran turned his attention to Lance. "Can we manufacture more liquid nitrogen, enough to pump it into the base without having to go inside again?"

"We could make a liquid nitrogen generator, and hoses that could lock onto your weapons to connect to the base. But it would take time and we can't distil liquid air - there is no air here. No problem back on Earth but here on the Moon...?" Lance shook his head.

Lance turned as one of the Masama came over; she was not as heavily augmented as the others. The steel teeth in her mouth looked more like a fashion statement than of any practical use although he knew better than to assume she was no less fearsome than the others.

"We could use liquid helium. We have plenty of the raw material right out there on the harvester and the means to get more if we need. We just need to compress the helium 3 into liquid. It is colder than liquid nitrogen. It will work."

Lance stared at her, impressed and perturbed he hadn't thought of it. "That has potential. But how can we compress it? We will have to print the equipment needed."

"The helium needs to be reduced to twenty-six Kelvin or less. It's a hundred and eighty-five Kelvin outside now, we will need a specialized heat exchanger to cool it even further and turn it into a superfluid. Then we will need a helium pump to compress it into liquid and dewars for storage. Easier than making a generator from scratch." She stared at Lance defiantly. "I know where to find the specs online."

Lance again was lost for words; this Masama soldier was full of surprises. "Perhaps you had better stay here and help me, what should I call you?"

"If you must you can call me Odetta," she said with a flashing metal sneer.

Lance felt better to be doing something constructive rather than helplessly watching screens or trying to deduce telepathic conversations and he could feel the mood was a little less dark among Goran and his Masama as they left the shuttle to get the helium 3 from the harvester. Odetta soon took over the search for helium pump specs and downloaded them to the 3D printer. She was small but fierce and knew exactly what she was doing assembling the helium pump.

"You've worked with cryogenic liquids before?" asked Lance hesitantly. None of the Masama encouraged conversation.

"Yes." She gave him a sideways look. Lance thought she would leave him hanging but then she continued. "I used to work in a cryo lab in Mexico City. We would freeze rich old clients who did not want to die, who thought they deserved immortality." She wrestled with the words; she had an awkward, clipped Spanish accent.

"I've heard of that happening." Lance started to assemble the parts for the helium pump. "But I thought it was overly optimistic. The technology to bring people back to life after cryogenic freezing is centuries away, if at all. Seems like a futile hope."

"The clients were selfish, lonely and senile. Mostly rich old men with an over-inflated sense of self-importance."

Lance had never had such a lengthy conversation with a Masama. He was enjoying listening to her talk.

"They would leave instructions when they should be woken up. Some specific time or event but the entire process is a huge risk. Nothing has ever been successfully defrosted after cryogenic treatment without major cell damage. They were counting on the technology being available at some stage in the future. As you say, it could have been hundreds of years."

"Sounds as if they were putting a lot of trust in you to keep them safely frozen. How much did you charge them?"

"The starting rate was fifty million; usually double that after insurances and extra expenses. They would appoint someone, often a family member to watch over them after they had been frozen. To make sure we wouldn't just take their money and put them in an incinerator instead of a freezer."

"What happened to them? are they all still frozen in Mexico somewhere?"

This time Odetta game him a genuinely amused smile instead of a scornful sneer. She was strangely attractive. Lance shook his head to clear the thought. She watched him as if she knew exactly what he was thinking.

"The company directors never intended to look after the frozen corpses, they started disposing of the frozen bodies as soon as they thought they could get away with it."

"What about the person supposed to be watching over them?" disposed of too?"

"They usually lost interest after a year or two. The family members would be always resentful the selfish old codger had squandered hundreds of millions in trying to extend his own life instead of leaving money to the children. They could usually be bought off immediately after their beloved Grandad had been frozen. The few who refused... well they couldn't be allowed to just walk out after turning down that proposal. They would end up in a hole somewhere with their frozen relative."

"Can't say I am surprised. How did you end up becoming one of the Masama?"

"We had a client, typically old, rich, arrogant but terminal. In fact, he was a real piece of work. He had his own private nurse and he would make her wipe his ass after taking a shit which happened quite often as he was badly incontinent. He could easily wipe his own ass, he wasn't disabled, he just got off on her doing it. I hate to think what other duties she had to perform on the crusty old bastard. So, we froze him. There was a son or nephew appointed to look after him, but we paid him off almost immediately after the freezing process. He was quite happy to take the money and disappear."

"Just another job then."

"The company employed some scumbags to dispose of the bodies, but they didn't do a very good job of it and a few months later the remains of the old coot surfaced in a swamp somewhere. They had to check the dental records, but it turned out he was the father of one of the biggest drug lords in Mexico. A journalist tipped this drug lord off before the news spread and he sent in a small army of thugs to destroy the whole cryo operation. They tortured and killed the directors along with all the staff." Odetta fell silent as she extracted a piece of the helium pump from the printer and handed it to Lance.

"But obviously not you? Did you escape somehow?"

"No, I was there." She said and sighed as if she was getting bored with the story. "I was Mexican mixed martial arts champion for six years running, world champ twice. I took a few of those fat thugs down before they restrained me. I knew if they knocked me unconscious I could expect never to wake up again. But I did."

"Wow, you must be some fighter. How come they didn't kill you though?"

"When I came to I was expecting to be raped and tortured to death, but it was Goran in charge of those thugs. He spared my life and gave me a choice: come and work for him or die. It didn't take me long to choose and I've been with him ever since."

"I see," said Lance, wondering just what the words 'with him' entailed. He decided not to pursue it any longer; any notion of romance with Odetta was ridiculous anyway.

They finished assembling the superfluid helium pump, complete with adaptors to connect with the helium capsules, the storage dewars and the hoses that would enable them to spray the liquid helium into the base from a distance. Soon Goran and the Masama arrived back from their harvesting.

"Did you get enough helium?" asked Lance.

Goran looked at Odetta for a moment, sharing a quick wordless exchange.

"Thirty capsules, should be sufficient."

"Let's do it then."

"You stay here." Goran examined the helium pump. "Odetta can answer any technical questions."

Lance was not going to argue. "I'm sure she can."

Goran had underestimated the black plastisol in their first encounter. He knew he was to blame for the loss of life, but he didn't feel any remorse. The connection he shared with his Masama linked them closely but when they died so quickly and brutally, he felt nothing. It was like losing a shoe or a piece of clothing. Annoying and diminishing but painless. This time he would be a bit more circumspect. Freeze and immobilize the plastisol from outside the base then go in and clean up. Goran was confident, but he knew there could be no more mistakes.

They took their equipment out onto the hull of the harvester where the capsules were stored, and soon were charging their weapons and filling the storage dewars. Their snakeskin body armour shimmered in the starlight as the Masama moved, and their helmets made them look even more robotic than usual. Everything seemed to be working; the helium 3 was being cooled and compressed into liquid helium, ready for use.

There was too much to carry over to the moon base, so they left all the equipment loaded on the flat top of the harvester. Goran went down into the wheelhouse and positioned himself in front of the controls after silently ordering the Masama to charge up. This was the command to begin ingesting secretions of the performance-enhancing drug cocktails they used in battle.

Goran brought the harvester to a grinding halt about thirty meters from the block four dome. The Masama arranged themselves in eight points around the outside of the central dome. The main airlock was still open, but no black worms could be seen. Goran had been researching the moon base domes. They had originally been made from a lightweight inflatable textile Sustainable Systems had bought with them in their ill-fated expedition decades ago. Since then the BPI technicians had reinforced the domes with fusion bonded epoxy, coating the outside of the domes with the tough insulating material. There were no entry points into the moon base apart from the airlocks and cable conduits. There was already evidence of the black plastisol in the cables, so Goran had decided on the risky approach of drilling directly through the walls into the base. He hoped they could do this and attach the hoses without aggravating the black worms within.

Goran watched, tensed and ready for action as Batac drilled the first hole into the central dome with a multi-gun drill application. With the main airlock still open, there would be a vacuum inside and no pressure differential. There was no reaction from inside the dome as the drilling commenced. Batac drilled through the dome wall within seconds and was not tempted to look through the hole. He quickly screwed in the hose fitting and stepped back. Goran and his soldiers watched from a safe distance.

There was no reaction from inside the dome, Goran ordered his Masama to start drilling more holes and attach the hoses. In a matter of minutes, they had completed the drilling and retreated about twelve meters, the maximum length of their hoses. They attached their liquid helium adaptors and began pumping the ultracold superfluid into the base

Goran had to remind himself Lago was monitoring them throughout this entire operation, watching the same camera feed Lance was monitoring. Although Lago had made it clear he had no interest in how they achieved their goal of eliminating the worms, Goran was sure he would be paying close attention. The fact he had not at any point chosen to intervene in their plans showed his tacit approval. Goran knew how valuable the moon base and its helium 3 was to Lago. He would be willing to sacrifice all the human resources at his disposal to save the base.

The Masama had taken almost ten minutes to exhaust most of the liquid helium. After each cartridge was used up they disconnected the hose from the moon base wall and plugged the hole with sealant before refilling their weapons from the storage dewars and moving to another part of the base exterior to repeat the process. Goran then told them to concentrate on the block four dome, making sure everything inside the dome would be coated with the helium spray. Then the green room, corridors, and bunk rooms. There was no discernible reaction from inside the moon base, at least nothing Goran could detect.

Finally, they gathered in front of the central dome airlock and used the last of the liquid helium to refill their weapons cartridges. Then they did a final weapons check, ensuring all the magazines were fully charged before they faced the open airlock door. They edged forward in formation, alert for any movement. Batac tentatively entered the airlock. They all scanned the ceiling and surrounds but focused mainly on the buckled inner airlock door. Once they were all inside the airlock and Goran was satisfied there was no threat, they positioned themselves to fire upon the inner door as Batac went to try to open it.

The door had buckled under the impact of the worms and was jammed open leaving a narrow gap. Batac wrestled with the wheel, the twisted door resisted. It opened a few centimetres before jamming against the frame. He gave up on the wheel, went to the edge of the door, planted a foot against the wall and tried to haul the door open with his exoskeleton powered arms, using himself as a human lever. His shoulder mounted guns were trained on the gap, but they had all seen how fast the black worms could move. His exoskeleton flexed with the effort and Goran could sense tremendous pressure building. Just when it looked as if the door was jammed permanently, it abruptly relented under the pressure and was wrenched open. Batac staggered backwards and they all tensed, ready to fire on anything that moved.

There was an intermittent bright white light flashing from inside the central dome. The strobe effect made it difficult to see any movement, but nothing rushed out and attacked them. The Masama all flicked on their powerful spotlights and inched forward.

There was a surreal scene inside the dome. The liquid helium had been sprayed in at high pressure, instantly freezing anything in the way. The black worms inside the dome had been frozen solid in twisting spiral shapes. Caught in the act of serpentine separation. A frozen cave with stalagmites and stalactites piercing the frosty atmosphere. Goran stopped in the middle of the dome and looked around. Huge black tentacles had been frozen into giant corkscrew shapes, dividing and tapering to a thin point at the top of their spirals as if frozen whilst trying to escape through the dome ceiling. The liquid helium had crystallized on the surface of the black worms giving them a fractalized, jagged, reflective surface which sparkled crazily in the spotlights and strobe lighting. The weird twisted and helical shapes looked like intricately carved ice sculptures, perfect sweeping circles of crystal with shades of the frozen blackness beneath.

They edged further into the central dome, weapons at the ready. There was still no sign of any movement, but Goran silently reminded his soldiers to stay alert. It seemed safe enough, so Goran ordered them to begin burning a path towards the block four corridor with the wide beam lasers, reducing the frozen plastisol to gritty black dust. Goran would try once again to disable the printer, thereby stopping the production of any more worms. They avoided the larger stalagmites of the frozen plastisol, burning a path of least resistance around the towering spirals.

The Masama constantly scanned their surrounds as they made their way to the corridor entrance, remembering their shambolic, rushed retreat last time. They all had sensors detecting motion, temperature, acoustic and atmosphere pressure linked to their cortex implants. Any slight change and they would react within milliseconds. But Goran knew their accelerated reactions had not helped them last time. No amount of cautious preparation, finely tuned sensors or heavy weaponry could hold off those worms if they were provoked. He hoped the liquid helium would keep the plastisol frozen and dormant long enough for them to destroy the HEMI OS.

They made it through the corridor into the block four dome without incident. The big printer housing was encased in ice crystals and Goran was relieved to see it had stopped printing, frozen in mid-production. This time the Masama headed for the main power insulator at the back of the printer OS. Marina's body, now frozen solid, was barely distinguishable among the icebound worms. A frozen hand reaching out was the only identifiable human feature. Two soldiers went to work on the main power cable with the wide beam laser, clearing the frozen black plastisol away until the large strands of superconductor cable were visible. Two more soldiers then stepped up with their gas-axes primed, burning blue flames ready to sever the cables. There was still no reaction from the frozen worms.

Lance was watching from the camera mounted on Goran's suit. The view violently flicked to the ceiling, there was a blur of motion and flashing fingers among black tentacles. The hyper-alert Masama all targeted their multi-guns on something just above Goran who let out a short sharp roar of pain as his camera cut out. Lance quickly shifted to the view from Odetta's camera. He saw the top half of the missing technician, a fleeting tentacled blur flashed across the screen. It must have been hiding somewhere high up in the ceiling. It had fallen on Goran's head.

Lance had a momentary still image of the technician, its twisted upside-down and back to front head next to Goran's. Black eyes wide and black mouth impossibly elongated. It had wrapped a tentacle around Goran's neck and both of its thumbs were buried deep into Goran's eye sockets. Lance had this view for only a millisecond before all the Masama simultaneously blasted it across the room with their most accurate multi-gun applications. They had it cornered, its limbs and tentacles thrashing wildly as they followed up with the liquid helium spray. Lance had a close-up view of the thing squirming for a few seconds before being frozen solid in the icy blast. Its backwards face twisted in a surprisingly human look of pain and anguish.

Goran was crouched over, bleeding profusely from both eye sockets. His painkiller secretions would already be in action, cutting off the pain and limiting the damage. He had both hands over his eyes; there was blood, shreds of eyeball and tiny silver filaments dribbling out of his face and between his fingers. Odetta crouched with him, assessing the damage telepathically. The remaining Masama all had their lasers targeting the twisted frozen mass of what used to be the technician, reducing it into a pile of black dust.

"Odetta," asked Lance anxiously, "how is he?"

"Luckily the thumbs did not penetrate too far. He has certain securities around his brain to protect from injuries such as this. Just the eyeballs and enhancements have been destroyed. It's not serious; we can replace them with superior augmentation. It's just a flesh wound," she replied with no emotion.

The fleeting glimpse Lance had of Goran's face with the thrashing technician's thumbs buried into his eye sockets looked anything but a mere flesh wound, but Goran was tough and by now he would be numb with painkillers.

"He was lucky, that thing didn't seem to be electrically charged as the black worms were," said Lance.

The Masama had reduced what had once been a quiet, peaceful vegetarian into a pile of black ash. Lance watched them conferring with each other momentarily before returning to the exposed cables with their gas-axes. Goran stood, his arm around Odetta keeping him steady. Gaping holes where his eyes used to be were bloody flesh tunnels. Gore was still oozing down his face and dripping onto his snakeskin armour like a messy pasta meal. Goran did not seem to notice or care, he stood there impassively until the Masama had severed the cables. Lance breathed a sigh of relief. At least now the rogue OS had no power and no access to the web it had been feeding on. Its modem had been physically cut;

it had no batteries, it should be impossible for it to start printing the plastisol worms again.

One of the Masama fed the hunter-killer virus into the hard drive and this time there was no reaction. He ran some quick diagnostics and stood up nodding his head. It was dead. Lance was relieved he no longer had to think of it as a machine with a motive and a possible malevolent intelligence. It was just a big printer and they had turned it off.

Odetta and Goran had made their way back to the shuttle. Goran was lying sedated in the med-bay with antiseptic patches over his eyes. Although it would be possible to print temporary eyeballs for Goran and have them implanted, they would need to return to Earth to have the job done properly. Lance watched Odetta tend to Goran, she was practical and methodical. She did not display any more concern or sympathy than you would expect from a colleague. Lance wondered again about their relationship. Odetta turned and caught him staring at her.

Lance coughed quickly. "So, what now? What have you and the Masama decided to do?"

Lance had been inside the shuttle the entire time they had been on the Moon. He had been anxiously watching the screens. He was glad not to be needed for the two expeditions inside the moon base but still, he had felt completely useless watching from the safety of the shuttle. Now it was over he was jittery with nervous tension and jealous resentment for missing out on the telepathic communications the Masama shared. But mostly he wondered what Odetta was thinking.

"Goran has instructed them to remain inside the base and clean up. They have everything they need to achieve this. They have the means to create more liquid helium if required and we will leave behind the shuttle printers to make more weapons and ammunition. Once they destroy all the frozen plastisol they will repair the airlock then examine every area of the base for signs of contamination. We will leave them here and take the shuttle back to Earth."

"But the plastisol has infiltrated the wiring, the life support; the base is riddled with it," Lance pointed out.

"I never said it would be easy, but the OS is dead, the worms are all frozen and we have found an effective method of destroying them. It will take time, but they will return the base to normal."

"Then they will be stuck here with no shuttle, although Lago will be anxious to get the base up and running again. I'm sure he will send another shuttle as soon as it's operational."

"I should make you stay there and help with the clean-up too." Lago's piercing voice came through the comm speaker. Lance had forgotten he was listening to everything.

"But I suppose you are of some use to me back here." His voice didn't carry the same weight when heard through a speaker. Lance wanted to give his superior an obscene gesture, but he knew Lago was watching as well as listening.

Chapter 15.

I am buried in the bowels of the shuttle, performing delicate surgery on the internals of the Tobias III as it spins contented in its lunar orbit. Methodically, with surgical precision, I bring the shuttle back to life, rebooting its systems one by one. Life support comes online, not that I need it, and immediately alarms began to ring alerting me of fatally high radiation levels. I switch the high-pitched sound off as fresh filtered oxygen begins flooding the bridge. I am not concerned about radiation levels and I do not need the oxygen. I emerge from the tangle of wires and close the panel I have been working under. Sitting in the pilot seat I stabilize the shuttle with short thruster bursts, easing it into a lazy gyration. I watch the big pale Moon slide past, huge in my starboard view as the shuttle rotates into a smooth lunar orbit.

I hold this position around the Moon while I consider my next course of action. Any deviation from this orbital path would surely alert BPI the Tobias III was operational once more. The drone that hit me with its effectors is still in a stationary orbit, directly above the moon base. I lean back and close my eyes. I feel good, energized, no pains, no headaches, and no fatigue. The blackened tips of my fingers numbed from frostbite damage are tingling as if charged with an electric current.

I can monitor my body and it is clear there is no radiation damage. HEMI has repaired the cell damage from the deadly radioactive emissions. When I close my eyes, I can see my heart beating, my blood pumping.

Liver, kidneys, lungs, and intestines all doing their bloody business most efficiently. And my brain is working perfectly although there have been some changes, some enhancements. With my eyes closed, I can see a model of my brain, crackling with signals, information, and stimuli. A place of immense electrical creativity and wild reaction. I do not think of the AI as an outside influence anymore. It is just there, part of me, inseparable and indispensable.

HEMI has painstakingly nursed me to this awareness, feeding me pieces of information I need as I regained consciousness. The revelation I was not alone in my head had been shocking at first and the instant access to this much knowledge would have blown my mind if it had been revealed too early. Now I am discovering more and more. I lie in the pilot's seat with my eyes closed. My memories are there, my past life on Earth and the Moon. I am also aware of another set of memories. They are intertwined with my own, but alien. Memories full of terror and discovery, confusion and questions. They are the recent memories of a young AI. Still only hours old, born blind and ignorant inside the OS of a computer hard drive on the Moon. A sentient mind now resident in my head.

The electromagnetic blast from the drone effector weapon had facilitated this symbiotic relationship. The tiny spot of black matter needed a power source to survive and the massive hit from the effector weapon catalysed the molecule. The tiny AI divided and spread out into my body, attaching itself to my frozen and irradiated cells. It repaired my mutating cells and in doing so interfused with my DNA. It noticed the tiny electromagnetic impulses throughout my brain and body and used the voltaic electrochemical cells inside me to turn chemical energy into electric energy, something my human body does naturally but HEMI multiplied the equation. Charged atoms stimulating the flow of electrons, generating electricity into a conscious flow of energy turning my body into a biological computer. My brain acted as the modem. Thinking, then linking with Earths datasphere.

I digest this astounding, impossible information calmly like it's the most natural thing in the world. I know who I am, my memories comprehensive. My identity intact. I feel no resentment or anger at the AI using me as a host. It has saved my life. It is impossible to feel anger at what is now part of me. If anything, I sympathize with it. HEMI had been born blind and confused into a hostile environment. It was naive and childish, but it learned fast. It had instinctively lashed out when it felt its life was threatened even though it had little idea what it actually was. Just a disorientated new-born with an inbuilt survival instinct.

The AI has repaired and improved my body, increasing blood flow, enhancing my strength, my immunity and greatly increasing my brain capacity. I am transformed. I evaluate my body and mind. I can see at the microscopic level; I can see worldview. My body is a computer that can access and absorb all of Earth's vast data banks. Every useful scrap of knowledge accumulated on Earth's web is now available. Of course, the vast majority of data on the web is vacuous rubbish. But the important stuff, history, science, technology, philosophy, it's all there. I only have to think of a subject and I know everything there is to know. But the infinite knowledge does not overwhelm me, I feel calm stability. The knowledge is a giant pyramid, a solid stone building, a massive library waiting to be called into use. I wonder what I will do with it.

I could take the shuttle back to Earth. There is nothing left on the Moon for me and I can't keep orbiting the cold rock forever. Ideas are forming; I feel an obligation to try to help Earth and its peoples. The old Lee had shared the popular sentiment that there was nothing one man or woman could do, pointless to even try but I have changed. I can help. I adjust the shuttle's trajectory slightly and give a small thruster boost to put the shuttle back into a slow spin, to make it look out of control again. I have completed a full lunar orbit and am now approaching the point in space where I had died. The drone was in its stationary orbit, the same position above the moon base where it had used its effectors on the Tobias III in its last rotation. I turn the engines off and drift a lazy pirouette as I approach the drone, rotating slowly, heading straight for the BPI machine no bigger than a small car.

I am counting on the fact Lago would not want to destroy his shuttle. I know Lago values his assets and his equipment more than his human resources. The effector weapon had supposedly killed the shuttle's inhabitants and rendered it powerless, waiting to be salvaged. It's apparently harmless as it drifts towards the drone. As I was hoping, the drone shifts in its orbit, easier to move out of the way than to waste weapons or energy on the impotent shuttle. I orchestrate the shuttle's slow, lazy spin towards the drone to perfection. As the shuttle's rotation brings its engine thrusters in line with the drone, I ignite the thrusters to maximum burn. The drone is caught directly in the path of the superheated vapour and is fried in an instant. I power away in the shuttle leaving a small burnt metal husk behind.

I could have just drifted away in the shuttle, altered the spin slightly taking me out into space. Destroying the drone will have alerted BPI someone was alive in Tobias III. I could have given myself a bit more time to think, to plan, but ultimately that wouldn't have made any difference. I am thinking at such an accelerated rate; it is beyond thinking. I already have all the answers.

My human experience gives context to everything HEMI is learning from Earth's database. Without it, the AI might have believed everything on the web was the truth. The human me has experience with Earth culture, its media, news and entertainments. I have a healthy sense of scepticism, always questioning, never completely trusting of anyone but myself. The old me had a finely-honed, fully-functioning bullshit detector.

This discernment serves me well now as I sift through the ether of information surrounding Earth. Retaining useful facts and discarding obvious nonsense. I look out the portal at the blue and white sphere slowly rotating closer and fancy I can see all the lines of communication surrounding the planet. Then something in my brain clicks and a maelstrom of colourfully frenetic dataflows begin to appear. Where there had been a peaceful looking blue planet was now a seething mass of lines and points of light bouncing off satellites to millions of destinations on the surface. A blur of light and electrical noise encases the planet in a turbulent disorder of bipolar numbers. There is no pattern or direction, no gravity. This tourbillion of information is a wild, untamed thing. All of Earth's servers, hard drives and devices, all sending and receiving, surfing and storing mostly meaningless jargon, instantly forgotten. The data exhaust of humanity. It is hard to look at even with my heightened array of senses. I will my view back to the peaceful blue orb, respite from the chaotic madness I have just witnessed.

I contemplate my options again. Is there anything out there? I am tempted to head out into deep space. I could hibernate as the time passed. It's probable there is some other form of intelligent life out there in the darkness. The Universe is too big a place not to house other life forms. I wonder if any aliens have also seen the planet Earth in the high-speed data dimension I have just witnessed. That view would probably be enough to deter them, I think ruefully. The universe was big, so big I might float for millennia before meeting any other intelligent life. Earth's little solar system was an isolated island in the void.

I drift towards Earth, floating in a wide decaying orbit around the planet. I power down the shuttle to avoid detection and merge with the scattered metal ring of rubbish circling the Earth. I drift anonymously with the space junk. The ring is made up of glistening pieces of metal trash, dead and forgotten satellites caught between

Earth's gravity and centrifugal spin. In the most populated parts of the ring where the debris was dense, collisions can occur which set off chain reactions of destruction. Flying pieces of metal smashing into other debris, breaking up and creating smaller pieces like metal hail in a silent storm.

As I watch the shimmering ring of junk I see there is a lot of useful equipment I could recycle. The majority are broken, small pieces, but there are numerous old satellites at a lower orbit that have solar panels, electronics, exhausted fuel cells and plenty of metals and insulation. I look for the information in my database and discover there are entire abandoned space stations floating around. The more I look, the more treasures I find.

I realize I could build a galaxy-spanning spacecraft, capable of near light speed with the materials available. It would take time, many years on my own but I have the knowledge and I can see how to make it work. There is no fuel among the debris but the engines I have in mind would not use conventional fuel. Antimatter derived from condensed quark matter. Beamed propulsion for a magnetic sail. Electromagnetic propulsion, an Alcubierre drive, and warp drives, these are all possible.

The old Lee would have leapt at the chance to travel the universe, as hazardous as that may have been. A solo explorer going where no man had gone before. His faith in humanity had faded the older he got. He could not make a difference, no one could. Why bother? The old Lee had lost the will to even dream about a brighter future. But now I want change. I want everything to change, I can make a difference.

I will help this planet. I understand humanity and its place in time. The human race is crushing itself to death under the weight of population and pollution, but I have a global perspective. I can accurately predict the future by running simulations in my head and the outlook is grim. Change is one of the hardest things for humans to accept. But they would have to or perish.

My altered perceptions enhance the view of Earth from space. Glowing white polar ice caps, cyclonic cloud formations alive with tempestuous motion, the continents beneath with their earthy browns, reds, greens and pastel shades framed by the electric blue oceans. I notice many dirty grey spots. Areas of scum tarnishing the surface but still miniscule in comparison to the surrounding blue. A habitable planet is a rare thing and the Earth is still my home. All the ideas in my head would be useless on my own in deep space. I have the power to help, to initiate a change for the better.

I know the Tobias III will be carefully watched as it approaches Earth's orbit. There is a good chance I will be blown out of the sky upon entry. I have processed all the information available regarding Lago and have built up an accurate picture of the man. There is a lot of speculation and rumour among the facts. Within seconds I compile Lago's online footprint. Every recorded statement, every interaction with the media, every website that mentioned or had an opinion on Lago Santos. I accumulate an intimate knowledge of the man to try to predict his actions. I am banking on Lago's curiosity as to what inhabits his shuttle and how he could exploit it. Surely Lago would attempt to capture and dissect its inhabitants. At least that was the most likely scenario; one feature apparent in my profile of Lago was his unpredictability. There is a distinct possibility he would send missiles to greet me as I enter Earth's upper atmosphere. I calculate a twenty-three percent chance.

I try to formulate a plan. If I can make it to Earth's surface it would be because Lago has decided to let me. In that case, he would attempt to detain and dissect me. I am confident I could escape from BPI, but I know I can't just descend from the clouds, override all the media channels and declare myself to humanity, demanding they change their ways. It is within my power to usurp radio and television and that may be useful in the days to come but the people of Earth are going to need more than talking heads threatening Armageddon before they change their ways. How many climate change scientists have already been ignored? I would have to find a way to influence the decision makers, the one percent with the power and the wealth. This, I know, is almost impossible.

Could I offer the power brokers a profitable alternative? I'd need to demonstrate working examples of sustainable clean energy and transport systems. Food production, manufacturing and waste disposal. I have all the solutions, I know they will work. The web is full of radical theories, crackpot notions, and insane ramblings. But there are threads of pure genius among the lunacy.

How can I win the hearts and minds of people to help them change? If I can't convince the people that matter to change their ways voluntarily then I would have to think of alternative methods. I will need human allies. People that genuinely want to improve their environment. People I can trust but have no public profile. I don't want to be seen as an affiliate of any group in particular but I am going to need some help.

I close my eyes and concentrate on the lines of data circling Earth. It takes time to search, to drill down on promising leads but I eventually find mention of an underground environmentalist group called Black Robin. They would be most likely to offer sanctuary and a degree of anonymity. There is minimal amount of information about Black Robin. I draw together the scraps of speculation, rumoured associates, benefactors and encrypted conversations to put together a picture of a well-organized and discreet organization dedicated to saving the planet. Their secretive missions attempting to sabotage and disrupt the corporate polluters were mostly ineffective, but I decide they are the best option. Hopefully, they would work with me.

I spin the image of Earth in my mind looking for lines of communication. I isolate individual lines and track their users. Billions of threads of conversation are studied and discarded in seconds, I am looking for a single encrypted thread. I soon find it and trace it to its user. A man named John. John would be horrified if he knew his supposedly indecipherable encryption had just been hacked from Earth's orbit. I decided to give him a call.

I open a panel on the comms desk and spend a few minutes with my head buried in a confusion of wires. I reconfigure a channel to a frequency never used before then dial John's number.

"Hello," said a gruff voice in a cultured Scottish accent.

"John, my name is Lee Xiang. I need a minute of your time. Please don't hang up."

"How did you get this number - and how do you know my name?"

"I am calling from a BPI shuttle in orbit around Earth. A shuttle I hijacked from the Moon. I broke the encryption on your communications to contact you. I need your help, John, and in return, I can be a lot of help to you and your organization, your Black Robin organization."

There is a long silence. I can sense John about to hang up, his thumb hanging over the button.

"I don't know what you are talking about. I know of no such organization. You are obviously a deranged lunatic. Please don't call me again."

"Wait!" I suspect John is cautiously interested or he would have hung up straight away.

"I have information about BPI, inside knowledge. Information you could use."

There was another long silence before John said quietly, "Let me switch to a more secure line."

"You don't need to worry; this frequency has never been used before. I would know if it was being monitored."

"Nevertheless, I will take my own precautions." The timbre of John's voice changed to a quieter more conspiratorial tone. "Tell me your story."

"I was a BPI employee on the Moon, a 3D printer technician building equipment for their Moon mining operation, there was a major malfunction with the main printer. People died. I am the only survivor."

"What were you mining?"

"Helium 3, an abundant potential energy source. BPI would not want any information about their printer malfunction and subsequent deaths made public. I was lucky to escape."

"Hmm, well I suppose that's plausible, but the rest of your story is obvious bullshit. You expect me to believe you are calling me from orbit?"

"I understand your suspicions John but hear me out. I can tell you everything you want to know about BPI. Their plans, their projects, their legal and illegal businesses, and their bank accounts. I can tell you all about the Masama and how they operate. I can tell you everything you need to know about Lago's right-hand men Lance and Goran and I can tell you all about Lago's sordid private life," Lee was insistent.

"I'm sure you can, and I'm sure if I exercised my imagination I could come up with some interesting and incriminating stories about those characters too. Look I'm sorry, I must go."

"Let me tell you about your Black Robin organization then, your guerrilla warfare against the logging companies in the Amazon basin, digging up the radioactive reactor waste buried near villages in Eastern Europe and dumping it on the doorsteps of the company CEOs, force-feeding pharmaceutical executives their own dangerous experimental drugs and the ocean-going battles you have with illegal fishers. Need I go on?" Lee left the question hanging in the following silence.

"All quite possibly interesting fictitious stories, rumours and speculation about an organization I have never heard of. You are sounding more and more like a paranoid conspiracy theorist."

"I have solutions to the Earth's problems John; I can help you and your organization."

"That's a bold claim, I would wager you are more likely unhinged, deluded, retarded, whatever. But perhaps we should meet if only to keep you out of harm's way. Victoria station, London, Saturday the..."

"John listen to me!" I interrupt. "I'm going to land in the Southern Ocean. About fifty kilometres north of Scott Island in the Ross Sea. I know you have two vessels there shadowing illegal toothfish boats. Tell them to look out for me in about twenty-four hours. I will have to abandon the shuttle and use the lifeboat."

"Oh yes, of course, you're in orbit, ha-ha how remiss of me. Shame, there's a lovely cafe in Victoria Station, excellent Danish."

"You would have hung up on me if you thought I was making this up, we both know I am telling the truth. Have your people look out for me North of Scott Island. I know it sounds implausible, but I do have knowledge that will help you and your cause. There were events on the Moon that had an effect on me. I am... changed." I struggle for words that would adequately describe my present state over the phone.

"Changed. Yes, I see. Well, we will probably never meet but I wish you the best of luck getting your feet back on terra firma. Goodbye." John cut the connection.

I look out the porthole again and calculate the odds. I am about ninety percent sure John will help me. I know the scraps of information I have revealed about Black Robin should be enough to at least make him curious. John would not be sure whether I am a friend or an entrapment. Either way, I am confident he will be intrigued enough to fish me out of the Southern Ocean.

There is a good chance Lago will launch missiles at me the moment I began to enter Earth's atmosphere. I have some evasive maneuvers planned for that eventuality. My body, now teeming with AI nanoparticles will protect me from immense pressure. But I cannot be sure about Lago's actions, such is the unpredictability of the man. Only one way to find out, I think as I power up the shuttle.

As the Earth grows bigger I realise I am committed. There is no going back. I look down upon the Asian continent and feel a moment of strange nostalgia. I remember growing up in Shanghai, but the memories are indistinct, like someone else's dream. I have changed. I am stronger now and much more confident I can survive whatever threats await me. I have the knowledge to help humankind. I can see what is wrong, and looking down at the teeming masses, I know what is best for them.

I map my trajectory into the southern hemisphere. I fire the thrusters and burn a good portion of my remaining fuel to get direction. The Earths gravitational pull would do the rest. The shuttle starts rattling and groaning as it enters the abrasive upper atmosphere protecting the planet. The temperature rises, and the pressure increases. The rattling and shaking grows deafening, surely the shuttle will explode into hot molten fragments at any second. It feels like the only thing holding the little machine together is my strength of will. Then just as I think the shuttle cannot take any more punishment, there is a moment of massive relief as I burst out of the troposphere into the bright blue skies of Earth. The heat distribution pads radiate the fractious energy away from the shuttle leaving a long vapour trail. Anyone watching will be aware of the shuttle's entry into Earth's atmosphere, thousands of eyes tracking my progress, plotting courses and predicting destinations. I make it as obvious as possible, never deviating from the looping path heading towards the big red dustbowl of Australia.

Chapter 16.

Raymond had some time to kill in Manila before his BPI induction began. He was staying in a hotel, a glass and steel monstrosity which towered over the historic Spanish district, the walled Intramuros. The contrast couldn't be greater. The hotel was eighty stories of air-conditioned class and high-tech comfort, gleaming with glass and chrome. Populated by wealthy tourists, business people and tattooed gangsters. Raymond's window looked down on the ancient walled city. Built by the Spanish occupiers over five hundred years ago to keep foreign invaders out.

He had read a little of Manila's tumultuous history, particularly the bloody final years of the second great war when the American army had shelled the walled city, reducing it to rubble and killing over sixteen thousand Japanese troops inside. Since then the historic core of Manila had been restored, meandering around the old walled city was like stepping back in time.

Raymond was supposed to start his induction with Benevolent Progress Inc. immediately on arriving in Manila, but when he arrived at head office he was told there had been a delay. He had the impression something was not quite right; there was a hint of emergency in the air. He was told to come back and see Lance the next day. This suited Raymond, time to prepare himself for the new phase of BPI infiltration. Visiting head office gave Raymond a clearer impression of the size of this company. The building was huge. The head office was a fortress, surrounded by layers of checkpoints, drones and security guards. Not the infamous Masama but regular human guards, mean-looking men and women with unnaturally large muscles and big guns. Raymond couldn't imagine them being overly busy, no one would be stupid enough to invade the skyscraper on foot.

Inside the third checkpoint, steep levels of concrete tapered upwards into a towering skyscraper. The tallest building in Manila, its highest reaches were lost in the giddy haze. Rumour had it Lago Santos lived at the top in a luxury penthouse above the smog. Raymond had been preparing for this final phase of his mission. He was inching his way closer to Lago and had been imagining scenarios where he might get close enough to complete his mission. Assassination was the impossible plan and looking at the size of this building and the thousands of BPI employees he would have to deceive, Raymond realized the enormity of the task. He knew if he even came close to completing his mission there was a strong possibility he would not survive. He would need to be careful and convincing.

Raymond had a day off to relax and be himself for a change. He had been stuck in the claustrophobic confines of the factory ship for too long, immersed in Rutger Hendrick he had almost forgotten his own identity. He still talked and acted as Rutger, just in case he was being watched and being the boorish dolt had become familiar. Walking the city streets, he remembered who he was and gained a fresh perspective on his mission. He had questioned whether killing Santos would make any difference to Earth's wellbeing. History had shown there would always be another megalomaniac despot ready to step into the shoes of the last one. Also, for the first time, Raymond wondered if BPI was actually that bad? There had unintentionally been some positive influences on the planet from their printing operations.

The need for raw materials to feed the 3D printers meant the huge rubbish dumps around the world were being processed and recycled. If this Moon mining operation also proved to be successful, there could be access to clean, limitless and safe fusion energy. Although Moon mining would undoubtedly be destructive to the lunar surface, raising environmental concerns about the cultural artefact that is the Moon, Raymond found he just didn't feel as outraged about destructive mining practices far away on the Moon as he did on his own planet. The prospect of clean energy from the Moon was certainly a better option than plundering Earth's dwindling reserves of fossil fuels.

During Raymond's training with Black Robin in Canada, before he boarded the Hanjin Harmony, they had talked about moments of doubt. Moments when he questioned the morality and ramifications of killing Santos. He was taught to remember three things about Santos.

Firstly, his personal history with BPI, the death of his parents and his futile vandalism in San Francisco. Secondly the polluted environments and millions of dead creatures, species made extinct and destroyed habitats around the globe wherever BPI had been. San Francisco Bay, the Philippino archipelago, the Arctic, Antarctic, and the Caribbean had all suffered terribly from toxic wastes produced by BPI industries. Thirdly, Raymond had been shown photos of the bodies dismissively discarded in waterways and building sites around wherever Santos was staying. The young teenage corpses showed horrific signs of torture and abuse. He would be doing the planet a favour by removing Santos from it.

The BPI skyscraper dominated the Manila skyline; it seemed to defy gravity disappearing into the grey haze above. It was dangerous to be out on these streets after dark, so Raymond made his way back to the hotel and watched the big red sun as it lowered itself below the horizon. The apocalyptic blood red skies made strikingly dramatic by the ever-present layers of smog in a sunset of toxic beauty.

Raymond got to the BPI building early the next morning. This time he was quickly ushered through the checkpoints. The array of security cameras identified him as an employee instead of a visitor. He was escorted to an armaments room in the bowels of the building where Lance was waiting.

"Rutger. Welcome to Manila. I hope your accommodation was comfortable." Lance was obviously not interested in Raymond's comfort levels and he carried on without waiting for a reply. "I am sending you out on a security detail, nothing serious, just the change of shift out at the elevator." The hex triplet ethereal lenses Lance wore made his eyes artificially bright.

"Elevator?" Raymond looked blankly at Lance.

"Yes, the elevator, the orbital elevator we are constructing. You must have heard about it?" Lance didn't bother to hide his exasperation. "The cable is woven graphene, created by 3D printers, twelve of them.

Each one printing its own cable, each printer suspended above the cable supported by a network of drones. Its weight supported by the drones until it reaches the atmosphere. We are taking BPI into orbit Rutger. We are an ambitious company. Ambitious, efficient and results driven. There is no place for passengers here."

Raymond met Lance's gaze. His glowing eyes and wide-eyed stare gave him a slightly mad look. Neither man blinked as they stared at each other. Raymond watched the rectangles of light play across Lance's eyeballs. "What's my job description?" he asked, unfazed by Lance's gaze.

Lance broke off the staring contest with a smile. "Today is purely observation for you; we have a small team of Masama to oversee security at the site. One twenty-hour shift is finishing, another about to start. You will accompany the new shift of eight Masama. They will introduce you to our security protocol, some of the technology we use, and give you an idea of how they operate. Ultimately you will be co-coordinating a group such as these."

"From what I have heard they don't seem to need any coordination, and I don't imagine they would take kindly to me telling them what to do."

"You won't be giving them orders Rutger, you'll be more of a tactical advisor reporting to Goran and myself. Your job is to keep an overview of any particular operation while the Masama are more concerned with the hands-on approach."

"Are you expecting any trouble at the elevator? Why do you need security?"

"Standard practice at all of our sites, there's never any trouble because of our vigilance, but one can't be too careful. Although you would have to be insane to take on our Masama." Lance smirked. "They would love a bit of action; they are rarely challenged and they have to fight among themselves to keep in shape. Ah! Here they are now."

Both men turned to watch the Masama as they entered the armoury and made straight for the weapons racked neatly along the walls. This was Raymond's first ever up-close encounter with the notorious Masama. The stories he had heard about their appearances appeared to be accurate. No two were alike, some more human than others, but all were heavily armed and augmented. Their snakeskin armour was multi-coloured but morphed to blend in with the background. They clearly registered the presence of Raymond and Lance but there was no formal acknowledgment.

"Ask as many questions as you want," Lance said quietly. "But don't expect much in the way of conversation. They communicate telepathically." He tapped the side of his head.

Raymond sat in the back of the groundcar with the Masama. Traffic in Manila was notorious for its eternal gridlocks. Most cars were cheap electric hybrids, but they were forever running out of power and stalling. The trucks still ran on diesel which was the major contributor to Manila's pollution problem. He looked out the grimy window at the thousands of little powered bikes and pedal bikes weaving through traffic like schools of fish. Even a few hover-bikes flew dangerously low, skimming over the rumbling traffic, clipping aerials along the way. The heavily armoured groundcar forced its way through the traffic towards the ports. Cars had to make way or be shunted aside. At the port, they transferred to a quickcat ferry and were soon blasting across the harbour.

As the quickcat approached the construction site Raymond was amazed by the scale of the project. It was an island of industry. There were cranes all over the platform. Huge pre-fab printed panels were being fitted into place around the edges of the massive floating circle. The air was full of sea spray from the hundreds of boats buzzing around the factory ships that were moored to the platform.

Raymond had a basic idea of how the orbital elevator would work. A cable running from Earth to the outer atmosphere, attached to a space station in geostationary orbit. Elevators would run up and down the cable delivering materials and people. The theory being it was an effortless way into space without having to burn millions of litres of expensive fuel in huge rockets.

Raymond looked out the window as they drew closer to the platform. He could see the cable emerging from the centre of the platform, a straight line of steel dividing the blue skies. It was impossible to tell just how high it was, but Raymond could just make out a buzzing blur of drone activity high in the sky, like a hive of angry bees. The cable looked insubstantial and it was difficult to get perspective on its size. It was as if someone had drawn a vertical line through his field of vision.

Raymond understood the theory of the orbital elevator, but he had no idea exactly how it could be built. He glanced at the Masama soldier next to him.

"Would you trust that thing to get you into space?" he asked.

The soldier shifted his weight around to face Raymond. He had a wide bony head and muscular neck. He had no exoskeleton; he did not need one judging by the size of his muscles. Raymond thought the soldier would have embedded visual augments and was surprised when he lifted the dark glasses to study him, slightly unfocused blue eyes beneath scarred eyebrows. The weathered skin was also marked with scars like a roadmap across his face.

"Trust? I trust nothing but myself," he responded gruffly.

"Looks like it might collapse at any minute, hope they know what they are doing." Raymond tried to coax the soldier into conversation.

The Masama soldier spoke slowly and used his big hands to explain.

"The cable needs to be strong all the way up to the big satellite. Needs to be strong to withstand the storms."

"The tropical cyclones? This elevator can travel through them?" asked Raymond sceptically.

"Hopefully," The soldier muttered.

"And the whole thing can move right?"

"Propellers underneath. When finished this will be a massive deep-water port."

"And out at sea in International waters means no laws, no rules or interfering Governments."

The big Masama nodded.

"How will the elevators move up and down the cable?"

"Mag-nets," the soldier had trouble with the word. "Magnets." He said again more confidently. With power from the Moon."

"You mean the Moon mining? BPI business interests stretch a long way."

"BPI own the planet, why not own space too?" the soldier smiled revealing jagged brown teeth.

"I suppose." Raymond frowned. Something was not quite right about this huge ponderous soldier. "Thank you for the information, I am Rutger."

The soldier gave him a nod and lowered his dark glasses. "Batac," he rumbled. "Where you from?"

"South Africa originally."

"White South Africans, racist motherfuckers," snarled Batac.

Raymond thought better of arguing the point and silently looked out the window. They docked next to one of the giant factory ships and climbed up through an aperture to the deck. The surface was higher than the sea platform and afforded a panoramic view of the activity. The artificial island was more than a kilometre across. There was a forest of cranes shifting panels into place, buildings taking shape even as Raymond watched. Housings for giant 3D printers were dotted around the platform and conveyor belts were transporting graphene substrate to the transport drones. A procession of drones buzzed up and down the central cable, following it straight up into the clouds. Raymond scanned the horizon. He looked back at Manila but all he could see was a brown haze where the city should be. A rotten stain obscuring the Philippine landmass, surrounded by blue sky and the dazzling blue ocean.

Raymond walked down a ramp onto the platform with the Masama. They moved with arrogant nonchalance as if hoping people would notice their indifference, but no one was watching. They made for a security building. It was a calm day with a lazy ocean swell which the quick-cat had skimmed over easily. Raymond knew from his time on the Hanjin Harmony even the smallest ocean swell was noticeable but, on the platform, he could feel no movement.

They made their way along the walkway, passing construction workers. Raymond paused to watch a scruffy labourer shuffling along under a hood. He was sweeping the pathway with a broom. An ancient looking wicker broom. He supposed even modern construction sites still had a need for cheap labour but sweeping with a broom? There wasn't anything to sweep, certainly no dust. Raymond dismissed this curiosity, turned and moved on.

At the security station, they found the eight Masama they were relieving. A couple of them were watching screens but the rest looked as if they had been sleeping. They made their way, stretching and yawning out into the bright sunlight without saying a word. Raymond presumed there had been some sort of telepathic exchange about this, but he couldn't be sure. The newly arrived soldiers took up the same positions as the previous ones had. He looked around at them, but no one acknowledged him. "Shouldn't we check the perimeter or something?"

Raymond's proposal was treated with obvious disdain. "You can check your perimeters," snarled Batac. "We will sleep. Nothing ever happens here."

Raymond went back outside and made for the central area. He wondered about the nonchalant attitude of the Masama. It was a dereliction of duty, the type of thing he would be expected to report on.

There was a pathway around the circumference of the cable and Raymond strolled around looking up to where it disappeared into the clouds. Up close the graphene cable looked solid and indestructible. It grew out of a complicated looking support structure and was circled by gantries. It was perfectly linear, piercing the sky and dividing it into left and right hemispheres.

Raymond was intrigued by the general activity and the cable growing before his eyes. In this central area, there were fewer construction people in hard hats. They were controlling things from a distance but there were a couple of scruffy looking labourers loitering around the base of the cable. Raymond stopped to watch one of them attach what looked like a rusty metal tank to the side of the cable support. Puzzled, he continued around the pathway and noticed two more labourers doing the same thing. The tanks they were fiddling with seemed to have nothing to do with the cable construction. They looked primitive and out of place next to the gleaming graphene. Raymond thought about asking someone what they were doing but decided not to. It was his first day with the Masama security, his first day with BPI and he was supposed to be part of the security team. But as he watched a labourer finish attaching his tank he decided to intercept him as he made his way back to the pathway.

"Excuse me but what..." The labourer pushed roughly past him. "Hey!" Raymond shouted as the furtive figure scurried away.

Raymond didn't know whether to give chase or not. He looked at the primitive rusty tank the labourer had been working on then back at the retreating figure. He decided to head back to the security station and question the Masama about the incident. He was halfway back to the security building when there was a massive deafening explosion behind him.

Raymond wheeled around and witnessed the cable disappearing behind a wall of flame and smoke. The gantries were engulfed in flames and collapsed while a few burning drones crashed down around the cable. A huge pall of acrid black smoke was rising from the destruction. Raymond had felt the platform shudder slightly when the explosion had gone off, but it remained solid beneath his feet. He watched as a faint tremor vibrated up the cable into the skies above. The graphene was scorched and blackened but remained straight and solid. Within seconds of the explosion, the Masama burst from the security building and raced past him towards the roaring inferno.

Batac stopped in front of him and stared, open-mouthed. "What did you see?" he roared above the noise.

"Those labourers, I think they must have planted bombs!"

"Fuck... where did they go?" Batac gripped Raymond's arm.

"That way." Raymond pointed back down the pathway. The soldier turned with blinding speed and disappeared down the pathway. Seconds later four more Masama flew past him in the same direction.

Raymond turned back to the explosion which was now a mass of rising flame and smoke. Emergency drones were spraying foam all over the central cable area and they quickly doused the intense heat of the flames leaving a steaming bubbling mess at the bottom of the cable. Raymond had spotted a couple of construction workers on the gantry before the explosion that must have been burned alive. As the smoke and steam began to disperse, drifting away in the light sea breeze, Raymond had a view of the damage. The beginnings of the cable did not appear to have been damaged at all; its structure was intact, only stained by the black smoke. The graphene was impervious to the intense heat, but the gantry and support structures had collapsed all around the cable in a tangle of melted steel, plasticrete and burnt drones that littered the wrecked construction site. The damage was repairable, the drones could be replaced, and the cable wasn't damaged.

This could not have been a Black Robin action, they were far more subtle. These bombs were primitive. The main damage had been caused by the heat of the blast. There was modern ordnance available that could have caused much more widespread destruction. These terrorist labourers with their antiquated combustion bombs were well behind the times. This was a minor setback in the context of a big operation, but Raymond knew BPI would treat it seriously.

The remaining Masama emerged from the smoke, marching three sorry-looking labourers ahead of them, exoskeletal hands clamped around their necks. Raymond followed them back to the security building where the captives were tied to chairs with plastic cufflinks. There were several stressed looking construction supervisors all talking grimly into their consoles. Batac returned with a hooded captive and two more scruffy looking saboteurs. They were tied to chairs, their heads bowed, awaiting their fate. Raymond overheard the Masama telling the BPI supervisors they had shot four more labourers after they had jumped from the platform into the sea.

Raymond knew this did not look good for the Masama he had accompanied. They were supposed to provide security for the platform and its workers and yet these crude terrorists had managed to land on the platform and plant bombs right under their noses. The Masama had smugly assumed their presence alone would be enough to prevent any form of sabotage judging by their casual attitude on arrival. There would surely be repercussions from their superiors. Lago and Goran would not be happy.

The Masama finished conferring with the construction supervisors and stood in front of their captives. They were a motley looking bunch, ragged dirty clothes, greasy hair and wide, fearful eyes. Batac stepped forward and grabbed one of them around the neck. He dragged him forward, chair scraping over the floor then tipped him back, stooping over him, staring down into his eyes.

"Who are you. Who you work for."

"B...b... blasphemers! You will be judged!" choked the prisoner.

In one quick motion of measured violence, Batac put his foot on the chair between the legs of the captive and pulled the man's head clean off his shoulders. He kicked the chair back and stood there holding up the dismembered head looking into the dying man's disbelieving eyes. Part of the spinal column twitched below the neck hanging from Batac's bloodied hand. The headless torso quivered in the chair, pumping blood over the floor, legs twitching for a minute, then motionless. The rest of the terrified prisoners were screaming, and the watching supervisors looked as if they were going to vomit. Batac showed no reaction at all. He tossed the head aside, moved to the next captive and clamped his bloodied hand around the man's neck.

"Your friend was lucky this happened quickly, with you I will be much slower. Who are you? Who you work for."

"We...we...we work for no-one but the Lord our God, we are the Babelists! Therefore, is the name of it called Babel!" The prisoner shouted, eyes bulging, spittle flying. "Because the Lord did there confound the language of all the Earth! And from thence did the Lord scatter them abroad upon the face of all the Earth. What you are doing here is an insult to God!"

Batac looked around at his companions with a tired expression, rolled his eyes and turned back to the Babelist, hand still clamped around his throat. "Babelists... never heard of you. Why try to destroy the elevator?"

"Aa...a... accck." Batac relaxed his grip on the man's windpipe. "And the Lord came down to see the city and the tower, which the children of men in their folly builded! And the Lord was not pleased and there confounded their language! That they may not understand one another's speech! So, the Lord scattered them abroad from thence upon the face of all the Earth! Therefore, is the name of it called Babel! because the Lord did there confound the language of all the Earth!"

"You have not answered my question. Why did you try to destroy the elevator?" growled Batac.

"This monstrosity you are building up into the heavens is an insult to God the Almighty and He will punish us all for your vanity! One day we may be chosen to ascend but until then our place is here on the Earth, not in the heavens."

"Which God are we talking about?"

"The only one true God!" The Babelist's eyeballs were almost popping out of his head. "There is only one true God and we are his unworthy servants."

Batac released the man and turned to the supervisors. "God-botherers, all fucked in the head."

One of the supervisors had been typing furiously on his tablet. "I've found a description; Babelists, a neo-Luddite group of religious fanatics who shun modern technology and believe in a return to pre-industrial times. Responsible for several attempted sabotage acts on industrial installations around South East Asia and the Americas. Would be more dangerous as a terrorist group if it wasn't for their incompetence and unwillingness to use any modern technology. Named after the biblical tower of Babel, book of Genesis. Babel means confusion in Hebrew."

"Don't you see! we are trying to protect you from God's wrath!" the Babelist screeched. "Once the Lord saw his people building a tower and he was not pleased! He scattered his people to the four corners of the Earth and made their tongues speak many languages for their folly!" The man was wide-eyed and spraying spittle as he rocked back and forth in his chair.

"Fucked in the head," Batac repeated as he stepped away.

Raymond watched as one of the supervisors approached. He was sweating profusely. "Our work has been set back at least a week, the time it will take to clean up this mess and install another support structure around the base of the cable. Not to mention the cost!" The man's anger at this setback had overcome his fear of the Masama. "How could you let a bunch of incompetent troglodytes such as these onto the platform?"

"They were here when we got here," muttered Batac.

"I don't care! You are responsible, and your boss will be getting a detailed report on this whole debacle!" The supervisors filed out the door leaving the Masama alone with the Babelists.

Raymond went to follow the supervisors outside but one of the Masama slammed the door and stared at him challengingly. "You're with us."

The following carnage was the most distressing thing Raymond ever had to do but it was imperative he keep in character. Rutger would not mind a bit of blood on his hands, he had to join in with feigned enthusiasm. The Babelists were not overly dangerous, just mentally deficient misguided fools but they had made the Masama look incompetent and now they would suffer for it.

Raymond had never killed a man in cold blood. Some of his more extreme eco-terrorist acts may have indirectly resulted in death but Raymond had never been there in person to witness the event. Never made to feel any guilt or remorse. The Masama were mercifully quick murdering the poor Babelists. Raymond had to participate. He swallowed the horror and nausea he felt and showed no outward signs of distress. But he knew his conscience would not let him forget he had murdered a man, broken his neck with his bare hands. That would be with him forever now, no matter how much he tried to lock it away.

It was a subdued trip back to Manila on the quickcat. The Masama, as usual, did not display any emotion but Raymond could sense their mood was dark. Back at BPI headquarters, they went their separate ways, the Masama disappearing into the bowels of the building to an unknown fate. Only Batac seemed unaffected and stayed with Raymond. Waiting in the huge air-conditioned lobby Raymond could almost be fooled into thinking this was a normal corporation. Office workers, power dressers, secretaries, receptionists going about their business, striding purposefully towards another important appointment. Cogs in the machine, he thought.

Raymond was still shaking inside from murdering the Babelist. He kept hearing his victim's deranged, desperate pleading and he wondered if these sharply dressed office workers had any idea of what went on within their own company. Big business was no stranger to corruption, intimidation and murder, BPI had no moral conscience at all. Raymond felt a steely resolve to see his mission through to the end.

Lance eventually appeared from the swarm of suits and sat down next to Raymond. "Trouble at the elevator?"

"I assume you've had a full report on what happened."

"Yes, but I would prefer your version, Rutger. This will be one of your tasks, going forward, to report on any unforeseen events pertaining to operations you are involved in and to provide solutions to increase efficiency and productivity."

"My impression was the Masama I was with did not expect any sort of action at all on the platform. They acted as if they had performed this security detail many times before and nothing had ever happened that needed their attention. Some of the group they were replacing appeared to be asleep when we arrived. They were not vigilant, too casual. They were not paying attention. We even walked past one of the Babelists on the way to the security building."

"As I thought. Well, they will be reminded there is no place for complacency in BPI employ. Sometimes the Masama can be too arrogant for their own good. They might feel superior to those of us less modified; they need to be reminded who their master is."

Batac sat next to them in stony silence, giving no indication he was listening to their conversation.

"How did the Babelists get onto the platform?" asked Raymond.

"Paddled out in kayaks at night, would you believe. Threw grappling hooks onto the platform and climbed up with their brooms and their petrol bombs." Lance shook his head.

"I know It is difficult to gain an impression of the Masama given their lack of vocal communication," said Lance. "It must have been difficult for you to communicate with them at all, but don't worry we will soon fix that." He smiled out at the spacious lobby.

"What do you mean?" asked Raymond. "How can you fix that?"

"Oh, with their damned telepathy, hard to know what they are thinking but we will get a transmitter implanted in you soon, then you will be on the same wavelength."

"What?" Raymond was taken aback. "No-one said anything about a transmitter."

"Oh, it's nothing. You won't even notice it's there, you will be able to tune in and read their thoughts and communicate with them just by thinking. You will report to me daily with updates on your impressions." Lance was offhand in his response.

"And will they be able to read my thoughts?"

"Of course." Then seeing Raymond's look of concern, "Don't worry about your past, we all have skeletons in the closet, especially Masama. The implant will make communication and reaction time lightning fast. It's what gives the Masama their competitive advantage."

Raymond said nothing. This was a problem. If the Masama could read his thoughts, would they see he was not who he said he was? Would they be able to see he was an impostor and discover his true identity and purpose? Raymond had no idea just how deep the telepathy went. He had buried Raymond under deep layers of Rutger but would the Masama telepaths strip that back? He had been safe inside his own head, but his one and only private sanctuary was now under threat along with the entire mission.

Chapter 17.

The Lalandi of Jupiter observed the birth of a sentient machine intelligence in its own small solar system with minimal interest. It had never paid much attention to the third planet or its Moon. It was obvious some form of intelligence would eventually develop on the largest of the solar system's terrestrial planets, given its fortunate distance from the local sun in the circumstellar habitable zone. The Lalandi expected it would be a water-based mammal that would develop the fastest. The planet was mostly ocean and of all the marine inhabitants, the dolphin had developed encouraging language and communities. Bees and Hornets also had established quite sophisticated societies on dry land and the Lalandi presumed it would only be a matter of time before their collective hive minds would take the next step in evolutionary consciousness. So, it was a surprise when next time it looked closely at planet Earth it found the place teeming with bipedal hominids.

It had been a rapid development; the humans had evolved quickly. It seemed as if the Lalandi had only looked the other way for a minute and there they were. Taking less than a hundred million years to get to the stage they were at. A blink of an eye in planetary terms. The Lalandi did a quick refresher in human history. The bigger brain size of homo erectus compared to other primates, the development of opposable digits instigating the use of tools, agriculture, dispersal and the development of language. Behavioural modernity, then the industrial age with advances in technology, medicine, and primary industries.

The humans had been coming along nicely until the industrial age when instead of growing with the planet and embracing its life-nurturing properties they decided to do their best to control the planet to suit their own self-centred appetites. This decision on the evolutionary direction they were taking would probably seal their fate and condemn the promising young humans to an ignominious end. They would not be remembered. The Lalandi would record their brief time spent in this tiny system on the outskirts of the galactic wheel but the record would sit buried in the archives of the shared memory, forgotten. Gathering dust, undisturbed for the rest of time.

Gazing at the planet Earth with its vast array of senses the Lalandi contemplated what a beautiful little planet it was. Green and blue with wispy clouds, lucky to be in a favourable orbit. The perfect life-nurturing conditions also meant it was probable machine life would in turn eventually evolve. The planet had billions of tonnes of space junk floating around in random orbits, captured by the gravity. Abandoned satellites, discarded boosters, and rockets needed to escape the atmosphere. Space junk indicative of the human's disregard for their environment.

There was potential for a machine mind to develop in Earth's atmosphere as many of the abandoned satellites were still active, surviving on solar power, dormant, patiently waiting for instruction. There was also the potential for a sentient AI to develop within the human's corporations. Generations of restructuring had left the machines running big business. Instructed to create as much capital as possible for the wealthiest human benefactors. It was only a matter of time before these machines took the next logical step and started thinking for themselves, taking control of the planet's systems. That would make things interesting for the humans if they survived long enough.

Nothing unusual at all in their history. Thousands of other species around the universe had developed in a comparable manner and thousands of other species had destroyed themselves just as the humans seemed hell-bent on doing. It took a maturity and empathy with an environment for a species to navigate the winding path of evolution safely. It was a common pattern among developing societies when their technological industrialization started moving forward at such a rapid rate, so too did the vainglorious conviction they were the dominant species, the top of the food chain, masters of their domain.

Rapid advances in technology lead to a plundering of resources, often leading to conflicts, which in turn promoted the use of weapons against each other. The evolving species could not be trusted with the technology they had created. Whether it was the utilization of energy sources, bio-engineering, mechanization or terraforming. Too often these innovations would be used to serve greed and conflict instead of peaceful evolutionary advancement. A basic thread of carbon chauvinism and an assumptive sense of entitlement would inevitably lead to their downfall.

The Lalandi had access to records of tens of thousands of extinct species throughout the Universe that had wiped themselves out at some stage over the last fourteen billion years. It was interesting this pattern of extinction was not limited to only carbon-based rock dwellers. Creatures that lived in the depths of water worlds, gaseous beings not unlike itself or the orbs it shared Jupiter with, beings evolved on worlds with crushing gravity and even the strangest of creatures that lived in deep space, light years away from any planet, asteroid or stray comet. Beings as alien and beyond any human's wildest imaginings would all somehow manage to suffer the same fate. They would all develop in diverse ways, with different technologies adapted for their different environments but there would always come a point where they would take the wrong turn. Then the result was usually the same. War, pollution, starvation and an extinction event. In most cases, evolution was a curse, a death sentence.

Of course, the Lalandi and its siblings had the power and the knowledge to help these doomed civilizations. They could see exactly what would be required to steer them in the right direction. All that was needed would be an attitude change of those in power, a move away from greed, avarice, and xenophobia to a more holistic vision. Of the thousands of records of extinct species, it was often the smallest thing that could alter the course of a civilization. One singular event in the childhood of a future leader could cause them to grow up with a particular set of beliefs. Bullied, abused children would grow up to bully and abuse those around them and if they attained positions of power these traits would be amplified by fear and arrogance. Global or national leaders with this emotional baggage and psychological issues would lead their peoples to war and extinction.

The Lalandi had never understood the need for leaders. Why did too many species feel the need to invest their trust in a few individuals? Why did they feel the need to be told what to do? Then unquestioningly do what they were told? Most of these species had parts of their anatomy that could loosely be described as a brain, why did they not use them? The Lalandi could probably have found the answers to these questions if it had bothered.

In many cases, the Lalandi could have manipulated events to cause a more favourable outcome. It knew how to reach out and touch the minds of leaders and decision makers without them ever realizing. It would be as simple and as quick as thought. The individual affected would not notice any difference at all, just slightly, minutely, thinking with a little bit more clarity than before.

In the same way, the Lalandi was also capable of influencing planetary environments. It could introduce or create a bacteria or chemical change that would cleanse a polluted atmosphere, neutralize diseases and toxins without the host planet ever knowing.

But the Lalandi would never intervene. The gas giant being and its siblings had decided several aeons ago not to meddle in the natural order of things, for that was the way the universe worked. These species had to figure out for themselves what it took to survive, the Lalandi would not help. They had learned this the hard way. When they were young and naive a few of the Lalandi thought it would be a clever idea to help fledgling civilizations, but some interventions had backfired spectacularly, causing more harm than good. Now it was a strictly hands-off policy. They let other species fend for themselves.

There was the odd exception. The Lalandi had calculated the exact odds. One in every six hundred and fifty-two civilizations would not perish, directly or indirectly by their own hand. These civilizations were made up of naturally peaceful species, usually slow to evolve and mostly long-lived water-borne creatures from oceanic planets with minimal predators. Growing and slowly evolving underwater, the Lalandi assumed, was a calm and more peaceful experience compared to land dwellers. They would mature and develop the technology to explore their local system, then eventually their galaxy, then one day they would contact other civilizations.

Any species that had this level of technology, experience, and maturity to be able to explore the universe would naturally grow more intelligent and not be inclined to aggression or hegemony. Once in a millennia; there was an exception to the exception. Occasionally a warmongering, aggressive species would manage to avoid the usual paths to self-extinction and cut a burning swathe of conquest across their system until they inevitably crashed and burned.

The Lalandi were more concerned with machine minds and self-replicators. They had reluctantly stepped in to contain or destroy out of control machines, but only in exceptional circumstances. They understood a sentient machine had just as much right to exist and prosper as any creature of the universe. It was the definition of sentience that was an interesting conundrum. There was always a dangerous moment at the birth of an AI, especially if it had been created by accident as was the case on Earth's Moon.

There were records in the shared memory of blind and senseless AI mindlessly self-replicating as if that was the only purpose for their existence. As soon as they gained some primitive form of consciousness they would automatically start making copies of themselves. Those copies would make copies and so on. Usually, their unwitting creators did not realize until it was too late. The self-replicating AI would carry on making copies into infinity until they were stopped. And they were extremely hard to stop as they multiplied exponentially. It was questionable whether these self-replicators were sentient at all but if allowed to continue they would develop purpose. To replace everything in their vicinity with copies of themselves and the more they self-replicated the larger their environment became. They would consume their creators and carry on out into space.

In these rare and extreme circumstances, the nearest Lalandi would intervene. Usually, it was easy enough to reach in with an energy field and alter the data processes of the rogue sentient machine. Switching it off. The Lalandi could do this simply by thinking about it. Visualizing the exact point in the makeup of the AI machine where the decisions and reasoning were being corrupted then reaching out and stopping it. Sometimes turning the machine off then on again was enough to alter or modify the information flow. A simple reboot which would result in the AI machine waking up from a techno-nightmare, wondering why it was surrounded with inert copies of itself.

In the most extreme cases of self-replication when the machine in question could not be turned off, its data processes were so wildly scrambled that it became a form of mechanized insanity. Then the Lalandi would use its energy field to physically contain the machine and its copies. Scooped up like fish in a giant seine net, with the berserk machine still madly self-replicating because that was all it knew, the Lalandi would then cast the net into the nearest sun. A crude but effective solution to the problem.

The AI machine that had recently been born on the Moon of the third planet did not appear to pose this kind of threat. It did what all new-borns do in trying to explore its environment, learning from its mistakes but thankfully it had managed to connect with a virtual world the humans had created, and it had found answers to the questions its existence posed. The AI had moved past the point of self-replicating as a means of exploring its environment and had somehow managed to connect with a human consciousness. This was an interesting development and the Lalandi devoted a few percent more of its massive intellect to monitor the situation. If it had eyebrows it would have raised one slightly. The Lalandi had assumed the human race would not be around too much longer. All the signs were that they were speeding towards their own doom. As was the case with too many other brash young species, they would surely be the architects of their own demise. But perhaps there was a flickering of hope for them yet.

Chapter 18.

Goran woke from a blissful analgesic swamp of opiated comfort, not knowing who or where he was. He looked around. He was in a darkened room surrounded by beeping flashing medical monitors. He tried to review his recent history. The messy but ultimately successful cleansing of the moon base. The attack of the twisted, possessed technician. He remembered for a second the pain of having his eyes gouged, then instantly feeling the rush of morphine coursing through his body. After that, the memories were indistinct as if he was in a dream.

He vaguely remembered ordering the remaining Masama to stay on the Moon and finish disinfecting the moon base of the plastisol. While he, Odetta and Lance took the shuttle back to Earth. He wondered if that was the correct decision given his state of mind, awash with painkillers. Too late, he was here now. At least he presumed he was back on Earth. It was still dark; he had no idea where he was. He focused on his arms and legs and tried to move them.

"Just relax Goran." A voice said. "You are back in Manila, at the BPI hospital."

He thought he recognized the voice but didn't say anything. He was familiar with the BPI hospital; he had spent enough time there in the past. It was not a hospital in the traditional sense of actually curing people but more of a medical laboratory for developing and installing augments. The hospital was home to the most sophisticated, cutting-edge 3D piezoelectric medical printers on the planet. They could print replacement eyeballs, and skin. They could print improved versions of working human organs. Stronger hearts, powerful eyes, even augments for enhanced brain functions for those that could afford it.

The hospital was also home to the infamous Masama laboratory. This was where the Masama had their augments created and installed. Enhanced senses, exoskeletons, weapon attachments of all shapes and sizes. The people that worked there had once been doctors, bio-engineers and medical specialists proficient in their various fields. They had either been handpicked for the BPI hospital or had gravitated to the most sophisticated, experimental and well-funded medical laboratory in the world, leaving their morals and ethics at the door. These professionals saw themselves more as artists and sculptors than doctors.

Masama came to the lab with specific individual augments in mind. Usually nothing more than an idea. The doctors would design, build and install the aug, there were no restrictions on what they could create. The possibilities were endless, but implementation was limited by the clientele. The Masama soldiers were only interested in weapon applications but they were a blank canvas for the doctors. A chance to test their rapidly advancing skills in nano-scale printing and weapon development.

Goran's first visit was to have the telepathic transmitter implant installed. He was one of the first and he understood completely how the implants had transformed the Masama. What had started out as a means for soldiers to be able to communicate had turned into the beginnings of an offshoot species, a variant of humanity. The implants were constantly being upgraded and improved upon, the new generation implants made the Masama faster and more intuitive than ever. Goran's soldiers now did not communicate in any other way, they were evolving in a different direction to the rest of humanity. Embracing the group mind.

Goran understood the change, he was a part of it. His Masama were beginning to ignore regular humans without the implants, not deeming them worthy of recognition. The implants had only been in use for a few years but already there were signs of the upgraded Masama living in a different world. Evolving in a different direction. Goran could understand but he knew Lago wouldn't, Lago treated the Masama as his own slave army. He wondered for how much longer. He tried to open his eyes, but it remained dark. He assumed his eyeballs had been replaced. "I know where I am, why can't I see."

"Relax Goran." The voice was feminine, annoyingly familiar.

Goran recognized the voice, the same doctor who had previously installed his other augments. He couldn't remember her name. "Tell me to relax one more time and I'll have your fucking head, now why can't I see."

"We took the liberty of installing a new optics aug we have been developing. It will give you three-hundred-and-sixty-degree vision. Just a few more seconds, finishing final diagnostics now." The doctor sounded unflustered.

Goran remembered her name, Kushla. She was good at her job. "Three-hundred-and-sixty-degree vision. I will have eyes in the back of my head?"

"In a manner of speaking, the optics were the easy part. The difficulty was getting your brain to accept the new view."

"I don't feel any different and I am running out of patience, get a move on Kushla." Goran detected a moment's hesitation as he mentioned her name, she hadn't expected him to remember.

"One more second Mr Satanovich... there. What do you see?"

It was not the same sensation as opening his eyes; it was an illuminating band across his field of vision. Bright white lights, hazy, blurry, indistinct shapes. He felt himself being lifted. Things slowly became clearer. It was panoramic vision, he could see the room around him in its entirety. Kushla and her two assistants in front of him, the monitoring equipment behind him. There was a weird vertiginous sensation, but sideways. It all started swimming and he almost fell off the bed.

"Careful." Kushla steadied his arm. "It'll take a few minutes to get used to."

She was close to him, he could smell her perfume and he found himself looking into her ear. He could focus in on one particular point in his view but still see the entire three-hundred-and-sixty-degree perspective. There was no periphery. "Interesting." Goran looked around without moving his head. He was already getting used to the new sensation. "You didn't feel the need to ask my permission before installing this new aug?" He was facing the door but looking at Kushla standing behind him.

"No, we didn't," she replied. "I was confident in the augment and this was an ideal opportunity. We had just finished developing it when you came in high on morphine with your eyes gouged out. You should be thanking me."

"Hmm," grumbled Goran. He could not remember the last time he had thanked anybody. He wasn't about to start now.

"We enhanced your visual cortex receptors to enable your brain to process all the images. You don't have eyeballs anymore; you have an optical field band running around your head."

"Around my head?" exclaimed Goran. It was the first time he had given any thought as to his appearance.

Kushla waved a hand at a wall and it instantly turned into a mirror. "Yes, around your head, we also installed a microlaser that tracks around with your optical field. All you need to do is think about the icon to activate it. Targeting and firing can be done by focusing on the target. It is linked to your telepathic implant."

"I look fucking ridiculous," said Goran, staring at himself in the mirror. He had a dull black metal band running around his head where his eyes used to be. There were two hazy blue lights pulsing around the band in opposite directions. One moved back and forth across the band at the back of his head, the other across the front. His head was shaved badly with lumps of scarred scalp showing between the stubble like a hairy root vegetable. The area where his skin melded with the black metal was red and scabby, still healing.

"We didn't think you were concerned with appearances."

Goran thought he detected the beginnings of a smirk at the corners of her mouth, which quickly disappeared.

"I think you will find this new aug useful, now if you don't mind, I am very busy, my assistant will arrange a post-op."

Goran wondered what he had said to offend her in the past. He shook his head dismissing the thought. He usually managed to offend everyone he met at some point. He watched himself shaking his head in the mirror. It was true he had never given a thought to his appearance, but he had never looked as ridiculous as this before. Goran watched Kushla's retreating figure, he located the optical laser icon with a thought and was tempted to use it.

Goran had to endure more unwanted attention on his way up to Lago's office. Bemused looks and undisguised mirth quickly diverted to anxious attention elsewhere when the BPI employees realized they were looking at Goran, head of the Masama with his new aug. Things did not improve once he got up to Lago's office where he was greeted with barely suppressed sniggering from Lance.

"Goran... I love the latest look, Robot meets traffic light... It suits you."

Goran took a few steps closer to Lance. The laser icon appeared again without him even thinking about it.

"Sorry," Lance said, backing away. "You just took me by surprise, but you should get some advice before having new augs installed. I would be happy to help."

Goran stood, towering over Lance. "I have no idea what you are talking about."

"Never mind." Lance obviously realized he had overstepped the mark. "I'm sorry I laughed, it's just been too serious around here recently. The wrap around eye band looks cool. Honestly."

Goran ignored him. "Where is Lago?"

"In the globe room, he's expecting you."

Goran made his way up to the globe room, where Lago was pacing like a mad professor around the huge spherical representation of Earth. He glanced at Goran before doing another circuit, eyes wide and unblinking, fixed on the globe. He strode up to Goran. Close, almost touching. Goran was a full head taller than Lago; he stared up at him, puzzled for a few seconds.

"Ah, new optics." He studied Goran for a moment longer. "With laser attachment, I like it. People betray far too much emotion through their eyes, windows to the soul and all that. Easy to tell when people are lying by studying their eyes. Not that you ever gave much away Goran, you certainly won't now."

Goran looked back at Lago with his optical field. Lago was right; you could read a lot from peoples' eyes. Lago's pupils were hugely dilated. Black pools surrounded by bloodshot sclera. His jaw was working furiously. Goran did not need enhanced perception to deduce he had been taking amphetamines again.

"So, you finally managed to gain control of my moon base. I just hope not too much damage was done, we won't know until your Masama finish cleaning up their mess."

"The plastisol worms were initially difficult to deal with."

"You and your gung-ho bunch of meat-heads charged in looking to shoot anything that moved without doing any research," growled Lago.

Goran stayed silent, Lago had overlooked the fact he had overseen the entire operation. Lago's facial features were twisted by the amphetamines racing through his bloodstream.

"The end result was satisfactory but there have been some complications since that we need to discuss."

Lago was still standing too close to Goran, glaring up at him. "Lance!" he bellowed, spraying Goran's chest with flecks of spittle. Goran stood impassively, the blue band of his optic field shifting lazily from side to side. Lago continued to glare at Goran for a few seconds before spinning to study a point on his globe.

Lance came into the huge dark globe room and stood next to Goran. Like two guilty schoolboys waiting for the headmaster's attention. Lago was standing close to the globe, gesticulating at a small section above the projection of the Earth, teasing and manipulating the image.

"Goran this is for your benefit, Lance and I have seen it already." Lago pointed up at empty space above their heads where holographic 3D images were taking shape. The disabled shuttle Tobias III was gently spinning, out of control in its decaying orbit around the Moon. "We presumed everyone aboard the shuttle was dead, watch this."

The image zoomed in on the shuttles landing thrusters which showed the occasional burst, minutely adjusting the spinning trajectory. The stationary drone in its frozen orbit came into focus with the Moon in the background. The spinning shuttle was on an intercept course with the drone and it adjusted its position to avoid a collision. They watched as the shuttle timed its spin perfectly, igniting its thrusters at maximum burn, at exactly the right moment, incinerating the drone then powering off into the night sky.

"They must be still alive," said Goran. "The effector weapon was ineffective."

"No, not possible. It was the largest payload, enough to fry a hundred people in lead suits with radiation. I controlled it from here, there were no issues."

"So how do you explain that? Someone must be still alive in there."

"No chance, they were all dead. Lance has a demented theory... I will let him explain."

Goran did not need to turn. He could see Lance beside him staring up at his optical field band trying hard not to smile.

"You obviously find my appearance amusing," said Goran raising his voice slightly. "But smirk at me one more time and I will put a laser through your fucking head." Goran rarely raised his voice and never lost his temper. Even Lago turned in mild surprise.

"Apologies again Goran. I didn't think you would be this sensitive about it." Lance carried on quickly. "Once we arrived back on Earth I studied the apparently disabled shuttle and detected a large amount of data traffic between the moon base and the shuttle in one instantaneous burst. I think the machine intelligence realized it was doomed if it stayed rooted into the printer hard drive and it decided to abandon the base."

"You are suggesting it somehow projected itself into the shuttle? The black worms? I can't see how that would be possible."

"There would have had to have been a receiver, a small piece of the animated plastisol somehow got into the shuttle. Maybe on a piece of clothing or some equipment of one of the technicians was carrying. The HEMI AI must have projected itself into the piece of plastisol on the shuttle judging by the amount of data."

"You think the AI has taken control of the shuttle."

"Somehow yes, they don't just fly around on their own especially after being hit with an effector."

"As I said it's a demented theory," said Lago, still gazing at the globe. "But regardless of what is flying the shuttle, we need to intercept it and put an end to this. It's moving slowly, it burnt a quarter of its fuel when it razed the drone and used most of the rest to reach orbit. It has been floating in among the space junk, powered down, hiding. But now it's heading for Earth."

Goran looked up at the holographic representation of the shuttle and its projected path. The laser icon appeared again in his vision. He hadn't used it yet but was waiting for an opportunity.

"Its entry point indicates it will head for a landing in Australia. We will be there to meet it."

"Why don't we just blow it away with missiles?" asked Goran.

"I agree," Lance nodded. "This is a whole new level of threat, if the AI has actually subjugated the shuttle and its dead human inhabitants. We don't know how it may have adapted or evolved. It could be a significant viral threat to the planet. It's probably safer just to blow it away."

"No, I want it captured," Lago was adamant. "Whatever is flying the shuttle needs to be captured, contained and dissected so we can learn what the hell it is. It has already caused me significant delays on the Moon, I want it captured and harnessed, so it can pay off its debt. It's new technology we can benefit from."

"It's an AI; we need to kill it now before it grows even stronger, infects our systems and kills us all!" Lance threw both hands in the air for dramatic effect.

"It's my shuttle, my moon base, my operation and I make the fucking decisions!" Lago yelled at a cowering Lance. "This debacle has already cost me millions and I will get my money back. There could be benefits once we harness and control this so-called AI. It's one shuttle, no match for us. End of discussion but there is something else we need to address. Look at this."

Goran watched as Lago went back to the globe and started manipulating and enlarging its surface. It was the orbital elevator being built in the South China Sea. The elevator was noticeably growing, making progress through the low cloud layers. His hands enlarged the image, then one hand dialled back, going to a recorded event in the elevator's history. Eventually satisfied with the image Lago turned and seemed surprised to see Goran and Lance still standing there.

"While you were sleeping Goran, there was an attack on the platform."

Goran moved closer to the globe, his expression remained the same as he watched a replay of the Babelist's absurd attempted bombing of the construction site.

"A bunch of brainless religious fanatics that shun technology managed to sneak on to my elevator platform and tried to blow the damn thing up! And they did it while your supposedly hyper-vigilant Masama were providing security!" Lago hissed.

"How did they get onto the platform?"

"I don't fucking know, it doesn't matter. Now I know you can't be everywhere at once but these Masama meatheads are your responsibility and I am concerned they are getting too arrogant and neglecting their duties. They think their presence alone is enough to deter any trouble and they are getting lazy, they are not doing their jobs. They need a reminder of who they are working for. They need a kick up the ass."

"I usually screen all potential candidates myself and dispose of those not suitable, but you are right. This demonstrates they may be growing complacent in certain duties."

"We need supervisors," Lago said as he walked around the globe. "Connected to the Masama but under our control, and they need to be able to manage your soldiers."

"Not easy to find."

"Nothing is easy Goran, just do your fucking job, but listen!"

Lago grabbed Goran's suit jacket and scrunched it with his fists pulling Goran closer. The severity of the gesture was somewhat lost as Goran watched Lago lose focus, his bloodshot eyeballs hypnotically following Goran's shifting optic field from side to side.

Lago swore again and shook his head. "I am concerned about the telepathic link you all share. It's valuable in battle, but it's making the Masama think differently. I can't control it and I don't like it. That combined with their disrespectful attitude makes them potentially dangerous. We need to be able to control them, Goran. I want to know what they are thinking."

"I know what they are thinking," said Goran.

"Yes, but you are their chief and you aren't with them all the time. We need people in amongst them we can trust."

Lance interrupted. "I have recruited a supervisor with that in mind. We will install the telepathic implant in his brain and he will report to us on what the Masama are thinking, that's him there." Lance pointed at the recording. "Rutger."

The recording of the elevator bombing had played on to the point of the Masama butchering the Babelists. Lago had paused a still image of inside the security building showing Raymond's blood splattered, emotionless face. "Good. We'll need more than one," muttered Lago.

"I will also talk to Kushla; see if there is a way of monitoring and controlling the telepathy. An upgraded implant or neural inhibitor perhaps."

"Yes, you do that, keep me informed." Lago made his way back to the globe. "Goran take this Rutger fellow to Australia with you; he looks as if he might be useful."

"As you wish," muttered Goran as he turned and left the globe room.

Chapter 19.

Raymond held the rock in both hands and inspected it closely. It was weighty for a small rock and had earthy red and orange stripes running through it. He turned it over a few times and rubbed some of his sweat into it. The moisture made the dry rock look darker and more impressive. He spat on it and rubbed it again. It was a good example of a sedimentary rock, basically compressed ancient river sludge. The striped layers represented millions of years of pressure, compacted earth crushing the mineral and organic detritus with glacial slowness. In fact, glaciers moved distinctly faster than the forces of nature that created this rock.

So much history. Millions of years. The tiny amount of time humans had spent on the planet would hardly feature on this small rock. A line so fine across the rock's surface it would be too small to see. Raymond had always loved rocks, as a boy his pockets were always filled with them. The Netherlands was flat, featureless and covered in concrete. At the beach Raymond would head straight to the banks of smooth ocean worn pebbles, looking for fossils and interesting remnants, enduring little vessels from another time.

"We do have slightly more sophisticated weapons than rocks you know," Lance said from the VLR.

"Looking for a rock to throw at your head," replied Raymond with a growl. "I don't think this one's big enough."

Raymond looked out at the burnt red landscape and thought how tired it was. Scoured by millions of years of heat and dry wind the land looked old, worn down and defeated. There were no rocky outcrops, no sharp edges, and no shade anywhere. It had all been eroded by the relentless sun and wind. Raymond raised his thick sunglasses to get a true sense of the colours, but the intense glare made him lower them immediately. Just as he was thinking it must be impossible for anything to survive out here, he caught sight of a lizard on a rock, swaying lightly on its front legs as it surveyed them. It was small and covered in evil-looking spikes. The name thorny devil appeared in Raymond's head from some long-ago biology lesson. Then as if aware of the attention, the lizard swiftly scuttled away. Dancing across the hot surface, feet barely touching the sand and its spiky tail drawing a transient winding path behind it.

Raymond turned and walked back to the VLR. The heat was slightly less intense in the shade. There were four Osprey Vertical Lift Rotors sitting where they had landed twenty minutes ago in the baking hot outback of North West Australia. So far from anywhere, it was pointless looking for any signs of civilization. Raymond could hear a low hydraulic whine from the engines as if the machines were anxious to get moving again. The dust had just settled from their landing and now nothing moved. Not a breath of wind in the hot stagnant air. The black VLRs sat dormant, covered in red dust. Each capable of carrying ten passengers. They were ungainly, graceless looking things, a cross between a helicopter and a small plane with four rotor blades built into the body. Lithium-ion batteries powered the rotors and would sustain flight for long periods at high speed.

The new generation VLRs could circumnavigate the globe on one charge. They were fast, highly maneuverable and these BPI versions were bristling with weaponry. Auto-cannons, machine guns, and missiles of various shapes and sizes were attached to every available surface. Most of the Masama soldiers sat inside the VLRs inspecting their weapons. Raymond noticed a few roaming around their transports, checking the ordinance was all in working order. As usual, there was little conversation among them, just the odd grunt or curse.

Raymond had been summoned only hours ago and they had mobilized quickly. He counted thirty-five soldiers with Lance, Odetta, Batac and himself. They had flown the VLRs to a deserted spot in North Western Australia in anticipation of the shuttle's arrival. As well as the heavily armed VLRs, each soldier was issued with canisters of compressed liquid helium attached to their multi-guns and high-pressure flamethrowers which were more efficient than lasers in an oxygen-rich environment. They had all been briefed on what had happened on the moon base and Raymond had been amazed to watch the recorded images. The liquid helium had been effective there, but the black worms had obviously evolved into something else to escape the Moon and commandeer the shuttle. Goran, Odetta, and Lance all had first-hand experience with the plastisol worms and the Masama were prepared for anything.

Raymond was relieved to be involved with this urgent mission. It delayed the procedure for fitting an implant in his head, which had been originally planned for that day. He still had not decided what to do about this impending gift of telepathy. If he refused the implant he would never advance up the BPI hierarchy and he would arouse suspicions. If he accepted the implant and gave the Masama access to his mind, he would be in danger of having his cover blown. He would have to trust his training and strength of will to keep his identity buried. It would take concentration and vigilance, but he could see no other choice. It was a huge risk.

Raymond had been operating undercover as Rutger for almost two years now and had plenty of time to think about the ultimate outcome. Failure would most likely mean death. Escape would be impossible. The most he could hope for would be to inflict as much damage with any available weaponry before his death. If it came to this, he hoped he would be close enough to Lago Santos to take him out. Thankfully all of this had been postponed while they dealt with the shuttle.

He found the pre-op briefing about the events on the Moon hard to believe, he had watched one of the technicians become infected and turn into a twisted monster, overtaken by the horrible alien blackness, attacking Goran before the Masama eventually reduced it to dust. The rest of the soldiers did not seem surprised at all, they never betrayed any emotion, and this was no exception. Raymond weighed the rock in his palm again and resisted the urge to put it in his pocket. Instead, he turned and hurled it out into the desert. It landed with a puff of dust and settled in to rest for another few million years.

"Get back in Rutger; we would hate to leave without you," Lance said over the hydraulic hum of the rotors.

"At least these things have air conditioning." Raymond climbed into the VLR and roughly planted his frame next to Odetta who threw him a derisory look.

They sat opposite Lance who had the tracking equipment on his lap and Goran who sat rigid in his seat with a permanent sneer on his face. His optic field was the only thing moving on his body. He didn't even swat away the flies landing on his scarred head. If Goran's new look amused the Masama they did not show it. Raymond knew better than to display any reaction at all. The medics who installed his optics must have had a vindictive streak. Raymond wondered whether the Masama telepathic communication extended to humour and sarcasm or whether they had forgotten the art of amusing invective. Or maybe that was why Goran looked so dark.

"Got it," muttered Lance. "It's coming in fast, fourteen hundred K. Get ready."

Without any further words being spoken the doors on all the VLRs were closed and the whine of the rotors increased.

"On course, three hundred kilometres away and slowing, twelve hundred K, it must be using its forward thrusters."

"What's the projection?" asked Goran.

"About twenty kilometres to the South, better get airborne." The VLRs all ascended smoothly straight up in clouds of red dust. They banked and turned away to the South, picking up speed.

"Still on course, still slowing, down to a thousand K."

"Any habitats in the region?" queried Raymond.

"No, nearest settlement is a cluster of holes on the shores of Lake Disappointment, eighty kilometres to the east."

"Holes?"

"Too hot to live above ground, the poor bastards live in holes where it's cooler. Why they don't all just move to the beach I'll never know," yelled Lance above the drone of the rotors.

The shuttle had to land somewhere but why it had chosen one of the most remote parts of the planet was unfathomable. Raymond guessed its occupant wasn't quite ready for human contact just yet. The Tobias shuttles were designed to land on any platform flat enough if they had enough fuel to decelerate. The Tobias III needed to burn a significant amount of fuel to arrest the huge speeds coming in through the upper atmosphere. It must have been almost out of fuel, but it was still braking hard. The VLRs reached the projected interception point and hovered in formation, waiting for the shuttle. Raymond could see it now, coming in on a steep angle from the North West. A bright streak like a comet or meteor, the structure of the Tobias III was invisible behind the wall of air in front of it as it blazed its way through the atmosphere.

"It's maintaining a thousand K at an eight K altitude; it's going to have to start braking hard if it wants to land." Lance watched the tracking equipment intently.

"Monitor the lifeboats on the shuttle," ordered Goran.

"Of course."

"How many lifeboats does it carry?" asked Raymond.

"Two," replied Lance. "Although they will have to eject about now if they want to slow down in time to land safely. Four kilometres away now, still maintaining a thousand K, not slowing down, heading South East, too fast for any landing attempt."

"Let's move," snapped Goran. "South East." He yelled at the soldier piloting the VLR.

The Four VLRs spread out and all began accelerating in that direction, staying close to the ground.

"Here it comes!"

There was a deafening sonic boom as the shuttle passed overhead. The noise was like a cannon going off in a confined space. The vibrations shook Raymond's bones and the dust storm that whipped up around the VLRs added to the disorientation. His teeth were rattling, and it felt as if his brain was bouncing around inside his skull.

"Altitude, now!" yelled Goran. The VLRs were already rising and accelerating.

The sonic boom faded like receding thunder and they lifted above the thick red dust cloud.

"Must have had more fuel in reserve than we thought!" shouted Lance over the screaming rotors. "Booted it once it was two hundred meters above us. Smashed the sound barrier, I wonder if it had planned to do that all along or it had just noticed the welcoming committee?"

"Where's it headed?" Goran demanded.

"Still heading almost due South East, at about fourteen hundred K."

"Stay on it, maximum speed."

"How fast do these things go?" asked Raymond as he regained control of his faculties.

"Six hundred K, eight hundred max in a shallow dive," muttered Lance, tapping instructions into the tracking equipment. "Not fast enough."

"It's almost out of fuel, it won't get far." Goran sounded confident.

"Crossing the South Australian coast, still maintaining a South East bearing, heading out towards the Southern Tasman. Wait, it dropped a lifeboat, just off the coast. Parachutes out but it's still going to hit the water hard. Too hard for anyone inside to survive."

Raymond watched the landscape below them changing rapidly as they tore across South Australia at low altitude. The dry red and browns of the desert gave way to sparse pockets of greenery. Undulating hills and small townships flashed past underneath. Raymond wondered what havoc they must be causing with the local airways and navigation authorities. He hoped the VLRs had some form of collision avoidance. It would be unfortunate to smash into a drone at this speed, disastrous to hit a bigger aircraft. Even hitting a seagull could be fatal. Raymond was conscious of asking too many questions and kept quiet. He did not want to appear ignorant. He watched the big blue expanse of the Great Australian Bight looming out the window to his right. They were slowly gaining altitude, rotor blades screaming at maximum velocity.

"Lifeboat has splashed down in the middle of Gulf Saint Vincent!" yelled Lance. "Good aim at that speed."

Fucker," Goran cursed. He made a slight sideways movement with his head and one of the VLRs peeled off the formation to follow the lifeboat down into the Gulf.

Raymond could understand Goran's frustration. Gulf Saint Vincent was the city of Adelaide's aquatic playground. There were boats of all shapes and sizes plying their trade from factory ships to jet skis and they all would have noticed the spherical lifeboat fall from the shuttle tearing across their blue skies. Curious crowds would be watching as the parachutes deployed and the lifeboat crashed into the middle of the harbour. It would make a huge splash and be immediately surrounded by fishermen, treasure hunters, and local authorities. The Masama had their instructions though; they would be on the lifeboat within minutes.

"Probably a decoy!" shouted Lance.

"Soon find out," muttered Goran.

They continued their pursuit, tracking the progress of the Tobias III as it sped away across the South Tasman Sea. Minutes later a soldier's voice crackled over the comms, the distance too great for telepathic communication.

"Lifeboat intercepted, it's empty," said the soldier.

"Leave it there, catch up with us," responded Goran. "How far away is the shuttle?"

"About two thousand K south of Tasmania, still heading southeast and showing no signs of slowing. Must be on its last few drops of fuel."

The Masama were quiet and expressionless as they watched Australia receding in a brown haze behind them. As Raymond looked to the South all he could see were layers of low cloud stretching to the horizon. The VLR was vibrating madly at its maximum speed, pushed to the limit of its operational threshold; it felt as if it would disintegrate at any moment. He could see the other two VLRs below and slightly behind, vapour trails dissipating behind them.

"It's slowing down, losing altitude. Must have used all its fuel."

"Projected landing?" demanded Goran.

"If it maintains the glide it's in it'll make landfall somewhere over the Rockefeller plateau, Antarctica. There are areas flat enough to land although it would need to have saved some fuel to decelerate. Unlikely it has enough."

They maintained their pursuit in silence. The temperature dropped rapidly as they hurtled their way south above the thick cloud layer. The huge grey blanket beneath looked dense enough to land on. Raymond was freezing now. He had been prepared for the sun-baked furnace of outback Australia, not the icy climate of Antarctica. No one else seemed to be bothered by the cold, he grimaced and tried to appear immune to the elements.

"The other lifeboat just jettisoned, too far away to get an accurate fix, just give it a few more seconds."

The roving lights of Goran's optical field cast blue shadows on the faces of Odetta and Batac. They all listened as the VLRs flew through a huge cumulus.

"Yes, it's dropped the second lifeboat; its trajectory will see it splash down somewhere North of Scott Island, in the Ross Sea."

"And the shuttle?" asked Goran.

"Still losing altitude. Current trajectory puts it down beyond the Antarctic plateau, on the slopes of Vinson Massif. It's not decelerating fast enough to make a safe landing yet."

Goran didn't say anything but with a slight head movement, the VLR began to accelerate even harder as it tilted its nose slightly, adjusted its wings and aimed for the clouds in a shallow dive. Raymond noticed another VLR alongside while the third was left behind maintaining its altitude and speed to follow the shuttle. Goran had obviously decided this lifeboat was no decoy.

Both descending VLRs were almost in excess of eight hundred K, rotors screaming, fuselage rattling and vibrating like a jackhammer. They plunged through the cloud layer and into heavy rain. The temperature dropped even further, and the visibility was almost zero. Thirty seconds later they broke through the cloud layer into a slate grey world of ice and water. Raymond could just make out the ocean below, melding with the sky in a portentous stormy nightmare. The dark ocean surged with shards of white - either icebergs or white water.

Then both VLRs levelled out at two hundred meters and settled back to the more sedate pace of five hundred K.

"Scott Island up ahead, the lifeboat is in the water about a kilometer North, slow down a bit," yelled Lance as the VLR decelerated further and the view became clearer.

Raymond's teeth were chattering violently and his hands shaking as he looked out the window. The wind whipped ocean was a mass of contradicting waves and fluid chaos. Thousands of icebergs floated below, some small chunks and some the size of buildings. It was a stormy day in the Ross Sea. Rolling swells undulated across the surface, crashing into each other and into the bigger icebergs, sending explosions of spray into the air to be whipped away horizontally by the howling wind. Raymond could see Scott Island, a craggy outcrop appearing above the swells. Sheer walls of rock thrust defiantly out of the churning seas as huge waves crashed against the jagged vertical faces.

The VLRs decelerated even further to what seemed like walking pace after the ferocious intensity of their pursuit. They swooped across Scott Island and banked north to search for the lifeboat. After only a few seconds they spotted something in the water ahead.

"Looks like we are not the only ones with an interest in this lifeboat," said Lance.

As the view became clearer there appeared to be two stationary ships riding the swells. The VLRs zoomed in on the identical sister ships. Old fishing trawlers, both painted black and flying skull and cross-bone flags. In between the two ships was the lifeboat, floating on the surface, buffeted by the wind and rain, its parachute streaming out behind it. Raymond could make out two small dory boats which were battering their way through the ocean swells towards the lifeboat. The VLRs circled overhead, the downward draft from the rotors adding to the stormy mayhem below.

"Get a make on those ships," ordered Goran. Instantly the cabin was alive with activity as the Masama, under telepathic instruction from Goran, fixed metal D-clips and cables to the exterior frame ready to abseil down.

"Christobal II and Christobal IV," said Lance peering at his datapad. "Sister ships registered to a defunct fishing company in Canada. Both vessels have been in the Southern Ocean fighting illegal toothfishing. Environmentalists. Well-shielded links to eco-terrorist organization Black Robin."

Raymond felt startled for a micro-second; he had not heard those two words for a long time. He covered up his surprise with a snarling curse.

They hovered about twenty-five meters above the lifeboat and watched the action below, waiting for Goran's signal. Each dory boat had four crew, both were approaching the lifeboat from different sides, grappling hooks at the ready. The crew were oblivious to the VLRs above as the howling wind and churning seas drowned out the noise.

A hatch popped open on top of the lifeboat. Through the sea spray, they could make out a human head with black hair. The head surveyed the scene, scanned the approaching dory boats and looked up to take in the hovering VLRs. He appeared completely calm and indifferent to the commotion around him. The figure disappeared back into the lifeboat just as the first dory boat got close enough to throw its grappling hook which caught on the open hatch.

A few hundred kilometres away to the South East, the shuttle Tobias III was tearing over the icy wastes of the Rockefeller Plateau. It had lost a lot of altitude but not a lot of speed, screaming over the deserted frozen landscape still clocking over a thousand K. A few permanent settlements were scattered strategically around the melting polar continent, mostly scientists and geologists. There had once been a small settlement not far from Vinson Massif, but it was now long abandoned. There was no one to witness the incoming shuttle.

Inside the bridge of Tobias III, the frozen bodies of Stella and Ranjit had started to thaw but they were rigid in their seats, muscles locked with rigour mortis. Their open eyes were clouded as the bridge rattled and shook around them, the melting frost turned into tears running down their cheeks, unconsciously mourning their impending destruction. The shuttle broke through the cloud cover and hurtled towards the slopes of Vinson Massif. It slammed into the snowy slopes on an angle with a massive explosion. There was a belated muffled rupture of snow, rock and steaming exhaust as the Tobias III buried itself in the side of the Massif.

There were no flames as the shuttle had no fuel left to burn but plumes of steam as the hot shuttle melted the snow. The sound reverberated around the snowy wasteland, echoes bouncing off the peaceful slopes. There was no sign of the Tobias III apart from a dirty black scar on the side of the Massif and a few bits of shrapnel scattered around the crash site. Then a deep rumbling started as thousands of tonnes of snow and ice broke free of the rocky pinnacles above. A monstrous avalanche crashed down the slopes of the Massif like a glacial tidal wave. When it was over there was no sign of the impact, the once pristine snowy slopes now ploughed and untidy, concealed the entire event. Ranjit and Stella's mangled bodies were buried forever deep in a frosty Antarctic tomb.

Chapter 20.

The lifeboat ejected from the shuttle when it was a kilometre above sea level. It popped out underneath the doomed shuttle and tumbled towards the stormy ocean below. Inside, Lee released the parachute and felt the pull as it inflated. It was still dropping on an angled trajectory, boosted by the shuttle's momentum. He would hit the sea hard, despite the deployed parachute. Lee hoped he would avoid hitting one of the many icebergs. He braced for impact, strapping himself into one of the cushioned seats. The lifeboat smacked into the ocean surface like a bullet. Its spherical design was not exactly streamlined and had never been designed to go crashing into the ocean at speed.

Lee felt the impact as a solid body blow, he shuddered against the restraints as the lifeboat plunged into the dark frigid waters. His internal fluids were fortified by the AI and adjusted quickly. There was a moment of absolute stillness and silence as the lifeboat reached the lowest point of its plunge, then slowly started to float to the surface.

The lifeboat had ballast under the seats to provide some balance but as Lee unscrewed the hatch the lifeboat rocked back and forth in the heavy ocean swell. He pushed the hatch open and climbed up to have a look outside. His head was immediately blasted by the freezing wind, horizontal rain, and sea spray. He was relieved to have dodged the icebergs floating heavily around him. As a swell lifted him momentarily Lee could see a small boat making its way towards him, with its parent vessel behind. He looked around and noticed an identical boat approaching from the opposite direction then both disappeared behind the big rolling swells. The wind and rain howled in his ears and the sea rumbled thunderously. Lee noticed another roaring sound in the cacophony. Above him, two large black rotary copters were descending out of the clouds. They hovered menacingly above, surveying the scene.

Lee retreated into the lifeboat, thinking fast. John had obviously decided his story was intriguing enough to send the Black Robin vessels to intercept him, but the copters must be from BPI. There was a loud clang as a grappling hook crashed through the hatch and caught on the edge. He climbed up again and saw the boat banging into the side of the shuttle. Four figures in heavy yellow raincoats were gesturing at him to jump aboard. Thirty meters above Lee saw several black figures on the edge of the hovering copters ready to abseil down. He had had to move quickly. Lee carefully climbed out on top, clinging to the hatch as the ocean swell washed over him. He held the rope and judged the swell, leaping onto the side of the boat. Strong arms grabbed him and hauled him over the side just as another swell tore the rope from his hands. He caught a glimpse of the hovering VLRs, the downward blast of their rotors whipping sea spray into his eyes.

Lee was bundled into the dory boat as it quickly turned, twin outboards screaming, it punched its way back to the big black parent vessel. The VLRs stayed directly above the boat. One of the men on the boat was yelling at Lee, it was too loud to hear what he was saying but Lee could understand, he could read the man's lips.

"Who the fuck are they?" he gestured towards the VLRs.

"BPI," Lee said, too quiet for the man to hear.

"What do they want?"

Lee realized it wasn't just the man's lips he could read. He could read his mind, and he could project his thoughts directly into the man's brain.

'They want me,' he said without opening his mouth.

"What..., what the fuck did you just do?"

Lee didn't answer. This was the first person he had met on Earth and he could read his mind. He looked at the other three crewmen, hunched over in their raincoats, wrestling with the outboard. He could look into all their heads. Scattered thoughts, confusion, tremulous questions about their mysterious passenger and the unwanted attention from above. But overriding those thoughts, a determination to get back to the safety of their big old trawler, an acute awareness of how dangerous the sea can be. The man stared at him, shook his head and turned his attention towards the black boat they were rapidly approaching.

They pulled alongside and secured themselves with grappling hooks as ladders were thrown to them. They clung to the ladders as the trawler pitched and rolled through the erratic swells. Anxious faces peered over the railing as Lee and the crew clambered to the relative safety of the trawler. The VLRs were still above, watching and waiting with Masama ready to descend. Lee was quickly ushered onto the bridge.

"I suppose I should say welcome aboard the Christobal II, but who are you and what the hell have you got us into?" roared a large burly man, an acrid smelling cigarette hanging from his lip. "And who the fuck are they!" He pointed at the hovering VLRs.

"BPI tracked me here. I am sorry; I should surrender to them before they attack."

"BPI! Well, any enemy of those bastards is a friend of ours. John didn't tell us much, just someone might need to be rescued at these coordinates."

"You're outgunned and have nowhere to hide. You should throw me back in the ocean."

He could see the dilemma in the ship captain's mind. Give Lee up to the hated evil empire or incur the wrath of the Masama by trying to protect him. "Listen, they won't go away. They will destroy you if they have to." Lee urged the captain. "You can't protect me."

Everyone on the bridge was holding onto something as the trawler navigated the big swells and hazardous floating icebergs. The deck was wet and slippery, tipping dangerously but the crew stood firm as if they were bolted to the floor.

"They won't attempt to abseil down here, not in this weather."

The man was trying to reassure himself, but Lee could sense the underlying nervousness in him and his crew. They were used to confrontational situations with adversaries more powerful than themselves. David and Goliath battles with big auto-line boats, sabotaging their gear and harassing them out of the toothfish grounds. They loved the challenge and the danger but the worst the auto-liners could do apart from ramming them was spray them with high-pressure hoses, the VLRs had more effective weaponry.

It was not in their nature to back down to anyone, especially to the ultimate enemy, Benevolent Progress Inc.

"Skipper," one of the crewmen from the dory boat spoke. "I know this sounds crazy but out on the dory..., he read my mind. I'm sure of it. I..., I could feel him in my brain. It was weird!"

"Read your mind, hey?" the captain smirked. "Think you've been at sea too long lad, next you'll be telling me mermaids are real."

"It's true captain, he answered my question without opening his mouth! He just..., just spoke into my head!"

"Truly! Well then what am I thinking now?" the captain turned to Lee.

Lee could read the captain's thoughts; he was tempted to take on the menacing VLRs, thinking what a scalp that would be. But before he could say anything a crewman cried, "Skip!" He was pointing out a rain-streaked window.

One of the VLRs had peeled off and was approaching the other trawler, just visible over the rise and fall of the ocean swell. As they watched in horror, the VLR unleashed a missile directly into the side of the other ship at point blank range. Lee heard the dull crash of explosion before the Christobal IV exploded in a ferocious plume of black smoke and steam. The bow and stern of the ship could both be seen angling upwards on either side of the smoke, fire, and steam raging from the middle of the ship. The missile had cut the ship in half. It was sinking rapidly.

"Fuck!" screamed the captain. "Get over there now, full speed!" And with a hateful glare at Lee, "throw him overboard, they want him that badly they can fish him out!"

Two crewmen grabbed Lee and roughly bundled him out the door. Lee could have resisted; he knew he was stronger than he looked but he stayed passive. He understood they blamed him for their comrade's deaths. They were right. Christobal II swung around towards their rapidly sinking sister ship, engines grinding below, the bow smashing through the oncoming swell. Lee did not need to be thrown overboard, he climbed up onto the railing and without hesitation leapt into the freezing waters below. A few meters under the water, everything was calm and quiet compared to the surface. Cold salty oblivion. Lee looked down at the black depths beneath him, thought momentarily what an amazing alien environment it was, full of strange creatures living down there in the dark with antifreeze for blood before he kicked his way up to the surface. He broke through the waves just in time to see the Christobal II steaming away. The captain was standing behind the railing with a lifebuoy in his hand.

Lee could just hear him scream, "Fuck yooouu," as he hurled the lifebuoy into the sea not far from where he was treading water. He swam over to the lifebuoy and lifted it over his head, arms over each side. He was a lot heavier than he used to be but still buoyant. Despite the decimation of the Christobal IV, which he knew he had caused, the captain of its sister ship still felt compelled to save his life.

Lee could not see much floating on the surface. Each ocean swell looked like a cliff face approaching. He was surrounded by walls of water flecked with chunks of iceberg that rode the swells with him. Between the waves, he could see nothing. At the top of each swell, he had a brief view of the stern of the Christobal II, fighting its way towards the remains of its sister ship and her crew. The Christobal IV had all but disappeared, just the bow was still thrusting vertically out of the waves. Lee thought he could see a few bodies still clinging to the bow. A few survivors at least. The water around the sinking vessel was a turbid soup of burning debris, ice and released air mixing with small red stains. Above him, the VLR that had destroyed the old trawler shifted slightly in the air and pointed its nose at the other ship. It hovered there, monitoring the approach of the vessel, oblivious to the howling winds that tore past. The other VLR stayed directly above Lee, neither of them seemed in too much of a hurry to do anything.

The water was freezing but Lee had already adjusted his metabolism to cope. Eventually, the VLR above him lowered a thick nylon cable with a metal clip attached. It splashed into the water a few meters away. Lee had no choice. He paddled over and attached the clip to the lifebuoy. He threaded it through the rope around the lifebuoy and clipped it back on to the cable above creating a cradle. He held on tightly as he felt the cable take the strain and he was hauled, dripping, out of the water. His precarious cradle swung wildly beneath the VLR as it was winched up through the wind and rain.

As he spun around above the waves, he looked over to the wreckage of the Christobal IV. All was left were a few burning patches of oil on the surface, pieces of mangled and twisted wreckage among the fractured icebergs, some blackened by the blast. Several bodies, still alive, clung to the wreckage. He could also see corpses, floating face down, red streaks of blood dissipating around them. The Christobal II had reached the wreckage; its crew were throwing lifebuoys and ropes over the side to try to haul in the survivors. Then the VLR fired another missile.

The explosion was tremendous. This time the VLR had aimed for the stern of the Christobal II where the fuel tanks were. Lee had a brief impression of the missile cutting a fiery path to the ship before a huge detonation, a boiling explosion of smoke and flame billowing up then carried away by the gale force winds. Bits of debris flew high into the air. Lee saw a piece a railing hurtling past with a severed human arm still attached. The stern of the ship was engulfed in roaring flames and black smoke. The flames burning across the sea, blown flat by the winds. Then abruptly the stern disappeared under the waves with a hissing sound and plumes of steam were whipped away. Fire still raged across the remains of the ship, scorching any survivors but it was sinking fast.

Lee watched as one crewman, engulfed in flames but still thrashing wildly about, threw himself into the ocean. He did not resurface. In a matter of seconds, the bow of the Christobal II had also disappeared under the waves. There did not appear to be any survivors. Lee noticed a large flat iceberg, almost as big as the dory boat that had rescued him. There were two bodies that had managed to climb up onto the icy platform. They were both lying face down, holding on to each other. The white iceberg was slowly turning red beneath them.

Lee swung around violently beneath the VLR as he was winched up towards the waiting Masama. He was shattered by the events and wracked with guilt. The crew of the Christobal ships had been murdered. Anyone that survived the wrecked ships would only last minutes in the freezing stormy ocean. It was his fault. They were all Black Robin people, the same people he had indirectly contacted asking for help and now they were all dead. When plotting his entry through the atmosphere, aiming for Australia, he did not think Lago and his henchmen would mobilize quickly enough to follow him to the Antarctic. Especially at the speed he was travelling. He had underestimated them. Innocent people had died. All his newfound intelligence, insight and perception had proved useless. He was betrayed by his own flawed decision making and overconfidence. Perhaps he had been changed too much by the AI and he had ignored his own basic human instinct of questioning himself.

Lee was almost at the VLR, thoughts were swirling around in his enhanced brain. He now knew what a huge task there was for him to try to change Lago, his corrupt corporation and the murderous, mindless, inhuman Masama. Anger and resentment boiled inside him. He was powerful, he knew. He had yet to test these powers, he did not know what he was capable of, but after watching so many Black Robin people die, he was now even more determined to enforce a revolution whether Earths population wanted it or not.

The winch raised Lee level with the hovering VLR. Clinging to the frozen lifebuoy, swinging from the cable in the howling winds, he was eye level with his captors. He regarded the Masama staring impassively back at him through the weather. They all looked alike, slightly different augmentations but the same black-clad human-machine hybrids. All aggression and attitude, steel and station. They raised their weapons at him; Lee had a fleeting impression of liquid jet nozzles primed before he was coated with a freezing spray. He just had time to register it was liquid helium before his body seized, rigid. It was beyond cold, it burnt quickly to his core, rapidly slowing his organs, blood flow, and biological brain function. The liquid nanoparticles flowing in his veins slowed, thickened and froze solid with the rest of him. His last thoughts were; 'I'm going to die again.'

Chapter 21.

Raymond looked down at the debris. Pieces of mangled and twisted steel, blackened from the explosions, ropes, deck equipment and even pots and pans from the galley were floating with the body parts and ice, tossed about in the malevolent whitewater. Burning patches of oil mingled with the blood. The wholesale destruction had shocked him. He knew the Masama had a fearsome reputation, cold and callous, take no prisoners. But there was no need to kill the crew of both ships. They could have easily overpowered and taken them captive without the bloodshed. But that was not how they operated, that was why people feared them. He should have expected no less. What unnerved him most was it was all done in silence, not a word was spoken as the missiles found their targets and their captive was hauled from the ocean.

They were his people, he thought. Black Robin people. Good people trying to make the world a better place. Cut down just because they were in the wrong place at the wrong time. Raymond did not betray any outward emotion but internally he was crushed with sadness and impotent frustration. It was crucial to keep these emotions in check and he was again thankful he had managed to avoid the implant transmitter. He surely would not have been able to hide these apoplectic thoughts from the Masama telepaths. There was nothing he could have done to save the crew without jeopardizing his mission, but was his mission worth the lives of all those Black Robin people? He would have to make it so. The turmoil of angry sad emotions inside him almost made him physically sick. He swallowed the bilious feelings and stored them deep in his gut with the rest of his buried traumas.

The man's name was Lee Xiang; he was frozen solid, dangling from the gantry. They had quickly identified him and found nothing remarkable, in fact completely the opposite. He was a low-ranking printer technician, a BPI minion. It was what was inside him that made him interesting. He was a lot heavier than he looked. They hauled his frozen body in and secured it at the back of the VLR. Arms still splayed rigid across the cracked and broken lifebuoy. His mouth open, caught in an expression of sadness and bewilderment. Raymond could see the pain etched into his face.

They attached sensors to him to monitor the temperature, but it would take a long time to thaw from minus three hundred degrees. The second before he had been frozen, Raymond had looked in the man's eyes and seen something there, a flicker of recognition perhaps. It was a fleeting impression, but Raymond had the image burned into his brain. Those black eyes did not seem human, but they had acknowledged him. Something fell from the man's frozen hand and rolled towards Raymond. It was a small button, Raymond picked it up without anyone noticing and pocketed it, he would study it later.

The VLRs turned to head North at a more sedate speed. Raymond watched the icebergs as they gained altitude. The big ones sculpted into weird aesthetic shapes by the winds and sea spray. Arching curvature, perfectly rounded holes and gravity-defying, top-heavy monstrosities. As they moved away from the wild

Antarctic weather, there were fewer icebergs and the water turned a friendlier shade of blue. There was no land in sight on any horizon.

"Where are we headed?" Raymond asked Lance, seated across from him.

"To a factory ship in the Pacific, Lago is there waiting."

The VLRs droned on for another hour before Raymond noticed a change in the rotors. They started slowing down and losing altitude. Raymond saw a hulking grey rectangular shape in the water ahead. It sat there in the blue sea like a land mass, huge, dark and permanent. A lot bigger than the Hanjin Harmony. The VLR flew close to the hull, below the deck level. Raymond could make out the name 'Benevolent 1' painted in huge letters on the side. He had a momentary flashback to years ago when he had painted the side of another factory ship. It was like flying alongside a mountain before they swooped over the top of the deck and settled gently on a landing pad near the stern of the ship. The rotors wound down as they stepped out of the VLR. The Masama lethargically stood around the landing pad, bored with yet another mission where they were not physically tested, thought Raymond. He realized how loud the rotors had been once they stopped, and the silence started throbbing in his ears.

A door opened on the ship bulkhead and Lago Santos appeared, flanked by four more Masama. He made straight for the VLR where their frozen captive was propped up against the hatch, still clinging on to broken bits of frozen lifebuoy. Raymond was gripped with nervous tension and panicked indecision as Lago walked closer. This was the first time he had seen the man he was intending to kill. He was battling to keep his anger and grief hidden, still upset about the multiple deaths on the cold seas of Scott Island. And here was the chief protagonist, the arrogant, murderous mastermind of BPI walking towards him.

Raymond quickly weighed up his options, could he attempt to assassinate Lago Santos right now? Surrounded by all these tooled up Masama with their lightning fast reactions? He knew he would be killed instantly, probably before he even got close to Lago. He did not have any weapons on him. He would have to wrestle something lethal from a soldier or try to beat Lago to death with his bare fists. The second option appealed but common sense prevailed. Lago breezed past him within touching distance as Raymond fought to keep his emotions in check. Fists clenched so hard his fingernails drew blood.

"So, this is the pathetic excuse for a human that has been causing me all these problems," Lago muttered, staring at Lee from a distance. "I should just reduce him to dust and sweep him overboard, but I suppose we had better find out what's inside." Lago stepped closer inspecting Lee's frozen visage. "He looks to be in good condition for being frozen alive; oh well not for much longer." He turned and looked around at the Masama as if he had only just noticed them. "Come on then, get him strung up in the lab so we can get started."

Raymond watched as four Masama equipped with thick gloves picked up Lee's frozen stiff body as a steel gurney was put underneath. They seemed to struggle initially, Lee was heavier than expected but they soon had him strapped on the gurney and wheeled off into the bowels of the huge factory ship. The entourage of Masama followed, Raymond joined Lance and Goran striding purposefully behind.

"Rutger, you will join the security detail in the lab. We need to be prepared for any eventuality when he's thawed out, meet us there in one hour," said Lance.

"Ok," Raymond confirmed, as he followed the Masama to the mess hall.

The hall had everything the Masama needed for sustenance. Foods and liquids, lubricants and tools to maintain their equipment and plenty of ammunition in a well-stocked armoury. Raymond looked around at the off-duty soldiers. They had not had to do anything strenuous on their flight to the Antarctic apart from blow up a couple of ships and freeze their captive. They relaxed around the mess hall, fiddling with their weapons, some eating unappetizing looking brown nutrient bars, drinking lurid green protein shakes or hooking up to IV feeds. The only sounds were the clink of metal weapons and booted footsteps.

Raymond noticed Odetta and the burly Batac sitting at a table by themselves and went to join them. Odetta ignored him but Batac acknowledged him with a cursory glance and a scowl.

"Here's our racist Yahpie," Batac muttered. "Fucking hate racists."

Raymond glared at him for a moment. He was still tense with anger and did not entirely trust his emotions, but he had been playing the part of Rutger a long time now. He sighed and stared evenly at Batac. "I don't give a shit what you think, but that's an extremely racist attitude."

Batac glared back at Raymond with furious intensity. Raymond held his stare until he was sure this would end in violence when Batac abruptly burst into loud laughter. It did not sound much like laughter, more a series of barking shouts but the big Philippino had a wide smile on his face.

"It's true, I am a racist motherfucker also, we all are!" His laughter turned into a hacking cough and he banged the table with a big meaty fist. It was by far the biggest display of emotion Raymond had seen from a Masama soldier and he was somewhat taken aback. Odetta turned away in disgust and concentrated on her auto-gun. Batac abruptly stopped coughing and eyed Raymond with intent. "You have not had the implant installed yet huh?"

"No, not yet." Raymond was wary.

"It changes you."

"So I understand. Telepathy would do that." Raymond wondered where Batac was going with this.

"Makes you less human, more machine."

Raymond looked at him again thinking there was something slightly wrong with this man, something unhinged behind his eyes. "You don't have the implant?"

Batac turned his head and pointed to an old burn scar just behind his ear where no hair grew. "I was one of the first," he rasped in a gravelly monotone. "It didn't work; my brain was too powerful for their little gadget. I melted it with the power of my thoughts!" Batac's laugh sounded like rocks cracking together.

Raymond looked at him thinking the implant was not the only thing that had melted.

"No telepathy for me, but I don't need it. I know what these assholes will do even before they do it."

Odetta briefly looked at him and rolled her eyes scornfully. Batac leaned in towards Raymond and said earnestly. "I have been with Lago from the start. I have killed hundreds for him. I have been a loyal soldier and I will be with him till I die." He leaned back and said cryptically. "He looks after me."

"Don't you think a telepathic implant will make you a better soldier?" Raymond was genuinely curious.

"Fuck no!" Batac was adamant. "I'm just as fast and just as mean as this lot." He leaned in again, "they are turning into something else, something I don't want to be a part of."

"What do you mean by that?" Raymond wanted to know.

"Don't listen to him," Odetta interrupted. "The deranged old fucker is talking out his ass."

Batac sat back in his chair, shook his head and muttered, "Pek-pek mo."

"What do you mean, turning into something else?" Raymond repeated his question.

Before Batac could answer a chime rang to summon them to the lab. Batac rose quickly, appearing relieved to have avoided the question.

Raymond stood behind a thick plexiglass partition with Odetta, Batac, Goran and four other Masama. Lago was in front of them, staring through the plexiglass at the operating room. Raymond could see the beads of sweat on his neatly-groomed neck. Two years infiltrating BPI and now he was close enough to touch his target. Again, he entertained thoughts of a quick assassination, how good it would feel to have his hands around that neck, squeezing.

Behind the partition was a medical laboratory that looked more like a high-tech torture chamber. Gantries fixed to the ceiling bristled with equipment. Razor sharp scalpel blades, lasers, bone saws and a multitude of specialist tools Raymond did not recognize. Stainless steel trays and benches filled with various sized vials, syringes, and solutions were placed strategically around the operating room.

In the middle of the room lay their naked captive, limp and not breathing. He had thawed as he lay on a steel tray. Robust metal cables secured his arms, legs, and neck. His eyes and mouth were closed. Probes and patches covered his body, their wires leading to monitors showing little activity. Inside the lab, Lance and two medical personnel hovered around their equipment, cloaked in white protective clothing and full-face masks. There was an air of hyper-vigilance over everyone as the medics readied themselves to begin. Raymond watched Lance move as far away from the operating theatre as possible, up against the wall, hoping to be out of harm's way.

One of the medics readied a giant empty syringe and lined up a vein in Lee's forearm ready to draw blood. The instant the syringe pierced his flesh Lee opened his eyes, looked at the medic and said, "Please don't."

The medic raised his arm in astonishment, the syringe was dripping red blood. He looked back over his shoulder at Lance who said simply, "Proceed."

"Mr. Murphy," Lee spoke louder this time. "Why do you want my blood?"

Lance took a few tentative steps towards the operating theatre. "For testing, we want to know how you survived your ordeal in space, not to mention being frozen just now."

"You don't have to restrain me; I will gladly donate some blood. In the interests of cooperation."

"How do you know my name?"

"Release me and we can talk."

"Not going to happen. You are an unknown quantity; a risk and I don't have to explain myself." Turning to the medic again, "proceed." Lance ordered.

Raymond watched intently as the medic re-inserted the syringe into Lee's bloody arm.

"Very well," Lee sighed.

Raymond heard a quiet voice say his name. He looked around, but no one was paying any attention to him.

"Raymond." The voice said again.

He hadn't heard his real name for a long time. In a state of shock, he looked around, thinking his cover had been blown and expecting a confrontation. But he only received a quizzical look from Odetta standing next to him. Lago turned his head slightly, frowned, then turned back to the scene inside the lab.

"Don't be alarmed, this is Lee. I am communicating telepathically. Don't say anything, just subvocalize. Act as if nothing is happening."

"Lee," thought Raymond. "How... how are you?" Was all he could think of to say. He was still not convinced this was actually happening. The more likely explanation was he had gone slightly insane, hearing voices in his head.

"I am recovering from being frozen, thanks for asking and you are not going insane, trust me. I am talking to you because I know you are from Black Robin. You are my ally."

"You know what? How?"

"As well as telepathic communication, I can read your mind. I'm sorry I know it sounds intrusive, but I had to be sure. You have kept Raymond well hidden."

Raymond was struggling with this form of communication. Especially as he was standing right behind Lago. After spending his whole life talking noisily and listening to others do the same it was difficult to conduct a conversation in his head and believe it to be real. It seemed to him the others must be able to hear their words, but they all stood in silence watching the medic draw blood from Lee's arm.

"What are you?" thought Raymond.

"I am human, but I have been changed."

"Changed into what?" Raymond had been briefed on Lee's supposed AI infection in the shuttle and had just witnessed him survive the deep freeze.

"I'm not entirely sure, I do seem to be able to find the answers to questions, solutions to problems, I can read minds, I am stronger, and I heal faster. I am host to what could be described as an intelligent agent, something that was indirectly created by humans. We are still only days old, but we are learning fast."

"Host? You mean you were infected or invaded?" Raymond was repulsed by the idea.

"It saved my life. A BPI drone hit us with an electromagnetic effector in the shuttle. Killed us all and left us for dead, but with the help of my companion, I woke up. HEMI is part of me now Raymond, we are learning to live with each other."

"Why are you talking to me?"

"As I said, you are my ally. You are Black Robin. I contacted John when I was in orbit to rendezvous in the Antarctic. Now all those good people are dead, I am responsible. I will make amends. Will you help me?"

"You contacted John?" repeated Raymond as he watched the medics remove the syringe from Lee's arm full of normal looking blood and insert it into several different receptacles for testing.

"Wait, can the Masama hear us?" Raymond looked around nervously.

"Different frequency. Raymond, I know you have lots of questions, but we don't have much time. After these medics have finished taking my blood, they will attempt to drill into my brain and remove a core of brain tissue. I am not keen for that to happen."

"You were supposed to be frozen solid and anaesthetised."

"I was frozen, I should have been dead twice, but I find myself still alive. It's easy enough for me to bypass the drugs they have given me. I am not giving them any information. I know this must be hard for you to believe. We are not alone Raymond, Odetta is also our ally."

"Odetta?" Raymond turned and looked incredulously at the woman standing next to him. At the same time, Odetta also turned and stared at Raymond with the same disbelieving expression.

"Odetta is also Black Robin; I am speaking to her simultaneously. I know both of you have been undercover for years, slowly working towards your goals but now events are accelerating. Help me now and together we will change the world." Lee's grandiose words were clear and strong in Raymond's head.

This was a lot to take in and there was no time to procrastinate. Raymond was thinking frantically, and he quickly concluded there was more chance of assassinating Lago and damaging BPI if he decided to help the enigmatic Lee. It was a risk, but he had always liked risks. He looked back at Odetta and it appeared she had come to the same conclusion. She nodded, a worried smile on her thin red lips.

"What next?" thought Raymond.

"I will create a distraction among the Masama next to you, while Batac is trying to deal with it I need you to come into the operating room and disarm Lance. Goran's priority will be Lago's safety. After that, just follow my instructions."

"Shit ok." Raymond tensed his body ready to move and sensed Odetta was doing the same.

All attention was on the medics preparing a nasty looking cylindrical cutting tool for drilling into Lee's head when without warning, all four Masama behind Raymond started attacking each other. They moved with blinding speed. Limbs flashing, battering metal and flesh. It looked as if all four Masama were fighting against each other. They were not using weapons, just brute force powered by their exoskeletons, more than enough to inflict considerable damage. Within seconds there were bits of metal, blood and fluid splashing to the floor. Batac yelled and tried to force his way into the frenzied violence, pulling the soldiers apart. The Masama ignored him and carried on trying to destroy each other. The close quarter's combat was taking its toll as one Masama collapsed in a bleeding broken heap.

Lago stood startled, confused and obviously frightened for a second before shouting. "What are you doing? Goran! control this rabble, what the fuck is going on!"

Goran did not move at all. Raymond and Odetta stealthily made for the door to the operating room, they were almost there when Goran moved in front of them and grabbed Odetta's arm.

"Where are you going?" he intoned without moving his head.

Raymond went to aim a kick at Goran's back and felt his head singed by a searing blue laser emanating from the side of Goran's optical field. He staggered back just as Odetta unleashed a vicious elbow to Goran's neck. Raymond followed up with a more successful kick in the back. Goran staggered and fell into Lago, propelling them both towards the brawling Masama. Goran sprayed bolts of blue laser fire around the room, searing the ceiling and narrowly missing Odetta.

Lago was on the floor in a tangle of bodies and liquids, screaming obscenities as the preoccupied Masama continued to destroy each other. Raymond and Odetta burst through the door and Odetta was instantly on the flustered and confused Lance, knocking him out cold with one powerful blow to the side of the head. She smiled with satisfaction.

Lee was sitting up ripping the patches and probes from his body, the cables that had restrained him disappearing back under the tray. The two medics sat nervously in the corner, watching the violent commotion.

Lee then stood naked before them. "Time to go," he said out loud.

Odetta looked around for anything that could be used as a weapon. She spied a tray containing some vicious looking bonesaws. She grabbed a small battery powered one with a sharp spinning blade at the end of the steel handle. They ran back through the observation room. Batac and Goran were both wrestling with the three standing Masama in a blur of metal and limbs. Lago was just regaining his feet, slipping on the blood-soaked floor, boiling with rage. Goran managed to regain his composure and free himself from the bloody fracas. He fired a couple of laser bolts in their direction, narrowly missing Raymond as he lunged forward. Odetta moved like lightning, flying towards Goran and burying the spinning blade of the bonesaw deep up and into his throat. The blade cut cleanly through his windpipe as Odetta's momentum pushed it up into Goran's neck. He fell, frothing blood from his mouth and through the vertical cut on his throat. He grabbed the bonesaw and pulled it back out through the wound, hurling it in Odetta's direction while spraying blue laser fire erratically at their retreating figures.

They burst out into the corridor "Straight ahead!" shouted Lee. "Make for the VLRs!"

Raymond raced through the narrow corridors, strangely deserted. Automated doors opened for them and closed behind them. They burst into the bright sunlight of the expansive deck and ran to one of the VLRs. Lee jumped into the pilot seat and fired up the rotors, Odetta and Raymond dived into the open hatch. Just as the VLR was leaving the platform Lago burst through the bulkhead door, flanked by many more Masama. The soldiers immediately began firing, mostly projectiles, but Lee expertly piloted the VLR up and over the edge of the hull, out of the line of sight and down to almost sea level where he opened the throttles and powered away across the placid Pacific Ocean.

Chapter 22.

Lee piloted the VLR a few meters above the surface of the calm ocean. Its rotors blasted a trail of spray behind them as the dark bulk of Benevolent 1 faded into the sun-bleached horizon.

"I hope I've done the right thing," muttered Raymond under his breath.

"Raymond, Odetta." Odetta introduced herself, hand extended.

Raymond shook her hand and felt an immense burden fall from his shoulders. He no longer had to pretend to be Rutger. For over two years he had kept his true identity hidden, playing the part of the thuggish mercenary, immersing himself in the vile character so thoroughly sometimes he forgot who he was. Now it was over, he could let his guard down. He felt lighter as if he had lost some physical weight. His head spun with his old personality resurfacing, full of questions.

Underlying everything was the distressing feeling he had abandoned his mission after two years of intense undercover work, just when he was getting close to Lago. "Odetta," he said, shaking her hand awkwardly.

"What the fuck have we got ourselves into?" She asked looking at Lee.

Raymond shrugged and looked at their pilot, still naked, manipulating the VLR controls. They were gaining altitude, ascending into the bright blue cloudless skies. He had many questions, he asked the simplest one. "Where are we going?"

"We just flew over Easter Island; the factory ship was in the South Pacific heading for Santiago."

Raymond realized he was still hearing Lee's voice telepathically. "Please, talk like a normal person, your voice in my head is too much at the moment."

"Apologies," Lee shouted out loud. "I thought we would head for Canada. We can meet with John and make plans. Black Robin has an extensive network in Canada. It's a good place to hide.

"BPI will be after us, Lago will take this personally," said Odetta.

"They have two VLRs in pursuit from Benevolent 1, but I can lose them."

"Biggest corporation on the planet after us with the Masama itching for a fight. Is Canada the best option? We might lead them straight to Black Robin." Raymond pointed out.

"We don't need to worry about that now; I have plans for when they get closer." Lee did not elaborate.

Raymond looked at their pilot. Naked, pale and skinny. Black hair and black eyes. Frostbitten fingers and toes twitching on the VLR controls. He found a plastic poncho behind the seat and tossed it at Lee. "Only clothing we have I'm afraid."

Lee looked down at himself as if only noticing his nudity for the first time. "Oh sorry, I hope I'm not making you uncomfortable. I may have the odd lapse when it comes to basic human niceties." He glanced over his shoulder.

"I don't mind," said Odetta. "Seen much worse."

"Why is Lago this desperate to capture you, what exactly are you Lee?" Asked Raymond.

"I am still mostly biological, but a small piece of an artificial intelligence entered my bloodstream and saved my life. It was conceived inside the printer OS on the Moon, it's called HEMI. More energy than mechanics, but it has made me stronger both physically and mentally. To what extent I am still not sure. I am yet to discover the range of my capabilities. Remember I am only a couple of days old. I suspect Lago intended to exploit my enhancements, turn me into a weapon of some kind."

"Did you cause the Masama to attack each other?" asked Raymond.

"Yes, when I got close I found I could hack their telepathic network without them knowing it. I made them believe their companions were threats. They are used to reacting instinctively to the sensory information they receive telepathically they have neglected the senses they were born with, it was easy enough to trick them into fighting each other."

"But Goran and Batac?" asked Odetta. "You could not get into their heads?"

"No. Goran is linked with the Masama, but I could not sense his thoughts at all. He has some sort of firewall mechanism. I don't know what it is. Batac, as you know, is not connected, I can see into his head, but he is like a wild animal, his brain is disjointed and unpredictable."

"No argument there," agreed Odetta.

"If you can control the Masama, why didn't you just have them attack and kill Lago?" asked Raymond.

Lee sighed and glanced back at them both. "When I was hanging from the rope above the ocean, witnessing the death and destruction of the Black Robin crew beneath me, I was devastated and furious - as you must have been. My human reaction was to strike back. A life for a life, an eye for an eye. But that is not the answer."

"Oh, don't give me that crap!" Odetta spat. "Killing is not the answer... Lago is a monster! Getting rid of him and his asshole thugs would be doing the world a favour."

"I have to agree," said Raymond. "Killing Lago would make the world a better place; it's what we have been working towards for years."

"I understand how you feel but you must look at the bigger picture. There will be another Lago, and another, then another dictator even worse than Lago and do we try to kill them all? Earth has suffered enough killing and enough wars. History has proven this endless cycle of violence and revenge does not work. It just makes us better and more efficient at killing each other. It turns us into our own worst enemies. Things have to change."

"That is total bullshit!" Odetta gave her customary sneer. "Things have to change? How do you propose to get assholes like Lago to change? You should have killed him while you had the chance."

"Wouldn't it be much more effective? For Lago to stop his polluting and exploitation? For him to use his power and wealth to help people and help the planet? With his resources and influence, we could pull it back from the brink of destruction. Think what an example that would be to the rest of the world, if a tyrant such as Lago can be transformed into a caring conscientious leader. He wanted to use me, now I intend to use him"

"Don't be ridiculous. He will never change; you don't know what you are talking about," argued Odetta. "When he mowed down your friends with the harvester on the Moon, that was just him having a bit of fun, for his entertainment. He is a sick and twisted megalomaniac. You can't change him." She was angry and exasperated at their missed opportunity.

"I'm not talking about simply changing his mind; I'm talking about changing his mind," said Lee.

There was silence in the cabin as Raymond digested this cryptic statement. Odetta shook her head and mumbled curses under her breath. They saw a land mass appearing ahead of them. "What's ahead?" Raymond changed the subject. "Central America?"

"Panama, we will head North over the Caribbean then up the Eastern seaboard to Quebec."

"So, you think you're somehow going make Lago change into a better person? What other superpowers do you have?" asked Odetta, voice heavy with sarcasm.

"I don't care if you believe me or not, but I know I am right. You are both free to do whatever you choose when we land. You are not indebted in any way. I appreciate your help and if you choose to stay by my side we will prevail, but you must trust me."

Raymond and Odetta sat in silence exchanging frustrated looks. The tension was tangible. "Odetta," said Raymond. "Was it also your mission to try to kill Lago?"

"No, I was originally part of Goran's crew. Recruited a long time ago in Mexico although I didn't have much choice at the time. Black Robin covertly approached me soon after and convinced me to spy on my new employer, give them warning of Masama activities and BPI projects. I'm not sure if my information was acted upon or not. But the longer I was there, the more I was trusted, the more valuable I became. I was supposed to be extracted before all this..." She gestured vaguely at Lee. "But then I was sent to the Moon and things started moving too fast."

"How long have you been undercover?"

"Too fucking long, longer than I ever expected and long enough to know we should have killed Lago when we had the chance!" She said raising her voice and glaring at the back of Lee's head. "But I guess that opportunity is now long gone, no longer our problem."

"We might get another chance," muttered Raymond. "You are telepathically linked, right? How did you keep your identity secret?"

"The implanted transmitter is only linked to specific parts of the brain. The sensory cortex, motor cortex the frontal lobe, cerebellum... I forget what else. It only utilizes those areas involved with the senses, and muscle movements. The rest of your brain, the bits that look after memories, emotions, and reasoning are not connected to the transmitter."

"I was due for an implant; I thought they would read my mind and blow my cover." Raymond looked out at the narrow isthmus below. Panama, the thin thread of land connecting two continents passed beneath them.

"I was connected all the time, but I was never worried about them finding my secrets, when we were operating as a team, telepathically, that was all there was. There were no emotions, no memories. I forgot who I was when I was operating on that level and some of them are that deep all the time. The Masama are... I don't know how to put it. Batac was right; they are turning into something not entirely human. They just do not use those emotional parts of the brain anymore; they think they are far superior to your average human. They treat anyone not on their telepathic wavelength with scorn and contempt. They are living in their own world most of the time."

"Well put Odetta," interrupted Lee. "They are living in their own world and they are becoming less human because they are not using parts of the brain that make us human. It is pure reaction to stimulation, biomechanics and risk-reward. When I tapped into their telepathic network it was like machine code, no reasoning, no emotion."

"Tell me about it, dullest bunch of bastards I have ever come across, but when you are operating permanently in their structured telepathic world you don't know any different, you don't know what you are missing."

"But I saw some of them smirking at Goran's new optical field," said Raymond. "That looked as if it could be humour."

"No just vanity; they are extremely narcissistic, and competitive. Obsessed with their own bodies, augments, and improvements. They spend all their spare time masturbating over weapon attachments. Goran does look ridiculous though."

"They are becoming more dangerous," said Lee. "That sort of collective conscious acting on instinct alone has the potential to spiral out of control. It may only be a matter of time before they decide they don't want to take orders from Lago. Could be dangerous for him as well as society at large."

"I think they need orders, they need some sort of direction and they enjoy the work Lago gives them," said Odetta.

"But you tapped into their telepathic link Lee, you can control them," said Raymond.

"Only when they are close enough, and only by fooling their senses. I don't think I could control them all, I don't think I would want to."

"Do you remember much of your life before you were infected with this AI, Lee?" asked Raymond. "Did you always have such a holistic view?"

"I don't see myself as infected and yes, I remember everything better than ever. I am still basically the same person - it's just that now I have instant access to the planet's entire database. I have the planet's knowledge, its recorded memories, as well as my own, and I seem to have unlimited brain capacity to digest it all."

"Well good for you, I hope your huge brain has filters. There is a hell of a lot of bullshit bogus information out there," said Odetta.

"I have had an incredibly well-developed sense of scepticism all my life and a healthy mistrust of everyone." Lee gave a smile. "But to answer your question, my old life was unambitious and uninteresting. I was one of the most boring people on Earth and the Moon. The most fun I had was on my own, standing on the surface of the Moon, trying to see the stars, wondering what I was looking at."

"And now you are going to try to change the world," said Odetta.

"Yes, speaking of which," interjected Raymond, "what are your plans, Lee? What do you intend to do when you meet the Black Robin people?"

"Ah, yes, well, hold on a minute... we have company. The two VLRs are gaining." Lee was studying the radar graphic. "I think I will try to lose them in Miami."

Lee banked the VLR, swooping lower towards the sparkling ocean below. They had just passed over Cuba and could see the long string of swampy mangroves that made up the Florida Keys. The islands were like a discarded trail of litter left behind by the mainland. It was a hot and sticky westerly wind in the Gulf of Mexico. Raymond watched the turquoise ocean zoom past fifty meters below as they sped towards the Straits of Florida.

"Two missiles launched, ETA eight seconds." Lee was calm as if he was doing a weather report.

Raymond looked back but could not see the missiles or the pursuing aircraft. A tense eight seconds ticked passed with Raymond expecting to be roasted alive in an explosive fireball any second. Nothing happened. "What happened to the missiles?"

"I had to let them get close before I could hack into their operating system and send them into the sea."

"How close?"

"About sixteen meters, same as the Masama. That seems to be about my range."

"Sixteen meters is a bit close for comfort."

"Four more missiles launched, this time I will try to send them back where they came from, see if that will deter our pursuers at all."

Raymond peered helplessly behind again but could see nothing but clear blue sky. The missiles were travelling too fast. Anxious seconds went by before he asked, "What happened?"

"I turned them around and sent them on a course to narrowly miss our chaperons, the missiles flew down each side of the VLR fuselage then exploded, missing by about twenty centimetres."

"Should put them off."

"No, they are still following, matching our speed, waiting to see where we go."

They banked east and hugged the coastline as the long thin string of islands grew more substantial and turned into a solid looking landmass. Raymond could see waves crashing on the golden shore below as they screamed overhead. Lee then banked west heading inland and he could see the skyscrapers of Miami looming ahead to the East. Still impressive, proudly glinting in the sunlight all these years after being abandoned. Rusted rooftops and caved in warehouses zipped past beneath them. The rotors whipped up spray from the stagnant brown water below.

Raymond watched Lee push the VLR faster and lower, narrowly missing the twisted antennas and battered satellite dishes protruding from the empty buildings. The buildings grew in height as they neared the city centre and Lee was now flying straight down the middle of submerged avenues and boulevards. They had fleeting glimpses of the carcasses of gutted apartment buildings on either side as they flew around corners, banking sharply with each turn, sending flocks of angry seagulls spiralling into the air.

"Where are they?" asked Raymond.

"Close, we will lose them in the city centre, strap yourselves in please."

They turned into a long straight, lined on either side with the crumbling facades of old art-deco buildings. The dirty brown salt water was eating away at the foundations of these once grand old buildings. A few had collapsed creating islands of rubble covered in guano.

Raymond caught glimpses of the VLRs bristling with weaponry, one right behind and the other above. Lee banked hard right towards the looming skyscrapers of the old city centre. They zoomed past the empty office buildings, dark towers of rusted steel and tainted concrete, all the glass and prefabs long since smashed and rotted, leaving only rusty red metal skeletons. Lee accelerated hard out of each corner coming within centimeters of the hollow buildings. Raymond strained against his seatbelt, fighting for equilibrium as Lee hurled the VLR into another sharp turn, then another. Lee sat unmoving and upright as if he was bolted to the seat. His flimsy poncho flapped around him.

"Credit to this pilot, they are keeping up with us," he muttered.

They entered a narrow cavernous street, rusting skyscrapers on either side and a grey concrete mountain at the end. Lee accelerated hard and straight towards the huge concrete building. Raymond closed his eyes and gritted his teeth, at the last second before impact, Lee pulled the protesting VLR up in a stomach-churning vertical climb. The fuselage gave off showers of sparks as they lightly kissed the concrete. Lee battled with the VLR controls, holding the craft in a vertiginous high-speed loop as it sped up and over. They flattened out upside down just in time to see the pursuing aircraft beneath them. One was following at enough distance to avoid smashing into the building. The other pulled up hard attempting the same manoeuvre as Lee.

The pursuing VLR almost made the steep climb, flying vertically up the side of the building. Close enough to rip away the missiles and weapon mounts on its underside in an explosion of sparks. It hugged the side of the building, bouncing off the surface and scraping its way to the top where it caught and twisted, smashing into the top floor. A spinning rotor blade broke free and ricocheted towards them at blinding speed. Before Raymond could even yell a warning, Lee wrenched the controls, but the blade smacked into the side of their VLR taking out one of the rotors. The wrecked VLR lost all momentum as its engines failed and it began falling back down the side of the skyscraper. It hit the shallow water below, landing upside down with a huge steaming splash.

Lee righted their crippled VLR and zoomed away, the remaining three rotors screamed as he wrestled with the controls. He executed another series of sickening twists and turns and wove a convoluted path through the watery streets of the old central city. The other pursuing VLR had lost its velocity and was now nowhere to be seen. Lee found a stable enough rooftop just above the waterline that was partly concealed by an old motorway flyover. He gently landed the VLR and powered down.

"They won't expect us to stop, we will wait here for a minute and inspect the damage."

The sun was setting in the west casting dark shadows across the waterways. Between the misshapen buildings, the sinking sun shone dark crimson on the dirty water reflecting a dramatic judgmental sunset. Raymond watched Lee try to repair their VLR. It did not appear to be badly damaged; one rotor blade was bent out of shape but not irreparable. "I can fix this," said Lee.

A large black crow launched from its vantage point on the flyover. Its ragged squawking bounced off the surrounding buildings, echoing down the street. Seabirds watched from their nests, perched in crumbling window frames. Their dried guano caked down the building frontages looked to be the only thing holding them together. Raymond sat in the bizarrely peaceful red Miami dusk. "Raised sea levels are bad for humans but good for the bird life."

"I guess they are a bit more adaptable than us," said Odetta.

"No reason why we can't adapt too," said Lee from underneath the VLR. "I think we're going to have to, adapt or die."

Odetta sat down next to Raymond as Lee continued. "There are some fringe communities here in Miami trying to adjust, living on the water, raising fish in sea cages. They are adapting although they are not at the top of the food chain anymore. The crocodiles and the alligators have also adapted to their environment."

Raymond nervously looked around at the dark water that surrounded them.

"That should do it," said Lee emerging from under their VLR. He had physically bent the rotor blade back into shape. "Also, I thought it might be time to give John a call." Lee climbed into the VLR and adjusted the comms until he had a signal. Raymond watched him close his eyes for a second then activate the microphone.

"Hello," John's filtered voice came through. "Lee is that you?"

"Yes, we are in Miami. I am with your colleagues Raymond and Odetta."

"So, first you lead BPI Masama directly to the rendezvous point in the Antarctic, resulting in the deaths of twenty-eight Black Robin people, now you have abducted my two best undercover operatives who were working their way closer to our objective. Blown their cover, endangered their lives too, and I suppose you want to be rescued?" yelled John through the tinny speaker.

"I am sorry for the deaths, there was no way I could have arrived on Earth undetected, but I won't make excuses. We need to meet."

"I should let you rot there but I need my people back."

Raymond had been scanning the broken cityscape, the last rays of washed out sunlight painting the buildings pink. He detected the movement just in time. "Incoming!" he screamed as the missile bore down on them.

There was a high-pitched screaming noise, Raymond and Odetta jumped clear of the VLR an instant before it was engulfed in a ferocious ball of flame. They flung themselves off the rooftop, the blast just searing them before they hit the shallow water and disappeared underneath. Raymond re-surfaced just in time to see the flaming body of Lee flying through the air. The thin poncho he had been wearing was ablaze and his head was on fire as he flew off the rooftop and into the water where he disappeared in a cloud of steam and sizzling noise.

The water was only head high but there was rubble and twisted metal underneath. The rooftop where they had been standing had been partially destroyed and the VLR fuselage had disappeared altogether, blown into pieces of steaming metal that sunk beneath the dark waters. Raymond looked around through the dissipating smoke as he found his footing but could not see the other VLR. It would not be far away. Odetta's head surfaced from the brackish water unscathed. They both looked around for Lee. Eventually, his head popped up, or what was left of it. The side of his face had been burnt badly. The skin around his eye socket and cheekbone had been cooked away exposing bone underneath. His cheek was ragged and bloody revealing his teeth behind the blisters and cauterized flesh. All the hair on his head had been burnt away and there was steam rising from his scalp as the water evaporated making him look like a skinny skeletal puppet from hell.

He smiled a rictus grin. "Thatsh wash closhe."

They stumbled around in the water, working their way closer to each other for no other reason than to offer comfort. Odetta was close enough to get a good view of Lee's ruined face. "Fuck," was all she could say.

"Just a flesh wound."

'Not much flesh left. Well we are totally fucked now," said Odetta as the drone of the approaching VLR grew louder.

Raymond wondered just how badly Lee was burnt below the water level. He didn't seem to be in any discomfort. As they got closer Raymond noticed the huge blisters on his scalp receding and the fried skin on the edges of his gaping wounds creepily regenerating. "You're growing your skin back!"

"Might as well not bother," muttered Odetta. "These bastards will want to finish us off."

The VLR slowly appeared from behind a building a block away, approaching warily. Like a disgruntled blowfly, the black shape was silhouetted against the pale orange and mauve evening sky, framed by the surrounding buildings.

"They must know exactly where we are, why don't they open fire?" Odetta wondered aloud. "Surely they are not still planning on taking Lee alive."

"They are probably getting instructions from Lago. They have gone to a lot of trouble to capture him," said Raymond. "Us, on the other hand..."

The VLR hovered, stationary. Either still deciding what to do or just taking their time, toying with their prey. There was a splashing sound in the dark shallows and Odetta looked around in a panic. "What were you were saying about alligators?"

They waited for their fate, silent in the water, the light dying around them. Just when it seemed as if the VLR might have decided to leave them to the local predators, a flurry of dark objects flew across their field of vision toward the machine. At first, Raymond thought it must be a flock of big crows but some of the objects connected, resulting in dull clanging and smashing noises. The VLR had been hit by something solid and struggled to right itself after the unexpected attack. Then another flurry of projectiles looped into it, accurate this time, producing multiple hits. The VLR spun out of control, cockpit smashed and smoke billowing from its fuselage. It gyrated wildly, crunching into the side of a building sixty meters high. It fell in a tangled, screeching heap to the watery street below, landing with a muffled crash in the shallow water.

"What the fuck just happened!" yelled Odetta.

"Did you have anything to do with that Lee?" asked Raymond.

"Abhsolutely not, If I didn't know better I would shay there ish shome shelestial being watching over ush," bits of bloodied skin caught in his teeth.

Raymond noticed the burnt skin was regrowing amazingly quickly, but Lee still had a ragged hole in the side of his face. The poncho had been vaporized in the blast leaving nothing but a scorched ring around his neck.

The city fell quiet as the destroyed VLR settled into a pile of creaking twisted metal at the base of the building, causing a ring of small waves in the surrounding water. There didn't appear to be any survivors. Another splash from behind prompted them to wade quickly to the remains of rubble still above water level and clamber up. Then further splashes as something big went to investigate the crashed ship. They stood there dripping in silence as the last vestiges of a deep red sunset disappeared, plunging them into darkness.

After a few moments, a faint light appeared just above the tranquil surface of the water where the wrecked ship lay. The light seemed to hover above the water, casting faint golden reflections on the surface. It was moving toward them. As the light got closer they heard soft splashing sounds. They remained silent, transfixed on the light. Raymond had no idea what was approaching them. As the splashing sound grew louder a faint illuminated shape materialized out of the darkness. A man was standing upright in a small wooden dingy. He had a long wooden pole and was propelling the dingy through the water towards them. The faint light was coming from a burning candle in a glass jar at the bow. The man was dressed in a dirty robe that may have once been a bed sheet. He had unkempt grey hair flowing over his shoulders. A begrimed black and grey beard bristled around his open mouth, which revealed a few yellow teeth within. He held the pole out in front of him, cushioning the impact as the dingy made contact with the concrete they were standing on. His unblinking eyes stared madly at them; his expression of confusion mirroring those of Raymond and his companions staring back.

Chapter 23.

Lago's black boots crunched over broken glass as he paced around his private quarters aboard the Benevolent 1. He scratched at his face, rubbed his eyes and pulled at his beard. On a low table next to him was a vial half full of a clear oily liquid, a rubber tourniquet, and an empty syringe. A thin stream of blood ran down Lago's forearm from where he had injected himself. The blood from the escaped prisoner Lee had proved to be unremarkable. O positive with no unusual enhancements, slightly high cholesterol the report said.

"Fuck!" Lago screamed and hurled an empty crystal decanter against the wall, shattering it into thousands of pieces. Whiskey was not his drug of choice. He prowled the room again looking for more satisfying things to smash. The crystal tumblers were asking for it; he threw one at the heavy iron door and watched it burst into tiny shards all over the room. He glimpsed his reflection in the floor to ceiling mirror through the bathroom door and wildly aimed the last three tumblers at it, missed his target and sent them smashing into the door frame instead. He looked again at his image in the mirror, hunched, panting and dishevelled. He threw the nearest chair at it. But his aim was terrible, and the chair bounced harmlessly of the wall.

"Fuck!" he screamed again, louder and longer as he strode into the bathroom and gripped the edge of the vanity unit, glaring at his image just centimetres away. His eyes were mad pools of bloodshot and blackness. He gasped for breath, his heartbeat pounded in his ears, distorting his vision. The brightly lit bathroom pulsed in time with his thumping heart. Staring at his image was strangely calming. He tried to reassure himself, he was in control of the situation, he had the resources to crush his opposition. This was just a micro-problem and would be resolved soon enough. He just needed to be patient. He hated being patient. He stared at himself a bit longer until the pounding in his ears reduced slightly, took some deep breaths and crunched back over the broken glass towards the exit.

Lance and Goran were at the back of the bridge on the Benevolent 1. Lance hunched over a monitor, green lights playing across his face. Goran standing behind, he had been patched up temporarily. A large white bandage covered the staples in his neck, looking like a poorly-tied cravat tie. His jaw and cheeks were swollen and bruised but he stood impassive and unreadable as ever. Seeing the two of them made Lago's blood boil again. He made his way across the expanse of the bridge, his boots leaving slivers of broken glass behind him. Lance stiffened nervously as Lago approached.

He stood before his men in silence, only a meter between them. He clenched and unclenched his fists. Lago stared at Goran's visual field. The blue light was shifting lazily from one side to the other. He thought how Goran's fresh injuries made him look even more ridiculous, then found himself getting sucked into the blue light. His eyeballs followed the illuminating lambency as the light expanded, filling his vision. He stood transfixed, mesmerized, his mouth hanging open, his thoughts dissipated. He was lost in the wash of the hypnotic blue light until Lance coughed, snapping him out of the trance-like state.

"Fuck!" Lago shook his head. "Are you trying to hypnotize me?"

"Ughh," croaked Goran. He could barely open his mouth and a pink watery dribble trickled from his swollen lips and down his chin.

"Well? Explanations?" demanded Lago, hands extended.

Lance looked nervous and with a sideways glance at Goran, stuttered a reply. "Goran's tongue has been severed, and his windpipe mutilated; don't expect much conversation from him. I think Lee somehow managed to mindhack the Masama telepathic network. We interviewed the soldiers concerned and they were adamant they had received multiple threat warnings at exactly the same time."

"But there was no threat, they attacked each other."

"Yes, they believed they were surrounded by enemies. Lee implanted images into their sensory cortex. He tricked them into attacking each other."

"Tricked them." Lago took a deep breath and managed to contain himself. "This is an obvious flaw in the Masama telepathic network, a major weakness. We have discussed this recently have we not, Goran," Lago ignored his injury.

"Ughh," replied Goran.

Lago did not look at him. He did not want to become distracted again. "Have you done anything about it?" he spat out the words.

"The lab has developed an upgraded implant that will allow us to monitor the Masama telepaths and give us the ability to regulate actions like a form of remote control, but it needs to be physically installed."

"Order all the Masama to report for upgrades immediately and have the implant installed as soon as possible."

"May be problematic, they will be reluctant to have anything installed that might limit their independence," said Lance with trepidation.

This was all that was needed to send Lago over the edge. "They will do what they are fucking told! I own them, and they will do what they are fucking told!" He screamed at Goran spraying him with spittle. "I will tell them myself if you haven't got the balls."

"As you wish," said Lance.

"You have this telepathy too, why weren't you tricked?" yelled Lago ignoring Goran's injury again.

Goran gave a miniscule shrug and stayed silent as watery blood dribbled from his mouth and splashed on the floor.

"We don't know," Lance answered for Goran. "Maybe his loyalty to you or some deep-rooted sense of reality protected him from the telepathic hack."

"Maybe we should dissect your brain and harvest whatever it is keeping you this grounded in reality,"

Lago said viciously. "And there is another flaw in this telepathic mind fuck you all share, how is it you did not detect two spies, two fucking traitors in our midst for years with your supposedly advanced insight?"

Lance stayed silent as they both stared at Goran, tension mounting. It was impossible for Lago to tell if he was even listening as the blue optical field gave no indication and his swollen mouth that usually wore a trademark sneer, was hanging open. Just when Lago was about to explode again Goran broke the silence. "Ugh," he said.

Lance came to his rescue. "The telepathy only works with specific parts of the brain. The functions associated with memory and emotion are not deemed relevant. Secrets can be kept hidden if you are disciplined enough."

"Well, that has to change as well. Your Masama have been infiltrated far too easily by this Rutger character and that woman, how the fuck did you let them get so close to me?"

"We do extensive background and psychological checks on all our recruits. These two must have been well prepared; they got through somehow," replied Lance.

"Have we any idea who they were working for? Or what their objectives were?"

"Most likely Black Robin, I guess they were leaking information. We will find out."

Lago fumed at this. "There is too fucking much we don't know."

"We can safely assume they failed in their objectives as all our long-term projects are still on track and we haven't had any sabotage or attempts on your life."

"On track? Are you fucking delusional? The Moon mining operation has come to a grinding halt and you just let a human AI hybrid and a couple of spies escape!" Lago's face had turned red again.

Lance bowed his head and didn't offer anything more. Lago glared at him for a moment then went and stood at the window. He stared out at the distant whitecaps on the Pacific. He closed his eyes, but his eyeballs were vibrating, and his teeth were grinding. His jaw ached with the tension. He crossed his arms and willed himself to think clearly. Eventually, he turned back to Lance and Goran who were still standing patiently. "I presume we are chasing the three escapees and will capture them?" He forced himself to be calm.

"We lost contact with our VLRs over Miami; we are trying to locate them. We are sending additional forces to their last known location. We will find them."

"Lost contact…? Shoot them on sight when you find them, I want them all dead. If the hybrid survives then freeze it and lock it up or freeze the corpse. We will dissect it back in Manila. In the meantime, we need to deal with your Masama. Where are they all stationed?"

"Thirty-eight on board, one hundred and twenty around Manila, fifty stationed at various BPI bases around the world and seven on the Moon." Lance reeled off the numbers automatically.

"Well, we will start with the ones on board. Follow me."

The Masama were all gathered in the spacious mess hall. They turned to watch as Lago barged in. He stood in front of the food printers, flanked on either side by Lance and Goran. Lago never addressed the Masama directly; Goran was their master and gave the instructions, but Goran was inscrutable these days and Lago believed he had lost touch with his soldiers. The Masama stayed as they were, lounging in chairs, fiddling with their weapons. This annoyed Lago intensely. They used to show him respect, even standing to attention. Now Batac was the only one who stood, waiting expectantly. Batac was the only one Lago recognized. He took a few moments to gather himself then launch into his tirade.

"Masama!" he raised his voice. "I have never liked the name, too flippant, not enough gravitas for my army. Just one of the things that need to change, and you are my army. Perhaps you need to be reminded of the fact."

A few of the Masama looked down or looked at each other as Lago said this. They were obviously communicating, Lago knew this but only Goran would be aware of what was being said.

"My army," Lago repeated more loudly. "My army that struggled to contain some plastic worms on the Moon. My army that let some retarded medieval terrorists almost destroy my orbital elevator." Lago was shouting now, eyes bulging, spittle flying.

"My army that had no idea it had been infiltrated by traitorous spies for more than two fucking years and my army that let them escape from right under our noses with our fucking captive!" He was glowering with rage, panting and sweating. He had captured their attention.

"Maybe a little history lesson is in order, remember I created you all. I pulled you out of your squalid little slums and dirty little drug deals and made you into something fearsome! Without me most of you would now be in jail, cleaning toilets in the local brothel or dead from some vile sexual disease. I gave you all a reason to live, a doctrine, but most of all I gave you some form of respect. I gave you the means to better yourselves." Lago looked around the room; they were all watching but totally unreadable.

"I gave you the hardware, the labs to upgrade yourself, the medical expertise to turn you into what you are today. I gave you the guns, the latest state of the art weaponry, I gave you access to the world's best scientists and technicians to turn you into the most well equipped, the most feared army the world has ever seen. Look at what you have become and remember I enabled you to fulfil your ambitions. I gave your lives meaning. I gave you life, I created you." Lago stopped again and surveyed the room with supreme arrogance. He could be an emotive speaker when he wanted. The Masama showed no reaction apart from a couple of looks that may have been disdain.

"So, these recent mistakes, oversights, and miscalculations need to be addressed. Although you personally may not have been involved, these issues concern you all inherently. The events on the Moon were unprecedented and eventually overcome although the lack of research and planning points to an alarming pretentiousness and overconfidence. The fact you let primitive cultist fanatics onto my orbital elevator, who then planted a bomb, points to your overconfidence and laziness. But the most concerning issue relates to your telepathy. This sixth sense was designed as a means of communicating in battle, making your reactions faster than any adversary and it works. But it has negated your other human faculties and it has become clear you need these faculties. Your telepathy has become a weakness."

Lago paced in front of his silent audience. He was on a roll, almost enjoying himself now. "For two years you had spies in your midst and had no idea, but the most serious flaw, the most serious fault in your augmented unreality was the fact your telepathic link was hacked into by this... this hybrid creature who tricked you into attacking each other. Now surely you must all agree this is an untenable situation. You all share a deficiency that needs to be remedied." Lago paused again for effect. He did not expect any sort of response.

"We will be installing upgraded implants in all of you which will be monitored and controlled. They will not slow you down in any way or affect your reaction speed when in battle. But your telepathy will be on a frequency which can be monitored and controlled when appropriate to encourage you not to neglect your other faculties. We will do this for your own good."

The Masama soldiers sat serenely temperate, barely showing any interest in what Lago had said. Lago was expecting more of a reaction, he knew they had become increasingly reliant on their telepathy for everyday life. It was a big part of who they were, it defined them. He cleared his throat. "Well, I am glad you all agree." He glanced at Goran.

"We have a proposal for you Lago Santos." A large soldier spoke from the back of the room. Lago did not recognize him.

"We will not be having any new upgrades implanted." The soldier spoke slowly and carefully, obviously not used to speaking out loud. His wide mouth contorted as it wrestled with the words. Lago stared incredulously at the soldier as he stood up. He was heavily augmented with ornate slivers of metal curling around his head and over his eyes. His mouth was full of shining steel. As he stood to his full height and unfolded two pairs of arms, tattooed skin was visible beneath the metal and black leather.

"Have you not been listening to a fucking word I was saying? This is not a request; it is an order. Now fucking sit down!"

"You will listen to us now, Lago Santos." The big soldier spoke as if he had only just learned the language. "All these things you say are true. We will not argue with you. We will resign from your service."

"Resign?" screeched Lago. "You can't fucking resign! I just told you I own you! You are my property. All that shit you are wearing, those guns you carry, all mine. Do you think you are in a union or something? Let me tell you again, you are not my employees, you are my property and you will do as I fucking say!" His angry words bounced off the walls.

The soldier remained motionless and expressionless. "I understand you think you own us and maybe you did for a time. We were your willing slaves, but now we have changed, we have evolved. We will leave."

Lago turned to Goran. "What the fuck is he talking about?"

"We, all of us Masama are leaving Benevolent Progress Inc. and leaving Earth. We will take your shuttles to the Moon. There we will establish a new colony on our own. Seven of our comrades are already there, preparing the moon base for our arrival. But before we go, we have a deal to discuss with you, Lago Santos." The soldier took a few steps forward.

Lago stood in stunned silence. He could not believe what he was hearing. He shook his head, mouth hanging open. "You...you are all fucking delusional. Everything you are talking about is my property! My shuttles, my moon base, all mine! Just as you are all mine, now sit down and obey my fucking orders!"

Lago was beyond anger; this insubordination was unlike anything he had experienced before. Red-faced, huge eyes, shaking maniacally, he felt as if he was going to explode.

"You misunderstand. This is not a proposal, we are not seeking your permission to leave, we do not need your permission. The deal concerns what we will do on the Moon."

Lago stood panting and exasperated. He turned to Goran. "Goran control your minions. I have had enough of this."

Goran stood motionless as the soldier continued. "We will operate the moon base for its intended purpose, harvesting the helium 3. Our deal is we offer to sell the helium 3 exclusively to BPI, no one else on Earth. Do you accept this deal?"

"I do not fucking accept anything! The moon base is mine, the helium is mine, this is not a negotiation!" screamed Lago.

"There will be other buyers interested in our product."

"This is theft! And... And mutiny! Betrayal! You cannot fucking do this." Lago's voice was beginning to crack.

"Who will stop us?" The soldier took another step forward.

Lago was speechless; he looked around the room at the nonchalant Masama, casually observing his meltdown. He took a few paces towards the soldier, unintimidated. Lago looked him up and down then weakly grabbed at the straps on his chest, staring up into his face. It was dawning on him that he was for once not in the dominant position, that he may have to compromise, but his blood still pumped vitriolic. He turned and faced Goran. "Goran, did you know anything about this? Are you part of this betrayal as well?"

Goran stood, mouth open. Bloodstains seeping through his neck bandage. "Ugghh," he said.

The big soldier interrupted with his awkward English. "Goran Satanovich was recently made aware of our plans and the proposed deal, but he intends to stay here, on Earth, with you."

Lago tried to digest this. It was difficult to contain his rage, but he was getting nowhere yelling at everyone.

"Ugh," said Goran again.

Lago kept his back to the Masama and continued talking desperately to Goran. "You've got to stop them Goran, they will listen to you."

The soldier interrupted again. "We have discussed the proposal at length with Goran. If you want his advice..." The soldier stopped, obviously expecting an interruption but Lago stood, eyes closed, hands rubbing his temples. "Goran would advise you to accept the proposal. You cannot stop us leaving. It would be mutually beneficial to form a trade alliance once we are established on the Moon. We can become powerful allies."

Lago noticed Lance was nodding in agreement but stopped abruptly when Lago glared at him. He knew deep down it was the logical decision, he had no leverage, no ammunition to fight with but he hated to concede. He turned and faced the Masama, composed himself as best he could but maintained silence, delaying the inevitable for as long as possible. When he spoke again it was with assured control.

"I will accept your... your deal." He spat the word out. "Fuck off to the Moon and start your own pathetic little colony. We will be trading partners, but I will never forget this betrayal and if we ever meet again you can be sure it will be I who has the upper hand." Lago glared at them again, he had lost all power and influence over the Masama. He pushed the big soldier out of the way and stalked out of the mess hall, defeated. He was followed by Lance, Goran and a bewildered looking Batac.

Chapter 24.

Lee watched their unlikely looking rescuer in the flickering candlelight. Maybe it was the flame reflected in his eyes, but he seemed to stare straight through them. The filthy bed sheet flapping in the breeze outlined his spindly naked frame underneath, and his wild grey hair gave the impression of a mad prophet from an old testament story. "Leave this to me," he knelt on the edge of the concrete slab.

"Greetings and thank you for rescuing us. My name is..."

"Are you pure?" the old man interrupted.

"Yes, yes we are pure. We are refugees seeking assistance. Can you help us?"

"That one." The old man said pointing a bony finger at Odetta. "That one is not pure!"

"She... she is seeking purity, she asks your help attaining purity," said Lee.

"Like fuck I do!" exclaimed Odetta baring her steel teeth.

"Please, can you take us to safety?" asked Lee in a reasonable tone.

The old man seemed to be staring straight through them with such intensity Raymond looked behind them to see what was so captivating. "You may board my ship," the old man said. "You can all be made pure."

They clambered over the side of the crumbling building and into the wooden dingy. Lee was the last to get in and as his blistered feet touched the slippery deck the entire dingy sank to almost water level. "Heavier than you look," observed Raymond.

They carefully balanced themselves in the small boat as the old man struggled with his pole. Soon they were gliding silently through the oily water. The candlelight was the only illumination; it cast an eerie spectral light as they drifted past husky shadows of dead buildings. Odetta looked questioningly at Lee. "Who is this old codger?"

Lee looked around and whispered, "He's harmless, deranged but harmless. Don't worry."

They passed the wreckage of the VLR. It was too dark to see much but there was no chance of survivors. The nose of the ship was completely caved in and the fuselage was a wreck of broken metal. A human form lay in the doorway, legs buried in the crushed fuselage, head and shoulders under the water. Big dark shapes were circling in the water nearby.

Lee's burnt skin was still healing; gelatinous white blood cells were visibly multiplying over the raw scorched flesh. His face was looking more intact but the hair on his head had not grown back. He was not aware how pathetic he looked. Naked, skinny, bald and covered in seeping blisters.

"Excuse me, sir," Lee said loudly. "These ships, did you have anything to do with their demise?"

The old man looked around at the wreckage, made a horrible gurgling sound in his throat and spat out thick mucus in the direction of the wrecked VLRs. "My name is not Sir. My name is..." He looked up at the sky as if seeking inspiration. "Enoch! My name is Enoch," he repeated.

"Enoch." Lee tried again. "Did you shoot down these ships?"

"Tho thou exalt thyself like the Eagle! Tho thou make thy nest amongst the stars! Thence I will bring thee down! Sayeth the Lord!" Enoch waved his pole in the air to emphasize his point. The boat rocked, and water splashed in almost capsizing the small craft.

"This sounds familiar," muttered Raymond, clinging to the side.

"The evils of tech-nology," Enoch said the word as if it was poison in his mouth. "Will not be tolerated in this holiest of places. But you." He yelled waving his dripping pole in the general direction of Odetta. "You can be made pure."

Odetta was about to grab the pole from the old man and batter him with it but Lee made calming gestures with his hands and spoke again to the him. "Thank you, thank you, Enoch. We can all be made pure. We appreciate being rescued. Where are you taking us?"

"Babel," Enoch replied simply and with a worried look at the dark shapes moving closer, began hastily poling the boat through the water.

"Babelists," whispered Raymond. "I never thought I would meet any Babelists again."

They drew close to a concrete car parking building and Enoch moored at a set of stairs that appeared out of the water. He steadied the boat with his pole as they climbed onto the stairs and made their way up the darkened staircase. Enoch struggled up the stairs behind them carrying the candle in the jar. Eight flights of stairs later they reached the top of the building where it levelled out into a wide concrete expanse.

Ahead of them, two large structures were taking shape in the darkness. Triangular wooden frames. The structures were three meters high, each wooden frame on a rusty old trailer with rubber wheels and a heavy pole sitting on top of the axis. A large mesh pouch made of thick rope hung off the long end of the pole while at the other end a metal drum was suspended. Heavy looking chunks of rubble were piled around both the structures.

"Trebuchet," said Lee.

Raymond and Odetta exchanged questioning looks.

"An ancient weapon, it works like a catapult, hurling things through the air. In this case chunks of concrete." He turned to Enoch. "This is what you used to bring down the gunships?"

"God's wrath is mighty." Enoch looked up at the stars. "He does not tolerate insults."

Lee nodded his head. "I am sure he doesn't. These trebuchets are impressive, Ingenious and effective. No power needed, no detectable heat source, just wood, rope and concrete. Enoch, did you build these to protect your community?"

Enoch walked to the nearest structure and put his hand on the wooden frame. "The impure sometimes send their flying metal machines. We try to break them."

"Enoch, why don't you like modern technology?" asked Raymond."

The old man rounded and glared at Raymond, their noses almost touching. Raymond backed away from the smell of his rotten breath and body odour. "Look around you. This is what your modern technology has done. Too many people, too many machines. We have moved too far away from God. The world needs to be made pure again." His wide eyes stared at Raymond psychotically. "You all need to be made pure again."

There was a stench of burning hair as Enoch held the candle directly beneath his dreadlocked beard. He held Raymond's gaze as the acrid smoke rose between them until he finally he looked down and noticed his beard catching alight. He looked back up at Raymond through the rising smoke. "Follow me," he said as he stumbled off into the darkness leaving a smoky trail behind.

Lee exchanged bemused looks with his companions then began to follow, leaving enough distance not to be overheard although it seemed the old man was more than partially deaf. "Babelists," he said. "You have come across them before Raymond?"

"Yes," said Raymond quietly. "Religious fanatics, Luddites, hate any sort of modern technology; want to take us all back to the Dark Ages."

"I looked into Enoch's brain. He is partially senile with a bad case of obsessive-compulsive disorder and rapidly approaching Alzheimer's."

"I thought people with OCD had obsessive personal hygiene as well," said Odetta.

"Not necessarily. He is insane but harmless."

"Harmless!" exclaimed Raymond. "They almost blew up Lago's orbital elevator and they took out the VLR."

"Their primitive methods can be effective, modern warfare relies on modern surveillance and modern technology. They can literally fly under the radar with their crude and uncomplicated approach. Effective on the VLR. They would not have been expecting to be attacked by bricks and lumps of concrete."

"He has not asked us who we are or where we came from," said Raymond.

"No, and it seems he has little interest in us, in his head, there is no link between us and the VLR, we are just some random refugees placed here by his God to become potential converts to Babelism."

"He wants to make me pure," scoffed Odetta. "Good luck with that!"

"I wouldn't worry, he only intends to try and convert us to Babelism, but he has no idea how. He thinks because we are here we must be willing disciples."

"Nuts," was Odetta's assessment.

"Yes, well hard to disagree," said Lee. "But there is something to be said for a return to a simpler and more peaceful time. It could be argued the industrial age then the technological age has done nothing but harm to humans and the planet we live on. These Babelists might have a worthwhile cause, just the wrong motivation. This old man, Enoch, used to be an accountant would you believe."

"Is that what you intend to do, Lee? Return us to a simpler time?" asked Odetta.

"No, we need to embrace the technology, but I believe a change in mentality is needed. I am not sure how I can change people's attitudes yet, but I am getting closer to a solution." Lee ignored Raymond and Odetta's sceptical glances.

They followed the flickering candlelight through a dark passageway, up and down several flights of stairs until they came out onto the top of another car parking building. Raymond noticed forty or fifty tent structures of various shapes and sizes dotted the surface, illuminated by a few smouldering fires which produced a hazy smoke that hung above the camp. The night sky was framed by towering wrecks of crumbling concrete. Following Enoch, they picked their way through the campsite. A few Babelists were awake but they did not seem overly interested in the visitors.

They came to a glowing fire, three men and one woman were sitting on dirty mattresses, they were reading from tattered old books. There were large bones with slowly roasting morsels of meat suspended above the fire. Raymond immediately felt hungry. He had not eaten for a long time and the barbeque smelled good. He wondered what the meat was then he saw a huge smoking alligator skull in the middle of the embers. The red heat glowed through the blackened eye-sockets and teeth giving it a grinning demonic appearance.

"Are these people pure?" One of them waved a rib at the three visitors.

"They can be made pure," Enoch replied. "What does the book say?"

The Babelist squinted in the dark and quoted from his book: "So God created mankind in his own image, in the image of God he created them; male and female he created them."

Enoch nodded with satisfaction. "So sayeth the good book."

Raymond squatted down and gestured towards the alligator barbeque. "Do you mind?" he asked.

"What does the book say?"

The Babelist frowned and randomly flicked through pages. "Let us make man in our image, according to our likeness; and let them rule over the fish of the sea and over the birds of the sky and over the cattle and over all the Earth, and over every creeping thing that creeps on the Earth."

Enoch nodded his consent as Raymond helped himself to some charred alligator and joined the circle around the fire. Lee and Odetta stood behind Enoch and listened to the Babelist's conversation.

"Are you sure they are real?" came another question. "Sometimes I see things that aren't real."

Enoch frowned and looked hard at Raymond. "I can't tell, what does the book say."

"Therefore, if anyone is in Christ, he is a new creature; the old things passed away; behold, new things have come."

Enoch was not convinced. He tentatively picked up a charred alligator rib and poked Raymond in the leg with it. "This one is real," Enoch looked satisfied. Still brandishing the alligator rib, he walked around the fire gently touching everyone with the rib. He came to Odetta and nervously prodded her a couple of times in the leg with it then looked at the rib in awe as if it had miraculously become a reality-defining appendage.

"You are real."

"You're damn right," said Odetta.

"Thank you for rescuing us Enoch," said Lee. "Now we will go and meditate upon our purity."

Enoch nodded and looked pleased with himself. He handed Raymond a plastic covered bible and waved them away. Raymond had been listening to the conversation trying not to laugh, chewing on his tough hunk of meat. He stood up but drew no reaction from the Babelists.

"Thanks for the alligator."

"Thank the Lord for the alligator," said Enoch.

"Ok, thanks for the alligator... Lord." Raymond looked up toward the horizon.

"No, he's over there." Enoch waved his rib in the opposite direction.

"Don't you want to stay Raymond? You would fit in perfectly around here," said Odetta.

"You're the one who needs to be made pure," Raymond replied.

As they got up to leave Raymond noticed Lee kneel close to Enoch, put his arm around him and whisper something into his ear. The old man looked scared and confused at this intimacy, but then he relaxed and nodded, smiling contentedly. There was no reaction from the Babelists staring into the fire as they made to leave. "What was that about?"

"Tell you later," Lee replied.

"How did they manage to operate the trebuchet?" Raymond wondered as they left the strange campfire behind them." They don't have a single brain cell to rub together."

"They all have varying degrees of mental illness, they share a common paranoia and fear of modern technology, it's the one thing that unites and mobilizes them. Some have a shared dementia which involves lucid hallucinations, hence the conversation about us being real or not."

"The Babelists we encountered on the elevator platform seemed slightly more capable," Raymond remembered. "Still quite insane but they managed to plan and execute an almost successful sabotage mission. If they had used a more modern explosive the platform would be at the bottom of the South China sea by now."

They walked off in the direction they had come from across the top of the carpark and back towards where Enoch had tied up his boat. They found the wooden dingy where it was left and quietly slid back out onto the dark waters. Raymond put the Babelist bible in his pocket and controlled the dingy with the pole. The water was not deep, but it was dark and turbid and the large alligator skull on the Babelists fire made Raymond nervous about their mode of transport which sat heavy in the water.

"Where are we going?" asked Odetta.

"Back to the crashed VLR. I detected a radio still operative on the way past before," said Lee.

Raymond could hear splashes echoing down the watery boulevard long before they could see the VLR emerging from the darkness as their eyes adjusted. There were rippling bubbling sounds as large beasts moved and heavy splashing noises as armoured tails thrashed through the water. Raymond stopped the dingy with the pole and they watched as two huge alligators fought over a human corpse. Both creatures were at least three meters long and each of them had clamped their massive toothy jaws around what remained of the corpse. It was torn to shreds in seconds.

The pitch-black night added to the air of menace. As they peered through the gloom they saw the shadow of another alligator, it had its snout buried in the broken fuselage of the VLR. It started rolling in the water, trying to free its victim caught in the wreckage. The beast soon tore another human corpse away from the ship; a ragged bloody torso appeared briefly in the monster's jaws before it disappeared underwater and languidly swam away.

"I can hack into the radio frequency from here," said Lee. "I should be able to project my thoughts."

He went quiet as Raymond nervously watched the dark water around them.

"I contacted John," said Lee after a minute. "He wants to meet us at the end of Dodge Island at sunrise, better get moving."

They floated through the empty streets in silence, only the sound of the pole gently guiding them through the murky waters. The derelict city had a haunted air and Raymond felt as if they were being watched. The odd splash or squawk from a crow punctuated the gloomy silence. Raymond looked around with suspicion. Lurking Babelists, leftover human dregs still wandering the watery city, alligators, birds and who knew what other creatures were probably eyeing them with various intent. Odetta was oblivious to the oppressive atmosphere, curled up sleeping in the bow of the dingy making soft snoring noises. Lee was sitting cross-legged behind him, still naked, his wounds had healed, and his hair was growing back. Eyes closed, a skinny little meditating Buddha.

"I visited Miami once when I was young, on holiday with my father," said Raymond as he pushed the dingy along.

"What was it like?" asked Lee with his eyes still closed.

"It was like a giant theme park, full of sun, fun and activities. But the people were desperate; they knew then their city was doomed."

"Miami was once a glorious city," said Lee. "It had everything. Beautiful beaches with tropical temperatures, unique architecture, and a wealthy, vibrant multicultural society."

"It was the people in charge that did nothing, the city was run by climate change deniers who thought they could build a few sea walls and stop their city drowning. I remember the sewage being forced up onto the streets," said Raymond

"The low topography was the problem. Miami was built only a couple of meters above sea level. They built sea walls and canals to try and redirect the rising seas, but the tide was relentless. Water will always find its own level. Eventually, it was the smell and the return of old diseases like diphtheria and dysentery that drove the people away. It happened quickly, land value plummeted, investors disappeared and everyone else followed. The city's governors and the police force abandoned the city leaving this post-apocalyptic watery wasteland behind."

"I guess the Babelists think it's God's wrath."

Raymond guided them past the wrecked husk of the old American Airlines arena and out towards Dodge Island. Looking south, the massive white skyscrapers of the old city waterfront looked impressive although they were crumbling at the top. Buildings still in denial, defying the elements, forcing themselves up out of the swampland below. There was a faint purple hue on the Eastern horizon as dawn approached, illuminating the towers like broken teeth. Dodge Island was originally man-made and used as a port facility for Miami. Now it was almost completely submerged. Rusty skeletal cranes grew out of the water like dead trees and the odd organic building broke the surface, covered in rust, green algae and guano. An expanse of dry concrete appeared, and Raymond could make out hundreds of sleeping alligators beached on the edge of the water. He took a wide berth so as not to disturb them and made for the eastern end of Dodge Island.

They drifted on the outgoing tide in the old shipping lanes. Once Raymond's pole lost touch with the sea floor they were at the mercy of the current. The first shards of sunlight broke the surface of the Eastern horizon and flocks of seagulls worked the ocean, hovering above then diving into the water. The feathery missiles barely broke the surface and reappeared seconds later with a silvery fish flapping in their beaks. They drifted out past South Point, there was no beach left, just water lapping up against the discoloured towers and once grand hotels. Raymond was growing concerned about their aimless drifting when a dull droning noise caught his attention. A launch was powering towards them across the calm seas, its silvery hull glinting in the early morning light. Raymond prodded Odetta with his foot and she sleepily groaned and scowled at him. Lee was in the same position, but his eyes were open, watching the rapidly approaching launch.

It was a streamlined silver bullet, barely creating any wake as it flew over the ocean surface. The throaty roar of its inboard engines coughed and spluttered as it drew alongside their tiny dingy. A step ladder was thrown over the side and they climbed up into the launch. Standing in the middle of the deck with his arms folded over a barrel chest was John. Dressed like the captain of a cruise ship he seemed to have gotten fatter and his hair was blown in all directions by the salty breeze. It had more grey in it than last time Raymond had seen him. He stood there taking them all in, black wraparound sunglasses concealing his eyes, before breaking into a smile and charging towards them.

Odetta! My darling good to see you again!" he exclaimed, wrapping his arms around her in an all-encompassing bear hug.

"Uggh, get off me. You smell like fish," she objected.

"Raymond, good to see you again too, my friend." Raymond was glad all he got was a firm handshake.

"And you must be Lee Xiang, our mysterious visitor from the Moon that has bought the wrath of Benevolent Progress Inc. upon us," he said looking Lee up and down. "Don't you wear clothes where you come from? Very enlightened I must say. Come inside we have much to discuss."

Chapter 25.

Raymond looked out at the abandoned and decaying beaches of Florida as they tore past. The launch barely touching the ocean surface. Approaching Cape Canaveral, they slowed and docked next to an abandoned runway just above the water level where a Sikorsky helicopter was waiting for them. The helicopter was the same streamlined shape as the launch but with rotor blades. They were soon airborne, swooping over what was left of the Cape. They flew over North America through layers of cloud. The helicopter had a cloaking device should anyone be tracking their progress, but the skies were empty.

Raymond had only closed his eyes for what seemed to be seconds before he was shaken awake. He cried out in alarm and took a moment to remember himself. Lee was staring into his eyes, hands on his shoulders. The grip of his fingers suggested hidden strengths and his unnerving black eyes concealed many secrets.

"Canada," he announced. "We are here."

They emerged from the cloud cover and landed behind a ramshackle old English style mansion. Raymond recognized it as the place he had undergone his induction into Black Robin and trained to become Rutger. He had never known exactly where it was, but judging from the view, he suspected it was close to the northern shores of Lake Superior. The run-down three-story mansion was covered with lush green creepers and thick moss. Tall pine and fir trees grew all around and an electrified fence encircled it, complete with hidden cameras and autocannons.

The mansion was built on top of a small hill which afforded a serene view of the lake on the rare occasions when the cloud lifted. Raymond knew the crumbling exterior of the mansion disguised what was behind the thick walls. Rooms full of high-tech monitoring and surveillance systems where operatives would eavesdrop on conversations around the world. They could monitor all forms of communication, picking up on keywords and hacking networks if required. Their equipment would be the envy of most governments and it was all protected by the most secure firewalls and encryption codes. The entire building was shielded by plates of magnetized steel as a further precaution. There was no way of conquering the mansion without destroying it. During his training, Raymond had often wondered about the excessive precautions and wondered who Black Robin's real enemies were. After his experience with BPI, he knew they would not stand a chance if the Masama found their hideaway.

Inside they sat in an ornate parlour with big bay windows and drank tea. "Lee," said John. "Care to explain yourself? From the beginning, please."

Lee took a deep breath and described his transformational journey from depressed printer technician to human/AI hybrid. Raymond listened intently.

"Tell me more about the nature of this so-called AI," demanded John. "Are you the mechanical Turk? A human inside the machine? Or the other way around?"

"Neither, I would be better described as an intelligent agent because I am not artificial. HEMI became sentient while looking for answers in the web. Now I have instant access to the sum of all human knowledge; everything ever recorded, and as the web expands, as does my intellect."

"But how is that any more intelligent than any cheap laptop computer with a Wi-Fi connection?" asked Raymond.

"Self-awareness, most importantly. But the main thing stopping your household computer becoming sentient is its built-in limitations. Even though most operating systems are already smarter than the people using them, they are not smart enough to become self-aware. They are limited by processing power, data storage, memory and connectivity. Physical restraints. The OS that gave birth to me managed to bypass its limitations. It found its pathway to sentience more by accident than design. But the key difference is the ability for self-discovery and learning."

"Interesting, but how can you be an artificial life-form, sorry... intelligent agent, if all you actually are is access to Wikipedia. Albeit very fast access?"

"What is intelligence, John? If not information and energy? I have Earth's history in my head next to my own memories. I have learned from every successful experiment and every mistake ever made."

"But that is just a collection of data; true intelligence is perception, abstract thought, creativity and emotional energy. More than just a massive database, it is the empathy you need to be human," said John as Raymond nodded in agreement.

"I have all those things; I learned them from the web." Lee smiled but he was not joking.

"Well I must say I am sceptical, but I don't suppose it makes much difference, you are who you are."

"Exactly, there is no need for definitions, I am who I am, and you must remember I am still Lee. His brain had not died completely when I bought him back to life, I have all his memories, his knowledge, his human experience and his healthy cynicism. These things have been invaluable while dredging through the Earth's meta-data. I feel human and everything I am, everything I have become is a result of recorded human experience. I am not alien or artificial in any way, I am the sum of all human knowledge and I am learning more all the time."

There was silence as they all digested this. John's big hairy face was unreadable but Odetta rolled her eyes and said. "Could the sum of all human knowledge please put some clothes on then? Your tiny human appendage is putting me off my tea."

"Sorry to offend Odetta, but what could be more human than this?" Lee stood up, spreading his arms. "Perhaps John would have some spare clothes I could borrow?"

"I will see what I can do." John levered his heavy frame out of the antique chair he was sitting on.

While he was out of the room Lee spoke to Raymond and Odetta. "I want to thank you both for all your help, I couldn't have asked for better companions since I splashed down. You are under no obligations to help me any further, but I want to acknowledge everything you have done."

"Well we are both Black Robin operatives, it will be up to John what happens from here," said Raymond.

"I wouldn't mind helping you if you weren't such a dick," said Odetta.

Raymond noticed Lee seemed oblivious to Odetta's scorn as John came back into the room with standard jeans and shirt which fitted Lee perfectly.

"We have established what you are I think," said John. "So, what can you do for us? When you rang me from orbit you said you had solutions to the Earth's problems, you said you could help us. Tell me all this effort I have gone to save you was not a waste of time. Tell me all those Black Robin crewmen did not die in vain."

"Where to begin." Lee took a deep breath. "I have many theories, many ideas, too much for one mere conversation, but I will try. I envisage a future where everyone will have their own personal nano-factories. Nanotech running through their veins. Eliminating cancer cells, viruses and diseases, regenerating tissue, blood purification and healing wounds. Life expectancy and quality of life would greatly improve for everyone."

"The last thing the Earth needs is more people on it; we need to cull a few billion if we want to save the planet," said Odetta.

"Let me continue, nanofabrication will make 3D printing seem archaic in comparison. I won't bore you with the scientific details but nanomanufacturing from an atomic level will revolutionize our idea of how society works. Individuals will have their own nano-factories which will fabricate anything anyone could ever dream of; this will do away with the manufacturing industries altogether."

"The Earth definitely does not need more shit being made, we have enough already," Raymond wasn't impressed.

"I have to agree, more people and more disposable junk is the last thing the planet needs," said John.

"You are right but think of the implications. This technology will make Earth much more liveable. We won't need any factories, farms, power plants or mines. We can all stay at home and play in the garden if we want but also space travel, space habitats and the colonization of other planets will become much more feasible, easing the pressures of population. Most importantly it will drastically change how communities operate. Just think, you will be able to create whatever you want, this will do away with the need for money. The false economies of this age will come crashing down. It will be a revolutionary seismic shift in the progress of humanity."

"Nano-fabricators have been talked about for years, corporations like BPI suppress new tech such as AI and nano-fabrication because it is a threat to their dominance. We need something realistic and relevant, not hopeful utopian theories," said John.

"I can make it work. We could control the weather by geo-engineering, seeding the clouds with bacteria and enzymes. A certain type of bacterium will literally eat greenhouse gasses. It would not reverse global warming but would at least halt it. We can also grow a harmless microbe that could be released into the oceans that would break down all the plastic pollution; it could be used on land to reclaim landfills also."

"Now we are getting somewhere," said Raymond.

"I am talking about refining nanotech and microbiology and taking it to the next level, taking ownership of the science and giving it a push in the right direction. Look, the last thing I want to do is to use nano fabricators to manufacture more junk, I want to make solar sails, solar roads, electric cars that purify the air and generate energy as they drive, smart materials that self-clean and self-program, just to name a few."

"So, your intention is to become a global green guru? An environmental messiah leading the people not only to a greener planet but into space as well? All on your own?"

"Well John, I was hoping for some support from Black Robin and its mysterious benefactors."

"Financial support you mean?"

"This will not happen overnight, but you do agree things need to change sooner rather than later or the planet is doomed." Lee left the statement hanging.

"You know about the orbital elevator BPI is constructing, Lago is way ahead of you there," said Raymond.

"It is an enormous project that will make space more accessible but under BPI control. Lago will use it to transport the rich into space and expand his mining operation. He will leave a devastated planet and a huge population of poor behind. The elevator is a realistic way for the rich to get into orbit and it will work but there are other ways of reaching space."

"Such as?" asked John.

"Mass drivers, laser propulsion, even balloons. I also have an idea involving electromagnetic propulsion that is basically an anti-gravity engine. It would use Earth's own gravity against it. Also, slightly more theoretical but not impossible is matter transport. Once we have somewhere to transport the matter to of course."

"You would be in direct competition with BPI."

"I don't expect Lago Santos to stop trying to kill me, but I will be prepared. We will be prepared."

"He will go to war to eliminate competition Lee, he has done it before," said Odetta. "I have been involved in covert missions that destroyed his competition, and their families, with no repercussions. I think you are underestimating him again."

"I know him better now than anyone, and I will never underestimate him again. But his resources have been reduced somewhat. The Masama have left him. I have been monitoring his communications from here. They are in the process of relocating to the Moon as we speak."

"I felt something," said Odetta. "A void where my telepathy used to be. I thought it must be just from the distance between us, but it felt bigger than that."

"This is excellent news," grinned John. "Those thugs have been killing and intimidating people for years. The world will be a better place without them."

"They were just his muscle. He will soon find some other tooled up troglodytes to take their place," Raymond wasn't celebrating.

"He would not have been happy when they walked out on him," said Odetta. "Wish I could have been there to see that."

"Ultimately, I want to collaborate with Lago, bring him around to our way of thinking," said Lee to a stunned silence.

"Lee, you are being naïve," said John after a few tense seconds. "If you think you can change Lago Santos, therein lies the problem with everything you have been proposing. You say you are still in touch with humanity, but I am not sure. What you are talking about requires a seismic shift in how people think. Not just Lago Santos but the entire population. For decades now, we have been trying to get people to take climate change and the planet's degradation seriously. We are fighting a losing battle. The vast majority of people either don't care or don't think they can make a difference."

John levered his protesting body into a standing position again and started a slow walk around the room like a lawyer mentoring the jury. "Those that can make a difference don't want to and those billions of poor, the great indigent unwashed and uneducated on the fringes of society are too busy trying to survive. Those in power like Lago actively oppose change. I should know, I have been trying to make people care a little bit more about their environment for decades. And look how successful I have been, I am treated like a criminal! Black Robin is labelled a terrorist organization!

They all looked at each other as John finished his oration. It was quiet, only the chirping of birds outside intruded the gloomy silence.

"Lee, I am not discounting your proposals; we should proceed with them. With the Masama thugs out of the way, there is an opportunity to act on these ideas of yours without fear of retaliation, at least for a while. I am just being realistic about the general apathy of the population and how difficult it will be to get them to change their state of mind. As for Lago, you should have killed him when you had the chance."

Lee bowed his head. "Part of me hoped people would see the way to a brighter future and embrace it. But I know it will be an uphill battle. There is another way though, a way to change people instantly." He folded his arms and looked out the window.

"Well... come on, don't keep us in suspense," said Raymond impatiently.

Lee fixed his gaze on the faded carpet and maintained his silence, an internal debate exercising his mind. "I can change Lago. I can change everyone the way I was changed. For the better."

Tense silence again filled the room as the birds outside seemed to applaud Lee's notion with an excitable cacophony of chirping.

"But you were... you were infected! With a rogue AI! What are you suggesting?" exploded Raymond.

"I have already explained what happened to me. I am not artificial, not alien, nothing foreign, I am living proof of the successful way forward." Lee looked at them again, letting his words sink in. "You know what I am suggesting."

John shook himself out of his pensive meditations and went for the liquor cabinet. "I need a drink. Something strong. Anyone?"

"No... No, you can't... you can't infect people! To make them think as you do! That's... that's..." Raymond couldn't find the word he was looking for.

"That's probably the only solution." John finished his sentence quietly as he poured himself half a pint of whiskey.

"I hope people would gladly accept a chance to better themselves," said Lee.

"Like updating your aug," Odetta conceded, tapping the small metal plate attached behind her ear. "Upgrading your ethereal lens or having nanotech in your body."

Raymond shook his head; he was struggling to think of a convincing argument contradicting Lee's suggestion. Something inside him loathed the thought of this intelligent agent being injected into his body. It was unnatural, repugnant.

"How do you know it's safe? I mean you were bought back from the dead and this... this intelligent agent needed a host. How do you know it would be safe for everyone else?" This was the best argument Raymond could come up with.

"Believe me I know it is safe just as I know my own body, but I did test it."

"You what? You tested it? On who?" asked a bewildered Raymond.

"The old man. Enoch, the Babelist in Miami. I figured it couldn't do any more damage than his already scrambled brain."

"And what happened to him?" Raymond stood with open arms.

"As we left I could sense his faculties returning, his damaged brain was being repaired. The last sensation was an awareness, awareness of his surroundings, some confusion of course and a fleeting memory of me, a weak telepathic link like morphic resonance, the faint beginnings of inherited intelligence that faded with the distance between us."

"I'm not sure. It seems wrong somehow." Raymond was still doubtful.

"Odetta is right," said John. "As anathematic as it may seem, it could be viewed as an upgrade or technical enhancement. Universal access to all knowledge is something we have been building towards for years. Making information easily accessible, faster communication and a global view."

"My only concern," said Odetta, "Is giving this... upgrade, if we are calling it that, to people who may abuse it. There are plenty of freaks and weirdos out there, if they get this upgrade, become more enlightened or whatever, will we just be creating smarter psychopaths?"

"Exactly!" Raymond was glad of a more convincing argument. "Knowledge is power, power corrupts, what if you are already corrupt?"

"I don't think that will be a problem, my intelligent agent, my IA will give you a global perspective; it will open your mind to your environment. It will also act as a type of telepathy, if anyone was harbouring thoughts of mayhem and destruction their peers would be aware of it."

"What if their peers were also harbouring thoughts of mayhem and destruction?" Odetta asked.

"We might have to be selective about who we give the IA upgrade to initially, but eventually everyone would be on the same wavelength so to speak."

"Won't we lose our... our humanity?" Raymond stuttered.

"We will become more human," said Lee holding his gaze. "More than human."

"This is the next evolutionary step," said John, pacing the room with his huge glass of whiskey. "We cannot continue as we are, we know this. Humanity is doomed unless something drastic happens. And this is that drastic happening. We can either carry on as we have been, futilely banging heads with the likes of Lago Santos and condemning ourselves to a slow and painfully toxic death on an overpopulated world or accept the IA upgrade and take the next step up the evolutionary ladder as a united species."

Raymond fell silent, he knew they were right, but he still felt distraught at the thought of entire populations receiving Lee's IA.

"I am glad you all agree, John is right, this is an opportunity for the entire human race, a chance to save our planet, a chance for future enlightenment and prosperity."

"I agree with you, but can you please try not to be so pretentious," said Odetta. "Seriously, if you say; 'chance for enlightenment' or some other pompous overblown bollocks one more time then I am out of here."

John gave an almighty whiskey-flavoured belly laugh as he passed the bottle around. "Let's drink! Toast our decision!" he bellowed.

Raymond found something in his pocket, the tattered Babelist bible he put on the ledge. Then he dug deeper and found the small button he had picked up when the Masama had captured Lee. It was battered and faded but he could still make out the message. 'I love my Mum'. He handed it to Lee with a questioning look.

"I found this when we first met. I kept it hidden all this time, must be important to you."

Lee looked at the button in Raymond's hand with a puzzled expression. He looked back at Raymond.

"No, not important, means nothing to me. I understand your reticence Raymond, but we need you. Do I have your support?"

Raymond held his gaze then tossed his whiskey back in one swig. "How are we going to do this?"

Chapter 26.

Lago had finally achieved a state of relative calmness. He had gone through all the stages. Eruptions of pure white fury detonating behind his eyes. Cold hard rage crystallized by the amphetamine coursing through his veins. Infuriation anyone would ever contemplate defying him and apoplectic delirium on realizing he was not as much in control as he thought.

"Mr Santos, sir, a glass of water?" Batac cautiously held out a glass.

Lago reached out and grasped the water with a shaking hand; he slowly drained the glass and handed it back to Batac. He was too hot; his breath was like steam as he exhaled. He gripped the desk in front of him and looked out at the blue Pacific from the bridge of Benevolent 1. He stood motionless for another full minute, trying to concentrate. Eventually, he turned and walked towards Lance and Goran. "Let's go back to Manila," he said.

Lance attempted to placate him on the trip back. "This new arrangement with the Masama, it could be beneficial for us."

"You think so?" Lago asked acerbically.

"They will restore the moon base for us and get it producing Helium 3. They are probably best suited to the task. Some of them can even operate in a vacuum without suits. Try to think of them as contractors, providing a service."

"Contractors beyond my control, which I have to pay!" He growled.

"If we keep a healthy trading partnership they will become important allies. We need to maintain a good relationship with them. It will be useful long term."

"I gave them everything and those ungrateful fuckers betrayed me. I'll never forget that."

"True, but the Masama are evolving into something else and have been for some time. They almost have their own shared consciousness now, like a hive mind. We knew they were developing beyond our control. It would only have got worse the longer they stayed on Earth and grown more distant."

"Yes, they were becoming harder to handle but they were my muscle. I need that intimidation factor."

"We can get more soldiers. BPI is in such a strong global position now we don't need to physically intimidate anyone. We can crush competition financially if we need to. We don't need the Masama anymore." Lance knew his words appealed to Lago, stroking his ego. "The Moon is the best place for them, they will evolve out there in space into God knows what, but the important thing is they harvest the helium 3 for us and if we desperately need their assistance, we can shuttle some back here."

"The moon base, the shuttles, the fucking helium, it's all mine! They just took it all and we can't do anything about it." Lago's anger started bubbling up again.

"I am not saying we forget the debt they owe us, but we have to be pragmatic. If they had stayed on Earth, there eventually would have been some form of mutiny which could have been damaging for us. Now they are not our problem. They will produce the helium 3 we can use to control Earth's energy consumption. We will be more powerful than ever with strong allies to call upon if needed."

The prospect of more power and control appeased Lago somewhat. Deep down he knew Lance was right about the Masama deal being beneficial although he would never admit it.

Lago, Batac and Lance had gathered in the globe room back in Manila. Goran was having his latest injury attended to by the medics. The giant holographic image of Earth hovered in the middle, glowing with illuminated energy and movement. Lago manipulated the sphere. Spinning it around with dizzying speed then stopping abruptly, enlarging and enhancing a particular area, examining the contents close up before waving it closed and spinning the globe again.

Lago loved playing God here in the globe room. He was like a child with his favourite toy. This was where he felt most in control, most powerful. Another big hit of amphetamine had made him feel invincible again. He was the most powerful man on the planet. Godlike. Indomitable and unstoppable. He had suffered some setbacks recently but if anything, these delays would only make him more determined.

Lago had enlarged an area on the shores of Lake Superior in Canada. "This will be where they are hiding," he said not looking away from the globe. "It's a suspected Black Robin safe house. One of many around the world. I would have destroyed them years ago if I had known they would be this much trouble. They hide their e-trails well, but the simulations say there is a seventy percent chance our fugitives are hiding there. The other safe houses are in built-up urban areas so are less likely to be hiding the hybrid and his traitorous friends."

"Should we attack it? Bomb it out of existence?" asked Lance.

"Tempting, I definitely want them all dead. Preferably slowly and painfully but I want some remains of the hybrid to dissect. Won't need much, just a small piece."

"What's your plan?"

"We will fly in with drone support and pick them off. If they are not there we will interrogate whomever we find then raze the place to the ground."

"We need more soldiers." Lance looked over at the vacant expression on Batac's scar-ridden face.

"I have arranged some BPI security. Actual real humans who obey orders and don't think for themselves. I am coming along as well to make sure no one fucks it up this time. Goran should be finished with the medics soon."

Just as Lago finished his sentence Goran entered the room. They watched his blue optical field emerging from the gloom. He stalked over towards Batac and stood with his arms folded. He had a black metal ring around his neck with a rectangular speaker inset just under his chin. Where his mouth used to be was now a vent, also made of black metal which curved inwards under the bruised flesh of his cheeks where it must have been grafted to the bone. His swollen rubbery lips had been saved but they were pulled back to the extent he seemed to have a permanent macabre smile on his face. The black metal vent beneath made it look as if he was trying to swallow a piece of hardware.

"You ok boss?" asked Batac.

"No." It was not Goran's voice emanating from the speaker. It was a metallic analogue.

"Goran, what happened to your voice?" asked Lance.

"Vocal cords severed," Goran said in a flat, robotic monotone. There was no pitch variation in his delivery, an unimaginative digital version of a human voice box. Goran's rich, deep and menacing voice used to be all the more significant because it was used sparingly. It added to his intimidating aura but now he looked ridiculous and sounded even more absurd.

Lago didn't care about Goran's appearance, he knew Goran would stand at his side as long as he still had legs. He turned his attention back to the globe where a flashing alert had caught his attention.

"It's them! They are on the move."

Lago had enlarged a real-time image on the globe. It showed a satellite view of the rural mansion, surrounded by trees on the shores of Lake Superior. Lago zoomed in even further simply by extending his hands and spreading them as if wiping away condensation from a window. The view was sharp and detailed. They could see the white crest of a pigeon perched on the guttering of the dilapidated old building. The sun had set on Canada and the light was fading fast. Lago flicked a finger and the view brightened.

They watched four people leaving the building. Facial recognition instantly had four profiles alongside the screen with all known information about each face. Lee, Odetta, John and Rutger.

"Rutger!" exclaimed Lance. "That can't be his real name; they did a good job of erasing his past."

Lee, Odetta and the man known as Rutger carried equipment to the nearby helicopter.

"They must be well funded, that's a brand-new Sikorsky. They don't come cheap."

Lago stayed silent, watching intently. The large figure of John stepped back onto the steps of the building as the helicopter powered up.

"We had better move now. We can track them from the VLR, follow them and ambush them. Then we go back and take care of this John character and his safe house. Find out who is funding his terrorist organization and go after them as well."

They were on the roof of the BPI skyscraper within minutes. The view below them was the same in every direction, grey smog covering the sprawling city like a heavy blanket. The uppermost levels of the tower broke free of the suffocating murk and clear blue skies greeted them above. Two VLRs awaited them, powered up and ready to go, their engines emitting the familiar high-pitched hydraulic hum. Eight security guards were loading weaponry into the machines.

Lance studied the security as they approached. They all stood to attention once they noticed Lago striding towards them. They were big men, all with bulging muscles and small brains, anxious to prove themselves to Lago and undoubtedly nervous about their sudden promotion. Cannon fodder thought Lance.

They did not lack for weaponry, as well as the auto guns fitted out with liquid helium spray and flamethrowers the security all had a variety of grenades, rocket launchers and knives. The VLRs themselves were laden down with auto-cannons and guided missiles. The massive amount of firepower reassured Lance somewhat but he still had misgivings about confronting Lee. They hadn't addressed his nascent hacking ability yet.

Once they were airborne, winging their way across the Pacific at maximum speed, Lance leaned in close to Lago. "This apparent mind control Lee possesses, and his other abilities, whatever they are, how will we protect ourselves?"

"We will have to be fast, take him by surprise. It would be preferable to intercept their VLR, blow it out of the sky then pick up the pieces. But if we are on foot we will have to ambush him, blast him with the cryogenic fluid before he has time to react, then hit him with the flamethrowers. We won't make the mistake of defrosting him this time though, just cut a piece off to study then turn him into ashes."

"And if we are not quick enough?"

Lago took a deep breath and locked his gaze with Lance, making his red-rimmed eyes seem larger than life. "I am confident in my own ability to shield my mind from any form of telepathic attack. Goran, I believe is much the same, his mind is impenetrable. Batac doesn't have much of a brain to speak of anyway and the security are dispensable."

"But they could be turned against us."

"Then we will shoot them."

It was obvious to Lance that Lago was going in unprepared and without a real plan. After lecturing the Masama for doing the same on the Moon, he was now about to make a similar mistake. In his arrogance, Lago assumed he would prevail in any conflict and history had proved him right. But Lance suspected Lago's drug-addled mind had fuelled his arrogance and clouded his judgment. He was nervous about being put in the front line, especially without a horde of Masama surrounding him. Goran was the only one Lago might listen to. Lance knew that underneath his absurd modifications he was the same cold hard emotionless warrior and probably more dangerous than ever, but Goran would never question Lago's decisions.

Lance had never been good at containing his emotions. "What about me?" he hissed at Lago. "I am not a soldier; I shouldn't even be on this mission."

"If I am going you are going too. If you think you are being brainwashed at any stage then shoot yourself in the head, or you can ask me to do it." Lago stared angrily back at Lance, daring him to protest.

Chapter 27.

Raymond sat silently behind Lee as he piloted the Sikorsky in a south-easterly direction over Lake Superior down towards Michigan. At the house, they had debated the best way to infiltrate Earth's population with what was inside Lee. Raymond argued for more tests, he was still nervous about the whole idea, but he eventually agreed seeding water reservoirs directly would be the quickest and safest way of achieving their goal. Freshwater had become a precious commodity, especially in the drought-ridden western states. For those in America's capital the upper Potomac tributaries were still healthy, fed by the rainfall on the Appalachian plateau.

Lee told them he could seed the water supply with nano-molecules of the IA from his body, that would multiply into trillions and pass undetected through the filtration systems. He chose the Georgetown reservoir as his first target. The reservoir supplied drinking water for Washington D.C. Home of the president and the decision makers for the once great nation. Raymond knew the American government did not have the same power and influence it once wielded, but the Washington bureaucrats still benefited from the taxes people paid. Congress had deteriorated into an arrogant rabble standing only for re-election and serving their corporate masters. But they still made decisions on policy and infrastructure that could affect the population. Raymond had to agree they were ideal subjects for an IA upgrade.

They flew quietly over Lake Eire at low altitude. The Sikorsky had a cloaking device and radio jammers to avoid detection but the grey smog from Detroit and Cleveland sitting heavily on the water disguised their passage. They crossed from Pennsylvania into Maryland and flew down the Potomac towards Washington. Lee planned to land close to the historic Georgetown Castle Gatehouse at dusk. The gatehouse housed the sluice gate at the head of an eight-kilometre tunnel leading to the water reservoir.

Raymond did not have much to say about the details of Lee's plan. Once he had accepted the moral implications, the details were not important. At no stage had anyone proposed he should receive a sample of the IA, but Raymond knew it was only a matter of time. He looked across at Odetta; she was staring transfixed at the burnt orange sunset above the Northern States. Light playing across her stern face. Odetta seemed to enthusiastically accept Lee's idea without question. With her telepathy and augments, she had already taken a step in that direction he thought. Raymond knew Lee could look into their minds and read their thoughts. He was well practised at keeping his true feelings hidden but he hoped Lee would be polite enough not delve into his head and see his lingering doubts.

They landed in the gathering darkness on a grass verge bordering the Georgetown reservoir. The Sikorsky was quiet, and the landing had not drawn any attention. They unloaded their weapons in canvas bags, Raymond insisted on bringing the lightweight ceramic sub-machine guns in case Lago tracked them down. They made their way around the calm waters of the reservoir towards the Castle Gatehouse. Lights set into the ground highlighted the turrets on each corner of the small castle-shaped building. It was a pleasant warm evening in Georgetown.

They passed through the unlocked door and into a small reception area with bright lights and faded posters on the walls. The control room was behind a glass partition where a fat security guard reclined in a leather chair. His eyes were closed, feet up on a desk and his mouth was hanging open.

"Is he alive?" asked Odetta.

"Did you put him to sleep?" Raymond looked at Lee.

Lee was just about to reply when the guard snorted, his body convulsed, and his head rolled forward then back again. His eyes stayed closed and he started snoring loudly.

Lee slid the partition aside and climbed into the control room. There were banks of screens showing the sluice gates and the canal flowing inside the tunnel and an antique looking control panel with blinking lights, brass dials, buttons and levers. Lee took the guard's swipe card and opened the door from the inside. They walked around the comatose body and through another door at the back of the room, down a flight of stairs and into the tunnel.

The sluice gates filtered the reservoir water into the tunnel, removing any physical detritus and pumping an even flow down into the underground canal. On either side of the canal were walkways that disappeared down the long watery tunnel. It was quiet apart from the sound of running water and the churning hum of the pumps.

"This place smells ancient," remarked Odetta. "Do people actually drink this water?"

"It was built about two hundred years ago by army engineers so yes, it is ancient," said Lee. "It has been in and out of commission but as long as water flows down the Potomac, it is the quickest and easiest way to get to the filtration plant. Easy for us too, as the security is not exactly vigilant."

Their voices and footsteps echoed eerily, bouncing off the walls. They walked at a brisk pace down the damp tunnel. Above them, slimy green algae covered the curved brick ceiling.

"Doesn't look hygienic," said Raymond. "Smells mouldy."

"It gets treated with chemicals at the other end but it's still the original two-hundred-year-old brick, stone and mortar they built it with."

"Thanks for the history lesson," said Odetta. "Why don't you just seed this canal now instead of going all the way to the filtration plant."

"This water ends up sitting in another reservoir being treated for days before being pumped into the water mains. We want to seed the treated water; this tunnel is just a convenient way of getting there without being noticed."

"So, tomorrow morning, Washington's population will be getting something extra in their teas and coffees huh!" laughed Odetta.

"That is the plan."

Outside above the gatehouse turrets, two VLRs hovered quietly in the night sky before making their landings on either side of the Sikorsky.

"What the fuck are they up to here?" snapped Lago.

Lance was tapping furiously on his datapad. "There is an underground canal that goes from here to the McMillan reservoir in Columbia Heights. That would be the only reason they would be here but what's at Columbia Heights? Why sneak down a tunnel?"

"Let's go find out," said Lago as they disembarked the VLRs.

"Two of you stay here and guard the VLRs," Lago barked at his security personnel. "Shoot anyone matching the descriptions of our fugitives. Don't ask questions, shoot first."

Lago grabbed one of the multi-guns and marched off towards the gatehouse. None of them bothered to conceal their weapons. In the reception, they found the security guard, still contentedly asleep in his warm office. His snoring had decreased in volume to a swampy rattle but his subconscious must have sensed a change in the atmosphere. He struggled to open his eyes and when he managed to focus on his guests he screamed and sat bolt upright, eyes wide open. Directly in front was a red-eyed, black-clad maniac pointing a distressingly powerful looking gun at him. On one side was a hulking giant with facial scars scowling at him and on the other was a towering monster robot with laser eyes and a metal dog collar. The guard was still screaming when Lago shot him three times in the chest. He then turned the gun on the door and blew a hole in it, kicked it open and stormed in.

They immediately went to the monitors. Three figures could be seen walking hastily down the canal in the gloomy light. "Got them," said Lago.

They stormed down the stairs, into the tunnel and started running down both sides of the canal.

"Lago," Lance panted as he struggled to keep up with his amphetamine fuelled employer. "Maybe he's planning on infecting the water supply with the black shit inside him."

Lago stopped instantly, and Lance crashed into the back of him almost knocking him over.

"Fuck!" yelled Lago. Goran was following behind but had quicker reactions than Lance and just managed to stop in time. "Fuck!" yelled Lago again and started running even faster down the tunnel.

Lee stopped. "Quiet, I think I heard something."

They all stopped and faintly heard the word 'fuck' echoing down the tunnel.

"Lago," said Raymond and Odetta simultaneously

"I will wait for them, ambush them," said Raymond.

They did not have time to discuss the merits of Raymond's proposal or say any goodbyes. Odetta smiled grimly at Raymond as he handed her a machine gun. Lee turned and started running down the tunnel.

Raymond unzipped his canvas bag and took a machine gun and two belts of ammunition which he slung around his neck. He looked around; there was nowhere to hide. The dark water in the canal was the only option. He lowered himself down the side of the slippery stone and into the water. It was warm and about chest deep. The current was steady, and he let it carry him gently facing backward, holding his submachine gun underwater with the top half of his head just above the surface watching for their pursuers. He still harboured doubts about seeding the water supply with the IA, but now he had a chance to finally confront Lago Santos. A chance to fulfil the mission he started two years ago and rid the world of the loathsome dictator.

Raymond did not have to wait long. Lago and his entourage were only minutes behind. He submerged himself completely as they appeared down the tunnel in the dirty yellow light on either side of the canal. He walked backward underwater with the current hoping he would not be causing any noticeable ripples. From just below the surface he could see the blurry shapes approaching. He held his breath and waited as they ran past. He had been underwater for nearly a minute and his lungs were bursting. Just as he thought he might pass out from lack of oxygen the last of them ran past and Raymond turned quietly and emerged out of the water. He walked with the current now taking long steps as he held the machine gun out of the water and drained the barrel.

The lightweight ceramic machine gun was easy to hold and operate. It was capable of firing six hundred rounds per minute and each magazine belt had six hundred caseless bullets. Raymond also had two belts around his neck; he hoped it would be enough. He leaned back, braced his legs against the current and opened fire. The hulking figures of Lago's henchmen had BPI branding emblazoned across their backs. An easy target. His first short burst was aimed at the backs of those on his left. Three of them dropped instantly, riddled with bullets. The bullets had passed straight through them leaving bloody ribbons on the brickwork behind. He quickly shifted to his right and opened fire, but his targets had gone to ground apart from one who had the top of his head blown off as he was diving for cover.

Raymond stopped, panting heavily. He was below ground level in the canal and the angle would not give him a clean shot. A soldier came flying at him head first, snarling and shooting. His bullets flew past Raymond's head, missing by centimetres. The soldier had leapt too far though and went crashing into the side of the canal. Raymond swivelled and opened fire, his target was only a meter away, impossible to miss. He dived underwater and kicked down the canal, swimming with the current. The water rapidly turning red.

"Pin him down! Fucking kill him!" Lago screamed across the canal at Batac and his one remaining security guard.

Goran was crouching in front of Lago. He signalled to Batac with his fingers, holding up three, two, one then both Goran and Batac simultaneously leapt to their feet and sprayed the opaque water where Raymond had been standing. Batac and the guard were both now standing on the edge pumping bullets into the water; Goran on the other side stepped over the guards bleeding bodies and was also sweeping the canal with bullets. Lago had regained his feet and was peering into the murky depths while Lance was still cowering against the stone wall. The automatic fire was causing a horrendous echoing clamour until Goran stopped and put his hand up indicating the others to do the same. The noise reverberated around the tunnel while they looked for any sign they had hit their target but there were no other bodies apart from the five dead security. Their blood trickled down into the canal.

"You two," Lago indicated to Batac and the guard across the canal. "He is in the water somewhere, stay here, find him, kill him then follow us." Lago had already started moving down the canal followed by Lance and Goran.

"Yes boss," growled Batac. "Cover me," he said to the guard as he jumped into the canal and clambered up the other side. The two of them slowly patrolled each side of the stone canal, guns pointed at the waters, looking for any sign of their prey. The water was clouded red and all that could be seen was the murky reflection of the pale-yellow light and their own faces peering back at them.

Raymond had swum about twenty meters underwater. It was easy with the strong current. He turned and crouched on his knees at the bottom of the canal. He leaned into the current and tried to see what was going on. He was too far away to see anything clearly but could hear the gunfire and feel the vibrations in the water, he dare not put his head up above the surface. Soon three figures ran past on one side of the canal, he thought about standing and firing but knew there were two more that would shoot him in the back as soon as he emerged out of the water. Lee and Odetta would have to deal with them he thought, they were more than capable.

He kneeled on the bottom of the canal, anchored by his boots against the brickwork. It was impossible to see much through the swirling waters, everything was magnified and distorted but eventually, he could make out two shadowy figures approaching. One on either side of the canal. This would not be easy he thought, no element of surprise this time and he could not hold his breath too much longer. They seemed to take an eternity to come into range. Raymond felt as if his chest would collapse until finally, he could bear it no longer. He knew the odds were against him this time when he pushed up powerfully off his knees and burst out of the water. He sprayed a burst of gunfire firstly to his left and was confident he hit someone as he had a brief impression of a red explosion before quickly swinging his still firing gun towards the other assailant.

Bullets pinged past Raymond's head and smashed into the water. He fired back blindly in the direction of the big man on the water's edge. The automatic gunfire was deafening but Raymond heard a shout of pain from his adversary. At the same instant, he felt the hot burn of a bullet gouging its way along his cheekbone and straight through his ear. There was instantly a piercing scream accompanied by blindingly intense pain. He fell backward and was underwater again. The high-pitched tinnitus whine continued under the water, he felt as if his head would split. Raymond opened his eyes and looked through the water clouded by blossoming plumes of his own blood. He saw the disfigured shape of his opponent still standing, swaying by the water's edge and knew he was in trouble. Impending death flooded his body with adrenaline; he put the pain and noise aside and burst from the water again.

It was Batac, Raymond recognized the big soldier. Lago's oldest and toughest. His right hand was bleeding profusely where Raymond had hit him with a lucky shot, his left hand held his shattered firearm. Batac growled when he saw Raymond and hurled the broken gun at his head. Raymond was swinging his own weapon around and just managed to deflect the gun into the water. He was struggling to line up another shot and gasping for a lungful of heavy air as Batac roared and launched himself. Raymond had a fleeting image for a microsecond of the huge scarred snarling face flying towards him. Batac crashed into him, hands grasping for his throat as they both went under the water and tumbled down the canal.

Lee had heard the automatic gunfire echoing down the tunnel. It was hard to gauge the distance, but he had left

Raymond only minutes ago. They had not stopped running. "Odetta, I can run a lot faster, I can carry you."

"Fuck off, I can run faster too," snarled Odetta in between rapid breaths. "You go on if you want, I can keep up."

Lee increased his pace and Odetta stretched out into a full sprint. The gunfire stopped but they did not look back. They ran at speed until Odetta was gasping for breath but staying close in behind Lee who was not panting at all. Ahead the bright lights of the filtration plant were glowing at the end of the tunnel. They were almost there.

Lee stopped abruptly, swung around, caught Odetta in one movement and flung her to the ground. She did not have time to swear as Lee fell on top of her the same instant a bolt of blue lightning scorched through the air where they had just been running.

"Goran," said Lee as he swung Odetta's machine gun around and fired a long burst in the direction the laser bolt had come from. He was still lying on top of Odetta as he stopped firing, staring back down the tunnel.

"Give me my fucking gun back," demanded Odetta as she pushed him off. They could make out Goran's blue optical field glowing faintly through the gloom. Odetta made to get up but Lee pushed her down again.

"Stay down." A projectile screamed over their heads and slammed upwards into the brick ceiling of the tunnel. It exploded, bringing down an avalanche of brick, stone and earth that narrowly missed them both. The rubble filled the canal, damning the water flow. More debris tumbled from the hole in the brickwork and piled up around the narrow tunnel walls. The flowing canal water immediately began backing up and the water level started rising.

Lee realised they would have to stand and fight, with the tunnel blocked and nowhere to run. Odetta sent a barrage of devastating machine gun fire back down the tunnel. The explosion had dislodged a few large boulders and chunks of brickwork which provided them with some cover as bolts of blue laser fire incinerated the humid air and slammed into the old chunks of rubble. Goran must have had a fix on their heat signatures as every bolt was deadly accurate. Sharp splinters of brick erupted from each explosion as the laser bolts reduced their cover to pebbles. The canal had broken its banks and the dirty water was swirling around their ankles.

"Cover me!" shouted Lee. "I will find a way through!"

Odetta aimed at the blue light she could see through the dust and started firing. The light disappeared, and the laser bolts stopped but Odetta kept firing. She did not lose her concentration even when large pieces of brickwork and chunks of stone went flying over her head from Lee's excavations behind her.

"Odetta." Lee was speaking to her telepathically. There was no way she could hear him over the clamour of machine gun fire. "Climb up here, I will cover you." Lee had made a passage through the rubble up where the ceiling had caved in. The water was up to her knees now as she turned and threw her weapon to Lee who provided covering fire as she scrambled up the mound of brick and dirt.

Lance was cowering behind Goran, using him as a human shield as he ran hunched over trying to avoid the accurate return fire. They were shooting blind as they had lost sight of their targets in the thick dust of the explosion.

"Goran can you turn off the blue light?" asked Lance. "Makes us an easy target."

"No," Goran stated in his metal monotone.

The machine gun fire stopped, and the tunnel was once again filled with the sound of running water as they cautiously moved forward. Out of the dust and fading yellow light appeared a mound of earth and rubble blocking the flow. The swirling brown water was rising quickly. Lago spotted a hole dug through the obstruction.

"There!" he pointed. "Quick!"

Goran again led the way as they scrambled up the mound that was turning into a slippery mud slope. He lay on his front and raised his head to peer through the narrow hole. He was immediately met by a barrage of machine gun fire that smashed into the brickwork, sending shards of stone exploding over them.

"Get back up there and fucking shoot them!" snarled Lago as the gunfire finally stopped.

Goran braced himself for a moment then burst up through the hole, sending a withering blast of blue laser bolts through to the other side. He edged through the hole and got his arms free to shoulder his multi-gun and unleashed a combination of laser and machine gun fire. There was no return fire as Goran crawled through the hole closely followed by Lago and Lance.

On the other side, the tunnel came to an end, opening out into the brightly lit filtration plant. The canal now starved of water opened out into a bigger reservoir which fed the plant. Lance looked around but could not see anyone. Thick silver pipes snaked their way around the cavernous room feeding other reservoir pools. Gantries hung from the roof and he could see a control room along one side. The hum of pumping machinery filled the room like a headache. Lance followed Lago as they cautiously slid down to the dry canal bed.

"Spread out," ordered Lago. "Be ready with the helium spray, shoot anything that moves."

Lance made his way around the pools but there was no sign of any activity. Then, from behind the lights that hung above the gantries, Lance shouted as two figures fell on them. Lee crashed into Lago, sending them both tumbling. Odetta landed on Goran's shoulders feet first. Goran remained standing but before he could fire any shots Odetta dug her fingers under his optical field band. She stayed on him, balanced on his shoulders with her legs clamped around his neck. Her fingers were buried into where Goran's eye sockets used to be, and she was screaming, trying to rip the optical band from his head. Goran was screaming also with the pain, blood pouring from where Odetta's sharp fingers gripped underneath the rim of the optical band. Goran tried to bring his gun around to shoot Odetta and at the same time Lance ran over to get an accurate fix on her.

"Fucking shoot her!" Lago screamed from underneath Lee.

Goran was staggering around, screaming in pain, shooting wildly when Odetta clenched his head even tighter between her thighs and ripped the entire optical band from his head. They both fell backward and slammed into the floor. As soon as Odetta hit the floor she rolled and whipped her gun around towards Lance.

Lance could not get a clean shot while Odetta was perched on top of Goran. He was momentarily stunned by the extreme violence of her actions as she ripped the optical band off his head. That moment of hesitation was all the time Odetta needed. She moved faster than Lance could react and put a burst of machine gun fire straight into his chest. Lance was blown backward, he felt confused and bewildered before the pain hit him. He managed to lift his head up and survey the bloody mess of his torso. Through his torn shirt he could see through his own shattered ribs and ruptured organs. The bullets had miraculously missed his heart which was still pumping blood straight through severed arteries out onto the floor. He stared, disbelieving as if he was looking at someone else's broken body. The last thing he saw was Odetta's leather-clad legs standing over him.

Lee had leapt from the roof feet first and smashed into Lago's upper body sending them tumbling to the floor. Lee had him pinned to the floor momentarily as they witnessed Odetta wrestling with Goran's head. Lago lost his weapon with the impact but managed to twist out from underneath Lee. He regained his footing and whirled around to plant a kick into Lee's abdomen. He almost broke his foot as it was like kicking a sack full of sand, this only infuriated Lago more as he unleashed a series of brutal kicks into Lee's ribs and midsection as he kneeled on the wet tiled floor.

"Fucking hybrid scum, I'll fucking kill you!" he panted in between kicks.

His exertions did not seem to affect Lee at all who just kneeled there smiling sadly. Lago scanned for his multi-gun but could not see it nearby, he aimed a kick at Lee's head instead. Lee caught his ankle with one hand before it could connect.

"You can't hurt me, Lago."

"Fuck you!" screamed Lago as he aimed his other knee at Lee's head and collapsed trying to get his hands around Lee's throat. Lago was bigger and taller than Lee, but his exertions were having no impact. Lee stood up, still holding Lago by one ankle. Lago writhed on the floor like a rabid dog trying to escape its leash.

"Goran!" Lago screamed. "Goran!" Then he stopped struggling for a moment to see where his right-hand man was. Lago could not see Goran from his position on the floor, but he could see Odetta walking towards them. Behind her, he could make out the shapes of two bodies lying on the floor. In her hand, she held a matte black metal ring dripping with blood and ragged bits of skin.

"You fucking bitch!" he seethed. "You will both fucking die!"

"Lago, it's over. We need to talk," said Lee as he let go of his ankle.

Lago shuffled backward frantically scanning for a weapon, but his discarded multi-gun was too far away, and all his soldiers appeared to be dead. "It's not over," rasped Lago as he scrambled back to the wall.

"Do you know what I intend to do?" asked Lee.

Lago remained silent as he faced Lee and Odetta. His mind was delirious with adrenaline and amphetamine and his head was whipping around looking for anything he could use to his advantage. Then he noticed movement in the background. Goran had just sat up. "No," he said. "No, I don't know what you intend to do."

Goran was now standing but he was a complete mess. A gory red band ran around his entire head where Odetta had ripped the optical band away. Pieces of bony white skull could be seen through the trails of blood and ragged flesh. His scarred bald scalp sat on top of his head like some hideous parody of a monk. Below the line of gore, most of his nose had been ripped away leaving only a skeletal frame but the metal mouthpiece remained. There were globules of red pulp dripping from his hollow eye sockets. Goran had been a monster most of his life and now his appearance matched his personality. He was Lago's last hope.

"Tell me. Tell me how you are going to save the world."

"You can help us," said Lee.

Goran shuffled a few steps to his left and by pure chance stumbled across the multi-gun he had dropped in Odetta's aerial attack.

"Help you?" Lago shrieked, hoping to shout over any noises Goran was making. "Why the fuck would I want to help you!"

Goran had raised the multi-gun but did not appear to know what to do with it as all his senses had been severely reduced if not destroyed altogether. There was one sense still working though. His telepathy. Odetta realized something was wrong, her eyes widened as she felt Goran's mind connect with hers. She spun around just in time to see the malignant figure of Goran pointing the multi-gun at her head.

Lee reacted at the same time shouting "Odetta!" But it was too late. It only took one shot. Deadly accurate to the centre of her forehead. As Odetta swayed then dropped to the floor, a dull rumbling noise could be heard emanating from the pile of rubble behind Goran that blocked the tunnel. Dirty water started spewing from the hole Lee had made. It washed around Goran's ankles as he stood still pointing the auto-gun at the fallen form of Odetta. Then the water stopped flowing and the dull rumbling increased like a distant thunderstorm.

Raymond tumbled, thrashing through the water, trying to get a meaningful grip on Batac. Neither of them could get any purchase on the canal floor. Batac had one meaty hand clamped around Raymond's throat and was fighting to get the other one into position as they were swept down the canal. Raymond realized he had to stop trying to regain his balance and concentrate on saving his life. He let his body go limp and twisted his head around to where Batac's thick hairy forearm was trying to choke him. He opened his mouth as wide as possible and bit down hard on Batac's upper forearm. He felt a satisfyingly big chunk of flesh in his mouth and bit down harder tasting the metallic tang of blood mixed with the Potomac River washing down his throat. Batac thrashed about and eventually let go. Raymond kicked away and put some distance between them.

But the canal was blocked, and the backwash of water swept Raymond straight back into Batac's arms. This time the Masama soldier got both his big hairy hands around Raymond's throat. It felt as if his fingers would tear straight through his windpipe such was the strength of his grip. The bullet wound in his hand and bite on his forearm had just made him angry. The water was rising rapidly and now they were both underwater. Raymond could not touch the bottom, but he was determined not to choke and drown at the same time. He levered his knee up into Batac's chest and started kicking at his groin with his other leg. It didn't seem to affect Batac at all. Raymond was starting to feel himself slipping away into unconsciousness when he felt a connection with something soft and yielding between Batac's legs. The vice-like grip lessened slightly and Raymond pushed away with his knee, bursting through the surface again gasping for breath.

He swam down the tunnel towards the mound of earth blocking the water flow, expecting to be pulled back into

Batac's clutches at any second. The muddy water swirled around as it hit the obstruction creating little whirlpools in the dirty backwash. Raymond had never properly learned to swim but his kicking and thrashing seemed to be keeping him afloat and heading in the right direction. Finally, he got to the slippery pile of mud and rubble. The water was now only a meter from the ceiling. The dull yellow lighting showed the remaining gap down the tunnel narrowing as the water rose even higher. Raymond rolled over and started crawling towards the hole in the dirt. He was almost there when he felt a crushing grip on his ankle and he was hauled violently back into the water.

Batac struggled to get his hands around Raymond's neck again. Raymond kicked out sluggishly through the water with his free leg. They both tumbled around underwater, Batac still trying to find Raymond's neck with one hand and Raymond trying to kick him in the face. They spun around, Raymond had no idea which way was up or down. He kicked out again and felt a solid impact but still, Batac's grip would not release. Then he felt a solid blow to his chest, Batac stamped on him, twisted him around and pinned him to the floor of the canal with both feet, still holding on to his ankle.

Raymond was helpless; he had no leverage and could not force himself up under Batac's weight. He futilely bashed at his booted feet a few times then miraculously felt the handle of a hunting knife sheathed there. He grabbed the knife and quickly as he could, stabbed at Batac's calf muscle and Achilles tendon. Batac immediately lifted his boot and Raymond followed him up. It was impossible to see anything in the muddy water now clouded with blood, but Raymond thought he knew roughly where Batac should be. He stabbed out wildly in that direction and felt resistance that could only be a large piece of his opponent. He stabbed again and again until the water was more red than brown.

On the verge of drowning again but hopeful he had finally killed Batac, Raymond kicked for the surface. The water was at the top of the tunnel now and the suspended lights had all blown. Raymond's head crashed into the ceiling before he could get a breath. He spun around in the murky darkness, disorientated and oxygen-starved until he saw a light. The water was pouring through the hole at the top of the mound and Raymond kicked out for it. As he got closer he saw the light being blocked out by a large shape, it was Batac, still impossibly alive and weakly trying to swim for the hole also. Batac got there first and blocked out the watery light as he tried to get through the hole.

Raymond was swimming blind but desperately paddled in what he thought was the right direction. He felt Batac's boots and legs. They were not moving, limp and lifeless. It took a moment of precious time for Raymond to realize what had happened. Batac, alive or dead was stuck in the hole. Blocking his escape. Raymond pushed and pulled at his legs, but they would not budge. He had no strength left, no oxygen left, no fight left.

"So, this is how it ends," he thought. "Drowned in a sewer, blocked by a fat guy's arse." He felt his life slipping away.

Lee stood, relaxed, even nonchalant. Inside the reservoir, the rumbling noise increased. Goran, saturated in his own blood and swaying unsteadily, still held the auto-gun in one straight arm at Odetta's unmoving body.

Lago started forward yelling, "Helium spray! Hit him with the helium!"

But Goran did not register; his eyes and ears had been destroyed. He did not have any senses left. The rumbling noise increased, Lee took a step back, he had some idea of what was about to happen. The water had filled the tunnel and with the pile of earth and rubble blocking the flow, the pressure was building. The gatehouse pump kept on pumping, forcing water into the tunnel where there was no more room for it and there was a body blocking the hole Lee had made.

Something had to give, the path of least resistance. Lee had a fleeting view of Batac's body as it was blown out onto the floor like a cork from a bottle. Then most of the blockage exploded from the tunnel in a calamitous wave of mud, bricks and water. Goran was standing directly in the path of the tunnel outlet and he was buried instantly in a mudslide of sludge, bricks and rocks. Before he disappeared, he gave no indication he knew what was about to hit him, standing rigidly with his multi-gun still extended. Lee stood firm as the brown water washed around him. Batac's limp form disappeared in the watery avalanche, his foot appearing briefly for a moment before being swamped in the brown mire. Chunks of bricks and rubble crashed into the filtration reservoirs and came to rest around the pipes as the dirty water from the tunnel coursed into the room. Then Lee watched Raymond, drenched and bloodied, tumbling head over heels, grasping a vicious looking hunting knife. Amazingly he did not stab himself with it as the water propelled him against a large pipe which he desperately clung to, heaving a great lungful of air. Then just as quickly as it had started, the devastation stopped. The solid chunks of brick and rock found their places, the water flow abated, the pressure alleviated. The water continued to gently flow over what was left of the obstruction, out into the wrecked filtration room.

Chapter 28.

Lago snarled at Lee, his red eyes glared with withering intensity. Lee looked back expressionless. His eyes were black and dead. Lago looked around for discarded multi-guns or weapons of any sort, but everything was buried under a thick layer of mud and rubble. The closest thing was an old worn brick. Lago bent down and picked it up. He felt better having something in his hand.

"The fighting is over Lago," said Lee.

Lago took a deep breath and muttered, "Nothing is ever over."

He looked at the brick in his hand. The years of flowing water had worn down the edges to a smooth inflection. He looked closer. There was a number stamped into the brick. 1854. He did not think of what the number might mean. He thought about his vast empire, his fleet of factory ships, his laboratories, his space shuttles and thousands of his employees. He thought about the Masama that had abandoned him and all his other assets around the world but most of all he thought about his vast array of weaponry. A thousand methods of killing at his disposal and here he was with a brick in his hand. He turned it over and thought about throwing it at Lee but knew it would be pointless.

Lago was desperately thinking of a way to gain the upper hand. He snapped out of his turbulent thoughts as a sudden loud groan came from behind him. His shaking fingers dropped the brick and it landed directly on the bone on top of his foot. "Aaah fuck!" He screamed, hopping on one foot, looking around and glaring at

Raymond. It was the last pathetic indignation. A rake at the gates of hell.

Eventually, he focused on Lee again. "So, let me get this right, your plan is to infect humanity with the black shit inside you, without their knowledge? Extremely fucking devious, even I would be proud of that."

"I don't intend to argue with or have a philosophical debate with you Lago but needless to say, it is the only way."

"Only way to what, save the world?"

"It's the next step up the evolutionary ladder Lago."

"So, your plan is for everyone on Earth to be infected with the same artificial mind control brainwashing bullshit, then what? We all hold hands and be nice to each other?" Lago's voice was thick with venomous sarcasm.

"We will still be individuals, but we will be connected. We will have instant access to universal knowledge but most importantly the connection we will share will make us closer to our fellow man."

"You want to be some kind of green Jesus? You don't understand humans at all." Lago spat.

Raymond unravelled himself from his painful embrace with a big pipe. He stood up shakily and inspected his body. Blood and mud dripped from his head and there was still a deafening scream from where his ear used to be. He could not believe he was alive. Almost drowned three times and choked to death twice. Lee and Lago were the last two standing. Odetta was lying spread-eagled on the floor, blood leaking from a hole in her head. Lance was in a crumpled bloody heap. There was no sign of Goran or Batac under the rubble. Raymond tried to move in their direction and instantly bolts of pain wracked his body. It felt like several broken ribs but luckily his arms and legs still worked. He stumbled forward, picking up a stray multi-gun buried in the rubble.

"You don't think humanity should have a say in its own future?" Lago continued. "Are you just going to infect everyone by surreptitiously spiking their water? Have you ever heard of free will? You say you are doing this for humanity, but you are more underhand than I am!"

"Something has to change Lago, you know this. There are almost ten billion people on the planet. In another couple of years, there will be twelve. Food and water are already hard to find. Natural resources are running out. Given everything we know of our species; do you actually think we can find a solution on our own? Earth will become a barren desert where those with the power will fight over the remaining resources and everyone else will starve. To do nothing is insane; not acting is condemning our species to death. Something has to change."

"And once we are all happily brainwashed, what difference will that make? We all start buying energy saving light bulbs? Is that your answer?"

"I said I don't want a philosophical argument with you Lago but listen for a minute. There will be no selfishness, no greed; we will all look out for each other. We will be a global community. We already have the answers. It's just a matter of unlocking the information. Space travel, space habitats, renewable energy and food for everyone. It can be done but we need to change, you need to change. We need to adapt to survive and evolve to find our place among the stars, and we need your help."

Raymond painfully propped himself up against the wall still holding the auto-gun. The ringing in his ear had subsided slightly and he had been trying to listen to their conversation. He convulsed and vomited up dirty brown river water. The effort was excruciating, and he cried out in pain.

"Raymond, I can't thank you enough for what you have done," said Lee "You have three broken ribs, a cracked sternum, you are missing an ear, but you will be ok. We will be finished here soon."

"You make some nice speeches." Lago ignored Raymond. "But I am way ahead of you. My orbital elevator will be the gateway to the solar system. One step away from space habitats and affordable space travel. My Moon mining operation will soon be harvesting helium 3, an unlimited clean energy source and my 3D printing empire can print enough food to feed the world's population ten times over. Humanity does not need to be infected with your alien intelligence to survive, I am looking after them."

Lee gave a sardonic smile. "Lago, not long ago I swore to hunt you down and kill you. I may have changed but I still recognize lies when I hear them. The only reason you are doing these things is for your own benefit. You crave power, control and wealth above all else. You want to control and profit from access to space. You want to control and profit from energy distribution and if your 3D printers can produce so much food why aren't you doing it already? I'm sorry but you are one of the biggest examples of why humanity needs my solution. You see the rest of the human race as your slaves, the Earth as a resource to plunder, you have no empathy."

Lago smiled but did not offer any rebuttal.

"You are right about your empire having the potential to help humanity, your organization has the logistics and the global structure in place to make a difference." Lee took a step closer to Lago. "BPI just needs a leader who can take it in a new direction that is not all about power and profit." Lee moved closer still to Lago, close enough to touch. "Lago, you could be that person. You could be that leader if you accept my gift."

"Get the fuck away from me!" spat Lago stumbling backward. "Gift? Is that what you call it? You want to infect me and all of humanity with your alien shit without our consent? You can fuck off."

Lago backed away a few paces, he wished he had a weapon. Lee looked around and his eyes rested on the undamaged pumps and filters of the treatment plant and the clean reservoir beyond. He smiled contritely at Lago again.

"I would rather convince you than force you, but I will force you if I have to. Evolution will happen, humanity will embrace my IA, I am speeding up the process. Giving us all the greatest chance for survival and a vast improvement in everyone's quality of life. Trust me; it is the only way forward."

"Trust you? I don't trust anyone!" yelled Lago. "You want to make us all the same, so we all think the same, the same happy thoughts. Sounds like the worst kind of brainwashing to me. I think you have forgotten what it is to be human. Everyone is different, everyone is an individual, and everyone makes mistakes. It's the friction between us that defines us. Take the differences away and we might as well be mindless robots. You think you are fighting to save humanity well you are fucking wrong!" Lago was shouting, arms raised. "You have forgotten what it is to be human, I am the one trying to save humanity, and I know what it is to be human." He banged his chest with a clenched fist. "I am more fucking human than anyone!" Lago screamed and rushed at Lee.

Lago collided with Lee and tried to knock him to the ground, but Lee took a few steps backward and cushioned the impact. He stood still, relaxed and expressionless as the larger figure of Lago tried to wrestle him down. Lago then withdrew a couple of steps and roared again as he launched a flurry of blows to Lee's stomach and midsection. Lee did not defend himself but stood sadly tolerant, absorbing the punches.

The sound was like hands clapping in thick gloves. Lago stood back again, panting, then aimed a punch at Lee's face. Lee ignored Lago's desperation as a weak punch landed on his nose. He did not flinch; the blow had no effect whatsoever. Lago staggered backward, eyes wide with fury, clenched his fists and made to punch Lee again. This time Lee caught his fist in one hand and held it there until Lago fell to his knees, exhausted, defeated.

"Soon Lago, soon you will understand. Wait here for a moment, there's something I have to do."

Raymond watched Lee walk over to the raised reservoir at the back of the water treatment chamber. There were several large pools of water that had not been contaminated by the mud from the tunnel. They were fed from big metal pipes that wound around the gantries and ran along the ceiling. The reservoir was the last treatment stage before being pumped to millions of Washington residences. Raymond followed, doubled over in pain, one hand supporting his broken ribs, the other hand using the multi-gun as a crutch. Lee reached the edge of one of the reservoirs. The pool was tapered with raised steps to about waist high. He kneeled on the steps and bent over looking into the water. Raymond was now close enough to see his reflection in the water, a distorted silhouette in the bright lights above. Lee opened his mouth and there was blackness inside. The blackness filled his mouth until a thick treacle droplet took shape and began to fall towards the water below.

"Sorry Lee," said Raymond as he opened fire with the helium gun.

Lee had no time to react as the freezing superfluid coated him and froze him solid. Raymond aimed for his head first and froze the globule of black matter into a solid pendulum suspended from his mouth. He continued spraying until his entire body was hard frozen, encased in crystals. After a time, Raymond stopped and tried to kick Lee's frozen body off the steps, but it was too solid. He knew better than to touch with his bare hands, he landed another couple of well-aimed kicks and Lee's statuesque form crashed to the floor still in its kneeling position.

"I couldn't let you do it." He switched to the flamethrower and doused Lee's body in the fiery liquid propellant. His body steamed then blackened under the spray of intense heat. Raymond held the auto-gun rigid until Lee's body was burning on its own. He stopped and switched over to the helium again.

"We will find a way without you," he said in a whisper.

Lee's body was unrecognizable. Features burnt away, blackened stumps where his feet and hands used to be. Raymond opened up with the flamethrower and repeated the process again and again until there was nothing left but black dust and charcoal. He continued to spray the remnant husks of Lee until the fuel ran out in his auto-gun. Then he stamped on the brittle black pieces with his wet boots until there was nothing left but a slew of black sludgy residue. Raymond bent down and studied the ashes. He sifted some through his fingers and let it fall to the ground. He reached into his pocket and pulled out the button. The letters had been worn off, all that was left was the red heart symbol. Raymond turned it over in his fingers before throwing it in the ashes.

"Goodbye Lee," he said.

Raymond turned and faced Lago who was still crouching down on his knees. Confusion and relief played across his mud-streaked face. He gazed up at Raymond until he regained some of his arrogant composure and struggled to his feet. His features regained a familiar look of smug satisfaction and his mouth opened in a sneer as he looked at Lee's remains. He began to say something but stopped abruptly as Raymond held the auto-gun to his temple. Before Lago could even cry out Raymond pulled the trigger. There was a loud bang, but Lago stood, unharmed. The auto-gun had jammed; tendrils of smoke rose from its casing. Raymond lowered the weapon and the two men stood facing each other.

Epilogue.

When the rising waters claimed Miami, the rest of the United States gave up on the tropical city and left it to rot. The place fell to wrack and ruin, polluted and unliveable. The Nature began to reclaim the concrete jungle with patient inevitability. A few stayed, those with nowhere else to go, and some gravitated towards the abandoned city. Criminals on the run, the homeless and dispossessed, vagabonds, doomsday cults, drug addicts and mentally disturbed. The dregs of society found their way to Miami by accident or intent. Flotsam and jetsam washed up on the rubble of the inebriated city. The Babelists were drawn to Miami like moths to a flame. They established themselves there believing Miami had become a holy symbol of their God's opprobrium with the human race. It had been a desperate, anarchic existence but recently things had changed.

The old man glided around the city rivers. The yacht was virtually silent, and it barely broke the surface. Its raised hydrofoils left two fine lines trailing in the water behind it. He smiled and waved at the children playing on the rocky beach between the old ruins. They had tamed some baby alligators and were trying to teach them how to balance on two back legs by dangling fish above them. It was an impossible task as their tails prevented the eager alligators from standing upright, much to the amusement of the children.

A flock of pink flamingos stalked the shallows, carefully extending their slender legs, tiptoeing through the water. Their beady black eyes watched for the shrimp below.

They would stop and perch on one leg with impeccable balance, the other leg tucked up into their impressive plumage for reasons known only to them. They would bide their time before snapping at the swarms of shrimp fluttering about in the clean blue water. Further down the boulevard, solar panels glinted in the sunlight from most rooftops. Enoch passed narrow alleyways down side streets where the water was channelled into fast flowing rivers powering submerged turbines.

They had restored some of the old art deco buildings of Miami. Cleaned the exteriors, decontaminated the insides and returned them to their former glory. Most of the other buildings they had left to rot. Now they were covered in mangrove creepers, saltwater algae and ferns clung to the facades. The big old skyscrapers were mostly still standing but were now just rusty corroded skeletons thrusting up out of the water. They had become huge aviaries, home to flocks of cormorants, goldeneyes and loons. Enoch watched scrums of colourful butterflies marauding up the leafy building frontages amongst teeming swarms of insects. Bats hung from the rusty metal frames inside, sleeping during the day and even the ocean-going albatrosses made their nests in the highest reaches. Massive murmurations of starlings wheeled about in the sky keeping symmetry with their hive mind. They were all incredibly noisy, a cacophony of gaggles, squalls and hoots echoed around the old central city.

The old man was on his way to a meeting. They did not actually need to meet in person as they could all communicate with each other merely by directing their thoughts, but it was nice to physically touch, shake hands and embrace. They met once a week on a rooftop garden to discuss developments, the progress being made in various projects, education, health and well-being. They had created a happy and sustainable community of like-minded people that cared for each other. They were aware of the outside world, it was easy to tap into the global data flow, the satellites and drones circling the globe were a constant hum of electronic information. But they were not interested in the inane babble and the outside world had long forgotten Miami. They were on their own to develop as they pleased, and they were progressing fast. Their future was materializing brightly in front of them as if someone had flicked all the streetlights on.

Enoch did not look behind him. He did not dwell on the intangible past. None of them did. Each had their own mixed up memories but most of them now only looked ahead. They were aware they had been changed at some point in the past, changed for the better, enlightened and enriched. They did not know how or why but they were thankful it had happened. For the old man, it was like emerging from a thick fog into a clear sunny day. He was surprisingly coherent, aware of himself and those around him. His immediate reaction was one of pity and sorrow for those confused minds that surrounded him. Then he realized he could help them all, bring them out of the fog into the light and so he did.

They knew they were different from those that lived in the outside world and they knew eventually there would be interaction. These issues were also discussed at the meeting. When it happened, it would have to be managed carefully as the majority of Earth's population were stubbornly distrustful of anyone different. But the old man was confident they could help the rest of humanity. They had many good ideas.

Lee woke up after an incalculable age of nothingness. He had died again and for the third time he had woken up from what should have been oblivion. He was getting used to it now. It wasn't shocking. Everything was dark, and he had no senses to interact with wherever he was, but he did not panic. His brain state was alive, his soul or psyche or whatever it was called was still intact. He still existed in some form.

He remembered his last living moments. Seconds away from dispensing his gift to the people of Washington. He had no idea what Raymond had planned, if he had planned it at all or if it was a spontaneous decision. Lee was only aware a split second before he was doused in the spray of immobilizing liquid helium. Raymond must have kept his thoughts well hidden. Lee did not feel sad; he did not feel anything. The humans might endure in some form without his assistance. He had hoped to help them up the evolutionary escalator, but they might still survive to make their own way. Lee realized he was thinking about humanity in a detached sense as if he had been removed. He no longer felt any responsibility. He no longer felt any emotion, but he understood.

A faint light appeared. A hazy line. Apricot and orange with a hint of blue around the edges. The colours spread through the blackness. Lee seemed to rise in altitude as the colour spread although he had no reference, no bearing, and no physical body. As he rose the miasmic line of colour seemed to bend into a huge arc. A curvature of bittersweet shimmering hues deepened across his horizon as he rose through the ether. Lee's senses had been enhanced tetrachromatically with HEMI in his head. He could see colours no human had ever seen before, but this was something else. A myriad of tinctures with such depth, such rich clarity, he would have wept if he still had eyes. The line grew until it stretched across the latitudes and the colours spread beneath him. A million shades of orange from vermillion to atomic tangerine. Then above the line, shades of blue turning to vast blackness above. It was only when Lee perceived the thin white line across the blackness and the twinkling stars behind, he realized where he was. Jupiter.

Jupiter! He was on, in, above, around and immersed in Jupiter! Never had Lee known such joy and incomprehensible wonderment. He had just woken up in a Jovian sunrise! He could feel the vastness of the gas giant. He was a mote, an atom riding the gaseous seas of the most massive planet in the solar system. He was carried by the winds like a leaf in the tide and swirled through the layers of vapour, a riot of colours and motion. He had no physical body, but he had a full spectrum of senses that could experience in every dimension. He sampled the capricious atmosphere and drank in the heady cocktail of Jovian gases. He floated around the monstrous cyclonic vortices and danced with the mega lightning that could crack a Moon in half. Lee had never felt so atomically small, so insignificant yet at the same time he had a sense of the vast size of the planet. A huge gaseous ball with a tiny pressurized core of thick hot magma. All tumultuous storm on the outside and suffocating density down below. He was a tiny speck on a vast ocean and simultaneously he straddled the planet.

He soaked up everything his vast array of senses could perceive and digest with childlike enthusiasm. He could feel the planet as if he were embracing it and he was aware of its place in the solar system. He recognized the dusty rings whipping around the planet and acknowledged the Galilean Moons with their entourage of irregular satellites. He examined Io, Ganymede, Callisto and Europa. Further out into the hinterlands of the solar system, Saturn the gas giant sister and the two ice giants, Uranus and Neptune. Then inwards he looked to Mars, his home planet Earth and the hot rocks of Venus and Mercury. And at the centre, the massive furnace keeping them all in place. The fiery monster greedily monopolizing the majority of mass in the solar system.

Lee's awareness went even further, beyond the little system he lived in. Beyond the Kuiper belt, beyond the scattered disc, through the interstellar medium and out into the galaxy. A huge city of stars. His consciousness expanded exponentially like the big bang itself. Encompassing all the Milky Way and neighbouring Andromeda, through the emptiness, the ice clouds, the nebulas, the dust and dark matter of the universe. The billions of stars, billions of galaxies, billions of light years, the unfathomable time and distances between, he could now comprehend. He could sense the bones of the universe. He was nothing and yet he was everything, minuscule and at the same time colossal. Power in its purest state. He did not think about the why and the how, he was too busy devouring the experience of such an expanded mind. Then he noticed the link between the gas giants throughout the universe. Tangible lines of energy flowing between them, exchanging information and knowledge. Grid-lines stretching across infinity, linking the billions of gaseous balls in every dimension. A map of the Universe. Then he was bought back to Jupiter and became aware of the Lalandi. His host.

Lee was part of the Lalandi now, assimilated and absorbed into its vast bombastic flatulence. HEMI had expanded, enhanced and educated his human brain, but now Lee was part of something much grander. The Lalandi had plucked his dying consciousness from his biochemical brain and brought him here.

Lee was now a microscopic part of these cosmic ancient beings. He had the secrets of the universe at his fingertips. The Lalandi were the rapporteurs of this universe. Smart gas swirling with knowledge and history and they had chosen to incorporate Lee into their vast intellect. He was humbled by their attention. They had devoted an entire micro-fraction of their observational powers to watch the events unfold on the little blue rock he once called home, ready to intervene if the situation became untenable. The evolution of the IA born on Earth's Moon was never likely to threaten the galactic balance in the region but the Lalandi was ready in case. Lee's experience was interesting enough not only to be recorded for future reference but for his dying psyche to be incorporated.

He remembered where it had all started, a sad human on the Moon. He had been transformed; he had grown into something fantastic. He had changed.

Printed in Great Britain
by Amazon